SPHINX'S P

D0728646

"Friesner imagines the early life of Nefertiti, crafting a complex teen character who is in turns intelligent and brave, impetuous and fiery, and has little concern for the prospect of marriage or trading on her remarkable beauty. . . . Dramatic plot twists, a powerful female subject, and engrossing details of life in ancient Egypt make for lively historical fiction."
—*Booklist*

"[A] satisfying foray into a time and place not often written about."
—*Kirkus Reviews*

"Readers will identify strongly with the intractable and wildly optimistic protagonist, and they will anxiously anticipate the promised sequel to see what lies in store for her."
—*The Bulletin of the Center for Children's Books*

"An exciting story, with an engaging young heroine. It will leave readers anxious to learn more of the historical Nefertiti."
—BookLoons.com

"Friesner creates an ancient Egypt that is lush and exotic, filled with beauty and sophistication, but which also harbors dangerous intrigues. I found this a suspenseful, well-paced and credible coming-of-age story about the young woman who will be forever immortalized in history as Nefertiti, 'The Beautiful Woman Has Come.'"
—*Historical Novels Review*

SPHINX'S PRINCESS

Esther Friesner

Random House · New York

Text copyright © 2009 by Esther Friesner

The Library of Congress has cataloged the hardcover edition of this work as follows:
Friesner, Esther M.
Sphinx's princess / Esther Friesner.
p.   cm.
Summary: Although she is a dutiful daughter, Nefertiti's dancing abilities, remarkable beauty, and intelligence garner attention near and far, so much so that her family is summoned to the Egyptian royal court, where Nefertiti becomes a pawn in the power play of her scheming aunt, Queen Tiye.
ISBN 978-0-375-85654-9 (trade) — ISBN 978-0-375-95654-6 (lib. bdg.) — ISBN 978-0-375-89330-8 (e-book)
1. Nefertiti, Queen of Egypt, 14th cent. B.C.—Juvenile fiction. [1. Nefertiti, Queen of Egypt, 14th cent. B.C.—Fiction. 2. Kings, queens, rulers, etc.— Fiction. 3. Egypt—Civilization—To 332 B.C.—Fiction.] I. Title.
PZ7.F91662 Sp 2009   [Fic]—dc22   2009013719

ISBN 978-0-375-85655-6 (trade pbk.)

Printed in the United States of America
10 9 8 7 6 5 4 3 2

First Trade Paperback Edition

*For Tom Hise,
one of the few real princes I know,
and for his wonderful wife, Jan,
the power behind the throne*

CONTENTS

PART III: THEBES

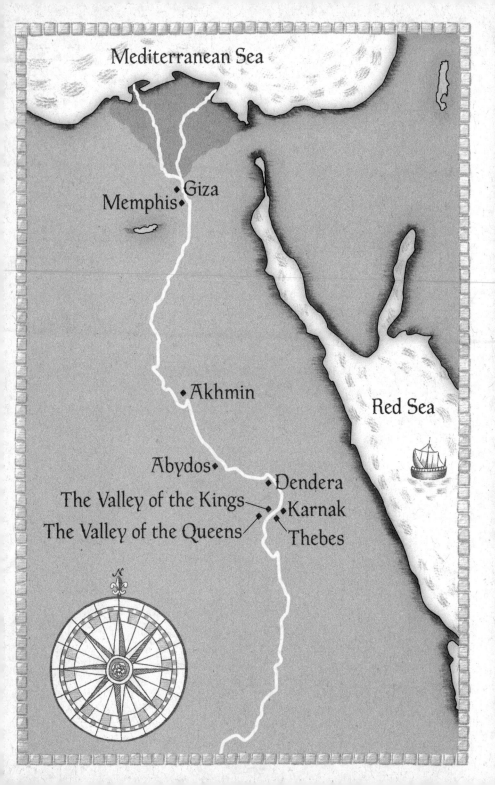

PROLOGUE

From the time of my first memories, my dreams were filled with lions—fierce, impossibly huge monsters with fiery manes and eyes black and cold as a starless night. There were no lions of such colossal size in all of Pharaoh's realm, not even in the wild Red Land, the desert where the waters of the holy Nile never reached. I was only a small child, barely four years old, but old enough to know that the lions haunting my dreams *could* not be real. And yet—I was still afraid.

The dreams were always the same: It was daytime and I was playing with my doll in the shade of the sycamore trees in our garden when suddenly the earth under my feet turned to sand. My doll sank out of sight as the lions clawed their way into the blazing sunlight, their mouths gaping, ready to devour me. I ran toward the house, crying for help, but no one came, and my home slipped beneath the surface of the sand before I could reach it. Then I was running,

running across the Red Land where nothing grew but stones and bones. I saw strangely shaped mountains in the distance, and though I somehow knew I would be safe if I could reach them, I never did.

No matter how fast my dream-self ran, the lions always caught me. When they did, they surrounded me in a ring, and that was when their faces underwent a frightening change: They became the faces of men. Before I could marvel at the transformation, their lips parted and I saw that though their mouths looked human, they still held the keen, bloodstained teeth of lions. Their roars shook the desert.

In every nightmare, the last thing I saw before I woke was their fanged faces. As soon as I felt the first hot touch of their breath on my cheeks, my eyes flew open and I found myself shivering and sobbing in my bed.

I can't count how many times my terrified tears brought Father running. He was a very patient man who never once scolded me for waking him. Even if my beloved nursemaid Mery was already there, trying to calm me, he would dismiss her. Then he'd pick me up in his arms and hold me until I fell asleep again.

My nightmares grew worse. Sobs and tears became shrieks and howls that roused everyone in the household. After one particularly harrowing night, I woke up to find myself not in my own bed, or even in Mery's comforting arms, but beside the pool of blue lotus flowers in our garden, only a stone's throw from the very spot where the lions appeared in my dreams. I sat bolt upright and screamed.

"Nefertiti, hush, it's all right, I'm here." Father's arms

were around me, strong and sheltering. He was down on one knee beside me, his face filled with sadness. "I thought that if I brought you out here to sleep, Isis would take pity on you and banish your evil dreams forever." He gestured to the delicately painted stone image of a woman whose serene face and welcoming arms were reflected in the waters of the lotus pool.

"Isis?" I was very young and the name was new to me, even if the statue itself was already one of the eternal, unchanging parts of my childish world, like our house, our garden, the city of Akhmin beyond our walls, and the great river that flowed beside them. "Will she make the lions go away?"

"Lions?" Father echoed. "What lions?"

"The ones that come to hunt me every night," I said. Though everyone in our house knew I suffered from nightmares, that was the first time I ever spoke about the images those nightmares contained. No one under our roof—not even Mery or Father—had ever asked me to describe the dreams that woke me up, screaming. By night, their chief concern was getting me to go back to sleep. By day, they might have been afraid to remind me of my midnight terrors. *If we pretend the evil dreams don't exist, maybe she'll forget about them tonight, at last!*

My father settled himself cross-legged on the ground and took me into his lap. "Tell me about the lions, Nefertiti," he asked as solemnly as if I were a grown-up, and not a child who had only lived to see four Inundations of the sacred river.

So I told him everything about the dream that haunted

me, and when I reached the part about how their faces changed, he hugged me close to his chest. "My poor little bird," he said. "The same dream, time and time again, and I never knew. All of your unhappiness for so long, and I could have put an end to it so quickly if only—" He sighed. Then his expression changed from regret to determination. "Never mind what's past. *Now* I can help you."

I never doubted it for a moment. Of course he could help me! He was Father, strong, all-loving, all-powerful, the only true god in my eyes. All the rest—Amun, Osiris, Thoth, Ra, Hathor, even Min, for whom our city was named—were only names to me. (Indeed, I had *heard* Isis's name many times before that morning in the garden, but I'd never thought to attach the sound of it in my ear to anything solid, the way hearing the word *table* or *cat* or *tree* called up a specific image in my mind.)

Now Father got to his feet, still holding me in his arms, and carried me to the statue of Isis. "Hail, Isis, lady of life, light-giver of heaven, queen of the earth, lady of the words of power!" he cried. "Have mercy on your servant, Ay, for he has been a great fool. O Isis, this is my sweet daughter, my only child, my Nefertiti, my greatest treasure. Banish her evil dreams and send them to haunt me instead as punishment for my stupidity. For this, I promise you many rich gifts. O Isis, hear my prayer!"

I was astonished to hear such words coming from my father's mouth. How could he call himself a fool and stupid? Didn't he know his own power? I had no time to ponder such disturbing thoughts: As soon as he ended his plea, Father bowed to the image, then turned and marched off.

His brisk pace jounced me roughly all the way to the edge of the raised bank where our property looked down on the green rushes and reeds bordering the Nile. Here Father lifted me so high that I was nearly sitting on his shoulder, then pointed upstream and asked, "Do you know what lies in that direction, my Nefertiti?"

What a question! Even if I was only four years old, I knew the answer well enough. It was part of a game that Father and I played, when he wasn't busy with whatever grown-up business filled his days. "The gates of the Nile," I replied. "The birthplace of the holy river. And—and—" I wanted Father to be proud of how clever I was. "—and that's where Pharaoh lives, too!" I cried in triumph, then quickly added: "May-Amun-bless-and-protect-the-living-Horus-son-of-Ra-lord-of-the . . . lord-of-the . . . um . . . I forgot."

Father chuckled. "Good enough. But do you know what wonderful birthplace lies *there*?" He pointed down the shimmering river. I shook my head. "Yours, my darling."

"I thought I was born here," I said, my eyes darting toward our house.

"You would have been, but then, as now, I served Pharaoh, and in those days it was Pharaoh's pleasure that I travel with him when he sailed down the river to view the great monuments and tombs of his ancestors. Ah, what wonders!" He lowered me so that I could put my arms around his neck. "There is one above all that steals your breath away, a pyramid of such size that it's like seeing a mountain. We call it Khufu's Horizon, because it is the place from which the soul of that Pharaoh rose to sail the heavens with the other gods. Its sides are sheathed in slabs of the finest white limestone, and the crowning stone is covered in a mix of gold and silver. When Ra's sunlight strikes it, it dazzles the eyes!"

"Oh! Can *I* see it, Father?" I asked, pressing my cheek to his. "Will you take me there with you? Please?"

He looked at me wistfully. "That was almost exactly what your mother said. You are very much like her, my dear, just as beautiful, just as charming. I couldn't tell her no, though I tried. I reminded her that it was almost time for her to give birth, but she argued that it wouldn't happen for at least thirty days. Then she reminded me that we'd be traveling with Pharaoh and his Great Royal Wife, Queen Tiye. 'Tiye, who is your own sister!' your mother said to me. 'You know she'll see to it that nothing happens to me or the child.'" He sighed.

I felt strange. This was the first time I'd heard Father speak about my mother for so long. I knew she had died very soon after I was born. That was why Mery—whose own husband and baby had also died—came to be my nursemaid. The three of us often went to Mother's tomb to leave offerings of food and drink for her *ka,* the part of her soul that remained in this world. Apart from those solemn occasions, Father seldom spoke of her at all, and he looked so sad when leaving the offerings that I didn't want to add to his grief by asking about her.

He looked even sadder now.

"It's all right, Father," I said, hugging him. "You don't have to talk anymore. I'll go to sleep. And I won't have any more bad dreams, I promise!" I knew the promise was empty, that the monstrous, man-faced lions would come back for me the next night, and the next, but all I cared about at that moment was easing his spirit. "Please don't be unhappy."

Father patted my head. Like all children, I had it shaved clean except for the youth-lock, a single braided strand of hair trailing down beside my right ear. The warmth of his hand was comforting. "Are *you* trying to protect *me*, dearest? Only four years old and already you're such a brave girl. Your mother named you The-beautiful-woman-has-come, but perhaps you should have been called The-beautiful-warrior."

I hung my head. "I'm not brave, Father," I said. "If I were, I wouldn't wake you up every night. I could fight my bad dreams myself. I'm sorry."

His smile, bright even in the moonlight, lifted my heart. "Don't you see, my sweet bird? Being brave doesn't mean *always* having to fight alone. You have me, and Mery, and as you grow older, you'll have friends who'll stand up for you, too. But on the night you were born, you were given a guardian who's stronger than all of us put together."

"Stronger than a lion?" I asked timidly.

"*Part* lion," Father replied. "Part lion and part man—the creature we call a sphinx, just like those in your dreams— except *this* one is mightier than all of them. His face is the face of Pharaoh—not our lord, but a Pharaoh who ruled the Black Land in ancient times. So you see, he is lion, man, and god. He ascended to Ra so long ago that his divine powers are more than a match for any bad dream. And he is *your* protector, my Nefertiti."

"He is?" I gave my father a skeptical look. I couldn't

imagine the almighty sun-god Ra making room in his Boat of Eternity for such a monster.

"Do you doubt me?" Father smiled and chucked my chin. "Someday, my princess, I will take you sailing down the river and show you the place where you were born, the place where the pyramid tombs guard the kings and queens of our past. That's where the Great Sphinx crouches on the sand and rock, greeting the sunrise. You were born in one of the rest houses that stand near the temple where our own Pharaoh worshipped his divine ancestor. Before you were one day old, I brought you out into the light of your first dawn, held you up before the god's eyes, and asked him to watch over you. He heard my prayer, and now he is your special guardian. I should have asked him to help you long ago, when your nightmares first began, but I wasn't thinking. Will you forgive me?"

I touched my forehead to his. "It's not your fault, Father," I said. "He's *my* guardian. I'll ask him myself." Then I yawned widely, making Father laugh before he carried me back to my bed.

The following night, before I went to sleep, I made Mery take me outside to the riverbank. There I stood, gazing downstream to where my unseen guardian kept watch over the splendid tombs of ancient rulers, until I found the right words in my heart to offer up to him: "O Great Sphinx, come into my dreams and don't let the bad sphinxes hurt me!" It wasn't much of a prayer, but the Great Sphinx must have made allowances for a four-year-old child.

It worked: That night, when the same old dream came

back to trouble me, when the lions surged out of the sand that swallowed our house, when they chased me and caught me, when their faces became the faces of men and their fanged mouths opened to devour me, I didn't scream. Instead, I stood my ground, stooped to pick up a rock, and threw it right at the biggest, fiercest one of all. The rock struck him squarely between the eyes and he broke into pieces like a clay jug dropped on stone. I grabbed more rocks and threw them as well, smashing sphinx after sphinx until my arms ached and I was panting like a dog at midday, but I was the only being left standing.

I did a little victory dance in the middle of that ring of shattered sphinxes until a shadow fell over me. I looked up and saw a sphinx so huge that he could have made a single mouthful of all the others. His human face was grave and severe, but somehow I knew that he wasn't angry at me for what I'd done to the other sphinxes. I raised my right hand to my chest the way Mery taught me to do when we prayed to the gods and he . . . he smiled at me. It was a smile of approval as beautiful, comforting, and good as when Father smiled at me. Then a whirlwind out of the Red Land swept over the two of us, he vanished behind a curtain of swirling sand, and I awoke.

After that night, whenever I dreamed of lions, I was the one who ruled them. I dreamed of riding them through the streets of Akhmin, or across the desert, or even from the earth to the heavens. They became as tame to me as the cats who blessed our house, and they never hunted me again.

But no matter how far I rode them—to the ends of the

world or the pathways of the stars—there was always a protective shadow over me. If the road grew too rough, or I became afraid that I had lost my way, I only had to glance up and he would be there, the Great Sphinx who had seen me born, the shadow of strength that was always near me.

Part I
Akhmin

1

GATHERING MAGIC

Almost a year after I tamed my dream-lions, during the Festival of the Inundation, my life began to change as surely as the rising river changes the deepest heart of the Black Land.

The Inundation is always a season of wild rejoicing. It's the time when the god Hapy, fat and generous, makes the river overflow its banks to bring new life to the farmlands. A good flood means a good harvest, a good harvest means we'll have more than enough to eat, that our Pharaoh's reign is blessed, and that the gods love us.

That year, when I was five, the priests of every temple in the city observed the rising of the Nile and declared that their prayers had given us a good flood and a fine harvest to come. All Akhmin filled the streets to celebrate the event with music, dance, song, feasting, and gladness. Sunlight flashed from the brilliantly painted walls of the temples and the enameled gold necklaces, bracelets, and earrings of the highborn men and women. The air was filled with a wonderful jumble of delicious scents from many food vendors. Everyone seemed to be laughing. Father carried me on his shoulders so that I could have a clear view of the festivities. I was pleased to be able to see everything from up so high, but when I caught sight of the older girls dancing, singing, and playing their harps, rattles, and tambourines, I squirmed like a fresh-caught fish.

"What's the matter with you, my little bird?" Father asked, grabbing my ankles when I wriggled so hard that I nearly fell off his shoulders.

"I want to get down!" I cried. "I want to dance, too!"

He chuckled, but he didn't let me go. "You're not a bird anymore; you're a kitten, wanting to pounce on anything that catches your eye. Well, little kitten, this dance is to please the gods and to thank them for all that they've given us. It's a sacred thing, not a game for little girls to play at. If you want to dance for the gods someday, you will, but not now. When you're older."

His voice was always loud, a trait he'd kept from his days commanding Pharaoh's troops on the battlefield. One of the dancers who was waiting her turn to perform overheard him and left her group to approach us. I gasped when I saw her: She was so beautiful! Next to her, my dearly loved Mery would have looked like a little brown hen beside a long-limbed, dark-eyed gazelle. The dancer's eyes were artfully outlined with black kohl, the lids glittering green as the reeds along the Nile, and her lips were tinted the rich red of sunset. I stared, fascinated by the dozens of gold charms adorning her tightly braided wig, but when she smiled at me and offered me her tambourine, I worshipped her with gratitude.

While I bounced on Father's shoulders, beating the little instrument with more enthusiasm than skill, she talked to him. At first I paid no attention to their conversation, but I soon began to feel Father's back growing straighter and straighter, his shoulders tensing.

"That will be enough, my darling," he said, reaching up to still my hands. "Give the tambourine back to this young woman now and thank her." I wondered why his voice sounded so strained, the way it did whenever I'd done something wrong that was too serious for him to laugh off.

"Why so eager to be gone?" the dancer drawled, glancing up at Father from beneath lowered eyelids. "She can play with the tambourine a while longer. The child has talent as well as beauty. You should stay at least long enough to see me dance. I promise you, you won't regret it." She gave him a strange little half-smile.

I didn't know what the stranger was trying to do, giving my father such odd, sidelong looks; I just knew that he didn't like it and neither did I. "I'm done," I announced abruptly, handing back the tambourine. "Thank you very much. I want to go home now."

I saw the dancer's lovely face turn ugly in an instant. She snatched the tambourine from my hands and muttered something under her breath. The only words I could make out were "that child . . . spoiled."

"I didn't spoil anything!" I protested as Father carried me off.

"And you never could," he said fondly. "So let's not spoil this happy day by going home *too* soon. There are still plenty of things to see and taste and try. Now tell me the truth, my kitten: Do you really want to go home, or did you just want to go away from that sharp-faced little dancer?"

"Away," I said. I took a deep breath and added: "I'm sorry."

"What for?" Father exclaimed. "For not liking her? That makes two of us."

"But I *should* have liked her," I said. "She was beautiful, and she was kind to me. She let me play her tambourine, and she said nice things about me."

"My sweet one, beauty and favors and flattery don't have anything to do with whether or not you *should* like someone. Affection isn't something you can *buy,* not if it's real. You still like Mery even when she scolds you, right?"

"I *love* Mery," I said loyally. "Even if she's not as pretty as that dancer. She was *much* prettier than Mery, wasn't she, Father?"

"Hrmph." Father coughed into his fist, or at least it sounded like a cough. "I don't think so."

"You *don't?*" What was wrong with Father, saying something like that? Mery was nice-looking, but nowhere near as lovely as the dancer.

"No, I don't," he said firmly. "Anyway, there are more important things than beauty, dearest."

"But she *was* prettier than Mery, wasn't she?" I insisted.

"Let's not worry about pretty and prettier," Father said hastily. "And we *won't* bother Mery with this. Besides, when you're near, all the other girls look like old crocodiles.

Now let's go enjoy ourselves!" He broke into a brisk jog that made me shriek with delight as we raced back to the festival.

We arrived home tired and happy that evening to find Mery waiting to share a festive dinner with us. I made a big fuss over how gorgeous our feast looked, but for some reason, Father didn't do more than glance at it. His eyes were on Mery, who met his warm smile with her own. Even though I was confused, I was also too hungry to wonder about it for long.

While I stuffed myself with roasted duck, fresh bread, and figs dipped in honey, Father sat beside Mery and kept taking the best tidbits of food from his plate, popping them into her mouth with his own fingers. I thought this was very strange. Was something wrong with my beloved nurse that she couldn't feed herself? Was Father teasing her somehow, treating her like a baby? Before I could put my thoughts into words, Father turned to me, smiling broadly, and said: "My dear little kitten, I have a wonderful surprise for you. I know how much you love Tey, so from now on you'll be able to love her even more because she's going to be your new mother."

I wrinkled my brows, completely confused. "I don't love Tey!" I objected. "I don't even *know* anyone named Tey, and anyway, I don't need a new mother. I have Mery."

Instead of thanking me for being loyal to her, Mery laughed and scooped me onto her lap. "Oh, my darling Nefertiti, *I* am Tey," she said, twirling my lone lock of hair around her long, gentle fingers.

"No, you're *Mery,*" I said firmly, wondering why my

nursemaid was saying such silly things. "That's your real name; it's what I always call you!"

Father put his arm around Mery's shoulders, embracing us both. "And *I* call you my little kitten," he told me. "Does that make Little Kitten your real name? Well, then! It's the same for Tey: As soon as you were old enough to talk and to learn the word for Beloved One, that's what you called her. But it doesn't change the fact that her mother named her Tey just as yours named you Nefertiti. Do you see?"

"I . . . think so." It was a lie, but I didn't want Father to think I was stupid.

"Never mind any of that," my nursemaid said, holding me close. "I'm still your Mery. You don't need to worry about calling me anything else unless you want to." She pressed her cheek to mine. Her skin was soft and warm and smelled like cinnamon. "So, are you pleased?"

"With what?" I asked. The whole business of names had distracted me so much that I'd forgotten to think about the more important part of Father's "wonderful surprise."

"With me becoming your father's new wife, of course!" Mery said, her face filled with joy. "And your new mother."

Well, I *was* happy to hear that Mery was going to be a part of our family; there was no question about it. Mery was the only mother I'd ever known. There was nothing "new" about her at all, except for the way I saw Father gazing at her. I'd never seen such a look in his eyes before, and for some reason, it irritated me. I suppose he must have been looking at her that way for a long time, except I'd been too busy with my games and toys and playmates to notice. Now that I did . . . I didn't like it. It reminded me a little of the way that dancer had looked at *him*.

Father was supposed to be *mine,* and only mine. Didn't they know that?

And so, even though I loved Mery with all my heart, I couldn't bring myself to say a single word to welcome her into our family. I only sat there in her lap, my thin little arms folded, my head resting against her heart, and I began to cry.

"Isis have mercy, what's the matter with her?" I heard Father slap the arms of his chair impatiently and stand up. His shadow fell over me, wavering in the light of the oil lamps brightening our evening meal. "It makes no sense. I know she's fond of you, and she can't possibly remember her mother, so why is she crying? Nefertiti! Nefertiti, look at me! Tell me what's wrong."

His voice was so harsh and insistent that he didn't sound like Father at all. I gave a little whimper of fear, threw my arms around Mery's neck, and buried my face against her shoulder.

"Shhh, let her be, Ay," Mery said softly. I didn't realize it then, but that was the first time I'd heard anyone call Father by his name, Ay. I felt my nursemaid—my new mother—stand up with me in her arms. "She's just overtired. Children need their sleep. I'll put her to bed and you'll see that everything will be fine in the morning."

Mery was right: I did feel better the next day. My life had altered, but only in a few small ways, nothing to shake the earth or pull the stars out of the sky. Mery began to wear finer clothes, and she no longer slept in the room next to mine unless I was sick; that was about the sum of the changes. I did catch her sitting on Father's lap out in the garden, and sometimes I surprised him kissing her, but the two of them always made such a big fuss over me when that happened that I stopped feeling annoyed with their silly winks and whispers and enjoyed the attention.

As happy as I was to have Father take Mery as his wife, I'd never suspected that the two of them were in love until they told me so. When the following year brought the next change into my life, it was no surprise. I knew all about it long before it happened. It's almost impossible to keep the birth of a baby secret. My beloved Mery began to grow fat and fatter with each passing day. I'd seen enough pregnant women in the streets of Akhmin to know what *that* meant. By the time Father and Mery decided to tell me about the baby, it wasn't news to me. I think they were disappointed by my indifference.

That changed on the day of the birth itself. Mery and I were eating breakfast together when suddenly she gasped and staggered to her feet, her hands on her belly. Before I could finish chewing the bit of bread in my mouth, a whirl-wind of shouting servants, running slaves, and bustling strangers swept through our house. Our oldest serving woman herded me toward the garden in spite of my hungry protests just as two unfamiliar women—the midwives—came hurrying past me, bound for the bedroom where Mery had vanished. I was still arguing with the slave about my abandoned breakfast when the younger midwife found me and let me know I had a new sister.

"Well, *that* was quick," the servant remarked. "You're good."

The young midwife spread her slender hands. "The gods be thanked, not me. The child is healthy and the mother is well." Then she turned to me. "You must be the young mistress. Your mama wants you to come back inside."

Mery was lying on her side in bed, nursing the newborn. She smiled warmly when she saw me. "Come and meet your sister, Mutnodjmet," she said. She'd named the baby Mut-is-the-sweet-one, but I didn't see anything particularly sweet about the red, wrinkled little person in Mery's arms. After only a glance, I decided she was boring and became much more interested in two big bricks left on the floor near Mery's bed. They were too heavy for me to pick up, so I squatted low and stared closely at the pictures carved on them.

"What are these?" I asked.

"Birthing bricks," the older midwife replied as she and her colleague went about the task of tidying the room. "Your mama crouched on them when it was time for your sister to be born. It's all right, you can touch them. I doubt you'll break them." She grinned, showing badly worn-down teeth. "Or their magic."

"Magic?" With one fingertip, I traced the images of a parade of carved and painted goddesses. I recognized some of them—Hathor with her cow's ears and horns, and of course Isis, but I was still too young to know all of the great divinities on sight. "Who's this? She looks like a frog. And this one? She's got a hippo's head!"

"Ah, the first is Heket, who protects women in childbirth, and the second, that's Taweret. Very few creatures are fiercer, more protective mothers than hippos. You must never go near them, young mistress."

"I know *that*," I said stiffly. "I'm not a baby." I cast a look back to where Mery was cradling my new sister and felt a pang of envy. *Now that* she's *here, will Mery still love me?*

"Of course you're no baby, young mistress." The younger midwife was done with her chores, so she knelt beside me and pointed to a very strange image, a brick with the head of a woman. "See this? This is Meskhenet, goddess of the birthing bricks themselves. All of them had the power to keep demons at bay, shielding mothers in childbirth and their babies."

I dared to trace the outline of Taweret, with her strong arms, bulging belly, and crowned hippo's head. "Are they good at it?" I asked.

"What a question, young mistress!" Out of the corner of my eye, I saw the young midwife clutch the amulet around her neck. "They are gods!"

Then why did my mother die when I was born? I wondered. But I didn't ask that out loud. I knew better. It was a very great sin to question the gods. It could bring horrible misfortune crashing down on your head in this life and condemn your heart to being devoured by a monster after you died. I loved Isis because she was beautiful, and the stories Mery told me about her proved she was also brave and clever—everything I wanted to be and feared I never would—but the other gods made me uneasy. Every morning when I stood with Father and Mery to offer up our family prayers, I felt as if I were giving honey cakes to a gang of bullies, hoping they would accept the bribe and leave me alone.

"Nefertiti, sit with me, please." Mery patted a place beside her and the baby. I clambered onto the bed, happy to be near her and to feel her fingers twirling my lone lock of hair the way she always did. "You are a very lucky girl, do you know that?" she said. "The gods favor you. They gave *you* the gift of meeting little Mutnodjmet even before your father does."

That was true. Father had left the house even before breakfast, because he had some unknown, grown-up business to discuss with the chief priest of Amun's temple. Still, I had to ask: "Why is *that* a gift? What can I do with it?"

"It's a good gift because it gives *you* a great power over your sister: the power to give her a name."

"She *has* a name!" I protested. "You gave it to her."

"Yes, but I don't want everyone calling her by that name. Names are magic. When Isis used her wits to learn the secret name of Ra, the almighty sun-god, she became as great as he! You and I need to protect this baby until she's old enough and strong enough to carry the name I gave her. Until then, she needs to be called something else, to keep her safe from evil spirits who could harm her if they knew her true name." Mery let go of my youth-lock and stroked my cheek. "Will you do this for my baby? Will you give her a good name?"

So that was how I became the one to call my sister

Bit-Bit, which means a double helping of honey. When Father came home from the temple and heard the name I'd chosen, he praised me. "Mut-is-the-sweet-one and honey is the sweetest thing I know. You're a very clever girl, my little kitten."

I shrugged. "I just like honey. Besides, she's too puny to have a big name."

"*That* will change," he replied. "Meanwhile, so you'll like your sister as much as you like honey, I'm going to give you a double portion of the best honey under this roof, right now. Does that please you?"

I nodded vigorously. "I'm glad I didn't name her Penu," I said. (And I almost *had* named her Mouse because she was so small.) "Even if you call me Kitten all the time, I'd never want to eat *that*."

The days passed and Bit-Bit grew quickly. She was a sweet-tempered baby, even when her teeth began to come in. Every time I was allowed to hold her, she smiled at me and patted my face with her tiny, chubby hands. Soon I was begging Mery to let me take care of her every day, and though it got harder and harder for me to carry her as she grew, I refused to give up the right to take my baby sister everywhere. My playmates saw less and less of me. When Mery finally insisted I spend time with someone besides Bit-Bit, they snubbed me because I'd ignored them for so long. I didn't care. I still had Bit-Bit.

One day, when Bit-Bit was old enough to walk and could even run a little, we were playing on a shaded bench in the covered walkway that faced the garden. It was the hottest part of the day, when the sun-god Ra blazed most fiercely.

"I'd better rub some oil on your skin, Bit-Bit," I told her. "Otherwise you'll dry up and blow away." But when I came back from the kitchen with the olive oil, Bit-Bit was hiding under the bench, and when I tried to put the oil on her, she squirmed out of my slippery grasp and took off. One of the servants must have left the garden gate unlatched, because before I knew what was happening, she'd pushed it open and was toddling swiftly down the street outside our house.

I raced after her. It was easy enough for me to catch up to her, running along on her plump little legs, but the instant before I could snatch her up, I heard her let out a horrible yowl. She sat down hard on her bare bottom, arms and legs flailing, and her cries rose to a shrill shriek of terror.

"Bit-Bit, what's the matter?" I cried, throwing my arms around my sister. Then I saw it.

It was a small insect, golden brown from the tips of its two clawed forefeet to the barbed end of the segmented tail arched above its back. My breath caught in my throat as I watched it scuttle away: My precious baby sister had been stung by a scorpion!

"O gods, have mercy," I whispered, kneeling in the dirt and holding Bit-Bit so close to my chest that I was almost crushing her. She howled louder, tears carving tiny rivers through the smudges on her cheeks, and fought me, but I held her in an embrace made strong by panic. A scorpion! I remembered Mery telling me the tale of how even great Isis had been powerless to shield her son, the child-god Horus, from the life-threatening sting of those venomous creatures, but I'd fallen asleep before she finished. If Isis was so helpless, what could I do?

I began screaming for help, but the street was deserted. The noontime heat was hammering the life out of the land. People were inside their homes, waiting for Ra's sun-ship to sail westward, bringing back the cool refuge of shadows. The house walls facing the street were thick and had no windows, so no one could hear me, no matter how loudly I yelled. I might as well have shrieked into a tomb.

"Merciful Hathor, what's the matter with you children?"

I looked up and saw the most remarkable person. He was tiny, no taller than me, with a perfectly round head on top of a perfectly round body that balanced on a pair of thick legs. I was surprised to see that he wore a fine white linen kilt and sandals adorned with sparkling jewels. Because he was so small, I expected him to go around completely unclothed, the way all of us children did. He carried a big palm frond over his head to keep off the sun, and his kohl-rimmed eyes were filled with concern.

"Help us! Please, help us!" I cried, getting a closer grip on my sister, who flailed her feet and bellowed like a whole herd of cows. With tears and snot running down my face, I told the stranger everything that had happened. His wide mouth fell open in alarm.

"A scorpion?" he said. He flung his little body down in the dust beside us and stared closely at Bit-Bit. "What color was it?"

Why does that *matter?* I thought, but I answered, "Brown."

"Mmm-hm. And where did it sting her?"

"I—I don't know," I said. "Her foot?"

"Let me look." His strong, square hands reached for my sister's feet.

Bit-Bit kicked him right in the chin.

He sprawled backward, his short legs paddling the air like a topsy-turvy beetle. The sight took Bit-Bit by so much surprise that she stopped hollering and began to giggle.

"Well, *there's* a fine thing," the little man said to me, shaking his oversized head with mock annoyance as he sat up. "Some magician's obviously pulled a trick on you, young lady. He's stolen your real sister and put an enchanted donkey in her place. I've half a mind to let the scorpion take her."

"Oh, please don't!" I cried, reaching across Bit-Bit to grab his arm. "This really is my sister. Don't let her die! Mery will be heartbroken."

"Mery?" The little man's brow creased with surprise. "Mery the wife of Ay? You're *their* daughters?" He glanced at our house, baking in the sun, and sniffed. "True, this is the place. How long it's been . . ." All at once, he looked at me so intently that it was frightening. "Ah, yes. I see it now. I would know that face anywhere. You're Nefertiti, aren't you?"

All I could do was nod. My lips were dry, and not just from the heat. How could he talk about knowing my face when we'd never met before? My head swam with memories of something I'd seen near Min's temple the previous year, when the priests hired workmen to add a magnificent new building to the god's shrine. The first thing the laborers did was set up a stone carved with an image that looked almost exactly like the little man before me, except the carved dwarf had hair and whiskers like a lion's mane and looked ready to fight. When I asked Mery, she told me it was the god Bes. *Always show him honor,* she told me. *He may be small, but he's a fierce fighter and especially devoted to protecting children.*

Bes! I thought. *It's the god himself, come to save Bit-Bit. And she* kicked *him!* My tears flowed freely as I finally found my voice and exclaimed, "Oh please, don't be mad at her! She's only a baby!"

"Of course, of course!" He clapped his hands and winked at Bit-Bit. "So, little donkey, will you let me save your worthless life? Or are you going to kick me again?"

Bit-Bit laughed and began clapping her hands, too. When he crouched in front of us and studied her feet— from a safe distance, this time—she sat docilely in my lap in the middle of the sun-drenched street until he was done.

At last he slapped his broad thighs and looked satisfied. "Just as I suspected. Dry your eyes, Nefertiti—and wipe your nose while you're at it—the time for tears is over. I know *precisely* the spell to drive the scorpion venom from this child's body. Moreover, it will leave her skin unmarked by even the smallest scar from the creature's deadly stinger." With that, he began to mutter in a singsong voice, all the while tracing line after line of pictures in the dirt between us. Bit-Bit squealed with delight but didn't squirm. As for me, I watched in fascination as the god performed his magic.

When he was done, he grinned at me and said, "Casting spells is thirsty work, especially at this time of day. Do you think I've earned a drink for my pains?"

In answer, I threw my arms around the god's neck, thanking him, praising him, and promising him every drop of beer that was in the house. Scrambling to my feet, I lifted Bit-Bit onto my hip, grabbed the god's hairy wrist, and dragged him with us around the corner and into the cool shelter of our home.

Once inside, I set Bit-Bit down gently and began shouting for someone to bring food and drink. I made so much racket that it fetched nearly every slave and servant under our roof. The four slaves didn't have much choice, but the servants weren't used to having a child give them orders. They glared at me, though as soon as their eyes lit on our guest, their scowls became gracious smiles of welcome. Obviously they, too, recognized a god when they saw one.

They were just beginning to bring in baskets of bread and fruit and a big clay beer jug when the room rang out with the sound of Father's voice demanding, "What's going on here?"

I rushed forward to tell him everything. Bit-Bit stayed where she was, happily bouncing on the god's plump knee while he shared the glittering, juicy red seeds of a cut pomegranate with her. I was so overwhelmed by what *might* have happened to my sister, if not for Bes's miraculous appearance, that I began crying all over again. Father picked me up to comfort me, then regarded our guest.

"So, you're a god now, are you?" he said lightly. "Does Pharaoh know?"

The dwarf spread his thick hands, casting all blame to the winds. "My lord Pharaoh declared himself to be a god, the earthly child of Ra himself. I, on the other hand, was named a god by a young woman whose beauty equals Isis's own! Tell me, Ay, who's the higher authority here, Pharaoh or Isis?"

Father gave me a helpless look. "Hmm. What can I say to *that,* little kitten? One answer will bring Pharaoh's wrath down on my head, the other will provoke a mighty goddess."

"Isis is right," I said firmly. "Pharaoh is Ra's son, but Isis stole Ra's power because she was more clever than the old sun-god."

The little man clapped his hands. "Well said, my pretty child! Only *don't* say anything like that if you ever find yourself in Pharaoh's court. You won't be popular."

"And how popular will you be when our king learns that you're parading around as the god Bes, eh?" Father asked, winking.

Our guest let loose a great sigh, so loud and so exaggerated that it sent Bit-Bit into fresh peals of laughter. "Alas, then it seems I have no choice. But will sweet Nefertiti still be my friend when I'm no longer a god, but only poor old Henenu the scribe?"

I made Father set me down and went swiftly to put my arms around our guest's heavy neck. "I will *always* be your friend, even if you're not Bes," I announced. "You saved my sister." I sealed my promise with a big kiss on his rough cheek.

Father laughed. "And how did he do that?"

"He made magic and took away the scorpion's poison and there isn't even a mark on Bit-Bit's foot where she was stung," I said, hugging Henenu harder. "I *told* you."

"Er . . . perhaps it's time I told you, my little lady." Henenu gently freed himself from my arms. "Your sister was never in any danger, may the gods be praised. The scorpion you saw never touched her. Even if it had, it was only one of the brown ones. Their bite hurts, but it can't kill us."

"But she was crying," I protested.

"Perhaps she'd just fallen down? And when I came upon the two of you, you were holding her tightly and screaming in her ears. She wasn't bitten, she was terrified." The dwarf bowed his head. "I deceived you, child, but only to calm your fears. I'll understand if you want nothing more to do with me."

I hesitated for only a moment. In the time it takes to draw two breaths, my arms were once more around Henenu's neck and I'd planted a second kiss on his brow. "I'm still your friend," I declared. "But you have to promise not to tell any more lies or Ma'at will be angry with you."

"Ah, so you already know about the beautiful goddess of truth, do you?" The dwarf was pleased. "Very well. In that case, I swear by the sacred Feather of Ma'at that from now on, I will always tell you the truth, Nefertiti. But you must swear that you won't hate me for it."

"Why would I?" I asked, genuinely puzzled.

"Because the truth holds the greatest magic, the greatest beauty, and sometimes the greatest danger," Henenu said solemnly.

I laughed and hugged him. "You're funny," I said, believing with all my heart that his words were another one of his jokes and that there was nothing in the truth that could ever harm me.

2

THE SCRIBE

"What are you doing, Henenu?"

If I'd been given a spoonful of honey for every time I asked that question during the first year after we met, I would have drowned in golden sweetness. During that time, the scribe became a frequent, welcome visitor to our home. This wasn't anything extraordinary: He and Father had known each other since boyhood. Both of them had grown up and left Akhmin to serve in Pharaoh's court, following the trail of good fortune my aunt Tiye had left behind her when she became Amenhotep's adored Great Royal Wife. Father and Henenu were inseparable friends then, but those days ended for Father soon after I was born. Mourning my mother, he requested permission to serve Pharaoh elsewhere and was sent back to Akhmin. Henenu stayed on, one of Pharaoh's best, most valued scribes.

In spite of how comfortably Henenu lived in

Amenhotep's shadow, he still made it a point to come home as often as possible, to visit his family and share the bounty he earned in the great king's service. It was only chance that kept us from crossing paths until the Day of the Scorpion, as he called it: Pharaoh sent him to Nubia as part of a diplomatic mission and the assignment kept him far from Akhmin for years.

"What does it *look* like I'm doing, Nefertiti?"

No matter how many times I asked my eternal question, Henenu's answer remained the same. He made me work for knowledge. Even though he was forever the size of a child, he was a grown-up. More important, he was one of those rare grown-ups who knew how to talk to children without treating us like living dolls or clever puppies.

"It looks like you're doing the same thing you did on the Day of the Scorpion," I said, standing behind him and peering over his shoulder. "You're making pictures, only you're not doing it in the dirt."

This was true. I'd found my friend sitting cross-legged in the shade of one of our sycamore trees, a sharpened reed in one hand, a piece of beeswax-covered wood in his lap. The wax was covered with line after line of pictures. Even though we had known each other for a year, this was the first time I'd discovered him busy with this particular activity.

"And why do you *think* I'm doing this, little kitten?" It hadn't taken him long to call me by the pet name Father had given me. It made me happy to hear him use it.

"I don't know," I admitted, settling myself on the

ground beside him and studying the lines in the wax. "Magic?"

"Maybe." The keen point of the reed flew across the board and a new row of pictures appeared. "There," he said. "That's you."

"That?" I pointed at the figure of a seated woman at the right-hand end of the line of images. "That doesn't look like me. She's too old and she's got long hair."

Henenu chuckled. "What I meant to say was, that's your *name*. This is how you write 'Nefertiti.' "

I looked more closely at the figures. "You're teasing me again," I said. "You're trying to trick me the same way you did on that day, pretending you were using magic to save Bit-Bit. But you were only pretending."

Henenu sighed dramatically and let his large head slump forward onto his chest. "So this is the thanks I get for helping you: nothing but cruel doubt and accusations of falsehood. If I were to die tomorrow, when I came before Osiris for judgment, the gods would hear your words and condemn me for being a liar. They'd feed my heart to the Devourer and that would be the end of me, body and soul."

"Nooooo!" I threw my arms around his neck. The Devourer of Souls was the goddess Ammut, a ghastly monster who was one-third hippo, one-third lion, and one-third crocodile. Any soul that failed to pass its trial of virtue was her lawful prey. There was no escape, no appeal, only oblivion. "I didn't say you *lied*," I protested. "I said you *pretended*."

"Some people might argue that those are the same thing," Henenu said, cheerful once more. He gently freed himself from my hold. "I did pretend to heal your sister, who needed no healing, but I assure you, whenever I write, I write only what I know to be true. The words I made in the dust on that day were a prayer to Hathor, asking her to calm and comfort you. Like this." He scraped the reed pen over the waxed tablet.

I studied the results closely. "Where is Hathor's name?" I asked. He pointed to a picture of a hawk inside a square. I frowned, skeptical. "That doesn't look like her. Sometimes she looks like a cow, and sometimes like a woman with cow's ears and horns, but never like a hawk."

"It doesn't need to look like her. There are plenty of painters and sculptors to make images of the goddess. But this symbol *means* her name."

"The way this means me?" I asked, fascinated. I pointed to the centerpiece of my own inscribed name, a row of four strange images between what looked like a pair of feathers. "But *how* does it do that?"

Henenu seemed to take real pleasure in answering my questions. "Ah, my lady is wiser than many of my students. They never take the time to wonder about the reasons behind their lessons; they only drudge away like oxen plowing a field, eager to have the task over and done. They memorize everything and learn . . . nothing. It's said that long ago, the god Thoth himself taught men the mysteries of writing. These are his sacred symbols. We are merely the servants that carry them from place to place and age to age. Now this"—he indicated the same symbol that had drawn my attention, a rounded object with a long, straight line rising from it—"this is a picture of the human heart and the windpipe."

"The what?" I knew about the heart, which was the house of the soul, but the other word was unknown to me.

"The path from your lungs to your mouth that carries the breath of life and lets you speak, cry, sing, laugh, and ask such interesting questions." He winked at me. "That's what the picture *is*, but what it *represents* is *nefer*, the part of your name that means beauty and goodness."

"I guess that makes sense," I admitted. "Mery taught me that my heart should always stay beautiful or Ammut will eat it, and it's good to breathe."

My words made Henenu laugh out loud. "I never thought of it that way! Very good, my lady: It's not every day that someone gives a lesson to a teacher. What would you make of the rest of these symbols, I wonder?"

I pushed myself closer to the little scribe and fixed my eyes on all of the writing on the waxed tablet. "Well, that one looks like ripples on the river, so it must mean water, and that one's a flower, so maybe it means beautiful, too, and that looks like Bit-Bit when she sucks her thumb, so I'll bet it means baby, and that one—it's just a bent line, I don't know what it's supposed to be. Oh! And there are two feathers in my name! Is it Ma'at's sacred Feather of Truth, the one that goes into the other side of the scales when the gods weigh our hearts?" I turned to Henenu, eager to see approval in his eyes.

I was not disappointed. His smile spread all the way across his broad face. "It's much more complicated than that, my dear, but you're not too far off the target. You have good eyes and a good mind. You're also not afraid to try to answer even though it means you might be wrong, and smart enough to confess when you don't know something. I'd love to see how well you'd do with some real instruction in the scribal arts. I wish you could be one of my students."

"Why can't I?" I asked.

"Scribes are men, that's why."

"But why is *that*?" I persisted.

"Because women have no use for such learning." He looked very sure of himself, very satisfied with that answer, as if he were repeating the word of the gods themselves. "You're going to grow up, get married, have children, and run a household. Why would you need to know how to write letters or keep records or make other important documents? Why would you want to take the time to learn something as difficult as writing when you could use your days better learning to do women's work?"

"What about magic?" I asked.

My question startled him. "What?"

"Well, isn't *that* women's work? Isis used it to win the sun-god's power by learning his secret name. *She's* a woman." It all made perfect sense to me, even if it left Henenu looking more and more like a goggle-eyed frog.

"Isis—Isis is a goddess," he stammered. "You can't compare her to ordinary women. You mustn't! She might become angry with you."

"No, she likes me," I replied confidently, thinking of my dream-lions. Even though it was the Great Sphinx who'd saved me from them, I still recalled Father's prayer to Isis and the sweet face of her image in our garden. Isis was brave but kindhearted, a loving wife and a devoted mother. She would understand and forgive sooner than punish. All I felt for her and from her was love.

Then I remembered something: "Once when Bit-Bit was a baby, she got very sick and Father had a healer priest come to the house, but Mery went to the *sau*, the woman who makes amulets to ward off demons. She took me along and I watched the *sau* make the amulet on a piece of baked clay. I thought she was only drawing pictures, but now I think she was writing, just like you. She's no goddess, so writing *is* women's work, too!" My triumphant voice dared him to contradict me.

He didn't. Instead, he laughed. "Ah well, who am I to stand against someone so fiercely determined to learn? I can almost see the divine Thoth smiling down upon you, giving his blessing."

I knit my brows. Thoth, god of wisdom, was a man with the head of an ibis, a bird with a long, thin, down-curving beak. "How can an ibis smile?"

Henenu chuckled and slapped his knees. "He's a god. He manages. Now let's see if *you* can manage to learn." He handed me the waxed tablet, showed me how to hold the sharpened reed, and our lessons began.

He must have been expecting me to lose interest quickly, either because I'd grow bored or discouraged trying to master all of the different symbols, their meanings, and their uses. But if he thought that writing was just another game to me, one that I'd soon tire of and abandon, I showed him otherwise. It was hard work, yet even if I sometimes wept with frustration, the satisfaction of conquering each new challenge lifted my spirit so high that I wouldn't have traded that feeling of exaltation for all the easy victories in the world.

Whenever Henenu was in Akhmin, he came to our house frequently to give me lessons and check on my progress. When he left to rejoin Pharaoh's court, he gave me plenty of work to do to fill the time until our next meeting, along with words of approval, of criticism, and . . . of warning: "Remember, Nefertiti, these lessons are our secret. Your parents don't need to hear about them."

"But why not?" I asked. I was proud of my achievement and, to be honest, I was also greedy for praise. I wanted Father and Mery to know how well I was mastering our complicated system of language. I wanted Henenu to tell them what he often told me, that he wished the boys he taught were even half as good at reading and writing as I was.

"Because I say so and I am your teacher," Henenu snapped. I was shocked. I wasn't used to getting such curt treatment from my friend. Usually he welcomed my questions during our lessons. He said that they kept his mind from sinking into complacency, like a fat hippo settling to the bottom of a river. But this was different. "Now you can choose: Either you honor my decision and we say no more about it, or you keep pecking at me like a plover at the crocodile's teeth and we end our lessons forever. Well?" He crossed his arms.

My choice was no choice. I wanted to learn. If the price of learning was silence, so be it. I gave in.

Henenu did his part to keep our lessons hidden. The

two of us shared a remarkable sense of timing: I was always within earshot of our home's entryway whenever he came by and he always seemed to show up when Father was occupied with official business, either at home or out in the city, and Mery had her hands full taking care of the household. No matter how busy they were, there was never any question of asking him to come back later. That would have been a great offense to an honored guest, to say nothing of an insult to a dear friend of the family.

Every time, the little scribe resolved the problem with the same solution: "Well, if you really don't mind, why don't I just go into your beautiful garden for a while? It's such a tranquil refuge. As much as I love my own family, our home can be a little rowdy. I won't be bored: I've got a number of official documents that I must review before amending for the royal court." He patted the always-full case at his belt that held a bunch of rolled-up papyrus scrolls.

Father and Mery were happy to consent. They went back to their work, Henenu toddled off into the garden, and I stole after him as soon as I could. I don't know how he managed it, but I was grateful for his cleverness. It gave us the time we needed to pursue my studies undisturbed.

There was only one problem: Bit-Bit. The older she got, the more time she wanted to spend with me. I loved her dearly, but I was jealous of the lesson time I had with Henenu. Every time we met, he showed me fresh treasures— new words, new ways to use them, new papyrus scrolls containing stories of the gods and goddesses, of pharaohs and queens from distant times, of love and adventure, even of the world that lay beyond the borders of the Black Land!

There was always something exciting to learn from the little scribe, whereas Bit-Bit—

Bit-Bit was Bit-Bit: always wanting to play the same games, sing the same songs, dance the same dances with me. If I tried to distract her with some new pastime, she turned up her nose and began wheedling for us to play "the *right* way." At best it was boring, at worst it was annoying, and trying to evade her when I had a lesson with Henenu was a challenge.

I admit it: I bribed one of the slaves to keep my little sister busy whenever Henenu came to visit. The slave was an old woman who'd been in our household for as long as I could remember. I didn't bother learning her name, or even if she had one. Slaves were slaves; they didn't have to be spoken to the same way as servants. They were something we owned, there to do a job for us, like a chair or a bowl or a pot of kohl. I didn't know how they'd come into our household, and if any of them died, it didn't affect me.

One day, in the year I reached my tenth birthday, everything changed.

I will never forget that morning. Bit-Bit and I were dancing in the garden. I loved to dance almost as much as I loved to write, and in my heart I cherished the secret ambition to dance at one of the great temple festivals with all of Akhmin looking on. I didn't even care which god I'd honor with my dancing, as long as the priests chose me. It was a great honor, because only the best dancers could be trusted to keep their steps and movements perfect. Anything less might anger the gods.

"Well, what do we have here?" Henenu's voice boomed through the sunlit air, such a big sound coming from such a small body. Bit-Bit and I stopped our dance and ran to greet him. The scribe was a great favorite with everyone in our family.

"What's that, Henenu?" Bit-Bit asked, clinging to his left arm while pointing at the object he cradled to his chest with his right.

"Don't tell me you've never seen my palette, little monkey?" he said, letting her get a good look at the long, narrow rectangle of polished slate with Thoth's image carved just below the two oval wells to hold the black and red pigments. "See how cleverly it's made. It even holds a small clay pot for water and a handful of the best reed pens, newly sharpened. If it only had a case for storing papyrus scrolls, I couldn't ask for a better tool."

"Oh." Bit-Bit sounded disappointed. "You're going to *work*. I thought you'd come to play with us. Does this mean we have to leave the garden?"

"Well . . ." Henenu gave me a conspiratorial look. This was my cue to find a way to send Bit-Bit elsewhere, so I could have a lesson.

"We can come back later," I declared, taking Bit-Bit by the hand. "The sooner we leave Henenu in peace, the sooner he'll finish his work. Then we can show him our new dance." I steered her firmly back into the house.

Once indoors, it didn't take me long to find an excuse for thrusting Bit-Bit into the old slave woman's care and to rush back to Henenu. I only delayed my return long enough to fetch my waxed tablet from its hiding place in my room. I found the little scribe seated under the tallest palm tree in the garden. Even though I was now old enough to wear a pleated linen sheath dress, I dropped cross-legged onto the dirt beside him. Mery would scold me for ruining my clothes, but I didn't care. I'd sacrifice a dozen dresses to learn how to write a single new word.

"Look at what I've done, Henenu," I said, eagerly holding out my waxed tablet. It was a surprise I'd been working on ever since our last lesson, something more than my usual practice lines. This time, instead of copying out someone else's words over and over, I'd written my own.

The scribe's brows drew together as he studied the lines I'd etched into the smooth wax. "This isn't what I gave you to do."

"No, it isn't," I said, grinning.

"In Thoth's name, *why*? What ever made you want to copy *this* stuff?"

My grin was gone. "It's—it's not *stuff*. It's a hymn in praise of Isis!"

"Yes, and every line of it seems to come from a different song. Here the goddess is soaring through the skies as a hawk, *here* she's swimming along as part of the Nile's waters, next she turns into a sacred cat for some reason, and the cat becomes a lion, and the lion decides it would rather be the moon!"

I felt as if he'd slapped my face. "Is it—is it *that* bad?"

"The pieces are all right by themselves—some even have a rough touch of beauty—but when they're thrown together like this, it's a worse horror than Ammut." He shuddered at the thought of the hippo-lion-crocodile monstrosity. "How did you find such a thing?"

I turned my face away from him. I wanted to crawl into a hole in the sand and die. "I wrote it."

"You . . . ?" I heard Henenu make a very strange sound, a noise that was as much of a badly matched mix as my miserable poem. It was part snort, part chuckle, and partly a failed attempt to hold back his laughter.

Something flared inside me. My chin came up sharply and I glared at him. "I *know* it's bad!" I shouted, slapping my hands on the earth. "You said so clearly enough! I won't write anything of my own ever again, but you don't have the right to laugh at me for trying!"

"Perhaps not. You're braver than I, Nefertiti. I never dared try my hand at writing anything of my own. But still"—his eyes twinkled—"still, if you reread it, I think you'll have to admit that it really is dreadful."

"It is *not*!" My voice rose to a shriek. "Take that back! I wrote this for Isis and if you don't apologize, she'll curse you for—!"

"Nefertiti! Nefertiti! What's the matter?" Bit-Bit came racing into the garden. She threw herself at me with such force that the two of us sprawled in the dirt. "I heard you yell! What's wrong?"

"Get *off*, Bit-Bit," I snapped, pushing her off me and sitting up. "Nothing's the matter. Go away!"

"But I heard—" She stretched out her hands.

I slapped them aside. "I say *go away*!" I didn't mean to treat my little sister that way, but I was blinded by anger. Henenu's words wounded my pride so deeply that I lashed out without thinking at any target that came too close. "Well? Why are you still sitting there?" I stood up, dragged her to her feet, and shoved her again. "Go, you stupid thing! *Go!*" She flew back into the house, crying.

Henenu looked at me wide-eyed. "Was that necessary, Nefertiti?" he said. "She only came running because she heard you making so much noise that she thought you were in trouble."

"I don't care," I said, folding my arms. "I'm tired of having to look after her all the time. I want to be free to do what I want when I want to do it."

The dwarf clicked his tongue. "And make everyone else dance to your music? You sound like your aunt Tiye. Unfortunately, she's got the power to do it."

"Good for her!" I wasn't thinking about what I said. I was still seething over how he'd criticized my song. "If *she* wanted to learn how to read and write, she wouldn't have to hide it, as if she was doing something wrong!"

Henenu's face hardened. "With Queen Tiye, there is no right or wrong. There are only her wishes, her plans, and her desires."

"And what's so bad about *that*? I wish *I* had her power! I'd have *real* lessons, then, not just a few crumbs dribbled out whenever you come back to Akhmin!" I was shouting again, carried away by my anger. I wanted to fight the whole world.

"Nefertiti, lower your voice. You'll draw attention."

"From Bit-Bit again? So what? If she does come back out here, I'll send her away again. What can she do about it?" I laughed and began to write *Bit-Bit is a jumping mouse* in the dirt. I couldn't think of a more easily frightened creature.

A shadow fell over me as my finger traced the last symbol. "*What* are you doing, Nefertiti?" I looked up into Father's stormy face.

3

SHE-WHO-WRITES

Henenu and I stood in the cool shadows of the room where Father often met with the local priests and other important city officials. I didn't know exactly what he did beyond the fact that he served Pharaoh, only that he had enough power in Akhmin to make great men bow to him, flatter him, and bring us gifts. He had left the house that morning in order to meet with the chief priest of the Isis temple. I thought he would be gone the whole day. How was I to know that his meeting would end early and that the first sight he'd encounter on his return home was Bit-Bit in tears, or that the next thing he'd hear would be me making such an angry uproar in the garden?

Now I waited to learn the price I'd have to pay for giving in to my temper. The secret between Henenu and me wasn't a secret anymore. Father had caught me in the act of writing.

"Is *this* how you honor our friendship, Henenu?"

Father demanded. There were three comfortable chairs in the room, but no one made use of them. There was too much tension in the air for any of us to relax enough to sit down. Bit-Bit was the only one not standing. She huddled at Father's feet, curled up in a shivering, runny-nosed ball. "Is *this* how you honor my wife's memory?" Father held my practice tablet in one hand. He'd seized it out in the garden and now he waved the piece of wax-covered wood in the scribe's face.

"Your wife, Ay?" Henenu repeated. "Your wife is alive."

"Don't try cheating me with your wordplay, scribe!" Father's knuckles whitened as he grasped my tablet with both hands and flung it to the floor. The sound of wood striking stone was so loud it made Bit-Bit yelp in fright and fall backward. I ran to her side and helped her up, holding her close while Father ranted on. "You know I mean *her* mother." He gestured at me. "Why have you been teaching her to read and write? Do you ever use that oversized head of yours to *think*? You know what Tiye will do if she finds out there's a second Seshat for her to exploit."

Seshat? I knew her well. She was a goddess whose name itself meant She-who-writes, the wife of Thoth, who first brought the gift of writing to mortals. Why was Father invoking her now? What did the goddess have to do with my aunt Tiye?

"And how will Queen Tiye find out any of this?" Henenu spoke calmly in the face of Father's fury. "*You* certainly won't tell her, and I hope you don't think I would do it. I never should have gone behind your back to teach Nefertiti, but I can't say I regret giving her lessons. Your daughter has her mother's gift for words. If I didn't nurture that gift, then I *would* be dishonoring her mother's memory."

"Even if that same 'gift' killed her mother?" Father had never spoken so bitterly before, or so fiercely.

"Killed her?" I echoed.

Father turned and stared as if he were seeing me for the first time. "Nefertiti, leave us," he said quietly. "Take your sister with you. This is between Henenu and me."

I didn't move.

"Are you deaf?" Father's voice filled the room. "I told you to leave!"

"I . . ." I hugged Bit-Bit closer. She was cold as deep water. I could feel her shoulders quivering as she tried to smother her sobs. My heart ached, knowing how terrified she must be, and how much I, too, had frightened her earlier. I knew I should get her out of this room, away from all the shouting, all the anger. But I couldn't do it. Not yet, not now. "How did her—her gift kill her?" I asked, forcing myself to meet Father's blazing eyes. "I won't go until you tell me."

"You're my child and you'll do as I say!" Father strode toward me as if to drive me off like a sheep, easily scared, easily mastered. He was startled when he almost knocked me down because I wouldn't move even one finger's width out of his way.

I stood nose to nose with him, and with Bit-Bit burying her head against my shoulder, I told him: "I want to know. You never mention her, except when we feed her *ka,* and as soon as we're done, it's as if she never lived. When I used to ask about her, you made me feel like I'd done something bad because you looked so hurt! But it's not fair. I *should* know about her. I'm her child, too!"

Father sucked his breath in through clenched teeth. He stepped back, retreating to one of the chairs. "Her child," he said. "Yes, you are her daughter. If you only knew how much you remind me of her, Nefertiti. She wasn't like other women. Her family came to the Black Land from the kingdom of the Mitanni, far to the northeast where the Tigris River flows. You have her face, so narrow, so delicate, her pale golden-brown skin, and her eyes—" He crumpled in his seat like an old man.

"Father . . ." Pity twisted my heart. I couldn't bear to see him in such pain. Suddenly my deep desire to know about my mother didn't seem worth the price. "You don't have to tell me now, but someday . . ."

He shook his head. "Let me speak, Nefertiti. If I don't tell you about her now, I won't be able to do it again. You're right, she shouldn't be a secret to you. She was my wife, your mother, and she loved us both very much. She was a scribe, as Henenu says. It amazed me, when I first met her in Pharaoh's court and found out why she was there. She was so beautiful, I was sure she must be one of the most favored dancing girls or one of the king's junior wives, but a scribe? I didn't think women could learn so many symbols, so many words, so many meanings. I know *I* never could!" His laughter was short and fragile.

"So I fell in love with my pretty scribe, and I did many foolish things to make her notice me. I used to tease her by calling her Seshat, the goddess She-who-writes. I must have made a good offering to Hathor, because my Seshat came to love me, too. We were very happy. When we learned we were going to have a baby, we were certain that the gods loved us as much as we loved one another." He closed his eyes. "We were wrong."

Bit-Bit stopped shivering. My little sister crept forward and took Father's right hand in both of her own. "Father?" He opened his eyes again. "Father, do you love *my* mother that much, too?"

He gave her a weak smile, then gently tugged her braided youth-lock the way he used to tug mine. "Very much, Bit-Bit. In fact, I'd like to give her an armful of flowers to wear in her hair this evening. Would you go into the garden and pick them for me? Take your time." Reassured, Bit-Bit nodded solemnly and padded out of the room.

Father sat up straighter in his chair and watched her go. "My little gazelle, so easily frightened," he said fondly. "She doesn't need to hear the rest of this." He looked at me sharply. "I wanted to spare you as well, but . . ."

"I *want* to know," I repeated.

"So you said." He shrugged and went on: "Your mother's beauty caught my eye, but I fell in love with her because she was kind and funny and *smart*. My sister Tiye is also beautiful, but *sly,* not smart, the mistress of plots and schemes. Even though plenty of other women in Pharaoh's house were prettier and more talented, she had the cunning to make Pharaoh fall deeply in love with her and name her his Great Royal Wife. Another woman would be content with that, but Tiye knows it's not enough to reach the stars; you must *stay* there."

"That's no easy thing," Henenu put in. "Queen Tiye always has many rivals among Pharaoh's other women. She knows she needs eyes and ears everywhere in the king's household to guard against conspiracies."

"Sometimes I wonder if my sister sees conspiracies that aren't even there," Father muttered.

"Was she—was my mother one of Queen Tiye's spies?" I asked. Already my imagination leaped to craft a tale of how one of the queen's enemies took my mother's life while trying to discover Tiye's secrets.

Father shook his head. "She used your mother's skill to help her spies do their work. The softest whisper can be overheard, but a written word is a better way to hold onto secrets. She made sure all her spies had some scribal training. But that means she needed someone to translate her orders and their reports into writing."

"Why didn't she learn how to read and write herself?" I asked.

"I suppose she would have, if there were fewer symbols to memorize," Henenu said.

"Besides, why bother learning how to use a tool when you can force someone else to *be* your tool?" Father said bitterly. "It didn't take long for Tiye to use your mother. My sister doesn't trust anyone outside of the family, so when she heard I'd married a skilled scribe, she praised the gods for giving her the perfect gift. My Seshat had to be ready at any time of the day or night to serve the queen. Even when she was expecting your birth and needed her rest, she had to rush to Tiye's side whenever she was summoned. It weakened her, and when we were commanded to accompany the king and queen on their journey to visit Khufu's Horizon—"

"The great pyramid?" I put in. "But—but you told me that Mother was the one who wanted to go!"

"Ah, so you remember that story?" Father's smile was thin and sad. "You were so small, so frightened by bad dreams. I had to tell you something that would comfort you, even if it meant twisting the truth. May Ma'at forgive me."

I remembered what Henenu had said to me not so long ago about the power, beauty, and danger of the truth. I walked across the floor to put my arms around Father's shoulders and kiss his forehead. "I know she will," I said. "But please, tell me the truth now."

"The truth is brief and ugly. One night during our journey when your mother was hurrying to answer Tiye's summons, she missed her footing and took a hard fall. The accident brought on your early birth. My Seshat was terrified that you wouldn't survive. How she smiled when you were first laid in her arms and she gave you your name! But then she closed her eyes, and—" His voice caught. "We never should have traveled. I should have stood up to my sister and told her to find someone else to take Seshat's place, but in those days, both your mother and I were afraid of her."

"And now?" I asked.

"I won't lie to you again: I still am," Father replied. "I'm not proud of it."

"You shouldn't be ashamed, either," Henenu said. "Pharaoh adores her and the passing years have brought her more and more power. Only a fool wouldn't be afraid of Queen Tiye." He turned to me. "When your mother died, Tiye lost a valuable strand in her web of secrets. At last, one of her own daughters mastered the scribal arts, but the queen finds Princess Sitamun to be a poor substitute for your mother. The princess has a life and a mind of her own and isn't willing to drop everything else the instant Queen Tiye demands her help. The queen can't bully her as effectively as she could bully—"

"—me." I finished the thought for him. "If she knew I could read and write, she'd use me the way she used my mother."

"You see, Henenu?" My father glared at the dwarf. "Even the child recognizes the danger she's in, thanks to your lessons!"

"What danger?" Henenu countered. "Until today, she and I were the only two people under the sky who knew about them. You're wary of your sister—good!—but you've let it get out of hand. She's controlling your life as successfully as though you'd never left the court. *And* the lives of your daughters! What next, Ay? Will you seal the girls inside your house with bricks to guarantee that Queen Tiye can never touch them?"

Father pushed himself out of the chair so violently that it crashed backward to the floor. "If I do, it's my house and they are my daughters!" he shouted. "And you won't see any of them again!"

"Father, no!" I cried, grabbing his arm. "He's your friend and he's done nothing wrong. Don't send him away because of me."

"This isn't your choice, Nefertiti," Father said. I'd never heard him use such a cold voice to me.

Maybe I couldn't choose whether or not Father banished his boyhood friend forever, but I could make a different choice. I knelt on the stone before Father and stretched out my arms as if I were praying. "I swear by Ma'at and Isis, by the goddess Seshat and by my mother's spirit, if Henenu stays welcome in our home, I will never have another lesson from him. Never!" I bowed forward until my palms and my forehead touched the ground.

I lay there like that for some time, nothing but stillness in my ears. I couldn't even hear Father and Henenu breathing. At last, the faint brush of a footfall broke the silence and I heard my father's weary voice say, "Get up, little kitten. You'll ruin your dress and Mery will blame me."

Slowly I raised my forehead from the floor. "So . . . you'll forgive him?" I looked from Father to Henenu. The scribe's expression was gloomy but resigned.

Father's familiar smile brightened his face. "Why should I forgive him when, as you say, he's done nothing wrong." He turned to Henenu. "It's you who should forgive me, my friend." I watched, lighthearted, as the two men embraced and began trading jokes as though nothing had ever come between them.

Henenu dined with our family that evening. He and Father drank a lot of beer and acted like rowdy boys. Mery wore the flowers Bit-Bit had picked in the garden earlier that day and looked as beautiful and serene as Isis, even when Henenu and Father got into a loud contest to see which of them could do a better imitation of a baboon's scream. Finally she tried to put an end to their nonsense by smoothly suggesting that Bit-Bit and I entertain everyone with a dance.

While Mery sang and the men clapped their hands, my sister and I danced. Bit-Bit forgot the steps three or four times, but as soon as I heard the music, it became a part of me and told my feet where to go, my arms how to gesture. I loved to dance, but that night my dancing was more than a pleasure: It was a refuge. It gave me a place to hide from the thought of everything I'd given up by making that promise to Father.

As I spun and leaped across the floor, I saw how happy he looked, laughing with his friend, and it made me smile. *I did the right thing,* I told myself. *Why do I need to know how to read and write anyway? I'm only going to get married and have babies and keep a pretty house here in Akhmin because—because that's all I want to do! It is! It is!* And I danced faster before I had the chance to doubt it.

When we finished our dance, Mery declared it was time for us to go to bed. We said good night to the grown-ups and I took an oil lamp to light our way through the house, leading Bit-Bit by the hand.

In our bedroom, I put out the light and curled up on my side, but I couldn't sleep. My head was filled with words, the dancing symbols from all of the lessons Henenu had ever taught me. There were proverbs and songs and stories and bits of history. One day, when he knew he was going to be gone from Akhmin for a long time, he had given me a piece of papyrus with the tale of a woman named Hatshepsut for my practice text. As I worked at copying the lines, I marveled at her story, the tale of a king's daughter who climbed the steps of the throne and ruled the Black Land not as queen, but as Pharaoh! I thought it was nothing more than a wonderful fantasy, but when Henenu returned to Akhmin, he told me it was all true. Hatshepsut *had* governed as Pharaoh for many years, bringing peace and prosperity to her people.

I want to know if there are other stories like hers, I thought bitterly. *I want to read about the great kings and queens, the adventures of the gods and goddesses, the beautiful songs! And I don't want to have to wait for someone else to tell me the stories. I want to find them for myself, whenever I want them.* I held my fist to my mouth. *But I can't. Not anymore. I promised.*

"Sister?" Bit-Bit's voice trembled in the dark. I felt my mattress sag as she climbed into bed beside me and cuddled against my back. "Can I sleep with you?"

"Bad dreams?" I asked.

"No." She put one arm around me and whispered: "I'm sorry."

"For what?"

"Father got mad 'cause of what you were doing in the garden. It was scary. He yelled at Henenu, and sometimes when he yelled at Henenu, it was like he was really yelling at you." I heard her sniffle in the dark. "He never would have gone into the garden if he hadn't found me crying in the house. So it's all my fault. I'm sorry."

I turned toward her and hugged my little sister. "No, it's not," I said. "It was my fault for yelling at you and making you cry. Forgive me?"

Bit-Bit burrowed her face against my chest. I felt her

small body shiver. "Bit-Bit, everything's all right between us. Why are you crying *now*?" I asked a little impatiently.

"You're not mad at me, but what about Anat?"

"Anat?" I was bewildered. "Who's Anat?"

Bit-Bit ignored my question. "You won't punish her, will you? You mustn't blame her for letting me run back into the garden. She's very old, and her bones hurt her all the time now, and . . ."

And then I knew who Anat was. She was the old slave I'd told to keep Bit-Bit busy during my lessons with Henenu. I hadn't thought about her at all until this moment, and now I realized that I'd never known her name. Yet here was my little sister, crying because she didn't want any harm to come to the old woman.

A woman, I thought. *An old woman with her own name and her own troubles. A woman, not a* thing.

We'd always had slaves in our house, the way we'd always had food and clothing and furniture. They were simply . . . *there,* like Mery's care or Father's love. Why would I ever stop to question something I took for granted?

I didn't, I thought. *But I should.*

I promised Bit-Bit that I wouldn't let anyone punish Anat. She was comforted, although she still insisted on sharing my bed for the rest of the night. "I *do* have bad dreams," she admitted.

"I know what that's like," I whispered back, but she was already asleep, her thumb in her mouth.

I rested poorly, scarcely sleeping. Long before the divine Aten sun-disk showed himself on the horizon, I slipped away from my sleeping sister, threw on my dress, and padded through the house to the kitchen. Our slaves and servants were already awake and working hard. I found Anat making bread for our breakfast, scooping dough out of a big bowl and forming it into loaves for baking. When she caught sight of me, she flinched.

She must think I'm going to punish her for letting Bit-Bit get away from her yesterday, I thought. *No servants ever fear me. And why should they? They're free to come and go as they please, free to complain to Father or Mery if I even raise my voice to them! Our cook is so valued that I think he* has the authority to hit *me if I interfere with anything in this kitchen. Even though I had to bribe her to keep Bit-Bit out of my way when I had my lessons with Henenu, she's still afraid of my displeasure.*

"Anat—" I began, approaching her. It was the first time I'd bothered to use her name. She refused to meet my eyes, so I said, "Look at me, Anat." Though I spoke gently, it was still an order to a slave. She had to obey. "I just wanted to tell you that everything's all right. I'm not upset that you lost track of Bit-Bit yesterday."

She lowered her eyelids. "My young mistress is gracious," she murmured. I heard relief in her voice, but no true gratitude.

And why should she be grateful to me? Even if it's not my fault that she's a slave, she's still my family's property. Who could ever be thankful for that?

"Anat—" It was still a strange new thing, calling her by name. "Anat, can I help you make the bread?"

"As my young mistress wishes." The old woman shrugged and waved her hands over the dough before going back to her task.

I helped myself to a handful of the sticky, floury mass. I tried to make a loaf that looked like the neat, identical shapes that came from the old woman's hands, but I couldn't get the raw dough off my fingers. In the time it took me to make one lopsided loaf, Anat had turned out five perfect ones.

"I'm sorry, it's a mess," I said, smiling at her. "Can you show me how you do it?"

She didn't smile back. "If my young mistress commands, I will stop my work and show you now. But the master will be wanting his breakfast soon."

"Oh." Suddenly I saw that my weak attempt at "helping" Anat was worse than no help at all. I was only getting in the way, keeping her from finishing her work. "Not now. I'm sorry I bothered you."

She gave me a funny look. "Sorry, mistress? You?" Now she did smile. "You are kind. I am the one to ask your pardon."

"You didn't do—" I began.

"For being as touchy as a sunburned dog. I always had a bad temper, even when I was a little girl, back home in Ebla. I am afraid that I woke up this morning with the bone-ache, which only makes it worse." She rested both hands on the small of her back and winced. "I will teach you how to make bread another time, young mistress, I promise."

I gazed at Anat with fresh awareness, seeing her as she was—gnarled hands, bent backbone, and careworn face, a stranger in our land, an old woman who would never be able to smile and declare: *That's enough work for me now. I'm tired and I'm going to rest.*

I remembered another of the texts Henenu had given me to copy. It was a song where the poet wrote about seeing his childhood playmate and suddenly realizing that he loved her. *The gods who give blindness and sight have opened my eyes to your beauty. They have given a new light to my eyes. I see you as never before.* My eyes were newly opened, too, but when I turned them to see the way I'd treated Anat and the other slaves—the other people in our home—I didn't like what I saw. I wanted to say more to her, as if my words would be enough to sweeten the life she led in our household. I couldn't think of a single thing to tell her that could do that, except—

"You're free," I murmured under my breath.

"Mistress?" Anat was old, but her ears were keen. She blinked at me, confused by what she'd heard.

"Nothing." I didn't have the right to give her the one thing she should have before all others. Suddenly I wanted that power more than anything in the world. I stood before her, twisting my fingers, helpless and miserable.

"Mistress, I must get back to my work."

I nodded and left the kitchen, but I couldn't go back to my bed. Instead, I made my way into the garden. It was still dark, but dawn was coming. The fresh air carried the juicy green scent of reeds and papyrus plants from the river. I moved carefully along the path until I found the statue of Isis.

When I was younger, the goddess towered over me. As much as I loved Isis, I was always a little afraid of her, too. Wise, kind, and loving, she was also capable of unleashing the destructive might of magic against her enemies. Now, however, I'd grown tall enough to look the goddess in the eyes. The goddess herself was only as tall as Bit-Bit when she'd been two years old. The rest of the statue's height was its limestone pedestal, all four surfaces covered with prayers and praises for Isis.

I sat in the dirt and leaned my head against the cool stone. I had to close my eyes tight or risk accidentally reading what was written on the base of Isis's statue. I'd read those words many times before, when Henenu and I sometimes had our lessons in the goddess's shadow, but I couldn't do so ever again. I'd made a promise to Father and I had to honor it.

"O Isis, there's so much I want to change, but—how can I? Help me be strong," I whispered. I wanted to pray more eloquently, but I didn't trust myself to find the right words. *Could* I pray for Anat's freedom? What about the rest of our slaves, then, and the slaves that the other families of Akhmin owned, and those who were the property of the temples? The priest of Isis had at least twenty. If Isis hadn't freed the slaves under her own roof, why would she do anything to help Anat?

Confusion set my mind whirling. Questions without answers made me so tired that I began to doze with the carved words praising Isis pressed against my cheek. I fell asleep where I sat.

Nefertiti, what was your promise? A soft voice breathed in my ear, the words lilting, like a song. *What did you tell your father?*

My eyes opened abruptly. I was still in the garden, but it looked different. The colors and edges of things were blurred. Only the image of Isis, smiling down at me, seemed real. I raised my eyes to the goddess.

I promised him that I wouldn't read and write anymore, I replied. *I swore it!*

Did you, my daughter? The goddess's face never moved, but I felt as if her smile grew a little wider. *Think, Nefertiti. Remember the words you* truly *spoke.*

And I did. As I sat at the feet of Isis, I saw the carvings on the base of her statue begin to writhe and shift shape, new words appearing out of the old, like a snake wriggling free of his former skin: *I swear by Ma'at and Isis, by the goddess Seshat and by my mother's spirit, if Henenu stays welcome in our home, I will never have another lesson from him.*

From him! *But that means—*The joy I felt was so sudden, so intense that I was breathless, my heart pounding. *O sweet Isis, thank you.* Thank *you!*

For what? The goddess sounded amused by my wild gratitude. *I've given you nothing. You are who and what you are, and if that means you must be She-who-writes, not even the greatest spell in my power can change it.*

4
SHADOWS ON THE RIVER

I woke from my dream with Bit-Bit shaking me, then laughing when I turned my face to her. "Oh, Nefertiti, you've got *squiggles*!" she exclaimed, pointing. I raised my hand to my cheek and discovered that the carvings on the base of Isis's image had left their mark on my skin.

I never did find out which words had marked me. The impressions faded before it was time to join Father and Mery for breakfast, but my memory of that vision of Isis never did. In the seasons that followed, I learned that the goddess spoke the truth: I was who and what I was, and that person was She-who-writes.

Whenever I left our house to accompany Father or Mery to the marketplaces or the temples, words were everywhere and I read them all. I couldn't help it. Without Henenu's lessons, I was famished for things to read. As for writing, I no longer had my practice tablet, but as long as I had a twig or a bit of dried reed and a patch of ground, I did my best to trace what I'd read that day, relying on my memory. I always stole away to some deserted corner of our garden, even hiding from Bit-Bit so that I could concentrate completely on my beloved work. When I had no new lines to practice, I began making up my own. I got Father to tell me tales of his early life as a soldier in Pharaoh's army, and I did my best to write them in the dust. The same happened with every housekeeping lesson Mery taught me, although I was often frustrated because I didn't know how to write all of the words. I even made up stories of my own. I wrote them down, learned them by heart, wiped them away, then crept out of hiding to share them with Bit-Bit.

Father and Mery smiled proudly when Bit-Bit ran to tell them: "Nefertiti knows the *best* stories!" No one suspected that my stories were so good because I'd practiced "telling" them over and over in writing before I recited them to my sister. Bit-Bit also bragged about my stories to her friends, and soon I was very popular. Everyone wanted to hear the tale of the Cat Who Thought She Was a Falcon or the story of the Cursed Prince and the Clever Maiden. I enjoyed the attention so much that I would have told my stories from dawn to dusk and beyond, though my throat became sore and my lips as dry as the Red Land.

Luckily I had Bit-Bit to look out for me. When it came time for storytelling sessions with her friends, my little sister appointed herself my keeper. She was the one who declared when I was done for the day. "Enough is enough for now. Nefertiti and I have *other* things to do," she'd say, looking so businesslike and self-important that I nearly burst out laughing. "We have to go practice our dancing."

Dancing! I loved it nearly as much as I loved reading, writing, and making my stories. When I danced, I felt free. I didn't need to hide what I was trying to accomplish or worry about what Father would say if he found me creating a new pattern of steps, a new way of moving my arms, a new song. And so I reached my thirteenth year with my feet on two different paths—one I could follow openly, one that had to cling to the shadows—both that I loved with all my heart.

That year, shortly before the great Festival of the Inundation, my father invited the high priest of Isis to dine with us. He told the family about it five days before, so that Mery would have time to place a lavish dinner before our honored guest.

"The priest of Isis?" I was astonished. "Father, you've never invited any priest here before."

"And with luck, I'll never have to do so again," Father muttered. "But it's not my choice. Pharaoh wants me to begin looking into how the different priesthoods use the gifts they're given by the people."

"Why?" Bit-Bit piped up.

"Because that's Father job," I told her softly. "He serves Pharaoh by helping to stop any wrongdoing in Akhmin." Over the years I'd come to learn what our father did for a living, but it was still a mystery to my little sister.

"You mean he chases *thieves*?" Her eyes grew wide.

While Father and Mery laughed discreetly, I said, "He

doesn't chase *common* criminals. When goods come into the city that are supposed to go to the royal storehouses but some of them . . . 'wander' into someone else's hands, Father has to find out about it and tell Pharaoh."

"Well said, Nefertiti." Father nodded approval. "I'm happy to say that we've had very few instances of such crimes in Akhmin. But now"—he sighed—"now that may change. Pharaoh has authorized me to investigate the temples. Do the riches that pour through their doors go to honor the gods or to let the priests live in royal luxury?" His smile was sour. "I already know the answer."

"Then why did you invite the high priest to dinner?" I asked. "If you *know* that he's stealing—"

"I'm doing it so *he* will know what I do," Father said. "Perhaps that will be enough to make him behave a bit more righteously. You'd be surprised how many offenders will mend their ways the instant that they realize someone's watching."

"What if he isn't one of those?"

"In that case, it becomes a matter for Pharaoh to decide." Father closed his eyes and pinched the bridge of his nose. "For all the good it will do. The priests have too much power, and the people believe they are the only ones who can keep things right between gods and mortals."

I thought about Father's words while I prepared for the grand dinner. Mery was obsessed with guaranteeing that every detail of the feast would be perfect. She sent all the slaves and servants running on countless errands. Bit-Bit and I were also put to work. Mery wanted to have professional musicians and dancers entertain the guests, but

Father forbade it. He said the expense would be hypocritical when he was about to reprimand the high priest for his lavish ways.

"So you girls will sing and dance for us instead," Mery concluded. "Now go practice."

Bit-Bit and I were overjoyed. She loved to sing even more than I loved to dance, and she had a wonderful voice—sweet, high, and clear. We rehearsed our performance constantly. Hearing Bit-Bit sing was like watching a lotus open its petals to the sun, something that became more lovely with every passing moment. She beamed when I told her how beautifully she sang, but as the day of the feast drew near, she began to panic.

"What if I'm awful?" she cried, clutching my hand as we practiced the steps of our dance in our room. We could no longer work in the house or even in the garden. It was the day before the dinner and Mery was turning the whole house upside down with the final preparations.

"Honestly, Bit-Bit, don't you *listen* when I tell you how good you are?" I demanded. "As soon as you sing one note, everyone will love you, and I'll become invisible."

"As if *that* would ever happen." My little sister's lower lip stuck out. "When people see you, it's everyone else that vanishes. I wish I were half as beautiful as you are, Nefertiti. Then it wouldn't matter if I sang well or if I croaked like a frog."

I stared at Bit-Bit as though she'd been sunstruck and was spouting nonsense. "I'm not beautiful."

"You *are*." Bit-Bit was as sweet as her name, but sometimes she showed a flash of temper. She stamped her bare foot and stubbornly repeated, "You *are* beautiful. Everyone says so—Mother, Father, the servants, the neighbors, all of my friends, *everyone*!" She took a calming breath and added: "Even me. I wish I looked like you. You're so tall and graceful, and your eyes are such a pretty shape, like willow leaves, and your mouth always looks like you know a wonderful secret."

"But you're beautiful, too, Bit-Bit," I protested. My sister's praise made me feel self-conscious, as if everyone were looking at me all the time. I didn't want to bask in so much attention, real or imaginary. I wanted to roll myself up in one of Henenu's old papyrus scrolls and hide.

Bit-Bit smiled and shook her head. "Not like you." She gave me a kiss on the cheek. "But I don't mind. I love you."

"I love you, too."

Her smile turned mischievous. "Enough to come with me to Isis's temple?"

"What? Why there?"

"I want to ask the goddess to bless my singing tomorrow so I don't make a fool of myself in front of the guests."

"Bit-Bit, if you want to pray to Isis, why don't you just do it in the garden?" I asked.

"Oh, that's only *our* Isis," she said with a wave of her hand. "There are much better statues of the goddess in her temple, and it's more impressive. The goddess is sure to pay attention if I ask for her blessing there. Please, Nefertiti?"

I couldn't say no. As soon as Bit-Bit gathered some flowers for her offering to Isis, we went to the temple. It was a fine building, with towering walls of yellow limestone and many open spaces, inside and out, for worshippers to gather. We hadn't purified ourselves properly, so we had to remain in the shadow of the great entryway, but that was good enough for Bit-Bit. While she prayed, I glanced into the temple courtyard. Because it wasn't a festival day, we were almost the only people there. Even the priests were absent, most likely preparing to perform a ritual later on. I took advantage of being alone to study the words carved on the walls, all praising the goodness of Isis. I missed Henenu's lessons, but I was delighted to see how much I understood without his help.

Bit-Bit was much calmer after her prayers, and when the next day's sun began to set, she was eager for Mery to summon us into the hall where the feast was waiting. We dined with wreaths of flowers in our hair and garlands around our necks. Bit-Bit and I were so excited by the many delicacies set out on the low tables near our chairs that we couldn't stop giggling and whispering about all the treats in store for us. Mery wore her best jewelry, a gold collar shaped like a hawk with outstretched wings, every feather starred with turquoise, carnelian, and lapis lazuli. She looked well satisfied with the way her plans for the night's festivities were being carried out.

We three were the only ones who seemed to be enjoying ourselves that night. Father was so solemn, he might as well have been made of stone. The high priest of Isis sat stiffly, his jaw taut, his kohl-rimmed eyes like chips of flint. He was attended by two lower-ranking priests, and all three of them were splendidly dressed, their pleated robes made from linen so finely woven that it was like a breath of mist. Gold flashed from their necks, ears, and fingers. Unlike

Father and Mery, they wore no wigs on their closely shaved heads. Like all priests, they took pains to remove every bit of hair from their bodies, to keep themselves pure enough to serve the gods.

The longer I looked at the grim-faced, hairless high priest of Isis, the more he reminded me of a cranky old bull-frog, puffing out his throat among the river reeds. I bit my lip to stop myself from giggling.

"Nefertiti, Mutnodjmet, it's time," Mery said. Because it was a formal dinner, she called Bit-Bit by her given name. I gave my sister's hand a quick, reassuring squeeze before we left our chairs and stepped into the middle of the floor. We took our places, posing with our arms raised to one side, our heads turned the other way, and our feet pointing straight ahead. I clicked my tongue quietly three times, the signal to start. We raised our right feet and stamped out the beat on the floor. Bit-Bit began to sing, and the two of us swayed to the tune, clapping our hands and moving into the first steps of the dance. Mery clapped her hands in time for us as well, with Father and the lower-ranking priests joining in. Only the high priest remained unmoving in his chair.

So, you're too grand to clap for us? I thought. *Sitting there like that, do you think you're the majestic image of Amun or Osiris? You're about as impressive as a dried-out stick! Bit-Bit and I worked hard on this dance, and we did it for you, old frog. I hope that every bite you ever eat is half as sour as your face!*

I took all of my fierce resentment for the priest's cold arrogance and poured it into my dance. I twirled and leaped across the floor, my arms weaving flowing patterns in the air, my feet riding the pure notes of Bit-Bit's song. I became the dance, and the dance gave me the gift of flight, of strength, of joy. When the music ended, I was breathless but smiling. I grabbed Bit-Bit's hand, we made a low bow, and I dragged her out of the hall.

Once through the doorway, I leaned against a wall and slowly slid down it, laughing. "We did it, Bit-Bit!"

My sister crept back to eavesdrop at the doorway. "Oh, Nefertiti, they loved us!" she exclaimed, her cheeks flushed. "Even the old priest is telling Father how good we were."

"Stupid frog," I muttered. But I smiled with satisfaction. It had been my idea for us to leave the hall after our dance. If we'd done badly, I didn't want to listen to forced, insincere compliments, and if we'd pleased our audience, we'd find out soon enough.

"Do we have to stay out here much longer?" Bit-Bit asked. "The honey cakes are being served." She sounded wistful.

"Then we'd better go back in before Father eats them all," I joked, holding out my hands for her to help me up.

We stepped across the threshold of the hall and into a river of praise. Mery and Father had to hold back the full measure of their pride in front of the guests, but the high priest and his attendants were under no such restraint. Bit-Bit and I had to stand in the middle of the floor to receive their acclaim. The longer it went on, the more ill at ease I felt. I was proud of my dancing, but so much admiration soon had me squirming, longing to be able to slip back into my chair and be ordinary again. I think that I could have enjoyed the attention more if my dancing were the only thing our guests complimented. But for every flattering comment about my dance, the priests poured out three times as many about how I *looked*.

Why *does* that *matter?* I thought, lowering my eyes so that I wouldn't have to look at them. *Wouldn't my dance be as good if I* didn't *have "gazelle eyes" or "skin like honey" or "the slender grace of a young palm tree"? I wish Father could say something to stop them. But they're our guests.* My stomach tightened and I prayed that Isis would silence her babbling priests.

My sister, on the other hand, reveled in the attention. She forgot all about the honey cakes and greedily devoured every word that commended her singing. I thought she was going to burst with pride.

"Such a gift should be treasured," the high priest said. "Most of our temple priestesses don't sing half as well as this child. It would please me to send one of our more adept singers to give her lessons and to teach her how to play the harp, so that she can accompany her song."

"You honor us too much," Father replied coolly. "Forgive me if I can't accept your offer until a time when our business is happily concluded."

The priest's eyes were as expressionless and unblinking as a lizard's. "As you will. May the gods in their infinite power bring us to a speedy agreement. Until then, I hope that you will give your consent to a different offer?"

"Go on." Father was on guard.

"At the Festival of the Inundation, we worship Hapy, who brings the rising of the river, but we do not forget our lady Isis, the god-mother, the giver of life. It would please the great goddess if your lovely daughter Nefertiti joined the ranks of the maidens who will dance for her beside the sacred river. Such an opportunity will honor your daughter's talent without giving anything to *you*." One corner of his thin mouth twitched up. "Well, Ay? Will you permit your sweet daughter to serve the goddess?"

My father's answering smile was as mocking as the high priest's. "How can I refuse?"

Bit-Bit woke me up on the morning of the festival by jumping onto my stomach. "Get up! Get up! You're going to be late!" she cried, trying to haul me out of bed by the shoulders.

"For pity's sake, Bit-Bit, do you want to wake me up or kill me?" I got free of my sister's grip before she could send the two of us tumbling onto the floor. "Is it even dawn yet? I swear, you're more eager for today than I am."

"How can you say that, Nefertiti?" Bit-Bit was shocked at the very thought. "You're going to get to dance in front of the whole city, and Mother will be letting you borrow her best necklace and bracelets *and* her jeweled wig! You've even got a new dress to wear! And afterward, I'll bet that every important family in Akhmin is going to want you to marry their sons."

"What, all of them at once?" I liked teasing Bit-Bit a little.

"You know what I mean." My sister folded her arms across her chest and glowered at me for making fun of something that was very important to her. In the past year, Bit-Bit had begun to take an interest in growing up quickly and having a home of her own. She'd also turned into quite the flirt, though her pretty attempts at getting noticed were wasted on the boys of her own age. They were more interested in their own games, sports, and adventures. If they had the choice between stealing a kiss from Bit-Bit and throwing rocks at a hippopotamus, the hippo would win.

"Are you in such a hurry for me to get married and move out of this house?" I asked.

"You wouldn't move far," Bit-Bit argued. "You'd still live in Akhmin. I could see you whenever I wanted to. I could have *two* homes!" She threw her arms around my neck and gave me a kiss, delighted by her vision of the future.

We joined our parents for breakfast. Because it was a special day for me, Mery had the servants add thick slices of watermelon, pieces of apple with honey, and sweet jujube fruit to our usual bread and beer. Bit-Bit and I stuffed ourselves until Mery put a stop to it.

"Nefertiti, if you eat much more, you'll be too sick to dance."

"And then I'll never get married," I said, with a playful glance at my sister. She made a honey-smeared face at me.

"What kind of nonsense is that?" Father asked pleasantly.

"Oh, Bit-Bit thinks that as soon as I dance, you'll be buried under a mountain of marriage offers for me," I replied, giggling.

But Father didn't laugh with me—he scowled—and Mery shifted uneasily in her chair. When their eyes met, they exchanged a look that sent prickles rushing up the nape of my neck.

"What's wrong?" I asked.

"If I don't start getting you ready for the dance, you're going to be late, that's what's wrong," Mery said briskly, rising from her place and taking me by the wrist. "You have to wash and perfume yourself, then I have to paint your face, help you into your dress, put on your jewelry . . ."

I jerked my hand free. "*What* is *wrong*?"

This time, Father did laugh. "What have I always said about this one, Mery? When she's determined to know something, my little kitten is too smart to be deceived and too alert to be distracted." He looked at me with a rueful smile. "Your sister has the gift of prophecy as well as song. I've already had to hear one marriage proposal for you."

I was astounded. "Someone asked to marry me? *Who?*"

"It doesn't matter," he replied. "You will not marry him. I sent him away."

Bit-Bit groaned dramatically. "Father, how *could* you? What if Nefertiti's in *love* with him?"

Father pursed his lips. "Bit-Bit, a *good* marriage begins with the man asking the woman, not her father. Now, Nefertiti, are you in love with anyone?" I shook my head, still stunned. "Then you don't have to worry about this. I promise you, when you find the right young man, one who will recognize what a treasure the gods have given to him, one who treats you like his second self and cherishes you for who you are, I won't stand in your way." He chuckled. "And if you love him that much as well, I'll get *out* of your way before I'm trampled into the dust. Now go with your mother and get ready."

With Mery's help I was soon ready to leave the house for the temple of Isis. Bit-Bit watched the whole process avidly, sometimes helping, sometimes getting underfoot. She held the alabaster jar of perfumed skin cream while Mery applied it to my arms and legs, to keep them soft and glowing in spite of the strong sun, and happily ran to fetch the smaller ivory container of red ocher mixed with fat, for staining my lips. But when Mery painted my eyelids green with powdered malachite, sacred to Hathor, Bit-Bit clamored so loudly to have her eyelids painted too that her mother lost more time arguing with her than she gained by not doing it.

After much wrangling, Mery decreed, "Come here and I'll outline your eyes with kohl just like Nefertiti's, but that's all."

Bit-Bit wasn't satisfied. "That's nothing special. You do that for me every day!"

"And I always will. It protects you from the evil eye and the demons of the Red Land. I'll do more when it's *your* special day. Today belongs to your sister."

While Mery drew an elegant black line all around Bit-Bit's eyes, I combed my hair and put on her best bracelets, earrings, and necklace. They were extremely heavy, but I'd practiced my dance at home while wearing them, so I was used to their weight.

When it was time for Mery to place her jeweled wig on my head, we hit a wall. I no longer had my head shaved like a child's, so the bulky wig wouldn't sit securely. "I don't know why you insist on keeping your hair," Mery said. "It's easier to stay clean without it."

"I like it," I replied. "I wash it every day. And I never liked how itchy my scalp felt every time you shaved it."

"Hmph. Children." Mery snorted, but she found another gold collar in her jewelry chest and anchored it to my hair with slender bone pins. "It almost looks like it was made to be a crown," she said, pleased with the effect. "Just make sure you don't lose it when you dance!"

I left the house alone, hurrying to the temple of Isis ahead of the rest of my family. The other dancers were already gathered in the shade of the wall that faced the river. There were nine of us, all daughters of the most important families in Akhmin. Our musicians were there as well, four girls who were temple slaves. One held a small tambourine that would help us keep our steps to the music's beat. One played the double flute, and two were harpers, including the littlest one of the group. She couldn't have been more than seven years old, yet her skilled fingers made the harp sing sweetly.

As I approached the other dancers, the oldest gave me a disdainful look. "Well, look who decided to show up: our little princess. What's *that* on your head? It looks like a collar. What are you, stupid?" She laughed raucously.

"Don't pick on Nefertiti," another girl spoke up. "She doesn't have to be smart; she's beee-yooo-teee-ful." She drew out the word until it was twisted and ugly.

A third cackled: "So what? The high priest's son would have asked to marry her even if she looked like a squashed dung beetle. His father made him do it. Anything to tie a rope around the jackal's jaws."

So that's *where my marriage offer came from,* I thought. *And as for the jackal* . . . "You'd better not be talking about my father," I said, closing in on the girl.

"Or what will you do about it?" she taunted. "Hit me? Then I won't be able to dance, and Isis will be angry. Even if your father is Pharaoh's pet, he won't be able to save you from punishment for *blasphemy*." She grinned brazenly.

I fought back my fury. She was right: I couldn't touch her. *Where did all this spite come from?* I wondered. *These girls were always friendly to me before today. Why are they suddenly being so mean?*

My answer came from a fourth girl, sharp-faced, tall, and gawky, but the best dancer of us all. "Shut up, you miserable swarm of locusts! You're all just jealous because the high priest's son wouldn't ask any of *you* to be his wife even if his father commanded it! He'd sooner throw himself into the river and let the crocodiles have him."

The four remaining girls gathered around me and joined their voices in agreement with my defender until the three who'd spit their venom at me retreated to one corner of the dancing ground, grumbling and making rude gestures. "Oh, I'm sure Isis likes *that* kind of behavior," the tall dancer sneered.

We sat in our two separate groups until one of the temple priestesses came out and ordered us to prepare ourselves. The townsfolk were beginning to arrive, eager to honor Isis and be entertained at the same time. Our dancing space was a large, square platform of beaten earth atop a high stone wall at the river's edge. It had steps leading down to the water, though at this time of year most of them were submerged. I wandered to the brink of the platform and enjoyed the fine view it gave me of the sacred river, with fine ships riding high on the current, smaller boats bobbing on the water or tethered to the bank nearby, and dense, green stands of bulrushes where crocodiles might lurk on the far shore. I was busy composing a poem in my head for Hapy, the god who had given us such beauty and bounty, when the priestess called me back to the shadow of the temple. It was time to dance.

The slave girls in their meager loincloths struck up the melody. Singing and clapping our hands, we wove across the dancing ground in single file, our feet tracing the path of the sacred river, our arms waving to imitate reeds bending beside the water. We sang as we danced, our voices backed by a choir of temple priests and priestesses who stood under a gaily striped linen canopy with the high priest and his most honored guests, the senior priests of Hapy's temple. The crowds of ordinary citizens didn't get to watch us so comfortably. They packed the two open sides of the dancing ground, their faces aglow with joy even though Aten's burning disk was already high enough in the sky to stripe their bodies with sweat.

We danced on, the music growing faster. Mery's gold bracelets and collars were heavy, but I refused to let their weight hold me down. The more I danced, the less anything else mattered—not the heat, not the stinging words I'd had to hear before, nothing. When we opened our arms to the heavens, threw back our heads and began to spin like lotus flowers caught in a whirlpool, I imagined that I *was* the flower and that I was blissfully free, riding the sacred river far into the north, to unknown cities, to marvelous adventures, to where my guardian sphinx stood watch over all, even over dreams.

I became so caught up in the spell of song and swirling motion that I closed my eyes, wanting to become a part of the music. I'd studied the steps of our dance so diligently that I was certain I could perform them in my sleep. I lifted my feet high, happily dancing in my chosen darkness, and didn't realize that I'd made a terrible misjudgment until I heard one of the other dancers shout my name. My eyes snapped open, but a step too late: I'd danced to the edge of the platform, one foot on the beaten earth, one on the air. I tried to pull back, flailing my arms to balance myself, but I forgot about my thick gold bracelets. Their weight threw me off-center, and with my next breath I was plunging over the edge of the dancing ground, into the depths of the river.

I hit the water hard. The impact struck the breath out of my body. I thrashed wildly, water filling my nostrils. Even with my eyes open, I could see only murky shadows. The sacred river was in full flood, carrying rich black silt out of the southern mountains. It fogged and darkened the bright blue water, blinding me.

O Isis, help me! I prayed in terror. *I danced for* you. *Don't let me die. Great Sphinx, you saved me once. Help me now! Stretch out your mighty paw and draw me out of the water.*

I kicked as hard as I could. My legs tangled in my clinging linen dress, but somehow I found the strength to break the surface. I coughed, gasped, and gulped air, shaking water out of my eyes. With blurred, stinging eyes I looked all around, frantic to find the shore. My heart froze when I saw how far the current had carried me. I was well downstream from the thronged dancing ground, though I could still see the horror-stricken faces of the people who were watching me be carried away.

Why are they just standing there? I wondered desperately. *Why don't they* do *something?* I was beginning to sink again, pulled down by my borrowed jewelry. I yanked off Mery's bracelets and gave them to the river. *Take these, generous Hapy, and let me go!* I tried to give the god the collar around my neck as well, but my fingers fumbled over the fastening knot and I swallowed a fresh mouthful of the river. It was the same when I tried to tear off the gold collar I wore on my hair. Mery had anchored it too well. Choking on the muddy water, I lost my struggle to stay afloat. The sacred river closed over my head and I was submerged in darkness.

As my thoughts faded from panic to nothingness, something dug into my shoulder so painfully that it jerked me back from the brink of the underworld. The grip shifted from my shoulder to under my arm and I found myself being hauled back into the sweet, beautiful, precious air. My back scraped against something rough, I heard a loud *whoof!* in my ear, and then I was yanked out of the river entirely. I sprawled in the bottom of a small boat made from thick bundles of papyrus plants, a common vessel on the sacred river, but the face gazing down at me didn't belong to a fisherman or a ferryman.

"Mistress, are you all right?" The temple slave who'd played the double flute for our dance sat on her heels beside me.

I tried to answer and wound up vomiting a huge measure of silt-laden water. I coughed so hard that I nearly drowned a second time before I was able to whisper "thank you" to my rescuer. By then she was already paddling the little boat back to the shore. I sat up in time to see the crowd that was waiting to greet us on the bank downstream from Isis's temple. The people gawked and clamored as we drew near, but no one came forward to help us land. I thought that was strange.

I saw the mob part as my family pushed their way through to the riverbank. Father waded out to us up to his waist into the shallows and I fell into his welcoming arms. Two other men, big and brawny, plunged past us as we came ashore. I looked back over Father's shoulder and saw them take the slave girl out of the boat, carrying her between them. I smiled, happy to see my rescuer being given such kind treatment, until I got a closer look at the men's faces. Scowling and cold-eyed, they dropped the girl to the ground as soon as they touched dry land, then got a fresh grip on her, dragging her away backward by the arms while she screamed and kicked in terror.

"No!" I cried, but my throat was raw from my ordeal and my protest was no more than a hoarse whisper. I dug my fingers into Father's arms, pleading silently for him to *do* something. Didn't he understand that I owed my life to that slave girl? Didn't he care?

"Hush, my dearest, hush," he murmured in my ear. "It can't be helped. It can't. She's going to die. It's the will of the gods."

5

THE HOUSE OF ISIS

I don't know how I came home again. Father must have carried me, even though I was much too big for that. I know I didn't cry. What roused me from my shock was the touch of Bit-Bit's hand ever so lightly on my cheek and her soft little voice whispering, "No tears. She hasn't shed a single tear, Mother."

"That's bad. The gods alone know where her mind has fled. My poor, sweet child, to suffer so!" I heard Mery speak, but I didn't see her or Bit-Bit, even though my sister was close enough to touch me. Slowly I became aware that I was lying on my back in complete darkness. How much time had passed since my return home?

"Is it night?" I asked.

"She's back! She's well! Her mind's whole! Oh, my darling daughter!" Mery scooped me up in a flower-scented embrace, wetting my cheeks with the tears I was still unable to shed.

"Is it night?" I repeated insistently. I was suddenly afraid that I'd been unaware of the passing of many days, not just part of one. I freed myself from Mery's arms and sat up on my own, peering into the darkness. "Where am I? Mother, *tell* me!"

I heard Mery gasp. In all the years since she'd come into our home as Father's wife, I'd never called her Mother. It wasn't because of any lack of love—I adored Mery, and she'd always treated me with the same kindness, care, and attention she gave to Bit-Bit, but even though I'd never known my birth mother, I felt that it would be disloyal to her memory if I called any other woman by that name.

"Oh my dear!" Mery exclaimed. "No, my Nefertiti, it's not night yet. We're only halfway through the afternoon."

"Why is it so dark, then? Where am I?"

"You're in your own bed. I had the servants hang a cloth over the door to keep out the light. I thought you would rest more calmly in the dark. Bit-Bit, see if you can fix that." At her mother's command, my little sister scampered away to yank the cloth aside. Daylight spilled into the room. Mery looked pleased. "Now, dear Nefertiti, what would you like to eat? You can have anything that would please you. I'll send someone to the market if we don't have what you want. Or we could go out together. The city's filled with people celebrating the Festival of the Inundation. You can't take three steps without finding someone selling delicacies to—"

"I don't want to eat," I said. "I want to know about the girl who saved me. Father said they were taking her away to die." Mery was silent. "He was wrong, wasn't he?" I pressed on. "He only saw them carrying her off, but how could he know what her master was going to do to her?"

Mery lowered her head. "When you fell into the sacred river, the high priest of Isis leaped to his feet and shouted that it was the will of the goddess and the desire of Hapy himself. Anyone who tried to pull you out would offend the god of the Inundation himself. She disobeyed him, and so—"

"That's ridiculous! The gods don't want our blood."

"My dear one, do you really believe the gods wanted any of this?" Mery turned her head abruptly and stared at me with grim eyes. "Your misstep gave the high priest a golden gift, the chance to rid himself of your father's troublesome investigation."

"But Father can't really *do* anything to touch him," I said.

"Thieves hate watchdogs even when they can't bite. Ay never would have let you drown even if it cost him his life, but that slave girl ran to the riverside, leaped into the first boat she found, and was paddling after you before he could take a step. She ruined her master's scheme. She will die for that, not for any false charges of sacrilege." She began to weep. "That poor girl. She didn't look much older than you. We must never forget her, Nefertiti. I've spoken with your father. We're going to build a small shrine for her, if we can learn her name, and honor her *ka* forever, even though she's not an Egyptian."

Bit-Bit and I both put our arms around her, trying to hug away her tears. It felt very strange. Usually Mery was the one who gave comfort to us. As we held her, waiting for her sobs to die away, my heart felt like a stone. *That girl doesn't need shrines or sacrifices or eternity in the Field of Reeds,* I thought. *She needs her life!*

I spent the rest of that day in my room, haunted by the slave girl's face. I did manage to leave my bed and put on a light linen dress, but I didn't have the heart to do more than pace from wall to wall or to sit on the edge of the bed, staring at the floor. If only I'd been less clumsy and avoided tumbling into the river! If only my fingers had been more nimble, I could have freed myself from all of the heavy gold jewelry that had pulled me down! If only I'd been stronger, or a better swimmer, I could have saved myself!

When Mery brought me food and drink, I couldn't touch a mouthful. She sighed and left me alone. Later on, when the sun was setting and the lamps were lit, Bit-Bit came to try to persuade me to join our family at the feast set out to celebrate the Inundation.

"There's duck, Nefertiti!" she cried. "Wild duck roasted with honey and onions. Can't you smell it? The skin is so brown and crackly, it'll be the best thing you've ever tasted! If you come, I'll let you have all the skin off my portion, too."

I smiled at my sister. "I'm sorry, Bit-Bit, but you'll have to eat my share of the duck instead. I still feel awful for having lost Mother's bracelets in the river. I don't deserve to share the feast."

"But it wasn't on purpose!" Bit-Bit protested. "And Mother hasn't mentioned the bracelets, not even once. She's just happy to have *you* back."

"Maybe so," I replied. "But I still feel responsible. You

go ahead and eat. Tell Mother and Father I'm sleeping so they won't make a fuss. I'll be better in the morning."

Bit-Bit looked reluctant to leave me, but the tempting smell of roast duck soon made her scamper off. I waited until I was sure that the family feast was well under way, then dropped to my knees beside the wooden chest that held my clothes. My cloak was at the very bottom. I swung it on over my shoulders, then pulled it up to cover my head. It was heavy, meant for winter use, but even though it would be stifling to wear, tonight I needed a garment that would let me go unrecognized through the streets.

As I crept out of the house, into the garden, I heard the sound of my family chatting over their festive meal. Rich, delectable aromas drifted from the hall and made my mouth water. For a feast like this, all of our slaves and servants would be busy either cooking, serving, clearing, or cleaning the dishes. It was easy to keep out of their way.

It was also easy to slip out of our garden and into the streets of Akhmin. I glanced left and right before running from the little gate into the shelter of the building across the way. Our neighbors lived behind walls that were higher than ours, and I kept them beside me, clinging to the added darkness they provided, for as long as I could.

I didn't have to worry about running into many people. By that time of night, the citizens of Akhmin were all safely home, celebrating the Inundation just like my family and probably talking about the spectacle of my fall, my near-drowning, and my rescue.

How many of them believed the high priest? I wondered. I felt a twinge of fear, and for a moment I stood still in the night, seeing the angry phantom faces of all the people who would turn on me if this year's crops failed. *Even if the harvest is good, how many of them will remember the high priest's words the next time something goes wrong? As long as I live in this city, I'll always be remembered as the girl who didn't become Hapy's chosen sacrifice. It doesn't matter if it's all a lie. When bad things happen, things that people can't control, they want to find a reason. They* need *someone to blame.*

A dog howled somewhere nearby. Another answered. I remembered Father coming home one night, complaining about the homeless city dogs. *They roam the streets in packs and they're vicious things. I was lucky I had this with me.* He waved the old painted war club from his soldiering days.

I had nothing. I readjusted my cloak and ran.

Isis's temple looked different in the moonlight. It was no longer the gaily painted, beautifully adorned building I knew by day. Though the night was clear and the moon and stars shone brightly, the temple was a dark hulk crouched beside the river. I heard the dogs howl again and hurried toward it. The tall face of Isis's house loomed above me, and I was close enough to see the words and figures carved there. It was so strange to stand before the temple alone, at that moment! The goddess's many images all seemed to be staring at me, demanding to know why I'd come there at a time when good daughters should be at home.

"Forgive me, divine one, lady of life," I prayed softly. "If you know what's in my heart, show me your favor. Guide my steps. Let me save the girl who saved me." I didn't expect a reply and I didn't wait for one. I turned sharply from the front of the temple and ran along the wall leading away from the river. Somewhere on the other side of that wall was the high priest's house. I had to find it. I had to find him.

If I stood some distance back from the wall, I could see the tops of many palm trees growing on the other side. It reminded me of our trees in the garden at home. A helpful breeze brought the scents of many kinds of food. I looked for a gate, but there was none. Perhaps I could have found a way inside if I walked all the way around the temple enclosure, but that would take me away from the place where I knew the priest's house waited.

I dropped my cloak, took a running start, and leaped for the top of the wall. Dancing gave me strong legs, but my arms were weak. I barely made it, clinging to the edge until I found the strength to haul myself up. The top of the wall was comfortably wide, so once I was up, I pressed myself flat against the mud brick surface and peered at what lay on the other side.

"Thank you, O Isis," I whispered, seeing the high priest's house. "And now . . . be with me." I took a deep breath, swung my feet over to the garden side of the wall, and lowered myself from my perch as far as I could before I had to let go and drop to the ground below.

I didn't land well. My left foot twisted under me, sending such sharp pain through me that I had to bite my lower lip to keep from crying out. It hurt to walk, but I *could* walk, so I thanked Isis again and turned my throbbing steps toward the priest's house.

Clusters of white-flowered jasmine budded and

bloomed on both sides of the open doorway. I slipped into the space between the sweet-scented plants and the house wall, thinking about what I ought to do next. I needed to find the high priest; I didn't want anyone else to find me. I strained my ears to catch any sounds, anything that would tell me if the people inside were still awake or had finished their celebration and gone to bed. Somewhere a child was wailing, but the pitiful sound seemed to come from farther away. I clenched my hands, fervently hoping that the house slept. I intended to find my way to the high priest's room and then—

And then—in the name of Ma'at who guards the truth—I didn't know exactly *what* I was going to do then, only that I had to do something to save the slave girl. If talk wouldn't sway the high priest, maybe I could bargain with him. It didn't matter that the few pieces of jewelry I owned were nothing next to the temple treasures. *The gods love justice,* I thought as I crouched in the shelter of the jasmine plants. *The gods love justice and I'm here to see that justice is done. The gods will help me.*

"Who's there?" A hand closed on my arm. Someone yanked me out of my hiding place and spun me around. I found myself facing a tall young man who looked almost as terrified as I felt. He didn't wear a wig to cover his shaved head, so I guessed he must be one of the temple priests. "Who are you?" he demanded in a shaking voice. "You're not one of our servants. You . . ." His forehead creased as he peered at me more closely in the moonlight. "Immortal gods have mercy," he breathed. "You're Ay's daughter Nefertiti."

I didn't respond at once. I was breathless and shaking

with dread. And then, a wonderful thing happened to me: I realized that because I'd been caught, because this young man knew who I was, I had nothing left to lose. My fear fled and a great sense of calm settled over me like the warm folds of my abandoned cloak. *If it can't get any worse, it can only get better,* I thought. I stopped trembling and drew myself up to my full height. I pictured a statue of Sekhmet, the lion-headed goddess of war, and gave my captor the same bold, commanding stare.

"I am," I replied coldly. "You will let go of my arm at once."

To my surprise, it worked! The young man released his grasp but stood close enough so that he would be able to grab me again if I ran. He didn't know that I had no such intention. With a nervous little bow, he said, "What—what are you doing here?"

"I have business with the high priest," I told him, still speaking with the self-assurance I'd borrowed from the goddess. "It doesn't concern you."

"But—but if you have business with Father, why were you hiding in the bushes?"

Father? "Are you the high priest's son?"

He nodded earnestly. "My name is Ikeni. My father wanted us to marry, but Ay turned him down." He looked dejected. "I wish he'd have said yes. You're very beautiful." All at once, his expression brightened. "Nefertiti, whatever your business is tonight with Father, if I help you with it, will you go home and persuade Ay that we should marry after all? There's some bad feeling between our families. Our marriage would smooth all that away."

I could hardly believe what I was hearing. Ikeni was a good-looking young man, strong and healthy, but when he spoke, nonsense poured from his lips. If not for the condemned slave girl's brave rescue, his father's command would have let me drown! How could he call something like *that* "some bad feeling between our families"? He'd probably call outright murder "just a little misunderstanding." I was in no hurry to marry, but I did know that when I chose a husband, he wouldn't be a handsome fool like Ikeni.

But a handsome fool who can help me, I thought. I offered him my warmest smile and chose my words with care. I didn't want to lie. Lies would weigh down my heart when the time came for me to be judged in the next world, and a heavy heart was doomed. "The sooner I speak with your father, the sooner I can go home and speak with mine."

I never said I'd speak to Father about *marriage,* but Ikeni heard what he wanted to hear. I saw a spark of hope flash in his eyes. "I'll take you to see him at once!" he cried.

I made a swift, silencing gesture. "Secretly," I said, keeping my own voice low. "No one must know I'm here."

"Why not? If we're betrothed—"

"Father would be angry." And that was certainly true!

"Oh." Ikeni nodded and led me into the high priest's house.

From the moment I crossed the threshold, I saw riches. I knew that my own family was one of the most prosperous in Akhmin, but next to the splendors of the high priest's house, we lived in a mud hut. The walls were painted with the same brilliance as the outer temple walls, the wooden columns supporting the ceiling so bright with gold that they shone even in the dim light of the oil lamps. And the lamps themselves! They were everywhere. Their sweet scent made me realize that they must be burning costly perfumed oil. Chests and tables and chairs shimmered with fantastic patterns of rare and costly woods from distant Punt and the lands of the Nubians, beyond the birthplace of the sacred river. Some flaunted exquisitely carved legs decorated with gold, ivory, coral, and turquoise.

Ikeni brought me to a doorway. The room beyond was small but even more brightly lit than the rest of the house. "Father?" Ikeni clapped his hands twice. "Someone important is here to see you." He took me by the elbow before I could object to his touch a second time and steered me inside.

The high priest sat in a splendid, high-backed chair, the gilded legs carved to look like lions' paws. There was one table to his left, laden with several small, ornate wooden boxes and many papyrus scrolls. The remains of a meal—a platter of discarded goose bones, half a pomegranate, a mostly eaten lump of bread—lay on the smaller table to his left. He was in the act of refilling his cup with wine when he saw me. He was so startled that he jerked his hand, staining his white linen kilt with red. For a few heartbeats, he looked confused and even a little afraid.

"What are you doing here?" he demanded. He glared at Ikeni. "Why have you brought her? If her father finds out, he'll use your stupidity to destroy me!"

"But Father, it's all right," Ikeni said, eager to restore peace. "I didn't bring her. She came here by herself." He laid his hands on my shoulders.

"She did *what*?" The high priest's eyes narrowed with mistrust.

I shrugged free of Ikeni's hold and stepped forward, bowed, and raised my hands in a sign of reverence. "My lord, I've come here by myself, of my own free will. My father and mother don't know anything about this. In the name of Isis, whom you love and serve, the lady of life, I ask for—"

"We're going to be married after all!" Ikeni blurted. "No one I know will ever have such a beautiful wife. Isn't it wonderful?"

The high priest looked from me to his son and back again. Our eyes met, and for an instant we recognized that we shared the same opinion of Ikeni's . . . wisdom.

"Most wonderful," he said dryly. "Ikeni, leave us."

Ikeni looked hurt and bewildered. "But she said she'd marry me! Shouldn't I be here for—?"

"Go." The high priest didn't need to raise his voice; his son hunched his shoulders as if protecting himself from a blow and slunk out of the room. When he was gone, the high priest turned to me. "Should I believe him?" he asked. "Do you want to marry my son after all?"

I shook my head. "That's not why I'm here."

This time his smile was almost sincere. "Good. I'd hate to think I misjudged your intelligence, Nefertiti. Not every girl in Akhmin knows how to read and write." Shock showed plainly in my face, making him laugh. "Don't gape like that. Of course I know. The gods have ears."

"More likely the servants have tongues," I muttered. It

would only have taken one eavesdropper during Father's argument with Henenu to shatter my "secret."

That made him laugh even more. "You *are* a sharp one. My own wife—may Osiris cherish her as I did—was also a woman of great wisdom. I wouldn't be where I am today without her by my side. And yet, as smart as you are, you've come to my house by night, alone. No one would call *that* wise. Whatever has brought you here must be very important indeed."

I bowed to him a second time. "Lord, it is. I've come to ask for the life of the slave girl who saved mine."

"Ah, Mahala the flute player? She was born in this house to one of my Habiru women. They say that those who are slaves from birth give you less trouble. So much for *that* theory, eh?" He smirked. "Her people don't know our gods, so the will of Hapy meant nothing to her, but the fact remains that she publicly defied her master. If such things go unpunished and other slaves hear of it, where will it end? I made the only righteous decision."

"A decision you can change," I said. "A decision you *must* change."

"Hmph! Strong words. And why *must* I? You look as grave as if the fate of all Pharaoh's realm depends on my obeying you!"

I lowered my eyes. "Lord, I have—I have had an evil dream." I told him my old vision of the lions, the way it had been before I dreamed of the Great Sphinx and defeated them. Many of the gods' priests understood the art of telling the future from dreams, and no one could possibly interpret my long-ago dream as a good omen. I never said that the dream was an ancient one, or that its fearful monsters were no longer a threat, or that it had nothing to do with the slave girl's fate. I had scattered a handful of truths in the high priest's lap and hoped he'd string them together in the way I desired. I felt a stab of guilt for my deceit and tried to comfort myself by thinking: *This is different from an outright lie. And is it wrong to mislead a man who spoke greater falsehoods in the god Hapy's name?* But I was still ashamed.

When I finished my story, the high priest looked suitably concerned. "What a terrible dream. My dear child, not even the most famous of Pharaoh's dream-readers could find a flicker of hope in such a dreadful message from the gods. How can I ignore it? If that's what moved you to come here so secretly, it must be a true vision. And if I spare the slave girl's life, all will be well?"

I knew he was talking about averting bad omens, but when I answered, "Yes, all will be well," I meant that an innocent life would be saved.

"So we're in agreement." He smiled at me with so much charm and kindness that I couldn't help smiling back. He no longer seemed like the disagreeable old bullfrog who'd shared our table. Maybe I'd misjudged him. Then his eyes flashed with malice and he said: "Too bad I don't have the power to bring back the dead."

"Then she's already been . . ." I choked on the words. My cheeks burned, but my eyes stayed dry. How I wanted to strike out at this mean-souled, leering man and his cruel game! My right hand lifted, as if it had its own free will. *Stop,* a level voice sounded inside my head. *If I slap that nasty grin from his face, he wouldn't hesitate to make Father, Mery, and Bit-Bit suffer for it.* I forced my hand back down and became Sekhmet again. "Then may the gods reward you for what you've done. Good night."

"Not so fast, girl!" The high priest sprang out of his chair and had my arms pinned to my sides before I could even turn toward the door. "We have unfinished business."

I squirmed and struggled in his grip. "Let me go! I have nothing more to say to you!"

"I disagree." He was a strong man and had no trouble hauling me across the floor and shoving me down into his chair so hard that it rattled my spine. "You wasted my time with that flimsy nonsense about your *supposed* dream, but I'm not the kind of man who wastes a good opportunity. Have you forgotten Ikeni? Your bridegroom?" His teeth were sharp and white, like a jackal's. "Once there's a kinship bond between our families, your father will have to treat me with more . . . courtesy. You'll stay here tonight, and in the morning you will be escorted back to your father's house with all the ceremony and spectacle suitable for such a happy occasion."

"Do it, then!" I snapped, digging my fingertips into the arms of the gilded chair. "The bond won't last a day! I'll be free of your son before noon. Even if people believe Ikeni wed me, marriage is a house with an open door. I can walk out any time I like!"

"And where would you go? If you leave my son quickly, after having rushed to his arms tonight, all Akhmin will see you as a common little slut. You'll never find another husband."

"I don't *need* a husband," I countered. "I can take care of myself!"

"But can you take care of your father's reputation? There are many men in this city who envy his success as Pharaoh's overseer. It won't take them long to send letters to the royal court, every one saying: *How can Ay look after Pharaoh's affairs when he can't even look after his own daughter?*"

"Pharaoh wouldn't believe them," I said staunchly. "He loves my father."

"No. He loves your *aunt*. If your father became an embarrassment to her, she'd turn her back on him in the blink of an eye and take all of her royal husband's favor and support with her."

I shook my head. "She's his sister. She wouldn't."

"She's Queen Tiye. I've met her." The high priest's grin grew even wider until the jackal became a crocodile. "She would." He shouted two names and a pair of gangly boys about my own age came running into the room. They were as thoroughly shaved as he, priests in training from the look of them.

"Master, is everything all right?" one of them asked, the lump in his throat bobbing wildly.

"Better than that, lads," the high priest replied easily, gesturing at me. "The house of Isis has a new mistress. Your companion Ikeni has taken a wife. We'll celebrate her arrival properly tomorrow. For tonight, she will be given the best room under my roof and the two of you will have the honor of seeing that no one enters or leaves. No one. Is that clear?" The boys bowed to show they understood and were ready to obey. The high priest turned to me once more. "Your escort awaits."

The boys marched me through the priest's house, one walking ahead with a lamp, one walking behind me. I didn't try to run away from them. They would have caught me, and I'd had my fill of unwelcome hands on me that night. It didn't take us long to reach my prison. "Best room" or not, a prison was its rightful name. The boy carrying our light went in first and used it to kindle the alabaster oil lamp inside. Soft radiance glowed over fine furniture and walls painted with a scene of dancing girls. The freedom of their movements seemed to mock me.

I sat down on the bed and stared at the wall. From the corner of my eye I saw the priests-to-be bow very low to me before leaving the room and pulling a blue and yellow curtain across the doorway. No doubt they were on guard just outside. I looked around the room for possible escape, but unless I could learn to be an earthworm and burrow my way out, I was trapped. The only window was too high for me to reach, even if I stood on the bed. There was a small storage chest in the corner, so I tried balancing it on the bed and using it to lift me higher, but the bed frame creaked and sagged so sharply under the extra weight that I toppled off. I landed on my feet without doing any further harm to the foot I'd twisted climbing the outer wall, but that was as far as my luck went. I was still a captive.

And in the morning, I'll be paraded back to Father's house as Ikeni's wife, I thought angrily. *Father will put an end to that "marriage" right away, but not before everyone in Akhmin starts jabbering about where I was tonight, and why. And if they don't know what happened, or if the truth's too tame, they'll make up a nastier tale to tell, just to amuse themselves. O Ma'at, how I wish your sacred Feather of Truth could send all storytellers' hearts straight down the gullet of the monster Ammut! My whole family will be shamed. And it was all for nothing. The girl is dead. I should have stayed at home and tried to find out if she were still alive before running headlong into this mess.*

I covered my eyes with both hands and sighed loudly.

"Mistress?" One of the boys spoke up in a reedy voice. "Do you want something?"

"Nothing," I replied. "Leave me alone."

"Don't call her 'Mistress!' " Now I heard the other boy's voice, deeper and scratchier than his companion's.

"Why not?"

"It's too soon, for one thing. For another—" His voice dropped so low that all I could hear was: "—old Mistress's spirit *mad.*"

Reedy Voice giggled nervously. "Why would she care if I call Ikeni's bride 'Mistress'? She's been dead for five years. Her spirit is living happily in Osiris's kingdom."

"That's not what the cook's son told me," Deep Voice said darkly. "Or the girl who used to be her maid. Both of them saw her. The girl broke one of old Mistress's favorite perfume bottles and the next thing she knew, her cheek was throbbing as if someone had slapped it hard! But she was the only person in the room. And the cook's son says that once, when he was hiding to avoid doing his work, all of a sudden his shoulders began to sting and sting and *sting,* just as if someone were beating him with a stick! He ran away, yowling."

"I thought you said they *saw* old Mistress." Reedy Voice sounded as skeptical as I was. By now I'd crept closer to the curtain, eager to hear more about the so-called ghost.

The other boy made an impatient noise. "They both said it was her! How would they know that unless they *saw* her? Thoth help you, you're stupid."

"I'm not the one who still can't read through the shortest scroll without making more mistakes than fleas on a donkey!" They bickered back and forth like that for a while and finally settled their quarrel by insulting Ikeni behind his back. While they chattered on, I went back to sit on the bed again but not to sleep. Those two had given me a most precious gift: an idea.

It didn't take me long to put my plan together. Once I'd found my inspiration, working out the details was surprisingly easy. *A plan like this is just another kind of storytelling,* I thought. I recalled my sister's face, so filled with fascination and delight when I entertained her with the tales I created. Somehow that memory gave me the confidence I needed to bring off the plan at hand.

I stood watch that night, holding on to my courage with both hands. Whenever I felt a twinge of doubt or hesitation, I thought of Bit-Bit. *I have such a wonderful story for you, little sister! Be patient. As soon as the right moment comes, I'll tell it to you.* I didn't dare to close my eyes until the high window showed that the night was fading. Dawn would come soon. It was time.

I stretched my arms and legs and body the way I did before a dance, happy to discover that my injured foot felt almost completely restored. I whispered a prayer to Isis for help and to Ma'at for forgiveness, then I threw myself backward onto the bed and began to thrash violently. Small, half-choked groans and whimpers poured from my lips, but I didn't make *too* much noise. I didn't want to attract the attention of every person in the house; just two.

The young priests-to-be tore the doorway curtain aside and burst into the room. Their faces looked white as sun-bleached bone in the lamplight. Before they could say a single word, I cried, "She's here! The high priest's wife is here! She's holding me down!" I had my hands hooked to the sides of the bed, and I kicked my feet as if I were fighting against a great weight on my chest. "She's trying to—" I made sounds like someone choking on a fish bone and did my best to look terrified.

The boys stood frozen in the doorway. "What did I tell you?" Deep Voice said, scared and triumphant at the same time. "It's old Mistress's spirit!"

"No, no, no, no, no, impossible." Reedy Voice wasn't ready to give up the argument. "She's just having a—a fit or something." He started toward me.

I sat up, transfixed with a look of blazing hatred. "How *dare* you!" I declared, pointing one finger at his heart. "How *dare* you try to touch your Mistress! In the name of Isis, if you lay one finger on me while I inhabit this miserable girl, your arm will wither, your skin will shrivel, your eyes will boil in your head, your—"

"All right, all right, I won't touch you, I swear it!" Reedy

Voice backed away quickly, holding his hands up before his face. How they trembled! I could hardly believe it: My plan was working! I began to enjoy myself.

"Disrespect!" I thundered. "Did you speak to me in such a familiar way while I lived under this roof?"

"No! I mean—No, O Mistress." Now Reedy Voice was completely a believer. When I rose from the bed, doing my best to look majestic and imposing, he fell to his knees and bowed at my feet.

Deep Voice was still standing like a statue, but his lips worked. "O Mistress, shall I—shall I fetch your husband?"

"Never!" I raised my arms high, my hands clenched. "After what he has dared to do to my precious son Ikeni, he doesn't deserve to hear my voice in this world again."

"I—I don't think we do, either," Reedy Voice muttered.

I ignored him. "He scorns my son, calls him stupid, wants to tie him in marriage to—to *this*!" Now I flung my arms wide and looked down at my own body in disgust.

"Um . . . what's wrong with her?" Reedy Voice asked. "She's really pretty."

"And we were just talking with Ikeni before your husband summoned us," Deep Voice added. "He's in love. He *wants* to marry her."

I glowered at him. "Did I ask for your opinions, you pair of squashed beetles? I know what's best for my son. The eyes of the dead see more clearly than the eyes of the living. I tell you, if Ikeni is married to this worthless creature for a day—no, for even *part* of a day!—I will take a hideous vengeance. My spirit will curse everyone and everything in this house. You will ache with hunger and burn with thirst!

Your feet will turn to stone, your hands to mud, your livers will swell, your blood will slake the thirst of poisonous serpents, and your manhood will be—"

I struck one final pose, gave the shivering boys a dire look, then uttered a tiny sob and fell into the best faint I could fake. As I lay in a heap at their feet, I heard Deep Voice ask: "Is she dead?"

"Of course she's dead! Old Mistress has been dead for years." A sharp slap rang out and Reedy Voice added: "Ow. Why'd you do that?"

"Because you're as stupid as Iken—I mean, you're just stupid. Is the *girl* dead?"

"I don't think so. I see her breathing." There was a pause. Then Reedy Voice spoke again: "We have to tell Master about all this. If he hears about the curse—"

Deep Voice cut him off with a snort. "You really are a bonehead. We both know Master never listened to his wife when she was alive. We have to get her out of here."

"But if we do that, Master will punish us!"

"Which would you rather have, one of his beatings or your feet turning to stone, your hands to mud, your manhood to—well, she fell over before she could say what would happen to our manhoods, but it's probably something awful. A curse is a curse."

Reedy Voice sighed. The next thing I knew, one of them hooked his hands under my armpits, the other grabbed my ankles, and the pair of them ran swiftly and silently through the priest's house while I jounced and swung between them like a goatskin filled with water. I kept my eyes closed and my body limp, but in my heart I was doing a dance of un-controllable joy.

At last I felt fresh air on my face and knew we'd reached the street. They set me down with a wall pressed against my right side. I had no idea where I was but I didn't care. I was *out*.

"Do you think she'll be all right here?" Reedy Voice asked.

Deep Voice answered: "The sun will be up soon. People will come out and find her. She'll be fine. Come on, let's go back inside. We've got to think up a good story to tell Master when he asks where she is."

I hope it's as good as the Tale of the High Priest's Vengeful Dead Wife, I thought and risked a smile. *Bit-Bit's going to love this one.*

As soon as I heard the last of their departing footsteps, I sat up, brushed myself off, and hurried home as fast as if there really were an angry spirit flying after me.

6

A WORD CAN CHANGE THE WORLD

I let myself in by the garden gate, went inside, and found the house in an uproar. Bit-Bit was wailing, Mery was praying frantically, and Father was nowhere to be seen. Had something evil happened to him?

"Mother, where's Father?" I cried, rushing in.

"Oh! The gods be thanked!" Mery clutched me to her so hard it hurt.

"I couldn't find you in our room after dinner," Bit-Bit said, wiping her nose on the back of her hand. "I thought you'd gone up on the roof or out into the garden, so I went to sleep. But when I woke up in the middle of the night you still weren't there, or on the roof, or in the garden, or *anywhere*. So I told Father."

"He's been searching the whole city for you," Mery said. "Where have you been?"

I took a deep breath. "You're not going to like this. . . ."

I was right; she didn't. Neither did Father, after Mery sent one of the servants to find him and fetch him back. I got such a scolding that my ears burned.

"What were you thinking?" Father shouted. "I never expected something like this from *you*, Nefertiti. You've always been so shy, so quiet, so *sensible*. Do you know how much trouble you could have caused? This isn't like you at all. My Nefertiti would never do such a rash, heedless, dangerous thing."

But I did *do it, Father,* I thought. *I chose to do it, and I don't regret anything except that it was too late to save that poor slave girl's life. You see only the risk I ran, not my reasons for deciding it was a risk worth taking. Oh, Father, you look at me and see* your *Nefertiti, but that's not who I am.*

Of course I didn't share my thoughts with Father. I was exhausted after my nightlong captivity, so I prostrated myself before my parents and begged their pardon for how much I'd worried them.

"I forgive you, little kitten." Father knelt and raised me back to my feet. "But for the next ten days you'll stay in this house. You can go into the garden, if you like, but not the street. Understand?"

"If that's my punishment . . . ," I began.

"It's not so much a punishment as a precaution," he replied. "The townsfolk are already talking about what happened to you at the Inundation, and if I know the high priest, he'll be sowing ugly rumors about you today. The crocodile doesn't like having prey slip out of his jaws. He'll do whatever he can to hurt you, even if it's only with words.

If you stay inside, the gossip won't have a visible target. It doesn't matter how much dung people throw if there's no wall for it to stick to."

"Listen to your father, Nefertiti," Mery said gently. "He loves you."

Yes, but he doesn't know me, I thought.

Father went to sleep even though it was morning. He was exhausted after his desperate search for me. Mery saw to it that I was given a breakfast that was more like the Inundation feast I'd missed. I ate ravenously. The last meal I'd had was also breakfast, a day ago. While I filled my belly, Mery and Bit-Bit left the house to go to the market. I was left to myself.

I finished eating and went into the garden. Early morning light bathed the statue of Isis in a golden glow. I recalled all the riches I'd seen the night before in the house of her high priest. *How much of that wealth was taken from the goddess?* I wondered. *Does Isis live in such splendor within her temple walls? No one but the priests would ever know. They're the only ones supposed to be pure enough to serve the gods face to face. That man, "pure"?* I shook my head, thinking of how the high priest had abused his authority, trying to take my life and break Father's heart. *Isis, forgive me, but I can't believe that we aren't just as pure as your priests and just as worthy to stand before you.*

I knelt before the goddess and gazed up into her serene face and spoke to her from my heart.

"O Isis, why can't Father understand that I've changed? I don't need to hide behind these walls, afraid of people's stares or whispers. What do they matter? Mahala the

Habiru slave had worse to fear; she didn't let that stop her from doing what was right. She had nothing—not even her own life—but she had courage. I can't give back her life the way she gave back mine, but I can give her spirit a better gift than a little shrine, a saucer full of grain, and a dribble of wine."

I went back into the house, to Father's office, where I found a small piece of papyrus. Next I went to the kitchen yard and took a bit of charred wood from underneath the cooling bread oven. It took a lot of work to get a fine enough point on something so crumbly, but I managed, and soon I was back in the garden, placing the papyrus scrap between the goddess's feet. If anyone in our house noticed it there, they wouldn't dare disturb it. It was hers now.

"Great Isis, be my witness," I said, weighing down the papyrus with a white stone. "This is my vow, my own words: I promise to live with the same bravery that Mahala taught me when she gave her life for mine. It's not enough to be born free; I have to *live* my freedom! I swear to do this in honor of her memory, no matter how many battles I'll have to fight. May you give me strength and blessing, and may Mahala's spirit find rest."

When I finished my prayer, I went straight to my bed and slept until it was time for dinner. The next morning I woke up at dawn and returned to the garden, expecting to find my small papyrus scrap gone, blown away on the night wind, but it was still there, at Isis's feet. "A good omen," I said with a smile.

The great sun-boat of Ra was only a sliver of gold in the east when the messenger arrived. We were eating breakfast, and Father had just made a joke about how glad he was that this day couldn't possibly be as bad as the past two. He was not pleased to have our meal disturbed when one of the servants brought the stranger in, but when the man bowed and stated his business, Father's expression went from mild irritation to outright alarm.

"My lord Ay," the messenger said solemnly. "I bring word from your august sister, Queen Tiye, Great Royal Wife of the divine Amenhotep, may he live a thousand years. You and all your family are commanded to travel to join her at Abydos, where it is her will to honor you as no servants of Pharaoh have ever been honored before. A ship awaits your pleasure."

"My pleasure has nothing to do with my sister's ship," Father muttered. If the messenger heard, he gave no sign. Father raised his voice and said: "You are welcome in my house. Eat, drink, and rest. Then return to my sister and say that we will obey her . . . *invitation* at once. We'll leave tomorrow at dawn."

"So much delay, my lord?" The messenger looked nervous. "Queen Tiye won't be pleased. She's *very* eager for your arrival. If I go back without you . . ."

Father laughed mirthlessly. "Then you'll go back *with* us. But we're not going to undertake the journey in haste. Who knows how long my sister will want us to stay? I still have business to conduct on Pharaoh's behalf. I have to make arrangements so that things here in Akhmin don't suffer in my absence, and I am *not* going anywhere if it means leaving my house in disorder behind me. When we reach Abydos, I'll tell the queen that the holdup was all my fault. You won't suffer for it."

The messenger gave him a look that said *That's what you think,* but since he couldn't do a thing to sway Father's decision, he submitted to it. "Lord Ay, I am your servant in all things. My mistress, Queen Tiye, also commands me to give you this." He reached into the leather pouch hanging from his belt and pulled out a many-stranded necklace of gold, lapis lazuli, and rock crystal beads, with an enameled pendant of the goddess Hathor. It was far more impressive than anything Mery owned. When he held the regal gift up for us to see it in all its splendor, the gems captured the shafts of sunlight pouring down from the hall's high windows. All of us gasped at such a rich gift, even Father.

"My sister is too generous," he said, holding out his hands.

The messenger looked uncomfortable. "Lord Ay, this gift—that is, *your* gifts from Queen Tiye await you in Abydos. It is the desire of her heart to fill your hands with riches, so that you will never doubt how much she favors you. But this—this is sent as a gift for your firstborn daughter, Nefertiti. I am commanded to place it around her neck with my own hands and let her know she has Queen Tiye's eternal love."

"Eternal, is it?" Father raised one eyebrow. "Well, do what you must. Nefertiti, receive your aunt's gift."

I rose from my stool and allowed the messenger to put the necklace on me. It was even heavier than the one I'd borrowed from Mery. Bit-Bit gazed at me with a mixture of admiration and envy. I smiled at her and made signs to let her know that I'd let her try on my gift. She bounced in her seat and grinned, all envy gone.

The rest of the morning became a flurry of work as Mery saw to the preparations for our departure. All of our best clothing was taken out of the storage chests, inspected, and given to the servants and slaves for any washing or mending that might be necessary. There was a moment of absolute panic when Bit-Bit discovered that she had out-grown her leather sandals. No one wore shoes unless there was a special occasion, so it was easy to lose track of such things.

Luckily for us, the news of our coming journey had raced through Akhmin like a fire in a dry field. Old Anat found a sandal maker who was more than happy to drop everything in order to make Bit-Bit a pair of shoes that might draw the attention of the queen. He brought them to our doorway by midafternoon.

He wasn't our only visitor. Every one of the most high-born families to Akhmin came to wish us a safe journey to Abydos. Some of them were our true friends, some sud-denly had a reason for wanting a closer relationship with our family. The same three girls who'd taunted me before we danced at the Festival of the Inundation showed up with baskets of honey cakes and armfuls of flowers for me. They made a loud fuss over my necklace, tried to kiss my cheeks, and begged me to remember all the happy times we'd shared. I didn't know whether I wanted to slap them or laugh in their faces. After they left, I ran back into my room, where Mery was folding my dresses, and flung myself across the bed with a dramatic groan.

"Is anything wrong, dear?" Mery asked playfully.

"Why is everyone so eager to be my friend *now*? They're like *fleas*," I declared. "I don't want them, but they keep swarming all over me."

"It's not that they want to be your friends, Nefertiti; it's that they're afraid of being counted as your enemies. Everyone in Akhmin knows that Queen Tiye has shown you special generosity and no one knows why. But they *do* know how powerful she is, so they're playing it safe and trying to stay on your good side."

"They think that if they make me mad, the queen will punish them? Ha!"

"Don't sound so skeptical. Your Father's told me a lot about his royal sister. She casts a big shadow and we'll all have to learn to walk cautiously around it."

A servant came into the room with word that we had yet *another* visitor, someone else who'd come asking specifically to see me. I groaned. "Tell them to go away. Whoever they are, tell them they're not my enemy. I don't *have* any enemies—I just hate all of my new 'friends!' "

"Nefertiti, stop acting like a child," Mery chided. "Go and greet your guest."

"But it's such a waste of time, Mother," I protested. "Every time a new visitor comes, we have to stop packing. We'll never be ready to go!"

"I'm the one doing the packing, Nefertiti," she replied calmly. "You're just the one complaining about it, and since it's you they've come to see, this visit won't delay our preparations at all."

"But—!"

"Now listen, it isn't that far from Akhmin to Abydos and we haven't got *that* much to pack. It would be easier to get ready for the trip if I had some idea of how long we'll be gone, but even if we haven't brought enough clothing, I'm sure Queen Tiye won't let her kinfolk go around naked. Go."

I couldn't argue with Mery's reasoning, so I pushed myself out of the bed and dragged my feet into the great hall, ready for another "friend." I wasn't prepared for what awaited me.

"Ikeni?" What was the high priest's son doing in our home? Possibilities whirled through my head like bats at sunset. Clearly his father's hand was behind it, but what was that man's scheme? To have Ikeni claim me as his "bride"? To have him confront me, in his father's name, for having wrongfully entered the temple grounds that night? To bring a false claim that I'd stolen something while I'd been in the priest's house? I wouldn't put it past the old bullfrog.

Then I saw the child. She was standing behind Ikeni, and she was so small that I hadn't noticed her until she peeked out at me. I recognized her from the Festival of the Inundation. Like poor Mahala, she was one of the temple slaves who'd made music to accompany our dance. I remember being impressed that someone so very young could already play the harp so well, with such sweetness. Why was she here?

"Hail, Lady Nefertiti. May holy Isis, queen of all the

gods, lady of life, the most mighty one, favor you with all her blessings." Ikeni bowed as deeply to me as he recited the stiff, formal greeting. He held that uncomfortable pose—bent sharply at the waist, his arms outstretched, his gaze fixed on the ground—the whole time he spoke to me. The words came out like a lesson that had been beaten into him until he had it memorized perfectly. "May she protect you and your august family on your journey. May you go in safety, abide in joy, and return in triumph. May you—"

"Ikeni, look at me," I said. He turned his head a little at my words but held his pose. "Ikeni, stand *up.*"

"As—as my lady wishes." He straightened slowly, relieved and uneasy at the same time. "I have more that I'm supposed to say to you, but it's hard to remember it. If anyone asks—"

"—you were perfect," I finished his timid plea for him. "We'll both be happier if you deliver your message in your own words. Why are you here? If your father thinks he can claim we're married—"

"Oh no!" Ikeni was even more horrified at the thought than I was. It was almost insulting. "He wouldn't dream of that. Not now. Not when your father is back in the queen's favor so much that you're all going away to join the royal court."

"We're only going to pay a visit," I said. "We're coming back."

Ikeni gave me a strange look. "If you say so. I hope you're right. Even if you're too pretty to marry me, I'd hate to think that I'd never get to see you again."

"Ikeni, that's not why I won't marry you," I said. Then I

bit my tongue. What if he asked for the real reason why I'd never marry him? I didn't want to tell him such a cruel truth, that his attractive face and his father's powerful position as high priest of Isis were his only good points in the marriage market. Plenty of other girls would jump at the chance to have him for their husband, but if I ever married, I wanted a man with whom I could talk, plan, share dreams, and even enjoy a friendly argument now and then.

I changed the subject as quickly as I could: "Who's your little friend? I don't know her name, but I remember her music." I crouched to be on eye level with the child and offered her a smile. "Hello, dear. Have you come to play the harp for me, as a farewell gift from Ikeni?"

"*She's* the gift!" Ikeni blurted. "And my father's very sorry about what he did—I mean, what *happened* to her sister, but it was the will of the gods, and we can't do anything about it, and her name is—um—I forget."

I stood up and stared at Ikeni as if frogs had just streamed from his mouth. "She's Mahala's sister?"

He nodded, cheerful as a well-fed dog. "Father thought that since he can't bring back that one and give her to you, the way you asked, this one will be all right instead."

I told myself that he wasn't being deliberately heartless; he simply didn't know any better. "This is . . . generous."

"I'll tell Father you said so!" Ikeni was beaming. "Oh, he'll be so happy! He was worried you'd complain about him to Queen Tiye, but you won't do that now . . . will you?" he added, still not entirely sure of me.

"By Ma'at's truth, I hope I never have to speak his name again," I replied. Ikeni gave a joyful yelp, bowed to me once more, and ran out of the house like a boy half his age. I turned to the high priest's "gift." The child gazed at me with large green eyes, her thin body trembling. "Why don't you tell me your name, little one?" I asked in a soothing voice. I got no reply. *She's scared and shy,* I thought. *The high priest's house was probably the only home she ever knew. I'll give her time to get used to this house, and to me.* I offered her my hand. "Are you hungry? Come with me and I'll get you some food."

The little girl continued to stare at me with owl's eyes, but after a little hesitation she took my hand. I led her out of the hall to the kitchen. The other slaves and servants regarded her curiously. She cowered under their stares and pressed herself against my side as if she were trying to vanish. I explained who she was and how she'd come to live here; they were unimpressed.

"Scrawny thing," old Anat muttered with a disdainful snort.

Our cook was no slave, and a valued servant, so he wasn't at all bashful about demanding, "What can she *do*?"

"She plays the harp," I replied.

"*What* harp?"

As if in answer to his sharp question, at that instant Ikeni came barging into the kitchen, led there by the same servant who'd first announced his visit. The high priest's son cradled the girl's small harp awkwardly in his arms.

"I almost forgot!" he said, setting down the instrument. "I ran all the way home and all the way here so I could give you this, too. I think she can still play for you, even if she can't sing anymore."

"Why can't she?" I asked. A dark uneasiness fell over me. I wasn't sure I wanted to hear the answer. It couldn't be anything good.

Ikeni shrugged. "She can't sing because she can't speak. Not now. When they took her sister away, she cried and cried for her until the cook's son said it wouldn't do any good because that slave had been tied hand and foot, then tossed into the river, so the crocodiles probably got her and—"

The child began to gasp, soundless sobs racking her thin body. She dropped to the ground in a tight ball, hands clamped to her ears, and a ghostly wail of pure grief escaped her lips. I thought my heart would break from that woeful sound.

"Get out of my home," I told Ikeni. "Never come back. *Never.*"

"What did I do?" he protested weakly. I took one step toward him, my hands curling into fists, and again I was Sekhmet, the lion-headed goddess of war and destruction. Even though I was much smaller than he, Ikeni saw the ferocious rage in my face, turned white as linen, and ran.

I dropped to my knees beside the child and tried to put my arms around her, but she pushed me away and crawled under the table where the cook chopped vegetables. I sat cross-legged beside her until she slowly uncurled her body and looked at me.

"It's all right," I told her. "He's gone. You live here now. No one's ever going to hurt you again." I held out both my hands. "I'm Nefertiti." She nodded, as if to say she already knew who I was, but she never made a sound.

I brought the child to Mery, who was just finishing the preparations for our journey. Bit-Bit, always inquisitive and enthusiastic, rushed up to greet us, scaring the little one into hiding behind me. She clung so hard to my dress that I thought she was going to pull it off. It was all I could do to have my sister calm down, get the child to loosen her grip on me, and explain matters to Mery.

"A fine apology from that man," Mery said tartly when I finished. "If ever there was proof that the gods don't choose their servants—! I pray that the divine ones find a way to repay the high priest *properly* for all he's done." She smiled kindly at the girl. "I'll also pray that this little one will recover her tongue someday and be able to tell us her name. In the meanwhile, we must find something to call her."

Her words provoked Bit-Bit into an eager burst of suggestions, though before Mery and I could say yes or no, my sister rejected each one as quickly as she proposed it. At last she exclaimed, "Let's call her Berett!" It was the name of the instrument she played, and as good an idea as any.

"Will that please you?" I asked the girl. "May we call you Berett?" She gave an almost imperceptible nod, and I added: "Only until you tell us your true name, of course." As if to prove her consent, Berett picked up her harp and began to play. I knelt beside her, my feet wanting to dance to the slow, sweet, tentative melody. In my heart, I made a promise: *Your sister gave me back my life, Berett. I will give you yours.*

Part II
Abydos

7

MEETINGS IN ABYDOS

We left Akhmin early the next morning. The first pale light of dawn made the river sparkle and revealed the glorious royal ship that my aunt had sent to bring us to Abydos. Bit-Bit and I were overwhelmed by the sight of such a splendid ship with its towering central mast, upcurved prow and stern, and the massive oar used to steer it and propel it when the wind or the current failed. I owed a debt to the magnificence of that ship. It dazzled me so thoroughly that it diverted my mind from thinking about the river itself and how closely the sacred waters had come to claiming me. Its sheer size and obvious strength lent me a measure of confidence, though from time to time I felt a small chill run over my skin when I gazed too long at the river.

Because we were heading upstream from Akhmin, the winds would carry us. We watched in fascination as the sailors unfurled the great sail with its painted image of Nekhebet, the vulture goddess whose mighty wings gave special protection to mothers, children, and Pharaoh himself.

Father and Mery retired to the richly decorated cabin in the center of the boat. Bit-Bit ran back and forth happily, investigating everything and crying out in delight when we pushed off from the shore and our journey truly began. She only settled down when Father stuck his head out of the cabin to command that someone tie a rope around my little sister's waist, in case her excitement made her careless and she wound up overboard.

With a strong wind filling our sail, the voyage to Abydos wasn't long. I was grateful. Even though I came to enjoy sailing, Berett was plainly terrified. As soon as I sat down facing the prow of the ship, she clung to me like a thornbush and wouldn't let me move. I should have thanked her: Her fear of the river forced me to banish the last traces of my own. Somehow I found it easier to be brave for someone who needed me than to be brave for myself alone. Father stuck his head out of the cabin a second time, saw how things were, and told Bit-Bit to bring Berett and me anything we needed. My sister was ecstatic to have an excuse for scampering around the ship again. She must have asked me at least fifty times if I needed a drink or something to eat.

"I'm fine," I said. "But why don't you ask Berett if she's hungry?"

"Why bother? She can't talk."

"She *won't* talk. There's a difference."

Bit-Bit shrugged. "Can't, won't, if I don't get an answer out of her, it's all the same."

"Until it changes," I maintained. I turned to the child. "You'll speak again someday. You *will*. Thoth will use his wisdom to heal you, Isis will comfort you, and the god of physicians, Imhotep, will send me a dream telling me how we're going to find your voice again. Until then, you're safe. Do you understand?" Berett stared, then began to suck her fingers. I heard Bit-Bit sigh deeply.

"I'll go get her some fruit. If she's hungry, she'll eat it; if she's not, *I* will."

By the time our ship reached Abydos, Berett had gobbled down three handfuls of dates, two of figs, a whole bunch of grapes, and was looking a little green. Her skin was much paler than mine, so the ill effects of her overeating were obvious. I held her by the shoulders and Bit-Bit kept her curly red-brown hair out of her face while she was sick over the side of the boat. Then I picked her up and carried her ashore. She hid her face against my neck, her thin arms and legs wrapped around me like a monkey.

"Nefertiti, you're going to have to learn that you can't give a child everything she wants," Father said as he watched me stagger along with Berett.

"She won't do it again," I said, resolute. "She's smart; she's learned her lesson. Haven't you, Berett?"

Father shook his head sadly over the child's silence. "How could the priest have done such a thing? I've known him for years; I used to admire him. He came from one of the poorest families in Akhmin and used his mind to work his way up to the high priesthood, but his past still rides him. Wealth means everything to him. Even if he had all of Pharaoh's treasures, he'd see it as nothing more than a strand of spiderweb holding him just above a bottomless valley of poverty."

The messenger who'd brought my aunt's command was already off the boat and out of sight by the time I set foot on land. We watched him race away; Father chuckled.

"Off to tell Tiye we're here, and probably praying with every breath that she's in a good mood. Poor man, what a way to earn his bread!"

I was only half listening. Between carrying Berett and taking in the wonders of Abydos, I was distracted. I had heard many tales about this city of temples, shrines, and graves. It was a place of immense age and holiness, where it was said that the bodies of our first pharaohs and their queens were buried. Even more awesome was the lore that named Abydos as the burial place of the god Osiris himself! We walked on sacred ground.

The messenger was back swiftly, accompanied by two teams of eight servants carrying heavy chairs on poles. The chairs themselves were made of gleaming black ebony wood, carved and enhanced with red and blue paint as well as flashes of gold on the arms, legs, and carrying poles. The seats were wide enough for two people to ride comfortably. Bit-Bit squeaked and clapped her hands in delighted anticipation of our glorious ride.

She thought better of it once we were on the road. The men carrying our chair couldn't seem to stay in step with one another. We jounced and lurched horribly. Berett still held tight to my neck, hiding her eyes, refusing to look at the marvels of Abydos. The tawny stones, the towering obelisks, the countless statues of gods and kings all slipped past her, unseen.

Our bouncy journey came to an end when our bearers passed under a massive gateway that opened into a broad courtyard. The walls were brilliant with the etched and painted images of gods and kings, but my eyes were drawn to the carvings I could read. Prayers and praises to Amun were everywhere, along with tributes to the kings who had enriched the god's temple. *Is this Amun's house?* I wondered, deeply troubled. *Why were we carried inside?* No one had the authority to enter a temple in such regal style. It was an insult to the god. *Even if it's not our fault, we'll still be punished. Oh, Berett, and after I swore I'd keep you safe—!* I hugged the child close. The instant that our chair touched the ground, I leaped off and away. Bit-Bit looked at me as if I'd lost my mind. My sister liked being treated royally and didn't seem aware of our surroundings. She stepped down from the chair with unusual dignity and plenty of reluctance.

I hurried over to my parents. "Father, are we in trouble?" I whispered.

"Why should we be?" My question puzzled him.

"Isn't this Amun's temple?" I glanced around at the words on the walls.

"You read too much, Nefertiti, when you shouldn't be reading at all." Father was suddenly serious. "Remember, I don't want my sister finding out about your . . . interest. There's no reason to fear: We aren't in the god's house. I remember this place from my younger days, serving in Pharaoh Amenhotep's court. It's where the king and his people stay while paying homage to the gods of Abydos. So many people make the pilgrimage here—nobles and commoners—that several temples maintain lodgings for them."

As he spoke, slaves came trailing in from the street, carrying our boxes on their backs. They grumbled to find us lingering in the courtyard, since they couldn't set down their burdens until someone let them know where we'd be staying. Just then, a tall man emerged from a doorway framed by the arched body of the sky-goddess, Nut. He carried an impressive staff that he struck against the ground and hailed Father by name and with a flood of flattering phrases. Unfortunately, his fine words were delivered in a singsong, nasal voice that grated on the ears. It was a relief when he reached the end of his recitation and said: "Your humble and unworthy lodgings are this way, if you will consent to follow me."

We followed. I can hardly begin to say how long we followed him, how far we walked, how many rooms we passed through, big and small, or how any human being could find his way through such a vast building without getting lost. In the end, we reached a garden that could have enclosed four of our green refuges at home. Our guide gestured with his staff, assigning us our chambers.

"My lord Ay, let it please you and your wife to accept *this* room. My lady Nefertiti, you will honor our house by entering *that* room, beyond the lotus pool, and your sister Mutnodjmet will take *this* room." He indicated the doorway next to the room he'd given to our parents.

I gazed across the serene surface of the lotus pool,

fragrant with vibrant blue flowers. Why was I being lodged apart from my family? I glanced left and right, seeing several other doorways, including one right next to Bit-Bit's room. Were they already occupied? *Oh well, it's not worth making a fuss about this,* I thought, and started toward my room.

The tall servant moved so fast that he seemed to appear in my path by magic. "If my revered lady Nefertiti will allow me, I will take charge of this"—he nodded at Berett—"for you."

"Berett stays with me," I said firmly.

"Ah?" One brow rose and vanished under the fringe of his wig. "I beg my lady Nefertiti to forgive me. I was told by the royal messenger who announced your arrival that you were traveling with a slave, not a . . . um . . ." His cool self-possession deserted him for a moment as he asked, "What *is* this child to you, great one?"

"She's—she's—" I paused. What *was* Berett to me? She was given to me as a slave and I'd done nothing to change that. My heart yearned to free her, but I didn't know how to do it. By our laws, slaves were property, the same as a cow or a house or a bracelet. I'd overheard enough of Father's conversations to know that if I wanted to give Berett a new life of freedom, it would have to be done exactly according to the law or she would still be a slave. *A slave—but I don't want to call her that,* I thought. "This child is—"

"Isn't it obvious?" A familiar voice boomed across the garden. "This child is the lady Nefertiti's friend and companion." I turned with a joyful heart to see Henenu come rushing forward with his unique, rolling gait, his arms held wide in welcome.

I wanted to hug him, but that was impossible. As soon as he reached us, Berett raised her head, took one look at the scribe, and squeaked like a newborn kitten in distress. Her grip on me tightened so sharply that it squeezed the breath from my body and made me stagger. Henenu couldn't help laughing.

"I've heard of close friendships, but this is astonishing. She's stickier than a split date, this one. Where did she come from? She looks foreign."

"She's a Habiru," I replied. "Her name is—we call her Berett. She's a musician."

"A good name for her, in that case." Henenu might have said more, but a sharp, insistent tapping drew his attention. The tall servant was drumming his staff on the ground impatiently and looked ready to bite someone. "Yes?" the scribe said, matching him glare for glare. "Did you want something?"

"I would never presume that my time was more valuable than yours, Master Henenu," the servant replied coldly. "However, Queen Tiye has given me word to bring her family into her royal presence as soon as they have been settled in their rooms. That cannot happen if the lady Nefertiti hasn't even crossed the threshold of her chamber."

"Don't let me stop you," Henenu said, his fat cheeks shining with deliberate cheer. It made the servant even crosser. "In fact, let me help. Nefertiti—I mean *Lady* Nefertiti, will you come this way?" Even though I was still holding Berett, he managed to take me by the elbow and steer us around the tall servant, who stood gaping at the scribe's audacity.

When I entered my room, it was my turn to stare open-mouthed at the luxury awaiting me. I'd never seen so much furniture, not even in the house of the high priest of Isis. The bed, the tables, the chests, the lamps, the chairs—all were beautifully made, lavishly decorated. The air itself was sweet with perfume. The slave who was carrying my belongings set down the box and left. It looked forlorn and small in the midst of so many luxurious things. A second slave brought Berett's harp and left it leaning against one of the chairs. I felt the child shift in my arms, her gaze going to her beloved instrument. I took advantage of this, setting her down and giving her a light push in the direction of the harp. She flew across the room, fell to her knees, and embraced it almost as tightly as she'd hugged me.

I sighed happily, letting my arms swing free. They felt drained and even a little numb from having toted Berett for so long. I was just starting to get full feeling back into them when a plump woman came in and began unpacking my things. I gave the tall servant an inquiring look.

"She is your chief maidservant, Lady Nefertiti," he drawled. "She's not attractive, but don't worry about that; she's only here to serve you temporarily. *Much* more acceptable women will wait upon you in the future."

"This woman is *very* acceptable to me," I snapped, bristling at his mean words. "And she's a lot more attractive than *you'll* ever be."

"If you say so, Lady Nefertiti," he replied evenly. "With your permission, I will go." He bowed low and backed out of the room, leaving me flustered and confused.

"Why did he do that, Henenu?" I asked.

My old friend wasn't smiling anymore. "A royal servant knows that his fortune depends on keeping the favor of the most important people at court. That man enjoys a good job with plenty of privileges that other servants can only dream of. He doesn't want to risk losing it."

"Oh, so he's treating me royally because of my aunt." That made sense.

"You could say that." His smile returned, twice as bright but strangely unreal. "Now tell me, dear Nefertiti, why are you traveling with this little harp player?"

I sat down in one of the chairs while Henenu assumed a scribe's comfortable, cross-legged pose on the floor, and I told my old friend all about the high priest of Isis, the Festival of the Inundation, my nearly fatal accident, the bravery of the slave girl, Mahala, and how she'd paid for her courage. I spoke in a whisper, so that Berett wouldn't have to hear about her sister's cruel death again.

"How could he do such a thing?" I hissed, digging my fingernails into my palms in anger. "She wasn't just an ordinary slave; she was a skilled musician! How could he destroy someone so talented just—just out of *spite*?"

"*Expensive* spite." Henenu stroked his chin. "Strong, young, healthy, *and* a musician? She was worth a lot, that poor girl. He might as well have thrown a handful of jewels into the river."

To throw away riches . . . I thought. "Henenu, Father told me that the high priest's family was poor and that he's still afraid of falling back into poverty." The scribe confirmed Father's story with a nod. "Then something doesn't fit. He might not spare Mahala's life out of kindness, but to kill her . . . He'd see that as a waste of someone—some*thing*—valuable."

"If that's true, my dear, then she must still be alive. But if you're right, then . . . where is she?"

"I don't know," I said. "But when we return to Akhmin I'm going to find out." My heart beat faster at the thought that I might be right, that the high priest had let Mahala live for completely selfish reasons. And what did his reasons matter as long as she was still alive? I couldn't wait for our visit, so newly begun, to be over. I had a great thing to accomplish, and I prayed fervently that the gods would show me the right road as soon as we went home.

"You don't have to wait, Nefertiti," Henenu said. "I could have one of my brightest students travel to Akhmin and begin asking questions on our behalf. I have at least one whom I'd trust enough to handle such a mission well."

"I'd rather do it myself," I responded. "I made a promise. . . ."

"As long as you find out the truth, it doesn't matter who does the actual work of investigation. If you wait too long, the trail will get cold." He spoke quickly and urgently, as if he weren't making a friendly suggestion but instead were trying to convince me to do this his way.

"A few more days can't make that much difference."

"But—but you don't know how long you'll be staying here." His eyes looked away from me. "The queen has waited a long time to reestablish good relations with your father. She'll want to keep you—all of you—with her long enough to entertain you well. She might even want you to accompany the royal court back to Thebes, so that you can enjoy the luxuries of the palace. Abydos is famous for its temples, not its lodgings. It can't compare to Thebes."

"I don't think Father will want to do that," I said, privately adding: *Neither do I. I need to go home.* "He's got work to do. He can't serve Pharaoh's interests in Akhmin if he's in Thebes. Even if the queen insists, Pharaoh's word overrules her."

Henenu sighed. "So young, and so sure that you know the way the world works." He reached up and patted my hand. "You're a strong-willed young woman, Nefertiti. I think that someday you might even be able to give our Great Royal Wife lessons in determination."

With the ability that came from years of practice, he got to his feet in one elegant movement and walked over to where Berett was just beginning to pluck a fragile thread of melody from the strings of her harp. She startled when she realized he was watching her, but then he soothed her by humming the same tune she'd been playing. Her fingers rose to the harp again, faltered, then resumed their dance over the strings. The dwarf lifted his voice in song, setting words to the music, a fanciful story about a shepherd who fell in love with a star. He had a remarkably high, honeyed singing voice, very different from the deep notes that rumbled from his broad chest when he talked. I couldn't sit still when so much beautiful music filled the air. I sprang from my chair and one after the other danced as the shepherd, the star he loved, and the goddess Hathor who lifted the faithful shepherd into the sky so that he and his beloved would be together forever.

When we all finished, Henenu smiled at Berett and

said, "I am a good friend of your mistress, Nefertiti. May I be your friend, too?" He cupped his hand as if he were offering her a drink of water. To my happy surprise, Berett didn't hesitate: She nodded readily and touched Henenu's hand lightly as a butterfly. For the first time, I saw the hint of a smile lift the corners of her mouth. Then the tall servant came barging back into my room, making his wooden staff thunder. Berett jumped straight up and dived under one of the chairs, letting her harp clatter and jangle to the floor.

"Greetings, my lady Nefertiti, may the gods favor you forever," the man's nasal voice pierced the air, as intrusive as he was. "It is the request of Queen Tiye, Great Royal Wife of the king, God's Wife of Amun, mother of princes, radiant lady, most gracious in all things, infinitely lovely . . ." He went on like that for so long that I was beginning to wonder if there was a message from my aunt buried somewhere under all those grandiose titles. I looked at Henenu, expecting the scribe to share a secret grin and a wink with me, but my friend's expression was dead serious. ". . . that you join your family and attend her at once."

"I haven't even had the chance to wash after my journey," I said.

"Indeed?" Once again the servant's brows rose to hide under his wig. "How unfortunate. There is no time for that now, my lady Nefertiti. Your parents and sister have already been conducted into the queen's splendid and revered presence. If you will consent to come with me, it shall be my extraordinary honor to bring you to them."

"Just a moment." I squatted beside the chair where Berett cowered. "Come along, dear one. We have to go."

"Oh no!" The tall servant reacted as though I'd announced my intention of finding a nice, fat cobra to drop in my aunt's lap. "That is not acceptable. Your slave must remain here."

"She's not my—" I stopped. By law, Berett *was* still my slave. "She's only a child, and she's frightened," I said instead. "I won't leave her alone like this, in a strange place."

The servant placed one hand over his heart and bowed, but it was only an automatic gesture, not a sign of surrender. "May you spare me your wrath and forgive me, my lady Nefertiti, but it is in the young slave's best interests to remain in your rooms. The Great Royal Wife was quite specific when she issued the command—the request—that you come to her. No one shall be there except those people to whom she is related by blood or the kinship of marriage. She will be displeased if you come with your slave in tow."

"Then she'll be displeased," I shot back.

Henenu's hand closed on my wrist. "Nefertiti, if you don't do as the queen wishes, her displeasure will fall on the child."

I met his eyes and saw that he was speaking the harsh truth. Still, I had to object: "I can't leave her here. She'll be terrified!"

"I can stay with her. It will be all right. Go." Henenu gave my wrist a brief powerful squeeze. "Don't keep the queen waiting."

I didn't leave immediately. I wasn't going to leave Berett without a word of farewell. I knelt swiftly beside her hiding place and said, "I'll be back as soon as I can. Henenu will look out for you. You're safe here, Berett. *Safe.*" I stood up and turned to the servant. "Take me to my family."

I followed him across the garden, past the open door-ways to my family's rooms. I couldn't help peeking inside as we walked by. Was it a trick of the light or were my parents and sister lodged in much smaller, simpler quarters than me? *There must be some mistake,* I thought. My aunt must have wanted Father and Mery to have my room. I'm supposed to sleep in the chamber next to Bit-Bit's. I'll tell her.

We passed rows of pillars whose tops were made to look like blooming lotus flowers and walls inscribed with the story of Isis's journey to return her dead husband to life. Osiris was murdered by his own brother, the evil god Set, ruler of the deserts of the Red Land, lord of destructive storms. He cut his brother into pieces and scattered them throughout the land, but Isis found them all. I paused before an especially beautiful image where the jackal-headed god Anubis, who taught us how to prepare the dead for their voyage to the Afterlife, bent over the reassembled body of Osiris, binding him back together with bandages.

"My lady Nefertiti, there will be plenty of time for you to see such things later," the tall servant said. He sounded edgy. "Please, we are expected."

I don't know exactly where he took me. The building where we were lodged was a maze. Hall after hall and great room after great room seemed to open up before us until without warning, we crossed the final threshold and were in a chamber twice the size of my room. There were many narrow windows high on the walls, letting in stripes of light but keeping out the worst of the day's heat and the night's cold. I saw my sister standing in one of the bars of sunshine and heard her call out, "Look, here she is! Nefertiti!" just as my guide bowed so low I thought his nose would brush his knees.

"O Majesty, lady of the north and the south, mother and wife of greatness," he told the ground. "As you have commanded, so it is done. She is here."

"So I see," said a voice from the far end of the room. There was the dry rustling of fine linen, the flash of gold, and Queen Tiye rose into the light to greet me.

8

GREAT ROYAL WIFE

I stared at the small woman who stood before me. She was very beautiful, with a softly rounded face and the sweet expression of a happy child. Her graceful body was dressed in a sheath of delicately pleated linen with a short cape floating around her shoulders. Over this she wore a necklace of so many strands that it covered most of her chest with gold, carnelian, turquoise, and crystal beads. Its centerpiece was a gigantic blue scarab with outstretched multicolored wings. And a gold crown shaped like a vulture framed her face with its jeweled feathers.

Even if she'd been dressed as simply as a farmer's wife, it was impossible *not* to stare at her. There was something about the way my aunt carried herself that demanded attention. I got the feeling that she had been exactly like this long before she married Pharaoh Amenhotep. *Born to be a queen,* I thought. I recalled all that Father had said about his sister— her ambition, her scheming, her way of using people—and couldn't make his words fit the pretty, soft-spoken little woman before me. Was this the same person he blamed for my mother's death?

Then I remembered my manners and bowed.

"Stand up, my dear child." Queen Tiye's voice was warm and caressing. "We are all family here. Or *will* be." She looked meaningly at the tall servant, who promptly scurried from the room. Satisfied, Queen Tiye smiled and motioned for me to approach her. Her large brown eyes shone with affection as she embraced me. Her skin was soft and luminous, scented with a haunting, spicy perfume that also clung to the tightly curled short wig under her crown.

"So you are Nefertiti," she said. Her eyes never left mine, yet I still felt as though she was looking me over from top to toe and evaluating everything about me. "What a foolish woman I've been, to have delayed this meeting for so many years. Your mother was one of my dearest friends; did you know that?"

I nodded, unsure of how else to respond. She was my aunt but also my queen. Was I supposed to call her Aunt Tiye or Queen Tiye or try to come up with a string of praise-names like the tall servant had used? Indecision left me silent.

She laughed and lifted my chin a little with the fingertips of her right hand. "Oh, such a joy! The resemblance is incredible. It's as if she were still alive. You don't look like your father at all, praise the gods." Her tone made it clear that she was teasing her brother.

"That seems to be the way it works in our family," Father answered genially. "Mutnodjmet doesn't resemble me, either, and you never looked anything like our father, Tiye. What about your own children? Do the girls favor you or their father?"

"You'll have to judge that for yourself when you meet them, Ay, though most people claim that all four of them look like me." A skeptical smile touched her lips. "More beautiful than Hathor, as charming as Isis, and so on and so forth. The magnificence of our beauty is determined by the size of the favors our flatterers come seeking." She cradled my face with both hands this time and added: "At least when people tell you that you are lovely, dear Nefertiti, you'll know they mean it."

Father laughed. "You've made her blush, Tiye! Nefertiti, your aunt's just paid you a compliment. Say something."

I lowered my eyes. "Thank you, Aunt—I mean, Queen Tiye."

She kissed my cheek and said, "You were right the first time. I have enough royal geese waddling after me, honking out empty titles. *You* will call me Aunt."

I was thankful to have that question settled. "Oh *yes,* Aunt Tiye!" I exclaimed happily.

She waved me to sit in a small chair close to her own. A table holding an alabaster fruit bowl and a pitcher of wine was between us. She served me with her own hands before telling Mery, "Don't stand on ceremony. Your husband and daughter must be thirsty. Take care of them."

I saw a hard look come into Father's eye. He had reason to be angry: My aunt had spoken to Mery as if she were another servant to be ordered around. She was also making no secret that she favored me above the rest of my family, even her own brother. *Why?* I wondered. *Is it for my mother's sake? She said they'd been friends, but Father told me she treated my mother like a tool to be used whenever it suited her.* Once again, my aunt's actions were nothing like her history and I was even more confused.

While we ate and drank, Aunt Tiye kept a close eye on all of us, but mostly on me. "Such a healthy appetite! And yet she doesn't gobble down everything in sight, like a hippo."

"Am *I* doing that, Aunt Tiye?" Bit-Bit asked plaintively.

"Certainly not. I would have told you. Really, child, can't anyone make one remark about your sister without your trying to grab their attention for yourself?"

Bit-Bit looked stricken at our aunt's casually harsh words, and Father's face hardened even more, but he said nothing. Mery was the one to speak up: "Mutnodjmet knows better than to do that, Great Queen. She's not one of those young women who have to have everyone's eyes on them all the time."

"Indeed? I'm comforted to hear it," Aunt Tiye replied blandly. "And how nice to hear *your* voice at last my dear. I owe you a very great debt for how well you raised Nefertiti after Ay lost his first wife. I know he's grateful to you as well. You must also be commended for how well you've steered clear of the stepmother's greatest snare: treating your true-born daughter better than your foster child."

"Nefertiti is a daughter to me as much as Mutnodjmet," Mery said. "What sort of mother would ever treat one of her children better than the other?"

"And yet it happens," Father said. "Once Tiye was chosen to marry Pharaoh Amenhotep, my parents had trouble remembering they'd ever had a son."

"You're exaggerating, Ay," Tiye said.

"I wasn't the one who could give them a tomb worthy of the richest noblemen in the Black Land. I couldn't send them all those luxuries, big and small, that let them live lives of royal splendor until the day they died. And when you became Great Royal Wife, I vanished like a shadow at noon, as far as they were concerned."

My aunt snorted. "Oh, rubbish! Our family members have always been faithful to one another. There are no exceptions. That loyalty is the source of all the power we have ever earned and the only thing that lets us hold on to that power. Don't try telling me that you have no enemies, my brother."

Father raised his wine cup to his lips, frowning. "I do."

"You'll tell me about them later," Tiye said, with a casual wave of her hand. "I'll see that they're made harmless."

"I can fight my own battles, Sister."

"If you could do that, you wouldn't have any enemies," Tiye replied with a wide smile.

"And what about you?" Father asked, flinging the challenge back in her face. "Are you saying *you* have no foes? If so, things have changed very much since the days before Nefertiti was born and you used her mother to—"

"I have *rivals*," the queen snapped, cutting him off. Her smile was gone. "There is a difference. My royal husband has many junior wives and concubines. I'm sorry to say that he is no longer here at Abydos to receive you, Brother. He's already returned to Thebes, supposedly because of pressing business. *I* know the truth: It's to be with his newest bride. That is his right as Pharaoh, the living god. I wouldn't dream of telling a god what he can and can't do. A pity that some of those foolish women see things otherwise and try to rob me of his devotion. They believe that just because they are royal by birth, they are better than I am."

"But, Aunt Tiye, you're the Great Royal Wife!" I protested. "How could anyone be better than you?"

My aunt's angry expression vanished as quickly as her smile had disappeared before. Her expressions and feelings changed so swiftly that watching her was like trying to keep your eye fixed on a single leaping flame in the heart of a blazing fire. She rose from her chair and seized both my hands, then stripped a silver bracelet from her arm and jammed it onto mine. I couldn't believe the richness of her gift—silver was much rarer than gold. I couldn't accept something so precious.

"Aunt Tiye, I don't deserve this. Please, take it back." I tried to remove the bracelet and return it, but she clutched my hands so tightly that I couldn't move.

"*I* decide what you deserve, my dear," she said. "Don't argue with me. I say that your beauty deserves this, and your wisdom seals the bargain. You're right, you know: I am Amenhotep's Great Royal Wife. It is the supreme honor for any woman, but even more so for me. Our family isn't of royal blood, Nefertiti. My father wasn't even born in this land. He came from the north, from the kingdom of the Mitanni."

"Like my mother," I said too softly for her to notice.

"There is no bloodline in all of the Black Land that is more royal than Pharaoh's," my aunt went on as she returned to her seat. "It's more than royal; it's divine, the blood of the gods. A Pharaoh can have as many women as he likes, but only one can be his Great Royal Wife, and that woman must come from the same family as Pharaoh. That way, the heritage of their child, the next Pharaoh, will stay pure, undiluted by the blood of ordinary mortals."

Father clicked his tongue. "She *knows* all that, Tiye. I didn't raise my daughters under a rock. You're wasting time, teaching a lesson she's already learned."

"Why, Ay, I'm surprised at you," Aunt Tiye said a bit too sweetly. "You should know that I never waste anything. I'm reminding her, not teaching her, because I want her to understand my position. It wouldn't hurt if you paid attention as well. My status as Great Royal Wife has been *your* good fortune. There are plenty of men who'd love to have your job as Pharaoh's overseer and investigator in Akhmin."

"Pharaoh gave me that job because I served him well, and I keep it by my own efforts."

My aunt's laughter filled the room. "You've been away from court too long, my brother. You've forgotten the way things work. Pharaoh's heart is big and generous, but it's also changeable and easily distracted. His eyes are drawn to whatever is freshest and most dazzling. Old achievements are covered in the dust of memory, and why should he bother making the attempt to brush them off when he has so many shiny *new* things to see? If some ruthless young nobleman decides he'd like to manage things in Akhmin, he's here to give Pharaoh gifts, entertain him with lavish banquets, fill his ears with flattery; flattery and poisonous whispers against *you*. Luckily, no man's ambitions can touch you as long as I am here. You don't know how many times I've protected and defended you already."

"And I doubt I ever will know the *true* number," Father replied.

Aunt Tiye ignored the barb. "You're my closest living relative, Ay. If we don't look out for one another, the world will devour us. Your happiness is all I care about. The gods have blessed you with two lovely daughters. I swear by Ma'at, I want both of them to have every opportunity to live rich, perfect lives. As Great Royal Wife of Amenhotep, it will be my joy to give your girls *everything*."

"Everything . . ." Father chewed over the word like a delicate quail bone. "And what will you want me to give you in exchange?"

Tiye didn't answer him right away. Instead she turned to me. "Nefertiti, will you please fill my wine cup?" As I rose to serve her, she said, "Look at you, so lovely, so poised. I've spoken to the scribe Henenu about you. He tells me you sing prettily, but that your most impressive talent is your superb ability as a dancer. Is that so?"

"I sing and dance," I replied. "I enjoy it very much, but I don't think I'm specially talented."

"None of *that*, young lady." The queen laughed again as she took her refilled wine cup from my hands. "No misplaced modesty. If you're good at something, you can admit it without being vain. So, here you stand, blessed by the gods with so many gifts. I had less than you do when I married, and I was younger than you are now, but I made the most of what I did have. Henenu also tells me that you're intelligent. That might be useful, too. Yes."

I began to feel an uneasy, prickling sensation running up my back. My aunt was looking me over closely again and talking about me as if I were a cow she was thinking about buying. But why?

Who cares *why?* I thought, suddenly furious at this treatment. *She doesn't have the right to do this to me.*

I pulled the costly silver bracelet from my wrist and dropped it onto the little table between us. "Aunt Tiye, this isn't for me. I'm not worth so much silver. Father and Mother can tell you all about what nearly happened to me at the Festival of the Inundation. Keep this and use it to buy yourself a more sure-footed dancer."

"What nonsense is this?" My aunt's soft, round face became a mask of indignation. She surged out of her chair, fists balled at her sides. "Was that miserable dwarf wrong or did he think he could lie to me about you and get away with it? This is *not* how an intelligent girl acts!"

"I don't know how smart you think I am," I replied. "But I do know I'm smart enough to tell when someone's trying to strike a marketplace bargain. Swear by Ma'at's sacred Feather of Truth that you *don't* want something in exchange for that bracelet and I'll apologize to you on my knees! But I don't think you can."

"Nefertiti! Don't you dare speak to Queen Tiye that

way!" Mery's voice shook. She wasn't just concerned about my rude outburst; she was afraid.

My aunt glared at me for what felt like an eternity. I held my ground, looking her steadily in the eyes. In the end, she was the one to pull back. Her expression went from blazing rage to mocking amusement.

"Oh dear, Nefertiti, I think we have a problem, you and I. I do swear by Ma'at's Feather that I gave you that bracelet freely, as a true gift, and yet"—she half-closed her eyes—"and yet, you are also right. I do want something from you, though not in exchange for the bracelet. You see, child, I don't have to make . . . 'marketplace bargains,' as you call them. I am still Pharaoh's Great Royal Wife. My word reaches to every corner of the Black Land and beyond. The kings of faraway countries call me sister when they send letters to my royal husband. They know I have great influence over him and that sometimes his treaties, trade agreements, and policies with them are really mine."

A shadow formed around my heart while I listened to her speak. It grew thicker and darker with every word. I wanted to run into Father's arms and cower there, but I forced myself to hold my ground. *You frighten me, Aunt Tiye,* I thought. *But I've stood up to worse terrors. You are just another dream-lion. You may have plenty of real power, but you have only as much power to scare me as I allow you to have.*

I got down on one knee. "So I owe you *half* of an apology," I said. "I'm sorry I misjudged your gift. I was wrong." I stood up again. "Now tell me, please, how I was *right.*"

The queen's elaborately painted eyes crinkled at the corners. "My poor, poor son," she said. "He'll have his work cut out for him with a wife like you." My jaw dropped and she drank in my shock greedily. "You might as well take back my gift, sweet girl. It's only part of the riches I intend to lavish on you when you become my new daughter."

"Have you been out in the sun too long, Tiye?" Father was on his feet and across the room in a heartbeat, placing himself like a shield between his sister and me. "Is this why you ordered us here? To marry Nefertiti to your son Thutmose?"

"You make it sound like a death sentence," Tiye replied dryly. "Thutmose is the crown prince, and I will see to it that he *stays* that way. My husband's junior wives who boast royal blood and younger faces are always scheming against us. They'd like nothing better than to have one of their nasty brats steal my boy's future."

"Are you sure of that?" Father asked sarcastically. "For as long as you've been Pharaoh Amenhotep's Great Royal Wife, you've seen sinister plots around every corner. It wouldn't be the first time that a ghost snake made you jump."

"I'd rather jump away from a thousand snakes that aren't there if it means I escape one real cobra. You have no idea what my life here at court is like, Ay. I've won many battles, but I've had to keep on fighting to hold on to my victories."

"And you want to drag my daughter onto your battlefield?" Father shook his head. "I want Nefertiti and Mutnodjmet to marry men they love. I want them to live peaceful lives, free from trouble and envy. What you're offering is nothing like that."

A sly look touched my aunt's eyes. "What about your girls, Ay? What do *they* want? To sink into the mud of Akhmin like turtles, watching the days dawdle by, as bland and boring and identical as grains of boiled barley dripping from a spoon? I may have to fight to hold on to my position, but at least I feel alive!" She looked at Bit-Bit and me. "Well, my dears? Do you share your father's vision for what you'll become? Do you want to live lives so ordinary that when you die, you'll hardly notice the difference? Do you want to marry dull men and fill the world with more dull children? The gods have given us only one life. Is that all you want it to be?"

Bit-Bit shrank back, nibbling on her knuckles, too overwhelmed by our aunt's forceful personality to answer. I stepped forward, out of Father's sheltering shadow. "Why should I have only two paths?" I said. "I don't need to choose between marrying your son and being the wife of some other man in Akhmin. What if I don't want to marry at all? There are other roads. Maybe even one I can make for myself."

Aunt Tiye put on a dramatically pathetic face and shook her head sadly. "Just when I think you're wise, you play the fool again, Nefertiti. You speak boldly, but you don't know anything about the world or how things are for women. Fortunately, you'll have a good teacher to correct that fault. When you marry Thutmose, I will look after your education personally."

"I'm not going to marry—"

"I'm not asking for your consent, girl!" the queen barked at me. "I don't need it."

"No, but you need mine," Father said. "If you try to force this marriage, I'll go to Pharaoh. I'm more than just Tiye's brother to him. He'll remember how well I served him in the past and how closely I'm looking out for his interests in Akhmin now. He'll stop you."

"And then he'll forget all about it the moment you're out of his sight," Tiye shot back. "If my son loses his claim to the throne because of your stubbornness, I'll make it my business to ruin your life, brother or not. Do you think I can't do it?"

Father breathed deeply. "On the contrary, Tiye," he said. "I've known you since birth. You're never more dangerous than when someone is standing between you and what you want. What I don't understand is why you're so insistent on turning my Nefertiti into your gaming piece. If your chief worry is the royal-born women in your husband's harem, why aren't you trying to marry Thutmose to a princess? Fight a sword with a sword."

"Princesses can be made," Tiye replied. "Beauty can only be discovered. Have you *looked* at your daughter, Ay? There isn't a more enchanting face in all of the Black Land. My husband is very fond of beautiful things. If Thutmose has such a lovely wife, Pharaoh will favor him for her sake."

"I'm not beautiful and I'm not a *thing*," I said hotly. "And I don't want to be a princess, or to marry Thutmose, or—"

"Nefertiti." Father's hand closed on my wrist. "Nefertiti, take Bit-Bit outside. I need to speak with my sister alone. We're going to settle this once and for all." He sounded confident. My spirits rose and I couldn't help giving Aunt Tiye a triumphant look as I clasped Bit-Bit's hand and left the room.

The tall servant saw us come out. He was waiting in company with five others, all of whom were holding trays piled high with succulent meats, fruits, and fresh, hot bread. He bowed low when he saw us and said, "Most noble young ladies, beloved of our revered Great Royal Wife, Queen Tiye, may she live eternally, is it time to bring in the banquet to celebrate the royal betrothal?"

"Not yet," I said. *Not ever,* I thought, exulting, though it was a pity to see the longing in Bit-Bit's eyes as she gazed at the delectable array of food.

"Nefertiti?" The bread and the roast meats were still hot enough to send trails of fragrant steam wafting through the air when Father stepped out to join us. An awful change had come over him. He looked haggard. He hugged us both so tightly it felt as if he never wanted to let us go. Then he noticed the waiting parade of servants. "The queen commands you to enter," he said. All the life had gone out of his voice. "Bit-Bit, go to your mother. Nefertiti and I will be just a little while longer out here." When Bit-Bit stayed put, he shouted *"Go!"* so loudly in her face that she yelped and fled.

"Father?" This was worse than the time he'd tried to force us away from his confrontation with Henenu. Then his anger sprang from grief, but now—now he looked crushed, broken. My father, the strongest, bravest man I'd ever known, was like a small slave boy who'd been punished harshly for some small misdeed. I tried to hug him again, but he held me at arms' length and shook his head.

"My little kitten, do you know how much I love you?" I nodded, my mouth dry. He sounded on the brink of tears. "I'd do anything I could to protect you, but sometimes— sometimes . . ."

I understood. "Sometimes you can't."

"She threatened us, Nefertiti." Now his face was streaked with tears. "I didn't know she had so much command. She's not just Pharaoh's Great Royal Wife; she's also the God's Wife of Amun, high priestess of the supreme god. The domination of the Amun priests is greater than anything you can imagine. Pharaoh Amenhotep is doing what he can to weaken it by declaring himself to be a god while he lives, instead of after death, but what strengthened him also strengthened her."

"What did she say she'd do?" I asked. I didn't want to hear, but I had to know.

"My sister is wise." Father uttered a hollow chuckle. "She didn't bother menacing me with poverty or exile. She simply reminded me that there was a high priest of Isis who'd be more than happy to add his testimony to hers that I'd blasphemed against the gods. I would die for that, my possessions would be confiscated, and my family— enslaved. I had no choice, little kitten." His laugh became a sob. "I had no choice."

This time when I tried to put my arms around him, he let me. "It's all right, Father," I said. "Maybe it will work out well. I might like Thutmose."

"May the gods grant it." He wiped the tears from his cheeks with the back of his hand. "To hear Tiye talk, it's impossible *not* to like Thutmose." He laughed again, and now it sounded a bit more natural. "Which is why I was able to gain you a *little* breathing space." He saw my questioning expression and went on: "My sister says she doesn't make 'marketplace bargains,' but the truth is that she's a born haggler at heart. As much as she likes winning, she likes a challenge even better, so I gave her one. When I saw that there was no hope of escaping this marriage, I began to plead that you were too young to marry just yet."

"But didn't she say she was even younger when she married Pharaoh?"

"Ah! But then *I* pointed out that she was an extraordinary woman. You can guess how much she liked that." His old smile was back. "I also said that it might be best if she used the time between now and your marriage to teach you all about the perils and practices of the royal court, making you into a worthy wife for her precious Thutmose."

"Time?" I echoed. "How much time?"

"Three years!" Father proclaimed his small victory over his sister as if he'd conquered an entire kingdom for Pharaoh. "With the condition that if you decide you want to marry Thutmose sooner, so be it."

"So it *won't* be," I said. "If I'm fated to marry him, I'll do it when I *must* and not a single day earlier."

"Don't close your heart or your mind, my sweet kitten," Father said, beginning to lead me back into the room where Aunt Tiye, Mery, and Bit-Bit waited. "You might like Thutmose. You said it yourself. Now come, let's enjoy your aunt's fine hospitality."

"I'm not hungry."

"Then come and stop your sister from stuffing herself with too much duck. You will stay here with the royal court, but your mother and I have to go back to Akhmin, and I don't look forward to sailing down the river with Bit-Bit being sick over the side of the boat all the way home."

Part III
Thebes

9

FAREWELLS AND GREETINGS

The next day, Father managed to persuade his sister to make a public oath before the temple of Amun, renewing her promise to delay my marriage to Thutmose by three years. The ceremony took place before many witnesses, not just the members of our family but also those nobles attending the queen, the priests of Amun, of Osiris, and of several other gods who were revered in Abydos.

I wore my best dress and sandals for the occasion and stood between Father and Aunt Tiye at the top of a wide flight of steps leading to Amun's sanctuary. Aunt Tiye tried to get me to agree to have my head shaved so that I could wear one of her finest wigs, with gold beads weighing down every one of the hundreds of tiny plaits, but I refused. As a compromise, I let her heap my body with the weight of enough bracelets, necklaces, earrings, and hair ornaments to bring a horse to its knees. One of those bracelets was the silver one I'd given back to her. She made it very clear to me that while she was only lending me the other ornaments, I had better not refuse the silver bracelet a second time. I was beginning to understand that with Aunt Tiye, you either gave her her own way, made a compromise that left things going *mostly* her own way, or fooled her into thinking she was getting her own way when she wasn't. The last option was very dangerous.

After she took that oath in Amun's sight, she dismissed Father and me. "We'll be leaving for Thebes tomorrow. I must make sure that everything awaiting you there will be perfect, my dear." She patted my cheek and swept away.

Father and I rejoined Mery and Bit-Bit in my parents' room. The queen's oath-taking had eaten up a lot of time, but I had no misgivings about leaving little Berett behind for so long. Once again, my good friend Henenu had volunteered to keep her with him while I was busy elsewhere. The child seemed happy in his company. Though Henenu was one of the most experienced and respected scribes of the royal court, he willingly tossed his dignity and importance aside in order to dance, sing, tell stories, recite poems, and even make fantastic faces—all to entertain one small slave girl.

I was glad. As much as I cared about Berett and as passionately as I wanted to help her out of the pit that had swallowed her voice, I knew that we two would have plenty of time together after we left Abydos. I couldn't say the same for my beloved family. Once the next day dawned, we would part ways, and the gods alone knew when we would see one another again. My heart ached, but I didn't cry during the short time we had left to spend together. I was afraid that if my tears started, they'd never stop.

We all sat together, Father and Mery on chairs, Bit-Bit and I on the bed facing them. Mery's smile wobbled whenever she looked at me.

"I'm such a silly woman, Nefertiti," she said, her eyes blinking rapidly. "Here you are, grown up enough to be getting married, and all I want to do is hold you in my lap the way I did when you were small."

"I don't think you're silly, Mother." I started toward her, but she held up her hands to stop me.

"Not yet. If I hold you again, I'll never let you go, and I know that's not possible." The room was not well lit, but I could still see the tears beginning to fall from her eyes.

I touched Bit-Bit's shoulder. "Sit with Mother." So my little sister took the place I longed to be and dried Mery's tears with her kisses.

Father looked at me intently. I think he couldn't bear the sight of Mery weeping. Perhaps he was afraid that if he looked at her too long, he'd cry too, and then we'd all be in tears. "My sweet Nefertiti, will you make me a promise?" he asked. "Be my voice when you next see Henenu. My poor friend! He sent me a message begging my forgiveness."

"Forgiveness? But he hasn't done anything," I protested.

"I know that, but he thinks he has. He blames himself for—for our parting." Father sighed. "He fears that by praising you to Tiye so much and so eloquently, he gave her the idea to make you Thutmose's bride. He's convinced I must hate him for it."

"But that's ridiculous!" I cried. "He was only telling her about her family. He's not at fault for what she did with that news."

"That's what I say, too." Father managed a weak smile. "You'd think Henenu would give me credit for having more sense than that, but the fellow's desolate. So promise me, dear one, that you'll let him know our friendship is secure."

"I promise," I said. "Gladly."

"Another thing," Father said. "When you reach Thebes, little kitten, be careful. You're a smart girl, but you're very young and you think that everyone can be trusted."

I laughed. "Not anymore. The high priest of Isis and Aunt Tiye already taught me that lesson."

"The high priest is a stupid bully and my sister is so powerful that she doesn't care if anyone trusts her as long as they do what she commands. I'm talking about the sort of people who'll *pretend* to befriend you. They'll seem exactly as faithful as your true friends, but they see you only as a step to help them rise high or a hoe to clear away the muck they don't want to touch with their own hands."

"If I don't trust anyone, I'll soon be like Aunt Tiye, seeing plots against me everywhere I look," I said. "Father, I can't live like that."

"I would never tell you to do that," he replied. "For now, rely on Henenu. Better to lean against a single wall made of stone than against a palace made of reeds. Not everyone in the royal court is a schemer, no matter what my sister thinks. If you go slowly, in time you'll find other trustworthy people, and you'll learn how to tell the difference between false friends and true. You'll be walking among lions. Promise me you'll always keep your eyes wide open."

"I will."

"And I will send you messages as often as I can, so you never forget how much we love you." He sighed. "I don't know if Tiye will let them reach you, but I *will* send them."

"Why would she keep your messages from me?" I asked.

"If I know her, she'll soon dismiss our bargain and want to push you into marrying her boy. The more you're reminded that you have a loving family in Akhmin, the less hope Tiye has that you'll embrace a new one in Thebes."

I hugged Father tight. "I have *one* family, and I don't need any message to help me remember that."

That night, I shared my sister's room. We lay in the same bed and spent the hours whispering memories, making promises, and wondering about what the future might hold. I'd brought Berett with me, and the little slave girl lay across the foot of our bed, the only one of us to sleep.

"Maybe you should marry Thutmose right away," Bit-Bit said. "Then you'll be a princess and you can order them to bring me to Thebes."

"And what would Mother and Father do without you? Besides, I haven't even set eyes on Thutmose. I might not want to rush into marrying him."

"Are you afraid he'll be that ugly?"

"I don't care about things like that," I said. "The high priest's son was very good-looking, but I couldn't talk to him. It was like talking to a child."

"I'm a child and you can talk to me," Bit-Bit pointed out.

"No one is asking me to marry you . . . *child,*" I teased.

Bit-Bit rolled over, turning her back to me. "You can't fool me, Nefertiti. You like pretty things. I'll bet that you'd choose a good-looking husband over an ugly one."

"I would not!" I protested. And I believed it.

The next morning, I took Aunt Tiye's silver bracelet off my wrist and slipped it over my sister's hand. Bit-Bit couldn't take her eyes off it. "Oh, Nefertiti, you can't give this to me! What if Aunt Tiye finds out?"

"Hide your hands behind your back when she comes to bid you farewell. Better yet, take it off and tuck it into your travel chest, but once you're away from here, put it on and never take it off until we're together again. I want you to have it, to look at it every day, and to remember me."

"I don't need a bracelet to help me do that!" Bit-Bit threw herself into my arms and clung to me until Father came to announce that it was time for my family to leave me.

Bit-Bit needn't have worried about Aunt Tiye spying her gift going to Akhmin instead of Thebes. The queen didn't bother to say goodbye to her brother. Instead she sent that tall, toadying servant of hers with a message saying that she was busy with preparations for her own departure from Abydos and wishing Father a safe voyage home.

I had to say my goodbyes at the gateway of the temple complex where we'd been staying. Henenu and Berett stood beside me as I watched the sedan chairs carry my parents and my little sister away. I didn't move from the spot until they were completely gone from sight, and even then I didn't cry. I didn't know if the gods would listen to a prayer that was half smothered by sobs, and I wanted to be sure that my words were heard.

"Blessed Isis, protect my father, my mother, my sister. Generous Hapy, give them a safe voyage home on your sacred river. Sweet Hathor, grant that we will meet again soon, in joy and peace. I don't care if I meet them as a princess or a beggar, only as myself. Great Sekhmet, give me your strength to stand firm against anyone—anyone!—who tries to change who I am into someone they think I ought to be." I stretched out my hands in the proper gesture for ending a prayer and wished I could still touch the loved ones who'd been taken from me.

A little later that morning, I found myself seated beside my aunt on the deck of her magnificent ship, watching the sailors unfurl a painted canopy to shield us from the sun. I'd given Berett into Henenu's care again and asked my friend the scribe to explain to her why she couldn't travel with me. I wanted to keep her out of my aunt's sight for as long as possible. Aunt Tiye knew I had a slave girl, but I didn't want her to know anything else about Berett. If she knew how deeply I cared about the child's welfare, she'd turn it into a tool or worse: a weapon.

My aunt is giving me my first lesson in court intrigue and she doesn't even know she's doing it. The thought pleased me. *Once we reach Thebes, I'll ask Henenu to help me give Berett her freedom. It has to be done the right way. I can't give her back her sister's life, but at least she'll have her own.*

I looked ahead to where Henenu and Berett were standing at the prow of the ship, mingling with the few servants important enough to sail in the royal vessel. The rest of Aunt Tiye's attendants were making the voyage to Thebes in smaller, much less luxurious boats. Thebes lay upriver from Abydos, so we had the advantage of the prevailing winds. Our sail bellied out, and though the current of the sacred river ran against us, the power of the wind was stronger. Aunt Tiye also insisted that the sailors man the oars. She was in a great rush to bring me to Thebes. She demanded that the men row day and night, though that meant they had to put a small boat made of bound papyrus reeds over the side at sundown, to light the water ahead with a lantern. When the sailors tired, she had her servants take their places. No one grumbled. No one dared.

I don't know how long it would have taken if we'd relied only on the wind, but by dawn of the third day, we'd reached our destination. I stood by the right-hand side of the ship and saw tawny cliffs and many buildings rising in the distance. I knew that rippling wall of stone was where the sun-god's Boat of Eternity sheltered the carefully concealed tombs of many kings. Their queens were also buried on that side of the river, as were all the nobles who could afford to build their tombs deep in the rock. The buildings I saw were temples, built to receive offerings for the royal spirits who thronged those eternal cities of the dead. I thrilled to imagine the astounding wealth that lay hidden in the depths of those cliffs, but my heart beat even faster at the thought of all the histories of life after life and age after age, preserved in words carved into the temple walls. Through them, the dead could live and speak again. They were the *true* treasures.

I turned my back on the western bank and crossed to the left-hand side of the boat. From there, the view was even more impressive. We sailed in the midst of many ships, large and small, glorious and humble, all gliding past the glorious temples, palaces, and gardens of Thebes. The shore teemed with life. All sorts of people were scampering back and forth on unknown errands, though some of the more richly dressed didn't seem to be in any hurry at all. Towering date palms cast their shadows onto the river. An old man poled a narrow papyrus raft through the shallows, singing lustily. Some women waded knee-deep in the water, filling pots. Others were hard at work, washing clothes and spreading them to dry on low-growing shrubs. Still others walked tall and straight, with baskets on their heads piled high with fruits, bread, and vegetables.

When our ship reached its berth at the dock, I was surprised to see that there were no sedan chairs waiting to carry us away. Instead, a troop of servants carrying sunshades and long-handled fans made from dyed ostrich plumes swarmed forward to greet the queen. Aunt Tiye beamed with satisfaction as they all raised their voices and welcomed her with every sign of delight. As soon as her foot touched the dock, her attendants surrounded her. "Well, my dear?" she called back to me. "What are you waiting for?"

I looked around for Berett and Henenu. There was no trace of them anywhere I could see on board our ship. Then I heard my friend's familiar voice hail me. He'd already disembarked and was waving to me from the shore. Berett stood as close to him as his shadow, her thin arms wrapped around her harp. Relieved, I left the royal ship and made my way to the queen's side.

"You look disappointed, Nefertiti," Aunt Tiye said. "Isn't Thebes grand enough for you?"

"I'm not disappointed, Aunt Tiye, it's just—"

"—you expected to be carried to the palace." She'd read my thoughts and relished my look of astonishment. "Don't worry. We'll arrive at the palace in much more magnificent style than any sedan chair. Such things are old-fashioned, after all, but Abydos nurtures the past. Here at Thebes, we turn to the rising sun. You'll see."

I fell into step behind her. With our escort before and behind us, we walked under our sunshades away from the dock and up a wide street where the people ran to clear out of our path but clung to the sides of the road to acclaim their queen. Their cheers worked a potent magic spell that made Aunt Tiye seem to grow taller with every step. I dropped back a little and made a subtle gesture for Henenu to catch up to me. The servants knew him well enough to recognize his status as one of the court's most respected scribes. Soon he and Berett were walking beside me under a sunshade of their own.

"I'm sorry I couldn't be with you on the ship," I whispered to the little girl. "I know you were in good hands with Henenu, but I missed you very much. We won't be parted again once we reach the palace. It will be a strange place at first. I don't know what to expect there, so I'm a little nervous, but I think your music will help me to be calm; maybe even to be brave." I smiled at her. "What do *you* think?" I didn't expect an answer.

Berett shifted the harp in her arms. One small hand clasped mine. A low, musical sound threaded its way shakily through the morning air. My heart leaped as I realized that my little Berett was humming a tune. It was the first sound I'd ever heard come from her lips. Those few fragile notes made me so happy that I wanted to stop in the middle of the street and sweep her up into my arms.

Instead, I was the one snatched off my feet and swung through the air. I screamed as a sharp-faced man lifted me in his arms and set me down again in the blue shell of a chariot drawn by a pair of brown horses. They whinnied and skittered in their harnesses, but the man leaped lightly up behind me, seized the reins, and brought them under control. My aunt's laughter sounded like a crow's rough cawing.

"By Amun, Nefertiti, haven't you ever mounted a chariot before?" she called out gleefully from her own place beside a white-kilted driver. The chariot she stood in was red and gold, the high wheels painted with multicolored bands and the two white horses in harnesses crowned with blue plumes. She pointed at the man behind me and added, "Go swiftly, but see to it that my niece reaches the palace in safety." She didn't threaten him with any dire consequence if I didn't survive my first chariot ride unharmed, but I saw him turn pale anyway.

"My lady, please hold on to the rail tightly," he whispered to me. "I'll hold you, if you'll allow it. It would be better if—"

"Wait," I said. I looked to the queen's chariot. Her driver slapped the reins on the horses' backs and they took flight like a pair of matched arrows, the light vehicle bouncing and swaying wildly as it skimmed the road. The instant it was out of sight, I jumped down from the chariot bed and ran back to Berett. The child crouched in the street, clinging to her harp as if it were the only thing holding her to the earth. Loyal Henenu stood by her, but every time he tried to coax her to look up at him, she shrank away. The sight of me being yanked away from her had renewed old terrors for the little one. If she curled up her body any tighter, she'd disappear.

I knelt in the dust beside her. "Little bird, look at me," I told her gently. "I'm here; I'm all right. Remember what I told you? We won't be parted once we reach the palace. I meant that. You must trust me, Berett. You aren't my slave or even my servant; you're my sister. I'd give my life to save you."

She lifted her head and looked deep into my eyes. Very slowly, very distinctly, she nodded, and then she put her fingertips to her lips, kissed them, and pressed them to my cheek.

Once I had her calm again, I let her know that I'd see her in the palace. I remounted the chariot without my driver's help and took a wide stance on the floorboards, my hands clutching the rail. A crack of the reins on the horses' rumps and we were off. The charioteer guided his team with one arm around me, which forced him to give up full control of the team. *This is stupid,* I thought as my teeth clacked together when he gave the reins yet another too-sharp jerk. *Riding this way isn't safer; it's only more awkward.* "I can hold on by myself," I spoke up. "Use both hands to steer. We'll travel faster."

"But, my lady—"

"*Faster,*" I repeated. "Or do you think the queen likes being kept waiting?" He did as I told him. I could hardly believe it!

When we reached the royal palace, Aunt Tiye was nowhere to be seen. The chariot that had carried her home stood empty, the driver stroking his horses' downy noses and lavishing them with praise. At first I thought that my driver had made a mistake and brought me to the wrong place. I'd expected Pharaoh's palace to be like the temples, made of monumental blocks of stone, a fitting home for the man who called himself a living god. Instead, the palace was built out of the same sun-dried mud bricks that were used to construct our home back in Akhmin and every other house I'd ever seen outside of a temple's precinct. The size of the building was much bigger and the decoration of the high facade was strikingly elaborate, but it was nowhere near as impressive as the houses of our other gods.

A group of three sturdy young women stood waiting in the gateway to the building. As soon as I set foot from the chariot, they approached me with words of welcome. "We are here to serve you, Lady Nefertiti," one of them said, her broad face friendly and serious at once. She looked about my own age, though she acted like a much older woman. "I am Kepi. Will you please follow us to your rooms?"

"Can we wait just a bit?" I asked. "There's a little girl traveling with me. She's coming here on foot with Henenu the scribe and I want her to see me before entering an unfamiliar place."

"A little girl?" Kepi repeated. "One of your relatives, my lady? The gracious Great Royal Wife didn't mention that. We'll have to prepare rooms for her as well." She turned to the other two girls and began giving quick, crisp commands.

"Please stop; that's not necessary," I said. The two girls, who'd started back into the palace in a panic-stricken rush, stopped in their tracks and looked relieved. "The child is my—my personal musician. She stays with me."

We lingered in the shadow of the gateway until Henenu and Berett arrived with the rest of the queen's entourage. The child's face broke into a smile when she saw me waiting for her. I embraced her joyfully. "See? What did I tell you?" I said. She nodded avidly, her tiny white teeth shining.

His purpose as Berett's guardian fulfilled, Henenu fell in with the rest of Aunt Tiye's servants as they entered the palace. "We'll see each other soon, Nefertiti," he called out to me as they left, then with a wink added: "My *lady* Nefertiti."

Now that I had Berett with me once more, I felt at ease following my new attendants deep into the royal house. I was quietly thankful for my journey to Abydos: The splendor of the temple-run lodgings there had prepared me for the sumptuous marvels of the palace. How odd to realize that my eyes were growing accustomed to seeing rare woods, brilliant wall paintings, and the gleam of gold everywhere I turned.

I was given a pair of rooms tucked away in a part of the palace where the air was sweet with perfume and bright with the sound of women's laughter. A slender pool like a captive portion of the sacred river filled the courtyard just outside my doorway. Green reeds and pink water lilies half-concealed the vivid flicker of a fish's scaly side. The rooms themselves were painted with riverside scenes of waterfowl—ducks, geese, herons, and cranes—and sometimes with the flight of a lone falcon above the water. The inner room, where my bed stood, showed a young woman on a raft, attended by two elegant cheetahs, watching while a royally dressed young man showed off his hunting skill in the thick of the marshes.

The chest of my belongings from Akhmin arrived soon after I took possession of my new place. It looked very small and shabby. Two of my attendants set about unpacking it for me, but soon enough they saw it was a job one girl could do in next to no time. As I watched them work, I wondered whether they were assigned to look after me from now on or if they were only supposed to get me settled.

What am I going to do with three servants? I thought. *All I need is one. I'm never going to be able to come up with enough things to have them do for me. Servants complain when they've got too much work, but they're bored and uncomfortable when they've got none, just like me.*

"My lady?" Kepi broke into my thoughts. "I'll have a sleeping mat brought for the child. Will that do?"

"I'd rather she had a bed," I said, glancing at Berett. She'd nestled herself into one corner of the room and was playing a lively tune on her harp. With her eyes shut, she wrapped the music around her like a comfortable cloak, content.

Kepi cocked her head. "If you wish, my lady. But I swear by the Eye of Horus that it's perfectly safe for her to sleep on the floor. For as long as I've worked here, and my mother before me, no one has ever seen a single serpent inside the palace walls."

"Nevertheless, please bring her a bed," I said. I wanted Berett to have every comfort now that we'd reached the place where I'd have to spend the next three years of my life.

Maybe more, I thought. *I suppose I* might *like Thutmose. If that happens, I'm here to stay, but at least I'll be happy. If it doesn't*—I tried to imagine myself three years in the future, telling Aunt Tiye that there was no way I could ever marry her son. How would she react? Would she let me go home with her blessing or would she force me into the marriage in spite of my refusal? *Three years is a long time. Maybe she'll find him a* real *princess by then and set me free. O Isis, let it be so, and soon!* I sighed. *I suppose there's always the chance that* he *won't want to marry* me. *That would solve everything. So much depends on Thutmose. I wonder when I'll meet him?*

I think that sometimes the gods hear our thoughts as well as our prayers. I was just about to ask Berett if she were hungry when an older woman came into the room and bowed to me. "Greetings, my lady Nefertiti," she said. "My honored mistress, the king's Great Royal Wife, requests your presence in the lesser hall of audience so that you may meet her son."

"Of course," I said, beckoning Berett to walk with me. I saw the woman frown and braced myself for an argument about why I couldn't bring the little girl with me. I was prepared to stand firm about that, no matter what. As things turned out, it was unnecessary. Berett looked at my hand, then pushed herself deeper into her corner, shaking her head forcefully.

"Sweet one, I have to go," I said. "Do you still want to stay behind?" This time she nodded, a stubborn look in her eyes. "Well, all right, if you're sure." I turned to Kepi. "Take care of her. She can't speak, but she can hear and understand. She might be hungry, so please see to it that she's fed." She bowed, but not before giving Berett a look that was pure kindness. I was able to obey Aunt Tiye's summons with no misgivings.

The older maidservant brought me out of the sweet-smelling part of the palace and into passageways where I smelled sweat, wood smoke, even animals. Then we made a sharp turn and the air was fragrant once more. She'd brought me to my aunt's royal apartments. We passed through room after room of furnishings and decorations so awesome that the sight stole my breath. Suddenly we left those treasure rooms behind and came out into the sunlight of a private garden filled with fruit trees and flowers.

In the middle of the garden, in the shade of a fig tree, Aunt Tiye shared a gilded bench with a dark-eyed young man and a slender woman who looked only a little younger than my beloved stepmother Mery. A speckled brown cat with a star-shaped patch of white fur on its forehead and tiny gold hoops dangling from its ears sat on the young man's lap and washed itself as if this were the most important occupation in the world. The woman was weaving a crown of sky blue flowers. They were two of the most beautiful people I'd ever seen.

She's probably one of Aunt Tiye's four daughters, I thought. *And he must be Thutmose. Oh! He's so handsome!* I told myself sternly that it was foolish to be so quickly snared by his looks, but he truly was stunning. I couldn't keep my heart from beating faster or my cheeks from coloring with embarrassment when I took in the sight of him. I came forward and bowed low to hide my face.

I was still bent at the waist when I heard Aunt Tiye's smug voice say, "Well, my darling, here she is. I doubt you've ever seen a more beautiful girl. Your mother will always see to it that you have nothing but the best. What do you think?"

"I didn't get a good look at her." The voice that answered Tiye's was deep, harmonious, and . . . bored. "If you say she's all right, I guess she must be."

"Now, Thutmose, don't be lazy," Aunt Tiye said. "I want you to see for yourself."

"Why? What will happen if I don't care for her?"

"Don't be a stupid boy! You *will* like her!" Just like that, Aunt Tiye's voice went from honey to flame. "Nefertiti, what are you doing, all bent over like that? You don't have to bow to us. Stand straight and come closer!"

I was way ahead of her. The blush in my cheeks was now an angry one. My heels thudded hard on the garden path that brought me right into the face of Pharaoh's queen. "Is *this* close enough?" I snapped. The young woman seated next to my aunt laughed.

"I don't know if *you* like her, Thutmose," she said. "But

I do!" She stood up and set the crown of flowers on my head. "I'm your cousin Sitamun, Nefertiti. Welcome."

Her sweetness stole the edge from my fury, but I was still mad. "Thank you, Sitamun," I said. "I hope that you and I will be friends."

"Never mind *her,*" Aunt Tiye demanded. "You'll have plenty of time for her and the others later. I want you and Thutmose to talk now. Sitamun, come!" She rose to her feet and for the first time I noticed how much tinier she was than her graceful daughter. It was hard not to laugh at the spectacle they made when Aunt Tiye grabbed Sitamun's wrist and dragged her out of the garden, like a flea trying to carry off a puppy.

I was left alone with Thutmose.

10

FAMILY SECRETS

"So you're Nefertiti," Thutmose said, not even bothering to look at me. The cat in his lap got all his attention as he scratched it between the ears and stroked it under the chin. "That scribe, what's his name, didn't lie. You *are* pretty."

"His name is Henenu and he's a friend of mine," I said. "I wish he'd told me about you."

That made Thutmose stop petting the cat and look up sharply. "Why? What would you need to know?"

I shrugged. "The things you like to do, how you pass your time, what amuses you, that you're fond of cats . . ." I gestured at the sleek, satisfied creature on the prince's knees. "If you ever smile."

He pursed his lips. "And of course you'd want to know what I look like, in case you feared Mother was bringing you here to marry a monster. She told me about that silly bargain she made with your family, putting off our marriage for three years. Now that you've seen me, perhaps we can forget about that and get it all settled sooner. Oh, not *too* soon—you're looking at me as if I'd said you'll have your head chopped off tomorrow—but sooner than three whole years in the future."

"Maybe . . ." My voice trailed off. "I think—I think that we should take a little time to get to know one another."

"Why?" His question was sincere. "My parents have had a satisfactory marriage for many years and the only thing Mother knew about my father before she wed him was that he was Pharaoh. That was good enough for her."

"I'm sure it was," I muttered. "Is that all you want? A 'satisfactory' marriage?"

He made a dismissive sound. "Do you always fasten on to one word and ignore the rest? My father is devoted to Mother. He made her his Great Royal Wife, he heaped her with riches, he permits her to give opinions when he deals with foreign princes, he had a whole *lake* built for her pleasure! If you don't like 'satisfactory,' call it something else, but know what you're talking about first."

How "satisfactory" is it if Aunt Tiye's so afraid of losing her power that she had to bring me *here to guarantee your future?* I thought. But because I still didn't have a secure footing in the royal court, I held my tongue. For all I knew at that point, one hard word said to the prince would rebound to harm those I loved. I remembered Father's counsel; he'd warned me to tread cautiously. So I guarded my thoughts, lowered my eyes, and said, "You're right. Please forgive me. I'm tired from my journey and it makes me speak without thinking."

"Fine." The cat leaped off Thutmose's knees and went

to investigate something at the roots of a nearby flowering shrub. "We'll have more than enough time to talk. Be welcome in this place." The stiff, formal words fell naturally from his lips, but there was no warmth in them at all. "You will be well served. Speak up when you want anything to eat."

"Won't we dine together?"

"Tonight, yes. You'll be presented to Pharaoh. After that, I doubt it, though if we must do so again, you'll be told." When he stood up, he looked exactly as handsome, strong, and imposing as a statue of Pharaoh striding forth to defeat his enemies: as handsome, as strong, as imposing, and as cold. "Where are you lodged? A servant should escort you back to your rooms."

"Don't bother," I said. "I know where to go."

"So quickly?" He looked interested but not for long. "As you like. Until tonight, then."

Well, that *wasn't pleasant,* I thought as I left him. *He didn't even try to know me. It's only our first meeting, but still—!* I turned down a corridor painted with scenes of Pharaoh hunting lions from his chariot. I thought it looked familiar. For a time I put away all thoughts of Thutmose as I tried to recall the route by which the older woman had brought me into the hidden garden. The more I walked, the more confused I became.

I'm lost, amn't I? I stopped in the middle of an empty room lined with storage chests and sighed. *I only told Thutmose that I knew my way back because he'd made me angry. I know he's the crown prince, I know he's more highborn than I am, even if we're kin. He doesn't need to remind me of it. So why did he act as if I was sunk in the mud and he was standing on a mountaintop?* I left the storage room behind and walked briskly on, cursing my hasty temper with every step.

My situation wouldn't have been so bad if I'd only been able to encounter another person, someone I could ask for directions. Alas, my luck led me to a part of the palace that was deserted, the gods alone know why. My steps echoed hollowly from the high ceilings. I sniffed the air, hoping to catch the scent of food or perfume or even dung—anything that might lead me to other living beings.

My efforts were rewarded: A wisp of flowers in bloom reached my nostrils through the dusty air of the vacant rooms. I followed the trail of scent eagerly, until I plunged through an archway crowned with an image of Ra's Boat of Eternity, bearing the blessed disk of the sun through the sky, and came out into a snug courtyard thick with small evergreens, nets of glossy-leaved ivy, henna shrubs, daisies, and other blossoms.

"Oh!"

I was so intent on my hunt that I didn't see the boy until I collided with him. Maybe it was the pattern of shadows in the garden, or how small a space it was to be holding so many plants, or the fact that his arms were filled with flowers that helped turn him invisible. Invisible but solid. The two of us tumbled to the ground. His flowers scattered.

I was the first back on my feet. "Oh, I'm so sorry," I exclaimed. "Are you all right?"

He clasped the hand I offered him and slowly clambered up. He was more than a head taller than me, and the most awkward collection of long bones and oversized hands and feet I'd ever seen. There wasn't one part of his body that was a match for the rest. Skinny as he was, he had a soft stomach that stuck out over the top of his linen kilt. His head was uncovered and so unnaturally long that it looked as if a pair of mischievous spirits had grabbed the top of his skull, the bottom of his chin, and pulled.

"I—I'm—yes," he said. It was hard to hear him. His voice was pleasant, but he scarcely raised it above a whisper. "And you?"

"No harm done." I smiled at him. "You'll have to teach me your magic."

"What—I—what magic?"

"How someone as tall as you can hide yourself in a place this small," I joked.

His laugh was startling. I never expected such a hearty sound to come from such a frail-looking body. "Hiding is— it's what I do best."

I'd been about to ask him who he was, but now I didn't have to bother: My ungainly flower gatherer was obviously one of the palace workers, and not a very good one. When Mery instructed Bit-Bit and me how to manage a household, she taught us: *Never keep a shirking servant. They're easy to spot. Many people try to disappear when there's work to be done, but lazy servants have a talent for it that's almost supernatural, and the laziest will even brag about it!*

"Hiding," I repeated. "I wouldn't overdo that, if I were you. It'll get you in trouble."

"No." He sounded wistful. "Sometimes it's—it's the only thing that keeps me out of trouble."

"I see." *Poor boy!* I thought. *Maybe he's not lazy after all. With those gawky arms and legs, maybe he's just not very good at—well, at* anything, *and he gets beaten for making a mess of his work.* My heart went out to him. I could just imagine how he'd fare if he displeased my aunt or my chilly cousin Thutmose! *I could do worse than making another friend here, especially one who knows his way around the palace, and I* would *like to hear him laugh again. Perhaps we can be good for one another.*

"My name is Nefertiti," I said. "If you don't mind coming out of hiding for just a little while, could you help me? I'm new here and I'm lost."

"I'd be happy to," he said, eager. "Where do you want to go?"

"Back to my rooms."

"Yes, but where are they?"

"If I knew that, I wouldn't be lost," I replied, but not angrily.

"Well, are they in the north wing, the south? Do you know where they lie in relation to Pharaoh's great hall of audience, the one where he receives foreign emissaries? Can you reach them from the river? I doubt they're near the kitchens or the stables. They'd never put someone as important as you there."

"How do you know if I'm important?" I asked.

"Oh, everyone knows about you." His thick lips turned up at one corner in a sad smile. "News travels very fast in this house. You've been brought here from Akhmin by way of Abydos and you're going to marry the crown prince."

"News may travel fast here, but it doesn't always arrive

in one piece," I said tartly. "Don't worry, you're not going to have to work on preparations for my wedding to Thutmose *too* soon."

"Really?" He sounded surprised, then grew thoughtful. "I'll bet you've been lodged in the women's quarters, then, with the junior wives and concubines. Otherwise you would have been put closer to the royal rooms."

I shrugged. "I smelled a lot of perfume and I heard a lot of giggling, but that's all I know about it. There's a garden with a long pool just outside my door, but this place seems to have a lot of gardens."

"It does. I think that's the only thing I like about living here. Well, that and the wall paintings. They're all beautiful, and all differ—By Amun, I *am* stupid! My lady Nefertiti. If you can remember how the walls of your rooms were decorated, I can help you find them easily!"

He listened intently while I described the painted marshes, the waterfowl, and the hunting scene, then smiled like the sun. "You *are* in the women's quarters! I haven't been there since I was a child. I can't take you all the way back—there are things I must do elsewhere before nightfall or I'll be neck-deep in muck—but I can set you on the right path."

"Wonderful!" I cried. "Let's go." I started back the way I'd come.

"Wait, please." He dropped to one knee and fumbled for something hidden in the greenery. "You lost this when you fell," he said, standing up and holding out Sitamun's crown of flowers. It was badly crushed, and it took him a moment before he realized he was offering me a handful of ruined blossoms. "Oh," he said apologetically. "I've done it again."

"You didn't do anything," I said. "I was the one who ran into you. Leave it."

As we walked out of the tiny garden, I looked up at my lanky escort and said, "You know who I am, but what's your name?"

"Amenophis." It was the last word I got out of him for a long time. It was as if once he'd solved the riddle of where to lead me, he'd taken fright and put up a wall between us. The farther we got from his cozy green refuge, the thicker and higher he built that wall.

Finally he stopped at a place where two palace halls crossed, and pointed. "The women's quarters are that way. Good-goodbye." He was gone before I could thank him. *So much for making a new friend,* I thought.

I had no difficulty making my way back to my rooms from that point. Once there, I found Berett merrily playing her harp in the corner of my bedroom while my three maidservants clapped their hands and danced. They stopped abruptly when they saw me, as if I'd caught them at some crime, and bowed deeply.

"Lady Nefertiti, pardon us," Kepi said. "We unpacked all of your things and we've laid out the dress you are to wear tonight. Since you hadn't come back to give us further orders and we had nothing else to do—"

"You knew *exactly* the right thing to do," I told her, smiling. "Berett, play some more for all of us. I haven't had the chance to dance for far too long." I didn't have to repeat my request. Berett's fingers skipped over the harp strings and one of the other girls raised her voice in a comical song about a baboon who kept stealing a farmer's grapes until the farmer tricked him into drinking wine. I did a clownish dance, pretending to be the baboon, Kepi played the farmer, and the others clapped in time to the music until we all fell down laughing.

There was more music and many more songs and dances before it was time for my maids to get me ready for the evening. I was bathed, rubbed with scented oils, and dressed in a flowing white gown that Aunt Tiye sent along with a cedarwood box holding a cascading necklace of gold and crystal beads. Last of all, Kepi painted my eyelids green and outlined my eyes heavily with black. She wanted to add a little red ocher mixed with oil to my lips, but I refused because I'd never used that before. I didn't want to spend the evening making faces if it tasted nasty.

I had a small pang of worry about leaving Berett behind in my rooms. The maids would look after her, but would she be afraid without me? It was one thing to leave her alone in the daytime, but at night, in a strange new place?

But Isis smiled on me: I was murmuring my concerns to Kepi when I felt a small hand pat my arm. Berett smiled at me, then slipped her fingers willingly into Kepi's palm. "Well, *good*," I said, pleased. I hugged the child and left, lighthearted.

The same older woman who'd brought me to meet Thutmose was waiting to lead me to dinner. My heart thudded louder at every step. This was not just a simple family meal: I was going to meet the lord of all the Black Land, the living god, Pharaoh Amenhotep.

What will I say? I wondered. *Should I say anything at all? How do I address him? What if I trip and fall when I approach him? What if I tear this dress? What if I lose my voice, or squawk, or get the hiccups? What if—? What if—? What if—?*

I was so absorbed in reviewing that unending series of humiliating possibilities that I barely noticed when the older woman stepped to one side at a lofty doorway and motioned for me to pass through. I obeyed her without thinking and found myself in a large room, bathed in the glow of dozens of lustrous alabaster oil lamps. A group of musicians sat in the corner to my left, playing sweetly on double flutes, harps, lutes, drums, and tambourines, while a choir of at least nine rich-voiced male singers sang to my right. As soon as they saw me, they stopped.

I almost didn't notice. My gaze was set on the group of seven people seated straight before me, behind a scattering of low tables covered with food, drink, and flowers. I recognized Aunt Tiye at once. She sat in the second-finest chair, her short wig crowned with a double ostrich plume and a gold disk and horns, so that she looked like the living image of the goddess Hathor. Anyone with eyes would have known her royal husband, whose seat was even grander than hers, although he was more simply dressed. He wore a striking gold pectoral, but no crown, only a wreath of blue flowers like the one Sitamun had given me and that had been destroyed.

Thutmose sat stiffly on a chair between his mother and father, his wig, clothing, and jewelry even more elaborate than Aunt Tiye's. *He's eating dinner with his family,* I mused. *Who does he need to impress?* Sitamun sat with her four sisters, on stools at Aunt Tiye's other side. The only other seat I could see in the twinkling light was an empty chair next to Pharaoh. My mouth went dry. I was nervous enough to be meeting the living god; I didn't know how I'd fare if I had to eat an entire meal with his eyes on me.

"My dear Nefertiti, come to us and be welcome!" Aunt Tiye stood up gracefully and swept her arms wide, as if they were divine wings. I bowed to Pharaoh, then crossed the floor until I stood with one of the short feasting tables between us and bowed again. All of the courage I'd learned from Mahala's brave and selfless act deserted me. I was a shy little girl again. I didn't know what to say, and my silence, like the sacred river at the Inundation, seemed to rise and flood the room, drowning me.

Running footsteps and jagged breath cut through the heavy hush. A wheezing voice cried, "I'm sorry! I'm—I'm sorry I'm late, but I had to make something for—Oh! You're here."

I raised my head and turned to face Amenophis, his hands quaking as he held out a wreath of flowers. "This is for you."

Gods, is he out of his mind? I stared at him in disbelief. *I thought he was a mouse, and yet here he comes, barging into Pharaoh's presence. And for* this? *Aunt Tiye's going to have him whipped, or worse!*

"Um . . . thank you," I said, and in a whisper added: "You should go now. Really." I took the wreath and tried to put it on my head, but I was so worried about the punishment in store for poor, frail, crazy Amenophis that I wound up with a loop of flowers tilted over one eye. Sitamun's sisters tittered and I heard Aunt Tiye muttering darkly.

But Pharaoh laughed. "Would you look at that? She's even beautiful when she doesn't look perfect! Ah, Tiye, what a treasure you've brought back to us. Amenophis, don't just stand there like a plucked goose; help your brother's bride!"

"Yes, Father." Amenophis carefully adjusted the wreath so that it sat properly on my hair. "Is that all right?" he asked me in quiet voice.

I couldn't say a word. My shock was so total that I couldn't even make a sound—no, not even if a jackal had been gnawing on my leg! The words *your brother's bride* and *yes, Father* resounded through my head like the throb of a giant drum. I was still speechless when Amenophis took me by the arm and led me to my place before taking the empty chair for himself. I was seated on a stool at Thutmose's feet. I hadn't noticed it at first because it was hidden by the feasting table.

Somehow I got through that dinner. The food was delicious, but I ate sparingly, still dealing with the revelation that my timid, awkward "servant" was actually the crown prince's younger brother. I kept darting incredulous glances at him throughout the meal. Pharaoh was tall and muscular, a good-looking man with a hearty voice who looked ready to take on the whole world just for the fun of it. My aunt was dainty and attractive. The gods had given

Thutmose and Sitamun the best parts of their parents' looks, and the other four princesses were pretty girls. Homely, rawboned Amenophis didn't fit in at all.

I was thankful when Pharaoh took one last mouthful of honey cake and stood up, the signal that the meal was over. "I hope you will be happy with us, Nefertiti," he said while the servants and slaves scurried to clear away the dishes and the tables and the entertainers bowed low and vanished from the hall. "We didn't speak much tonight, but you're tired from your journey here. You and I will have plenty of time to talk in the future. Would that please you?" All I could do was nod.

He strode out of the hall and his family fell into line behind him. It was all very formal: None of them looked at me, not even my aunt, though I thought I caught sight of Amenophis's head turning just a bit in my direction. Though the royal family left, I wasn't abandoned. As if by magic, two female servants appeared beside me the instant that the last princess crossed the threshold. They escorted me back to my rooms, where I found Berett comfortably asleep on the folding bed I'd requested for her. Kepi was waiting up for me and helped me undress. I fell into my bed exhausted and slept like a stone until late the next morning.

I woke up to the sound of women laughing and the smell of fresh, hot bread. For one brief moment I thought that I was home, hearing the voices of Mery and Bit-Bit, and that everything from our departure for Abydos through last night's feast was only a dream. My sweet illusion only lasted long enough for me to rub the sleep from my eyes and see sunlight streaming across the marsh scene on my bed-room wall.

So this is real, I thought, hugging myself. *It's real, and I'll have to get through it on my own. Three years . . .* It seemed like an eternity to be away from my beloved family, but also much too short a time standing between me and marriage to Thutmose. *O Isis, be with me. Show me the good path here and spread your sheltering wings over those I love in Akhmin.*

I got out of bed and looked around for Berett. Her bed was empty, though her harp was still there, leaning against one of the legs. *She's probably with Kepi and the girls,* I thought. I found that my servants had already brought me water for washing and a dress to wear. I was happy to discover that it was one that I'd brought from home. I'd had enough of Aunt Tiye's gifts. I couldn't shake the feeling that she was keeping count of everything she gave me, and that someday she'd demand repayment in ways I wasn't going to like.

When I stepped into the outer room of my lodgings, I saw that I'd been right: There was Berett, sitting on the floor with a basket of small, round rolls and a drinking bowl of milk. Her cheeks were stuffed and she was chewing happily while Kepi and the other maids stood around, encouraging her to eat even more.

"Do you like that, my duckie?" Kepi crooned, stroking Berett's hair. "Do you like bread? Say *bread* for me, won't you? Come on, I know you can do it. Say *bread.* Listen, if you'll just say *anything,* any kind of food that you can think of, I'll bring it for you, but you'll have to—Oh! Lady Nefer-titi! I didn't know you were awake. Good morning." She and the other two bowed, then began fluttering around me, fetching a chair, a table, and my breakfast.

After I'd eaten, I sat back and looked expectantly at my servants. "That was very good, thank you," I said. "Now tell me, what am I supposed to do today?"

The girls frowned, perplexed by my question. As usual, Kepi spoke for them all: "Why . . . whatever you like, my lady."

"Isn't there someplace I need to go? Something I ought to do?"

She shrugged and turned up her hands, empty of answers. "You have the freedom of the palace. You can go anywhere you like. If there are places where you're not permitted to be, you'll be told."

"Only the palace?" I asked. "What about the city? I'd like to see Thebes."

Kepi's face became troubled. "I—It's not for me to tell you that you can't leave the palace without an escort or—or permission."

"And yet you just did." I smiled to let her know I didn't blame her for being the messenger who brought me news I didn't like. "Never mind. I think it would be better for me to be able to find my own way around the palace before I start trying to make sense of the city."

"That's a *wonderful* thought, my lady!" Kepi exclaimed. "We will be honored to help you."

"Thank you, but Berett and I are going to explore on our own."

I hoped that my refusal hadn't hurt Kepi's feelings. She was such a friendly, capable girl that I caught myself forgetting that she was a servant. The other two did what little work there was in my rooms, but they never spoke much. Either they were too timid or they wanted to keep me at arm's length, except when they had to serve me. Kepi was different, and thinking about that gave me an idea for something I *could* accomplish that day.

With Berett holding my hand, I walked out into the sunlight. The halls of the women's quarters were bustling with activity. We saw faces whose complexions ranged over every color from deep ebony to dark brown, to the golden hue of well-baked bread, to the palest tan. Most of the women wore white dresses like mine, though some chose to go bare-breasted and some wore simple sheaths instead of intricately pleated gowns. There were also a few exotic clothes, brightly colored garments from distant kingdoms that were no more than names to me. The ceilings echoed with many different languages, chattering, whispering, arguing. Even though I only knew the tongue of the Black Land, it was easy to tell a curse from a blessing. Sometimes I heard the sharp report of a slap, a distant wail of pain or sorrow, and the ripple of muffled tears.

Then there were the children. Aside from the babies and the toddlers who were still in their nursemaid's arms, children ran wild everywhere. Their braided youth-locks swung and bounced as they skipped, scampered, and tumbled through the halls and gardens while gold earrings and necklaces with charms to repel demons and the Evil Eye twinkled against their naked bodies. Their laughter was sweeter than any music.

Every so often, one of them would rush up to Berett

and demand to know who she was and if she wanted to play. My poor little girl pressed herself against my side and buried her head in the folds of my dress until the other child gave up and ran off to find another playmate. *It's only her first full day here,* I thought. *Things will change.* But I wondered if they ever would.

"Why don't we go somewhere else?" I suggested gently to Berett after about the sixth such encounter. "Yesterday I discovered a lovely little spot, a garden that's so far from all this tumult that I only found it by accident, because I got lost. Would you like to see if we can find it again?" Berett nodded.

I concentrated on backtracking a path based on the different wall paintings Amenophis and I had passed the other day, but my memory failed when Berett and I reached a series of rooms where swarms of men, young and old, trotted by looking very serious and self-important or sat crosslegged, reading or copying heaps of papyrus scrolls.

"Scribes!" I cried in delight. "Maybe Henenu's nearby. I'm sorry I can't find that garden, Berett, but we ought to be able to find him." She didn't need to speak to let me know that she thought this was a brilliant idea.

It took me three tries before I could get one of the scribes to agree that I was important enough for him to stop his work and answer my question. "Ah yes, Henenu, I know him well. At this hour he'll be with his students. Follow me." He led us to a room where our old friend sat supervising rows of very young boys as they practiced writing, copying texts onto pieces of broken pottery. When Henenu saw us, he let out a shout of joy so loud that several of his pupils made a mess of their lessons.

"My dear friends, you've found me! This is a blessing. How did you sleep? Are your rooms comfortable? What did you think of—?" He bit off the end of his question and cast a wary eye over his students. "Perhaps we ought to go elsewhere to talk."

He told the boys that he'd be gone a short while, gave them orders to copy a page of tax records, and warned them against acting up until he came back. We hadn't taken five steps out of the classroom before we heard the sounds of laughter, crude noises, and scuffling.

Henenu sighed. "Boys. Sometimes I think the only difference between my pupils and donkeys is that if you beat a donkey for misbehaving, he won't do it again." Still complaining, he walked down the hall ahead of us, peering into every room we passed until he found one that was unoccupied. It was lined with many storage chests and baskets full of poetry fragments. Plopping down on the floor, he let out a deep breath and said, "*Now* I can speak freely. What did you think of the prince?"

"Which one?" I asked with a wry grin, and told him about my odd introduction to Thutmose's gangly younger brother. "The weirdest thing is, Aunt Tiye never mentioned him once," I finished. "If he hadn't been at dinner last night, I never would have known she's got two sons."

"The queen . . ." Henenu clasped his hands in his lap and didn't look at me directly. "The queen has put so much of herself into grooming Prince Thutmose to follow in his father's footsteps that she may—she must be forgiven for overlooking her second-born son." Lifting his plump chin, he added: "You haven't answered my question, Lady Nefertiti. What do you think of Prince Thutmose?"

"I think that it's too soon to judge him," I replied, keeping my tone as neutral as my words.

I would have done better to speak normally. By trying to say nothing, I'd said too much. Henenu was a smart man and a longtime resident of the royal palace, with ears attuned to what you *didn't* say as well as what you did. "You don't like him," he stated.

"Oh, Henenu, he's such a *cold* person," I cried.

"Hmm, yes, that's Prince Thutmose. I've known him since he was born. He was a merry child, but then the queen began teaching him that a future Pharaoh must always be dignified, as befits a god on earth. It didn't matter that his own father, as much of a god as our prince will ever be, is one of the best-humored men I've known; Queen Tiye insisted on training all the joy out of him. The only time we get a glimpse of the old Prince Thutmose is when he plays with his cat, Ta-Miu. She must be a sorceress in disguise; she owns the secret for making him happy."

"Is that so?" It was an empty question. Henenu wouldn't lie to me. I felt a deep pity for Thutmose, and sorry that I'd judged him so hastily, after only one conversation. "Well . . . he might be a warmer person once I get to know him. Perhaps I could talk to Ta-Miu and find out how she does it," I joked, wanting to lighten my mood.

"Ah, you know how to talk to cats?" Henenu teased back.

"Not yet, but I've got more than enough time to learn. Three years is a long time, and what else will I have to do?"

Henenu shrugged. "I know only what a scribe does all day, not a princess."

"Princess?" I repeated.

"You weren't told?" Henenu looked as surprised as I felt. "By the divine will of Pharaoh Amenhotep, you were named Lady Nefertiti, Royal Daughter, Excellent in Grace, Beloved of Hathor, and a string of other titles that all mean you are now as much a princess of the Black Land as Sitamun and the others. It was one of the first things the queen arranged when she came home yesterday. Prince Thutmose can't marry a commoner."

"His father did," I said. Meanwhile my thoughts swirled around my new status: *A princess! If Bit-Bit was here, she'd want to know why I'm not leaping for joy. A princess! That's my little sister's dream, not mine. It's supposed to be an honor, but it feels like a rope's been tied around my neck, dragging me down the one road Aunt Tiye wants me to walk. What can a princess do except marry a prince? No. I'm not a princess. Who cares what Aunt Tiye made Pharaoh decree? If he decreed that she was a hawk, would she jump off a roof and expect to fly? I say what I am, who I am, and I say that if she thinks plain Nefertiti of Akhmin isn't good enough for Thutmose, she should send me home tomorrow. Three more years and all the titles in the world won't change a thing.*

"Merciful Isis, what's the matter, Nefertiti?" Henenu asked. "What a face! I just told you that you've been made a princess, and you look ready to tear me to shreds with your bare hands."

"Is it that bad?" I asked lightly, forcing a smile. "I don't think it's right that I'm the last to know about being a princess, but was I *really* making such a monstrous face about it?" I struck the same dramatic pose I'd seen in paintings and carvings of past pharaohs triumphing over their enemies in war. "If only Aunt Tiye had made me a princess years ago, I could've used my *great* and *mighty* royal authority to *command* Father to let us continue our lessons!" I dropped the arm that was holding an invisible war club. "Then I *know* what I'd do all day."

Henenu tilted his large head and gave me a thoughtful look. "Why not?"

11

THE KNIFE AND THE REED

"Good morning, Nefertiti! Did you sleep well? No lions?" Sitamun called out to me gaily as I climbed the last of the steps leading up to one of the palace's flat roofs. It was the same greeting she gave me every morning since the day I'd confided in her about my childhood nightmares. I didn't mind: Her words were a never-failing reminder that I'd made at least one true friend since my arrival at Thebes nearly half a year ago. I only wished that Aunt Tiye's oldest daughter were someone closer to my own age. There were at least ten years between us.

The time of the Inundation had passed and we were well into the season of Emergence. From the rooftop I could see how far the sacred river's waters had receded from the fields. The freshly fertile soil was thickly planted with new crops, and the tender growth turned the Black Land green.

"No lions," I replied as I joined her under the vividly patterned cloth sunshade. Sitamun had already spread out her scribe's kit and was using the flat-edged burnisher to smooth the final rough spots from the blank piece of papyrus in front of her.

"Maybe no lions, but I'll bet you were followed by our favorite cub," she said.

At that very instant Berett's head popped into view at the top of the steps. My little musician climbed up the rest of the way, carrying her harp with her. The past months of good food and peace in the royal palace had been very good to her. She'd grown taller and stronger, though she still clung to silence. She crossed the rooftop to kneel in her favorite shady corner and began to play.

I laid out my own set of palette, brushes, and pens, taking water from Sitamun's small flask to make the red and black inks, then indicated the papyrus my friend was finishing. "Is that mine?"

"It is." She gave it one last scrape with the burnisher and slid it over to me. "Are you sure you're ready?"

"I've practiced enough," I said. "I'm as ready as I'll ever be." I stretched my hands out over the papyrus and my tools and prayed aloud for Thoth to bless my task. Then I picked up a brush and began to write.

Sitamun watched me intently. "Very nice, Nefertiti. You have an elegant style, but I still don't understand why you insisted on doing this yourself. Henenu could have done it for you, or any of the other scribes."

"These words have to come from my own hand," I replied. "It means a lot to me."

"You'd think you were writing a love poem!"

"I wouldn't know how."

"That's a shame. Thutmose should send you one."

I frowned. "That wouldn't be *dignified* enough for him."

Sitamun laughed. "He *is* a stick! But a stick can become a roaring fire if it meets the right spark." She turned to Berett. "Dear one, can you play us a love song? We need to put your mistress in the proper mood." Berett tilted her head and gave Sitamun a doubtful look but did as she was asked.

I snorted. "*Stop* that, Berett," I said. "Stop that and come here. I want you to see this. It's almost done, and it's very important for you."

The girl put her harp aside, drew near, and squatted next to me, questioning me with her eyes.

"This is your freedom, Berett," I said softly. "I'm sorry I couldn't give it to you sooner, but I had to find out the right words to use so that after today, no one will be able to call you a slave ever again. This document also gives you some of my jewelry, so if you ever want to leave Thebes, you can take it with you and nobody can accuse you of theft." My pen added a few more characters to the papyrus. "Once this is finished, carry it with you always and you can come and go as you like. No one will be able to hold you captive anymore."

Berett heard me out, then pointed decisively at one group of characters on the papyrus. I stared, taken by surprise. "Look at that, Sitamun! She recognized her name!"

"Pooh. It's a coincidence." Sitamun waved away anything marvelous about it. "She just *happened* to point at it. How would she know—?"

"Hasn't she been with me every time I come up here for

our lessons? Whether it's just the two of us or if Henenu's here as well to teach us some new characters or a better brush technique, month after month, she's always close by."

"It's not as if she's sharing our lessons," Sitamun argued. "She plays her harp the whole time, and she's usually over *there*." She indicated Berett's favorite spot.

"She starts out over there, but you know she always creeps closer and closer to us while we work. She's interested in what we're doing, Sitamun. She's been watching," I said. "*And* learning, I'll bet. In fact, I *will* bet you that she knows more than you think."

Sitamun's eyes glittered. She loved to gamble, and she'd been known to wager a fortune on the outcome of a game of Hounds and Jackals. "I like those jade earrings of yours. I'll bet my new gold and turquoise cuff bracelets against your earrings that Berett pointed to her name by pure accident."

"Done." I sat back on my heels. "How will we settle this?"

Sitamun studied the document I'd been crafting. "You've written her name more than once," she said. "If she can show me every place that it appears, I'll concede."

I faced my little harper. "Do you understand what Princess Sitamun wants you to do, Berett?" I asked. "Do you want to try?"

The words were just out of my mouth when Berett began pointing at the papyrus here, there, there, and again until she had jabbed her small finger at five out of the six places I'd written her name. Then she looked from

Sitamun's stunned face to mine and gave us both an impish smile.

"Uhhhh, I think you owe me a pair of bracelets," I said.

"Not so fast. She missed one." Sitamun was joking, but the joke bounced back at her when Berett pointed at the last repetition of her name in the document and then, very deliberately, put her first two fingers in her mouth.

It was the symbol for a child. It belonged next to the other characters that spelled out Berett's name, to indicate that I wasn't writing about a grown woman. I'd included it five times, but not the sixth.

Berett saw it, recognized it, understood it. Berett could read.

A little while later, when Henenu joined us, Sitamun and I nearly bowled the scribe off his feet in our eagerness to tell him all about the miracle. He thought we were playing a prank on him. Even when we got Berett to repeat what she'd done, he claimed we'd trained her to do it. The three of us were arguing about how we could prove the truth when Berett stuck her finger into the water for making paints and traced Sitamun's name on the rooftop.

"Did she just—?" I began. As if to remove all doubt, Berett made a sweeping gesture from the fast-fading symbols to my cousin.

"By Thoth, how did she learn that?" It was Henenu's turn to be astonished.

"Sitamun and I often practice by writing funny messages to each other," I said. "Then we read them aloud. Berett probably knows what my name looks like, too."

Berett nodded and tried to demonstrate, but she became confused partway through and slapped the floor in frustration.

"There, there, my girl," Henenu said. "Nefertiti's name is much longer than Sitamun's, so it's much harder to write. Would you like me to help you?" This time Berett nodded so vigorously that I thought her neck would snap.

As Sitamun and I looked on, Henenu sat cross-legged on the rooftop and began instructing the child. "Well," I said with a gesture of surrender. "There goes our harp music."

Later that day, while Berett napped, I sat beside the long pool just outside my door and marveled over the morning's surprise. *Isis be praised, she wants to learn! Oh please, kind goddess, grant that someday she'll be willing to write the words she still can't bear to say. It's so hard, not being able to talk to her, to know if I'm really taking good care of her or not. But if she can write—!*

I jumped to my feet. I was so happy, I had to dance. I hummed an old song Mery used to sing to me, about fishermen casting their nets in the river. I stamped my feet, clapped my hands, twirled, swayed, leaped, and burst into full song out of the gladness of my heart.

"So pretty! So good!" An unfamiliar voice put a stop to my dance. A majestic-looking young woman with light brown skin and startling green eyes stood at the far end of the pool, clapping her hands.

During the past months in this part of the palace, I'd come to recognize the most important women—those few junior wives Pharaoh preferred over all the rest, either for their looks, their youth, their importance as the daughters of his foreign allies, or for the sons they'd given him. This green-eyed beauty was one of the two Mitanni princesses, and though I'd often crossed her path, we'd never exchanged a single word.

Now she approached me, and though she hadn't mastered our language, she managed to let me know that she admired my dance. "This is good to see. Again? Please?"

So I danced for her, and she praised me even more loudly, so loudly that she attracted a crowd of other women. I felt self-conscious, dancing and singing alone for all of them, but soon the Mitanni princess began to sing one of her own people's songs and to share a dance from her homeland. Others took turns, bringing out their memories as music. Berett woke up and brought out her harp. Together we turned yet another ordinary day into a celebration.

That evening, a servant presented herself at the doorway to my rooms and asked if I would join the two Mitanni princesses for dinner. I was overjoyed. In the past six months, none of the other inhabitants of the women's quarters had said more to me than a simple greeting when we crossed paths and it was unavoidable. My own attempts at making friends were always turned aside, politely but firmly. Even if I'd overheard one of the foreigners speaking our language fluently, the moment I tried to introduce myself, she acted as if she couldn't understand a word I said. As for the women of the Black Land—the daughters of nobles whose fathers had given them to Pharaoh as a mark of respect or a bribe—they couldn't avoid me by hiding behind our different languages, but they always managed to re-member someplace they had to be immediately. After two months of such rejections, I gave up.

Who would have guessed that a simple dance could have built such a strong bridge? The Mitanni princesses greeted me warmly, and though they weren't fluent in our tongue, they still managed to share stories, jokes, and an invitation for me to return to see them as much as I liked.

"Next time, bring little girl who plays harp," one said. "Very *good* little girl."

"She looks like people from near our home," the other said.

"She's a Habiru," I responded. The princesses nodded.

"You, too, look like us, some," the first one remarked. She indicated my nose and my high cheekbones.

"My grandfather came from your land," I said. "And my mother also had Mitanni blood."

"So that is why you are so pretty!" the first princess exclaimed with satisfaction. "All Mitanni women are, much more than Black Land women." Then she made a comically serious face and laughed, to let me know she was only teasing.

I returned to my rooms with a happy heart. Aside from my writing practice with Sitamun and Henenu, this was the most company I'd enjoyed since my arrival. There were some times that I was summoned to dine with the royal family, but they were formal occasions, often attended by foreign dignitaries. Pharaoh was the only one who dared to break the solemn atmosphere with a joke. Everyone laughed dutifully, but no one tried to tell another one.

As for my husband-to-be, the last time I'd seen Thutmose, apart from the formal dinners and our initial meeting, was a month ago when Aunt Tiye had the two of us brought back to that same garden to share a very awkward meal while servants filled the air with soft music and passionate love poetry. Thutmose ate without enjoyment, asked me a series of dull questions, and didn't bother to listen to my answers. I prayed that I'd get a fish bone stuck in my throat to put an end to the torture.

The next morning, all of my joy at finally making new friends in the women's quarters was snatched from my hands and shattered. Instead of Kepi's murmured, "Mistress, it's the hour you asked to be awakened," I was roused from sleep by an anxious, "My lady, the queen wants you. Now."

I sat up and rubbed my eyes. Kepi hovered by my bedside with a clay lamp in her hand, her broad, pleasant face transformed by apprehension. "At *this* hour?" I protested, shivering. The air still held the chill of night, the windows were still dark, the holy sun-disk still hidden below the horizon.

"Yes, my lady. At once. I have your dress waiting, and a robe. Her messenger said—she said that *all* of us must come with you." Her fingers flew to her simple necklace and closed tightly around the amulet she wore to ward off evil. "Even the child."

Even though the palace came to life very early every day, with slaves and servants hastening to stoke the cooking fires, bake the bread, and fetch all the things that their masters needed to start the morning, we walked through deserted halls. I still had three maidservants looking after me—my efforts to make do with only Kepi had been countermanded by Aunt Tiye—and now I was glad to have them. I didn't dare to be caught holding Berett's hand when I presented myself to the queen. No matter how special the child was to me, Aunt Tiye could *not* be allowed to discover that. So Berett walked behind me, with the rest of my servants, and took comfort from the two who clasped her small hands and whispered for her not to be afraid.

We were taken to a part of the palace whose sumptuous rooms were decorated with scene after scene of Aunt Tiye receiving gifts from her husband. The flickering lamps that lit our way let me glimpse some of the writing on the walls, all praising the beauty, charm, and wisdom of the Great Royal Wife. The woman herself was waiting for us in a room that looked like a miniature version of Pharaoh's principal reception hall, where he sat on a raised platform under a colorfully striped and gilded canopy and accepted the tribute of lesser kings.

Aunt Tiye was not seated. She stood with her fingertips just touching the arms of her chair and looked ready to spring straight down my throat. In spite of the hour, she had seen to it that her attendants dressed and adorned her to the point where she might have been mistaken for a goddess—a goddess of wrath.

"Are these *all* of your people?" she thundered when we all bowed before her. "I'll know if you're lying, Nefertiti. I know everything that happens under this roof."

"Yes, Aunt Tiye," I replied calmly. "This is everyone who serves me."

She pointed at her messenger. "Take them out of my sight! Let no one know they're here." The woman bowed and ushered everyone else away. The look of stark terror in their eyes was appalling. I saw Berett press both hands to her mouth, as if to make doubly sure that no sound would escape her lips.

"Aunt Tiye, what's wrong?" I asked. "I don't understand."

"Is that so?" She mocked me. "But you're such an *intelligent* girl, so talented, so perfect to become the next Great Royal Wife. So why aren't you intelligent enough to remember that everything you are or ever hope to be, you owe to *me*? Why have you decided to reward all I've done for you with *treachery*?"

"What treachery?" I asked, unable to believe my ears. "I'm your niece, not your enemy. If I've done anything to offend you, I apologize, but I don't see how I've—"

"You were with *them*!" Aunt Tiye's teeth clashed together in her fury. "You shared food and drink and laughter with the women who'd like nothing better than to steal our rightful thrones from my son and me!"

"The Mitanni princesses?" So that was it. "All we did was—"

"I know what you did. How could you even think of befriending the very people who want to destroy your family? Does loyalty mean nothing to you? Are you so stupid that you'd betray the ties of blood between us for a mouthful of cake and wine? Do you love those foreign dogs so much that you'd gladly cover yourself with their fleas?"

I held up my hands in surrender. "Aunt Tiye, I swear by

Ma'at that I would never side against you with any of the other royal women."

"*Royal* women," she repeated scornfully, then narrowed her eyes. "Prove it."

"What do you want me to do?"

"Forget your foolish reluctance to do what you know you must, sooner or later. Marry Thutmose now." She was smiling again, a thin, disturbing smile.

I shook my head. "Not yet," I said. "Ask anything else but not that. Not yet. He's still a stranger to me."

The queen's smile blinked out. "You have too many scruples for somebody who's entitled to none. If I say you will marry my boy today—"

"You took an oath before Amun," I reminded her. "There were witnesses. If you break it, the gods will be angry."

"I would risk that for my son's future," she said. I could tell she meant it.

"What if they didn't punish *you* for oath-breaking?" I asked, desperate to turn her thoughts aside from forcing me into that unwanted marriage. "What if they punish *him*?"

I saw her face grow pale. I'd reached her. "Don't even say such things! Niece or not, princess or not, you can still be punished for ill-wishing Pharaoh's son."

"I wish Thutmose well," I said. "Just as I wish you and all my kin well. No matter what you think of me, I'm loyal to my family. But I can't marry Thutmose yet. Please, Aunt Tiye, honor your oath to Amun."

The sly smile crept back across her lips. "Will *you* take an oath of your own to prove your words, Nefertiti? Will you swear before Ma'at or Amun or any of the gods that from now on, you will have *nothing* to do with any of those devious little vipers in the women's quarters?"

"Why must I—?"

"Or will I need to show you that bad choices yield worse consequences? I promise you, the next time word reaches me that you've done more than exchange a nod or a greeting with any of Pharaoh's women, I will take one of your servants and see to it that she suffers for your selfishness and disloyalty. I hope it won't take you four lessons to learn that I'm in earnest about this."

Four—? Berett! I didn't want my aunt to harm Kepi or the other maids, but the very idea of her taking out her mad spite on Berett made me tremble down to the marrow of my bones.

"You won't need to teach me anything," I said, standing tall and holding the queen's gaze. I refused to let her see how distraught her threats had made me. It would give her a fresh advantage over me. "I swear by Isis, I won't have anything more to do with your rivals." And then, because I was so angry at my aunt for how she'd cut me off from any friendships, I added: "I hate to see you so afraid."

I turned my back on her and left, not even waiting for her messenger to bring back Berett, Kepi, and the others. *She knows I care about their fate or she never would have tried to control me through them, but she doesn't know how* much *I care,* I thought. *My words stung her—I saw it—but if she takes it out on them, she'll be tossing away all of the playing pieces she's got. Aunt Tiye's too good a player to do something that brash over such a little barb.*

I'd gambled well: Before I'd gone half the length of the hall, I heard a patter of many feet and I was surrounded by my girls.

The days that came after my clash with Aunt Tiye were doubly lonely. Since that dawn-light meeting, my servants did their scant few chores in a state of jangled nerves, even Kepi. She and I used to share funny stories about my life back in Akhmin and her own experiences growing up as the daughter of a wine merchant, but Aunt Tiye's threats had opened up a canyon of silence and fear between us. It didn't matter that she and the others had been taken out of the room when the queen and I tangled; there were always ears and eyes and eager lips to carry news of supposed "secrets" through the palace.

I thanked Isis that no such gap had yawned between Berett and me. She'd endured worse ordeals of terror in her short life. My aunt's attempt to tighten the reins on me by menacing her and the rest was just a passing shadow to Berett. I was glad of that but regretted that the one person in my immediate household who wasn't afraid to talk to me couldn't do so.

The situation grew worse. The Mitanni princesses and the other women who'd joined me in that happy dance were taken aback when we crossed paths and I only spoke a word or two to them. Their expressions went from surprised to hurt to resentful, and I heard their whispers behind my back, calling me proud, arrogant, two-faced, high and mighty, cold. Any child of the women's quarters who took so much as a step in my direction was grabbed away by his or her mother as if I had leprosy. I couldn't set foot out of my rooms without overhearing cruel jibes. So what if they weren't true? They still had the power to draw blood.

I tried to take refuge in my friendship with Sitamun. Our morning lessons became my only diversion, but they weren't enough to chase away the full measure of my loneliness.

"Why do you look so glum lately?" Sitamun asked. "Something's eating at you. Tell me."

"It's nothing." I wasn't brave enough to confide in her fully. I was afraid that if I told her about what her mother had done, she'd confront her. Sitamun had a bold heart, but I knew she didn't have the power to protect Berett and the others if she made her mother mad. "Just some bad dreams," I replied.

"Lions?" She winked, trying to cheer me with our old joke.

"Lions." I bent over my work, unsmiling, and focused on the papyrus, the pen, and the words.

Henenu joined us, but he had little to offer me. All of his attention had shifted to teaching Berett how to read and write. It was anyone's guess how well she could read, since there was no chance of having her do it out loud, but he assured us that she managed to let him know, in her own way, that she understood the symbols he placed before her. As for her writing, her rapid achievements sent the little scribe into gleeful ecstasies.

"Why are all of my best students *girls*?" he exclaimed. It wasn't a complaint at all.

I was pleased for Berett's sake. The child now had something more with which to fill her days when she wasn't playing the harp. When we weren't on the rooftop with Sitamun and Henenu, she reviewed her lessons with a waxed tablet I'd given to her, just like the one I'd once used. I was very serious with her when I explained why she couldn't practice her writing on shards of pottery, like Henenu's official students did. One of the servants might find them. Even if the maid didn't understand exactly *what* she'd discovered, she would know it was something out of the ordinary. She might go running to tattle about it to Aunt Tiye, in hopes of buying herself the queen's protection.

"So you see why this must stay a secret," I told Berett. She looked solemn and nodded. Unfortunately I'd stressed the need for secrecy too well. There were many days when my little musician would grab her tablet and vanish from dawn to dusk, holed up somewhere in the palace where she could practice her beloved new skill, safe from spying eyes.

So Berett's days were occupied, but what about mine? I was left behind, alone more often than not. The women's quarters held nothing for me but sneering looks and hostile whispers, so I wandered aimlessly through the palace, looking for nothing except a way to make the hours pass until dinner and bed.

On a cool day toward the end of the season of Emergence, my wanderings brought me to an open space planted with tall palm trees, a terrace with a sweeping view of the sacred river. I looked across the water to the western bank and the yellow cliffs in the distance. When I turned back, I almost walked right into Thutmose. I let out a small yelp of alarm and jumped, but he stood unruffled, studying me in that unnerving, detached way of his.

"So you are here after all," he remarked.

"What do you mean? You sound as if someone told you where to find me, but I didn't even know where I was heading today."

"You do that a lot, don't you? Roam the palace? I don't see why. You don't even pay attention to where you're going. Yesterday you nearly walked out one of the side gateways, into the city."

"I wish I'd known," I said bitterly. "I would have kept going."

"No, that would not have been permitted."

"How do you know so much about my comings and goings?" I asked, suspicious. The obvious answer came to me almost before I finished the question. "I'm being watched, amn't I?"

His eyebrows rose sharply. "You didn't know that? You must be joking."

"It's true? I'm spied on all the time?"

"You are being *looked after*," he corrected me. "You should be grateful that someone thinks you're valuable enough to deserve so much attention. And no, not *all* the time. Don't flatter yourself. Not even I am that important."

The way he spoke—as if losing your freedom to privacy was a privilege and not an assault—made my skin crawl. I decided to change the subject.

"You have a very light step, Thutmose, very soft and graceful," I said, trying to turn our conversation into something more pleasant by flattering him. "Did your cat teach you to move so silently?"

His face lit up with a smile so natural and unexpected,

it was startling. "My beautiful Ta-Miu! She's as unique as that white star on her brow. I've never seen another cat with such a mark, so it must come from the gods. No mere human can move as gracefully as she. She's a shadow on the water, a wisp of cloud drifting across the sky. She steals through the house like twilight. The best dancer in all of Thebes would be a crippled hippo next to her."

"Then I'd better not dance for you," I said, pleased to see that there was some hope of human warmth from the crown prince. "I don't want to know what *I'd* look like in comparison to your cat." I glanced around. "By the way, isn't she with you?"

His smile died. "She's with Mother. She'll be given back to me in three days, provided that I earn her return." He looked at me as if I were a cup of sour wine, but only until he forcefully twitched the corners of his lips back up again. "My beautiful Nefertiti, forgive me for having neglected you for so long. Tomorrow I'm going hunting on the river. It would make me very happy to spend that time with you. Please join me."

Isis help me, she made *him do this,* I realized. *Aunt Tiye took his beloved pet to make him woo me. Am I that repulsive or is he simply that indifferent to me? But if neither one of us wants this marriage—*

"Thutmose?" I said. "Thutmose, if you could marry anyone under the sky, who would you choose?"

His forehead creased. "Why do you ask such a question?"

"Your mother would be happy if you married soon and had a son of your own, but I'm not ready for marriage or motherhood yet. Why not take the wife that *you* want now? That would please everyone."

"You mean it would please *you*." I didn't think it was possible for Thutmose to become even colder toward me, but he proved me wrong. "Who put that question in your mouth? The Mitanni worms? *You* will be my wife; none other."

"No one told me to ask you anything," I argued. "If you don't want to marry anyone except me, so be it."

"If I *want* to marry you?" he echoed. "You don't *know* what I want."

"You could tell me."

His laugh was a slap. "And then what? Will you bring me my heart's desire freely, asking nothing for yourself in return? Or will you play the same games with me that they all do? This for that, that for this, keeping a handful of game pieces hidden or shaving the toss-bones so they show the numbers *you* need in order to win?"

"I only asked a simple question," I said, feeling my temper slipping out of my control. "I didn't want to upset you like this."

"There are no simple questions inside these walls, Nefertiti," he told me. "If you ask me whom I'd rather marry than you, it means that there's someone *you'd* rather marry than me."

"No, it doesn't, I swear by—"

"Stop. I hear too many oaths, too many promises. Let's forget you ever asked me anything. I would rather have your answer."

"To what?"

He made a small sound of exasperation. "To my invitation. I'm going hunting for birds in the marshes tomorrow and it would make me deeply happy if you'd come along."

"Thank you, but I'd rather—"

"*Please,* Nefertiti." Thutmose's mask slipped and I was looking into the eyes of a young man who had lost the one thing he actually cared about.

"All right, Thutmose," I said, relenting. "Until tomorrow."

I tried to resume my aimless exploration of the palace, but Thutmose wouldn't leave me alone. He spent the rest of the day stuck to my side like a burr. There was no question about why he was doing it: He saw his mother's spies everywhere and wanted them to report that he was doing everything he could to win my heart and hasten our marriage.

The next three days were filled with more of the same uncomfortable togetherness for Thutmose and me. We ate every meal together except for breakfast. I think we both liked those mealtimes best because we didn't have to make conversation while we were drinking or chewing. Thutmose was perfectly polite when he did speak to me. His words were thickly laden with praise for my eyes, my skin, my mouth, my voice, every part of my body he could list. He even recited poems that claimed how deeply he adored me, how painfully he missed me when we were apart, how ardently he wished for my love. He sounded like he was counting the number of steps from one end of his room to the other.

I was polite, too. I never laughed at him once. Aunt Tiye

would have found out and she wouldn't have liked it. Neither one of us wanted her to become cross enough to punish Thutmose through his innocent pet. It was the only thing we had in common.

So the days went by and I watched him kill whole flocks of wild ducks, watched him practice shooting the bow and arrow with the nobles' sons, watched him throw hunting spears at straw targets, watched, watched, *watched* him until I closed my eyes and cried out from my soul, *O Isis, let Aunt Tiye give him back his cat already! And thank you for showing me that there are worse fates than always being alone.*

My prayer was heard. Thutmose and I were eating our midday meal together under the shade of a date palm when Amenophis came out of the palace with Ta-Miu in his arms. "Look who's come to see you, brother!" he called out joyfully.

Thutmose was on his feet and across the garden in one bound. He plucked Ta-Miu out of his younger brother's arms and lavished the cat with all kinds of affectionate babble. Then he carried her back to where the servants had set our table and began offering her tidbits. Amenophis and I might as well have been on the moon.

I reached over and tapped Thutmose on the arm. "Aren't you going to thank your brother for bringing back your cat?"

Thutmose didn't bother taking his eyes off his pet to answer me. "Why? He only did what Mother told him to do." He tore off another shred of roasted goose and fed it to Ta-Miu.

I saw Amenophis turn to go, crestfallen. *That's not right,* I thought, and ran from the table to stop him before he could leave. "Come and eat with us," I said.

"I'm not hungry." He sounded miserable. "I'm going to take a walk."

"Then I'll walk with you," I said.

"Are you sure? Thutmose will—"

"Thutmose won't notice, and if he notices, he won't care." I laid one hand on Amenophis's scrawny arm. "Can you do me a favor? I've been blundering everywhere in this palace for months, but I've never been able to find that tiny garden where I met you. Can you take me there? Just so I don't start believing it was a magician's illusion."

"I wouldn't make a very good magician," he said, with a faint smile. "I'll show you how to find it."

We walked through the palace together with Amenophis taking special care to point out landmarks along the way so that I'd be able to find my way to the hidden garden whenever I liked. "It's a good place when you want to be alone, but you can't do that if you need someone else to bring you here," he said as we finally crossed the threshold into the garden.

"I don't have to go somewhere special to be alone," I replied, running my fingertips across the leaves of a fragrant shrub.

"Really? But the women's quarters are so busy." He pulled back the fronds of a very young date palm, revealing a stone bench, and motioned for me to sit down. Then he sat as well, though so far from me I thought he was going to fall off the edge and land in the dirt. "Haven't any of the ladies spoken to you?" he went on. "Are none of them willing to make friends?"

"A friendship takes two," I replied dully. "It doesn't work out so well when one of them doesn't dare to talk to the other."

"Well, you *are* a royal princess, betrothed to the next Pharaoh, so the concubines might be shy about approaching you, but the junior wives wouldn't hesitate. Some of them are princesses in their own right, like the two Mitanni women Mother is always complaining about."

"Your mother does more than complain about them," I said, and to my surprise I began to tell Amenophis all about how my first tentative efforts to make friends in the women's quarters had been yanked from my hands by Aunt Tiye and thrown to the winds. When I finished, he looked very uncomfortable.

"Oh, I'm so sorry, Amenophis!" I exclaimed. "I shouldn't speak ill of Aunt Tiye to you like this: She's your mother. I'm—I'm sure she has very good reasons for acting the way she does. I shouldn't speak ill of her at all, it's just that I'm so *frustrated*. I'm not used to being so alone. I didn't have any *close* friends in Akhmin, but I knew lots of other girls. We danced together and chattered about silly things and had a wonderful time. And at home, there was my little sister, Bit-Bit. She must have changed so much, even in the short time I've been here. I wish I knew how she's getting on. I'd do anything to hear any news about her or my parents."

Amenophis was puzzled. "Doesn't your father write to you?"

I shrugged. "I don't know. He said he would, but he also said there was a chance that his words wouldn't reach me because . . ." I stopped. I'd already embarrassed him by criticizing his mother once; it would be mean to do that to him again. "Because so many things can happen to a message between here and Akhmin."

"I don't understand. Father receives letters from as far away as the kingdom of the Mitanni to the north and the heart of Nubia."

"My father isn't Pharaoh. Nothing is at stake if his letters don't arrive." Before Amenophis could pursue the matter, I diverted him. "I shouldn't complain. Henenu and Sitamun are good friends, but they're both much older than I am. I don't have anyone closer to my age that I can really talk to here."

He mumbled something and looked away. When I touched his arm and asked him to speak up, he softly said, "You've got me."

12

TWO PRINCES

It was good to have a new friend. I enjoyed talking with Amenophis very much, and our conversations ranged over everything from the latest palace rumor to the news from other kingdoms allied to the Black Land to the problems the royal baboon-keeper was having training his newest animals to pick dates from the tallest palm trees.

"You should have seen it, Nefertiti! The creatures are supposed to pick the dates and throw them down to the men below who're holding the catching cloth," Amenophis told me as we walked along one of the palace rooftops, enjoying the view and the fresh air.

"But they ate the dates themselves?" I guessed.

"Yes, but that wouldn't have been so bad. It's what they threw *instead* of the dates that—"

"Ugh! Stop! That's awful! Don't tell me any more!" I said, laughing so hard that he knew I didn't mean it. "Why can't *I* ever see something that funny in this place?"

"It didn't happen in the palace. It happened in the royal groves, past the farthest downstream limit of Thebes."

"Oh." I sighed. "All the best things lie beyond the palace walls."

My friend looked concerned. "Haven't you ever left the palace?"

"I can't. I've tried. Whenever I go to one of the gateways, the guards are very respectful but they always turn me back, saying it's forbidden." I didn't tell Amenophis that I'd flirted with the idea of sneaking out, only to set it aside. If I wasn't careful enough, I'd be caught and Aunt Tiye would hear of it. I'd risk that if I were sure she'd punish me and only me, but I knew she was more likely to make someone innocent bear the penalty for my daring. I refused to gamble against those stakes.

"It's not forbidden," Amenophis said.

"What?" If he was teasing me . . .

"It's only forbidden for you to leave the palace *alone*. You aren't a prisoner here, after all; you're family. You don't know your way around Thebes, so you could get lost easily if you went into the city on your own, or worse."

"Worse?"

Amenophis looked sheepish. "There are some parts of the city and some people that aren't very . . . nice. We have plenty of police patrolling the streets—you can't miss them, they're all members of the Medjay tribe from Nubia—but they can't be everywhere all the time. A beautiful girl like you, alone, unfamiliar with the city—"

"I'd be a target for thieves," I finished for him. "Or worse. I know what you're hinting at, Amenophis. We had all sorts of crimes committed in Akhmin, too." I sighed again, more deeply. "I wouldn't have to worry if I could go into the city with some kind of weapon to protect myself— a club, a staff. But even if I did, I'm not strong enough to use it effectively. My arms are too soft. Prisoner or not, I'm trapped."

"I don't like seeing you so disappointed, Nefertiti," Amenophis said. "Why don't you ask Thutmose to take you for a chariot ride through Thebes? I'm sure he'd be happy to have the chance to show you the city."

"I suppose," I said, but in my mind my answer was: *Do you want to bet on that, my friend?*

It was too bad that I didn't make that wager with Amenophis; I would have won with ridiculous ease. That night we had one of those formal dinners to attend. I'd come to dread them. Aunt Tiye always made sure that I was seated next to Thutmose and kept a stern eye on both of us, to be certain we were speaking to one another. She'd never wanted to postpone our marriage and kept pushing us together, hoping that the more time I spent in the crown prince's company, the faster I'd become enchanted with him.

It wasn't working. Thutmose and I still talked like strangers, or the priests and priestesses who sometimes donned masks and acted out stories of the gods at festivals. He only spent time with me when Aunt Tiye insisted on it, and then he spent most of our visits playing with his cat. I doubted he'd jump at the chance to drive me through Thebes, and I was right.

"Why do you want to see Thebes all of a sudden? What

put that idea into your head?" he asked without bothering to look at me.

"It's nothing new. I've wanted to see the city since I got here," I responded. "The temples, the marketplaces, the people . . ."

"I thought you had such things in Akhmin." He clicked his tongue. "Anyway, I can't take you any time soon. I'm very busy. I'm spending a lot of time with the priests of Amun these days, learning how to serve the god so that when I rule, I'll do it with his blessing."

"How could I ever hope to compete with Amun?" I said dryly.

My sarcasm went right over the crown prince's head. "I'm glad you understand."

Amenophis was seated near enough to overhear our conversation. I gave him a look that said: *What did I tell you?* He replied with an apologetic expression, and the very next morning he sent a maidservant to invite me to join him for a tour of Thebes.

Berett was already up and gone, along with her writing-practice tablet. Ever since Henenu had begun giving her proper instruction, the child got into the habit of running ahead of me to our rooftop classroom in order to have extra time with the scribe. Once those two sunk themselves in the day's lesson, they probably wouldn't even notice that I wasn't there.

Amenophis was waiting for me at the main gate of the palace. The guards didn't even blink when he led me outside to where a blue and gold chariot waited. A groom stood holding the reins of a pair of magnificent horses with pure white coats whose trappings matched the chariot. Ostrich plumes dyed red as pomegranate juice bobbed and nodded atop their heads.

"Will you be all right riding with me?" Amenophis asked anxiously. "We could walk, if you'd prefer."

I remembered coming to the palace in a chariot so many months ago. At the time, my mind had been too preoccupied for me to enjoy the experience. I wasn't going to make that mistake this time.

"I want to ride," I said. "But only if you promise to drive *fast*."

Amenophis looked dubious, but he gave me what I wanted. I held tight to the chariot rail as he slapped the reins crisply over the horses' rumps and they took flight. He was a masterful driver. Those skinny arms of his were strong enough to steer the horses with precision, to slow them smoothly when we entered streets where speed would have been folly, to let them race like twin dragonflies skimming the surface of the sacred river. The wind of our ride whipped through my dress and sent my hair streaming behind me. I laughed aloud at the joy of being free.

Oh, how I hated it when he brought the horses down to a walk, then made them stop. I wanted to keep on flying! I wanted to outrun my own shadow, and the palace that we'd left behind, and the day when my three years of reprieve would be over and my aunt wouldn't have to take "Not yet! Not yet!" for an answer.

"Can't we ride some more?" I asked, and was ashamed to hear my own voice sounding so much like a spoiled child's.

"Of course, Nefertiti, but—but I—I thought you might like to see this first," he said bashfully. "It's the great temple to Amun that Father is enriching." His arm swept up and my eyes followed, filling with awe.

Such majesty! I had grown up with the temples of Akhmin, I had seen the ancient monuments of Abydos, but this was a holy place of such colossal size that any person seeing it would know how insignificant he was in the presence of the gods. I was only half-aware when Amenophis took my arm, helped me down, turned over his chariot to one of the waiting temple slaves entrusted with such tasks, and began to lead me through the sacred place.

Though I returned to the great temple complex many times, my first impression remained my most treasured and—embarrassing to say so—my most jumbled. The grounds were filled with priests and worshippers, workmen and artists, servants and slaves, yet they were little more than phantoms to me. I moved through a dream of looming walls, towering obelisks, sprawling flat-roofed halls whose ceilings were supported by a grove of titanic stone pillars, all carved with images of gods and kings and words that were a resounding shout of self-glorification by one Pharaoh after another. Amenophis's father was only adding to this place; many other kings had left their mark here before him. Generations of unborn pharaohs would do the same when he returned to the gods. I looked down the long line of pillars and saw eternity. I should have been afraid.

I wasn't; I was overjoyed. "This is beyond belief, Amenophis! I don't know what to say. It's all so . . . so . . . ." I couldn't speak. My heart was too full, yet I wanted him to know how thrilled I was to stand in the midst of so many wonders. Without thinking, I threw open my arms and hugged him the way I'd hugged Father when I was small and he brought me some new "treasure."

Father never broke out of my innocent embrace so suddenly or moved away from me so fast that he staggered and nearly fell over backward. "I—I—Nefertiti, you shouldn't . . ." Amenophis gulped out the words, the bulging lump in his throat jerking up and down rapidly. His eyes darted left and right at the people surrounding us. Most of them went about their business, but a few smirked and snickered.

I clapped a hand to my mouth, mortified. "Oh! I'm so sorry! I don't know why I did that."

"It's—it's all right. I was only—surprised. Come, there's a lot more to see." He loped away on his long legs, leaving me to pick up the hem of my dress and try to keep pace.

I wanted to see everything, but that was impossible. The day wore on, and I became drunk with the glow of sun on golden stone and jewel-hued paints. Soon I was outdistancing Amenophis, who began to weaken as I kept him on the run, not even pausing for food or drink. I didn't notice anything was wrong until he finally staggered into the shade of a sycamore and dropped into a crouch, his head between his knees. *That* yanked me out of my trance. "What is it, my friend?" I asked, kneeling beside him.

He raised his head and let me see a wobbly smile. "How do you do it, Nefertiti? We've been here for hours, and you're not hungry or thirsty. Do you live on air?"

"I think I must live on stupidity," I said, and hailed the first likely person I saw, a junior priest, judging by the look of his clothes and his hairless body. Once I told him that the lanky young man curled up under that sycamore was Pharaoh's younger son, he summoned up a whirlwind of servants to carry Amenophis to more comfortable quarters and saw to it that my friend was given everything he needed to restore him, body and spirit.

"Thank you very much," Amenophis said to the junior priest once he'd recovered. "Your kindness won't be forgotten. I wish we could enjoy your hospitality longer, but I think it's time that the lady Nefertiti and I returned to the palace."

"Certainly, certainly." The junior priest nearly snapped himself in two bowing to the prince. "I will send for your chariot and escort you to it personally."

Amenophis tried to decline, but the man wouldn't be dissuaded. He accompanied us every step of the way and insisted on pointing out special parts of the temple complex as we passed them.

"Now *this* should be of interest to the lady Nefertiti," he said, gesturing at an odd piece of construction. "It is the obelisk of Queen Hatshepsut, stepmother of our revered Pharaoh's great-grandfather."

"What obelisk?" I asked. All I saw was a mud brick tower.

"Look up," our guide said. When I did, I saw that where the walls ended, the pointed top of a carved stone shaft rose above them.

"Why would anyone build walls around an obelisk?"

The junior priest was only too happy to explain. "Queen Hatshepsut did not conduct herself the way a woman should. When Pharaoh's *great*-great-grandfather ascended to stars, his son was too young to rule, so she became regent. It is said that she ruled well, but that she became arrogant and wicked, sinning terribly against the gods."

"What—what did she do?" I wasn't sure if I wanted to know the answer. I expected to hear horrors.

The junior priest lowered his eyelids as if looking away from a hideous crime. "She declared herself Pharaoh, as if a woman could be the equal of a man." He sounded very satisfied when he added: "When she died, her stepson saw to it that her monuments were all removed from sight so that her name and achievements might be forgotten."

I looked at the obelisk, soaring regally above the inadequate mud brick walls. *Well, he didn't do a very good job of it,* I thought.

That was only the first of many times that Amenophis took me riding in his chariot to explore the city. I continued my lessons in the scribal arts with Henenu in the mornings and sometimes spent afternoons helping Berett with her lessons or enjoying her harp music while I lost myself in dancing, but whenever I could, I'd slip away and let Amenophis show me yet another face of the royal city I was condemned to call my new home.

On one such day, when the season of Emergence was beginning to turn into the season of Harvest, I was sitting beside the long pool with Berett when Sitamun joined us unexpectedly. My older friend looked as mischievous as a child.

"You're grinning like a crocodile, Sitamun," I said fondly. "What sort of tasty gossip are you keeping to yourself?"

"Why would I tell you, you stuffy old thing? *You* don't like gossip. You've told me so repeatedly." She opened her hand, revealing a piece of broken pottery. "This is for you. It isn't gossip . . . yet."

I took the shard and read a message from Amenophis, inviting me to join him for another of our rides. My heart fluttered as I read the words: *I've been thinking about what you've asked of me so many times and I surrender. I'll let you do it.* My eyes flashed to Sitamun. "Did you read this?"

"I tried not to," she said, hedging. "My younger brother writes very large. He'd never make a good scribe, wasting space that way." In a more serious tone, she added: "I love Amenophis, Nefertiti, and you're my dear friend, but Thutmose is my brother, too, *and* the next Pharaoh *and* your chosen husband."

"*I* never chose him."

"Do you think *that* tiny point changes anything important? Then you haven't been paying attention to Mother, and that's not smart."

"Amenophis is my friend," I said defiantly. "*Only* my friend. While your mother refuses to let me have any company except our family and Thutmose leaves me to gather dust and cobwebs, Amenophis has been *here* for me! He worries that I'm lonely, he cares if I smile. Aunt Tiye sends me flasks of rare perfume and makes Thutmose give me earrings and bracelets—though I doubt he even looked at them before he had his servants deliver them to me. Amenophis gives me the gift of his *time*. We aren't doing anything wrong, and if you go running to your mother or Thutmose with any false tales, I'll—"

"Hush, lioness, smooth down your fur," Sitamun said kindly. "Do you think Amenophis would have entrusted that message to me if he believed I'd tattle about it? He's just as vehement as you when he insists you're just friends, but I wanted to hear the same thing directly from your lips."

"Oh."

"Why do you sound so disappointed?"

"I'm not," I protested quickly. "Why do you make a pebble into a pyramid, Sitamun?"

"What else have I got to do with my days?" she replied a little sadly. "Thebes holds nothing new for me to see, and I will never leave my father's house to marry. Foreign kings send us their daughters because we are the more powerful nation and they want to buy Father's good will. Father knows this, and so he'll never let any of his daughters be sent as brides for other kings. The most my sisters and I can hope for is that some noble performs such a heroic deed on the battlefield that Father rewards him with a royal bride, but how can that happen? We're at peace."

I hugged my friend. "Is it so bad, just being Princess Sitamun? Do you *have* to be someone's wife?"

"No," she said with a wan smile. "But I'd like to have that choice." She paused a moment, then pushed aside her regrets. "So! If you and Amenophis are just friends, what is this great, mysterious, totally innocent thing you've been nagging him to do? He surrenders, but I want to hear about the battlefield."

"Is it any of your business?" I asked, mimicking her lighthearted tone.

"It is if you want me to continue serving as your trusted messenger."

"He's going to teach me how to drive a chariot."

I might as well have said: *He's going to teach me how to weave a garland of horned vipers.* Sitamun was appalled. "Are you *both* crazy? He can't do that!"

"Why not? Because I'm a girl?"

"Because you'll *die*. The horses will bolt. The chariot will break, or turn over, or bounce over a rock and send you flying. You'll be trampled. You'll break your neck. You'll smash your skull. You'll break every other bone in your body and never be able to walk again, or dance, or—You'll *ruin* your face!"

"Well, we can't have *that*," I said. "Aunt Tiye would never approve."

Sitamun tried talking me out of my plans until she saw that it was useless. She contented herself with making sure that I picked up a big rock and smashed Amenophis's message to dust, then whisked the dust into the long pool. She left threatening to "talk sense" to Amenophis.

"Don't you dare!" I called after her, then hurried to prepare for the adventure awaiting me.

Amenophis drove the chariot out of the city to a flat space out of sight of Thebes and the sacred river. "This is where I learned how to drive," he told me. "The ground is nice and smooth, with no surprises. You ought to be all right." He jumped to the ground and took hold of the horses' bridles.

He spent some time showing me how to hold the reins. "Whatever you do, don't lose your grip or the horses will get away from you and run wild. And use both hands. You won't be hunting lions."

"What do you mean?" I asked.

"When Father hunts, he doesn't like to have a driver with him. He says it crowds the arm he uses to hold his bow. But he still needs both hands free to shoot his quarry, so he tucks the reins into his belt."

"He can *steer* that way?"

"His horses are the best of the best, well trained. I think that if you set them loose, they'd bring back a lion on their own!" We both laughed over that.

"Can you do that, too?" What I really wanted to ask was, *Can you teach* me *how to do that?* but I thought it best to approach that question stealthily.

"Not yet. Father has been hunting for many more years than I. The best I can do is steer with one hand."

"Like this?" I grabbed the reins loosely with my right hand and flung my left over my head.

He climbed back into the chariot and made me hold the reins in both hands. "Like *this* or like nothing."

Under Amenophis's nervous eyes, I was forced to keep the horses to a walk while he kept up with us. Back and forth across the plain we went, slow as a pair of oxen instead of a team of wing-footed steeds. *How much longer is he going to hold me back?* I thought crossly. *I can do better than this.* And with that thought, I gave the reins a slight flick.

The horses were just as eager for more speed as I. That glancing sting on their rumps set them off like a green branch tossed on the fire, exploding into a shower of sparks. As Sitamun had predicted, they bolted. I tried to clutch the reins and pull the horses back, but my palms were sweaty and they slithered out of my grip. I lurched backward, but by some unmerited mercy of the gods, I didn't fall off. In a desperate heartbeat I threw myself forward after the vanishing reins and grabbed the chariot rail. Bones shaking, teeth clashing, body jouncing, I got a bellyful of speed until the horses had enough of a gallop and came to a stop.

"Nefertiti! Nefertiti! Are you hurt?" Amenophis caught up to the chariot, seized the trailing reins, and looked fearfully at me as I huddled on the floor of the chariot, covered in dust from head to foot.

I shook my head no, and for the first time saw my friend's homely face transformed with dark fury. "If you *ever* do something like that again—!"

"I'll do it right," I piped up.

His anger broke into shared laughter, and for the rest of the lesson I didn't try any more silly tricks.

I was very glad that Amenophis didn't hold my little escapade against me. The chariot lessons continued whenever the two of us could get away. One day, when the season of Harvest was two months old, we rode with a bundle of straw and Amenophis's bow and quiver sharing the ride. He set up the target, showed me how to draw and aim the bow, and was kind enough not to mock me when I lacked the strength to make the tall weapon bend more than a finger's breadth.

"Keep trying," he said. "It will get better."

"I'd rather be driving the chariot," I said, in a bad mood because of my repeated failures with the bow.

"Wouldn't you like to do both someday?" He gazed at me proudly. "I believe you could."

What could I do after that but go back to wrestling with the bow? By the end of our time together that day, I'd gotten it to bend halfway, sending the arrow tumbling to the ground not far from my feet. Then Amenophis took some practice shots of his own. It was incredible how the bow changed him from an ill-assorted collection of knobby joints, spindly limbs, and bulging belly into a noble figure, fit to be included among the royal images at the great temple.

My arms were aching when I came back to my rooms that afternoon, but I didn't mind. I found Berett beside the long pool, playing her harp for her own pleasure. I sat beside her, paddling my feet in the cool water, and said, "You'll never guess what I did today." She looked interested, so I told her all about it. We often had those one-sided conversations. I hoped that if I talked to her enough, the day would come when the countless silly, happy, pleasant, ordinary fragments of life *now* would beat back the past horror of her sister's cruel death and let Berett speak once more. I ended my story as I always did, by asking, "And what did *you* do today, Berett?"

Usually all I got for an answer was a shrug, a smile, a few vague attempts at gestures that told me very little. Berett would mimic the acts of wandering through the women's quarters, of eating, of drinking, of writing. Sometimes, if she'd seen something remarkable, she'd draw a picture of it in the dirt for me.

This time, everything changed. Instead of her customary gestures, Berett got up, ran into our rooms, and came back with her practice tablet. She wrote out a few lines of clean, precise symbols, then handed it to me.

Now why didn't we do this earlier? I mused as I took the tablet from her and began to read: *My name is not Berett. I am Nava the Habiru. Thank you for being good to me. May the One bless you always. I love you very much.*

"Oh, Bere—Nava!" I cried, dropping the tablet and embracing her. "I love you very much, too."

Even though Nava and I now had a better way of communicating with one another, I didn't abandon my intention of getting her to talk again. What would help achieve that goal? What could have the power to draw her back into the world of voices? I kept my eyes open, eternally on the alert for some new trick to try.

I found one from an unexpected source: When the season of Harvest was nearly over, Thutmose came seeking me in the women's quarters, his cat Ta-Miu in his arms.

"Nefertiti, I need you to look after Ta-Miu," he said, putting the cat in my lap as I sat cross-legged in the shade, playing a game of Hounds and Jackals against myself.

"Well, since you ask so *nicely,*" I said. It was nearly a full year since I'd met Thutmose, and I no longer bothered to refrain from sarcasm when he annoyed me with his high-handed ways. And why should I hold anything back? Nothing I said or did made any impression on him.

"I'm serious," he said. "I have important things to do today and I can't bring her with me."

"She's a *cat*," I said, as if speaking to an infant. "She'll be happy roaming the palace until you return."

"If she wanders free, she'll be caught. I can't stand the thought of that happening again."

"Again? You mean that time your mother used Ta-Miu to make you court me?" He nodded. "Why would she want to do that again?"

"Because *you* are a stubborn donkey." Thutmose's fear for his beloved cat flared up against me. "You know that you'll have to marry me one day, but you insist on putting it off, making Mother angry, making her blame *me* when it's all your fault! We haven't spent any time together all this season except for when we have to share meals with the family, and she's noticed."

"I've—I've been busy," I said, praying that he wouldn't care enough about me to demand details.

"*You?*" His scorn was poisonous. "Busy with what? Your mirror? Your little songs and dances? I've been busy, too, but my time's been spent on *important* matters. When I am Pharaoh, I still won't be safe from those who plot against me. I'll need strong allies to guard my back from traitors. That's why I've spent so much time with the priests of Amun. They have as much wealth and influence as Pharaoh himself; maybe more. I want that."

"If they're so strong, don't you think it's foolish to give

them even more power?" I said. "Who's going to rule this realm, Pharaoh or the Amun priests?"

He sneered at me. "Now you sound like Father. He's tried to cut away some of their influence, and he's had some success, but ultimately he'll fail. No man can stand against the supreme god!"

"And you're talking as if the priests *are* Amun and not just his servants," I countered.

Thutmose shook his head. "I knew you couldn't understand. Try to grasp this instead—it's simple enough: If my mother's agents get their hands on Ta-Miu while I'm away, you and I are going to be spending a *lot* of time together, like before. Except this time, Mother might insist that we stay in each other's company for as long as it takes to make you accept our marriage *now.*"

I put my arms around Ta-Miu protectively and kissed the white star that marked her brow. "I won't let her out of my sight."

Thutmose was amused. "That's what I thought."

I kept my word. There was no way I'd risk being shoved into a renewed "courtship" with him. Fortunately, Ta-Miu was willing to cooperate. The small, spotted cat was very affectionate, soaking up head scratchings and belly rubs like dry earth at the Inundation. She even let me tap her gold ear hoops with my fingertip as long as I atoned for my impudence by feeding her. I sent Kepi to fetch meat from the kitchens and was just giving Ta-Miu the last bite of a baked fish when Berett—I mean *Nava*—came in.

Those two took an immediate interest in one another. Nava awakened the kitten in Ta-Miu, and soon Thutmose's cat was bounding all over our rooms, chasing the supple branch Nava had plucked from one of the trees outside. When Thutmose returned to claim his pet, Nava's sorrow was real.

"You know, if you ever need to leave Ta-Miu again, I'll be happy to help you," I told him.

He gave me a mistrustful look. "Why?"

"One, she was no trouble. Two, I like to watch her play. And three, we both know *why* no one else will guard her as faithfully as I will." I crossed my arms, challenging him to argue that last point.

He couldn't, and so Nava's heart was gladdened nearly every day when Thutmose gave us Ta-Miu and went off to his strange business with the priests of Amun.

Now that the cat was a frequent visitor, I decided to try to use her as a means to coax Nava out of her silence. The child had gone almost a full year without speaking. I thought that was long enough. As we sat together one afternoon, I casually said, "Ta-Miu is such a pretty cat, but do you think she's smart?"

Nava stopped feeding the cat—she was *always* feeding the cat, who was beginning to look like a fur-covered cheese ball—and nodded emphatically.

"Really?" I acted surprised. "But . . . how do you know? They're sacred animals, yes, but so are some fish, and how smart are they? A dog will come when you call him, do what you tell him to do, answer to his name. It's why we *do* give dogs special names, but not cats. They're all called 'cat' or 'she-cat,' because it's a waste of time naming a creature that doesn't come when you call it. I knew at least twenty Mius and Ta-Mius back in Akhmin, and not one of them under-stood a single word you said to them."

Nava glared at me and shook her head again, with more vigor. Then she looked left and right, on the hunt for something.

"You don't have to fetch your practice tablet, dear one," I said mildly. "You could fill line after line with your opinions and I still wouldn't be convinced. It will take proof I can see and hear to make me believe Ta-Miu is as smart as you think." With that, I left the two of them alone in the safety of our rooms. I didn't know if I'd succeeded in using Nava's devotion to Ta-Miu to plant a good seed or a speck of dust. I hoped I'd stirred her up enough so that she'd find her voice again, if only to call out a cat's name and show me I was wrong.

I made a lot of noise as I left, then stole back to our doorway to eavesdrop, silently praying that there would soon be something to overhear. The day was warm and still, with most of the inhabitants of the women's quarters taking their midafternoon sleep. A child's fretful cry drifted across the garden and was soon hushed. Ta-Miu's purr from inside my apartments was loud.

Then I heard something else come from that room. Faint, tremulous, and hoarse, it was the tentative sound of someone clearing her throat. I held my breath, closed my eyes, and prayed.

"There you are!" Thutmose's voice boomed in my ears, drowning all other sounds. He grabbed me by the shoulders from behind, spun me around, and pushed my back against the wall. His jaw was clenched, his face bloodless with rage.

"Traitor," he rasped. The fingers of one hand dug painfully deep into my arm, the other shook a piece of broken pottery under my nose. I glimpsed a thread of writing, but I could only catch sight of a few of the words—". . . meet me again . . ."

"Let me go," I growled, giving Thutmose scowl for scowl. His grip didn't slacken. "I said, let me *go*!" I shouted, and kicked his leg as hard as I could. My own legs were strong from many years of dance and from learning how to stand solidly balanced in a moving chariot. My heel struck his knee with all the force in me. He howled in pain and let me go.

"Don't *ever* touch me again!" I shouted.

"You dare to tell *me*—?" Thutmose gasped, indignation overcoming pain. "After what you've been doing? I ought to—"

"Be quiet," I said, dropping my voice abruptly. I held up a warning hand, laid one finger to my lips, and looked at Thutmose meaningly. "Listen." My skin was prickling; I felt a host of curious eyes peering at the scene the two of us were making. The midday peace of the women's quarters had become a low hum of many voices, a windstorm of whispers.

He looked around. Though no one else was in sight, he, too, could sense the hidden watchers. "In there," he snarled, and dragged me into my own rooms before I could stop him from laying hands on me a second time.

We stood facing each other in the outer chamber. Nava and Ta-Miu were nowhere to be seen. They'd remained in the inner room, and after hearing Thutmose's outburst—

the blessed dead could have heard that!—the two of them were probably hiding under my bed. I folded my arms. "Well done, Thutmose," I said. "You just made a fool of yourself in front of all of your father's women. And over nothing."

"*This* is not nothing." He waved the shard. "I caught my miserable brother in the act of writing this. The palace teems with people continually conspiring to rob me of what's mine, rightfully *mine,* and Amenophis knows it. It's been that way since I was born. Why must he be like them? Why is he trying to steal you away from me?"

"And why are you making me sound like a pair of earrings or a box of incense or—or a slave?" I returned. "I can't be owned or given or stolen. Even if I could, your brother would never—"

"Don't try denying that this is meant for you. Your name is here for anyone to read." He threw the pottery fragment in my face.

I snatched it from the air before it could hit me. "Did you bother to read the whole message?" I said. "That's no love note. Amenophis and I are friends, friends, *friends*! He helps me spend my days in this place happily, seeing new sights, learning interesting things, opening doors for me when everyone else keeps trying to seal me up behind stone walls! He *talks* to me."

Thutmose's upper lip curled. "He would. He's got nothing better to do with his time, and he's so soft, he might as well have been born a girl. What delightful times the two of you must spend, gossiping, dabbling with perfumes, trying on each other's jewelry! Don't let him wear anything too heavy, Nefertiti, none of the big pectoral necklaces, no thick gold bracelets. The weight would snap his flimsy bones."

The same flimsy bones that master a team of spirited chariot steeds? I thought, fuming. *The flimsy bones that can bend a strong bow and send an arrow through the heart of a distant target?* I wanted to shout those words at Thutmose but thought better of it. *If I lie down with pigs, I'll get up covered in the same muck as they. I won't let his cruel words turn me into someone just as cruel.*

"You don't know your brother very well," was all I chose to say.

"I don't want to. He's useless to me. No, he's even worse than that for stealing your attention from me."

"My *attention*?" I was flabbergasted. "If you wanted that, why did you leave me alone except when your mother forced you to keep me company?"

"*Pffff!* My brother's given you a false idea of your own importance. You are a beauty, Nefertiti, and it will do me good to have someone as lovely as you for my Great Royal Wife, when the time comes. Meanwhile, it will please Father and keep his favor with me. But you're the one who's got the most to gain from this marriage. Marrying me will make you *somebody*. You're the one who should be courting *me*."

I was so angry by this point that I could feel hot tears rising. *I won't let him see me cry,* I thought, clenching my fists. *But O sweet Isis, what I really want to do is kick him again, and I can't—I shouldn't do that.* With intense restraint, I answered him: "I see. So I have no one to blame but myself for my past loneliness?"

He smiled. "Well! So you *are* a smart girl. Maybe we can make a fresh start. I'll make sure that Amenophis doesn't take up any more of your time, and you can turn your attention to better things. You know, if you're so terribly bored, all you have to do is agree to marry me immediately. Once you become the crown princess, you'll have plenty of new duties to fill your time, and if you're a *good* wife and give me a son as soon as possible, I'll see to it that you get a nice present."

I wondered how he'd react if I'd asked for a chariot of my own, then and there. He'd probably gape so much that his eyes would pop out of his head. The thought made me smile, and he took it for a sign that I'd conceded the quarrel.

"You agree with me. Good." The passion he'd shown during our argument was gone; the old, familiar coolness was back. "All will be well between us from now on. Where is Ta-Miu?"

I motioned for him to step into my rooms. As I'd imagined, Nava and Ta-Miu were under the bed. When I called to the child, she and the cat poked their heads out side by side, four green eyes peering up at me.

"There you are, my treasure!" Thutmose exclaimed, kneeling. He turned to me and added: "You won't need to look after her again."

"Oh, but I don't mind," I said anxiously. The memory of how close I'd come to hearing Nava speak taunted me. "She's a lovely cat, so sweet, so well-behaved!"

Thutmose beamed. "She is; all the more reason to

guard her. I didn't think things through. I forgot that there would be times when neither you nor I would be free to keep her out of the wrong hands. Tonight, for instance, both of us must attend a banquet honoring the ambassadors from Kush. If Mother's agents wanted to seize Ta-Miu then, who'd stop them?"

"Nava could take care of Ta-Miu for both of us," I said, indicating my little musician. "She loves her."

"Nava—?" Thutmose glanced at the still-cowering child. "Oh yes, *very* formidable. I'm sure *she'd* be able to protect Ta-Miu against whole armies!" He snorted. "I've entrusted the task to one of my strongest slaves, a Nubian with hands that can crush baked bricks. He won't fail me—he has a wife and children to think of."

With that, Thutmose scooped Ta-Miu into his arms and stood up. The cat was still a little unnerved from the shouting match she'd just overheard at such close range. She squirmed, which only made him hold her more tightly. The cat made a low, warbling noise deep in her throat—half meow, half growl—and lashed out viciously with her hind legs. Thutmose uttered a sharp cry of pain and dropped her. She was back under my bed with Nava before the first drops of blood oozed from the gash she'd opened on his arm.

"This is *your* fault!" he bellowed, whirling to confront me. "My Ta-Miu has never hurt me before. *Never!* What did you do to her? How did you turn her against me?"

"I won't listen to this nonsense," I said, keeping as calm as I could. Nava didn't need to witness any more uproars. "As if *I* could make a cat do anything it didn't want to do?

As if *anyone* could do that? You're not being rational, Thutmose."

A dangerous look came into his eyes. "So that's his plan." And before I could ask him what he was talking about, he threw himself flat on his belly, wormed under my bed, emerged with a struggling Ta-Miu in his grasp, and stormed out, leaving me to cope with a silently weeping Nava.

I sat on the floor and held her in my lap, rocking her like a baby. I was trying to cheer her with silly songs and funny stories when I heard someone rapping on the wall just outside of my bedroom doorway. "May I come in?" It was Amenophis.

"Why are you here?" I asked sharply, still upset from all the nasty things Thutmose had said.

"It's not forbidden," he said, taken aback by my hard words. "The only reason I haven't done it before is . . . is I was afraid."

"Of what?"

"Gossip. You've been here long enough to know how it is in the women's quarters. So much gossip, so much jealousy, and everyone looking for the chance to turn the most innocent act into a knife to use against her rival."

"I wish I had a rival for Thutmose," I muttered. "I'd let her have him and go home." I sighed. "If you were afraid to come here before, what changed your mind?"

He smiled sadly and knelt beside Nava and me. "Wasn't my brother just here?" A beam of sunlight from the high window fell across Amenophis's face, revealing a large red mark that was swiftly darkening into a purple bruise on his cheekbone.

"He hit you?" I was outraged. "I wish I'd kicked him harder when I had the chance."

"You kicked Thutmose?" Amenophis stared at me, then let loose his wonderful laugh. "I wish I'd seen that. It would be worth suffering *twenty* blows."

And yet, for all Amenophis's brave words, that was the last time I saw him, apart from formal occasions. I missed him, and I made up a dozen excuses for his absence. When Sitamun, Nava, and I gathered for our lessons and were waiting for Henenu to arrive, I casually wondered aloud if there was some official business or princely duties keeping Amenophis more than ordinarily busy.

"Thutmose told Mother about the quarrel. She ordered Amenophis to keep his distance from you."

"And what did he tell her?"

"Tell her? What *would* he tell her? He might defy her wishes on the sly, but I've never known him to stand up to her for anything." Sitamun looked at me with compassion. "I'm sorry, Nefertiti. It looks like my brother fears Mother more than he loves you."

I felt my face heat with a blush. "I know he doesn't love me. That's not the way it is between us. I only thought that our friendship was worth fighting for."

"I'm sure he feels the same way," Sitamun said. "He would fight for it against anyone else, but this . . . this is Mother."

I bent my head over my pens and palette, pretending a

sudden interest in examining them. As I ran my fingertips over each part of my scribal kit, my heart was heavy. *Oh, Amenophis, my dear friend! I know you're strong, even if your body looks weak, but why can't your spirit be strong, too?* A tear splashed onto the stone palette and I wiped it away with my thumb.

13

WHISPERS

As the season of the Inundation approached and the end of my first year at the court of Pharaoh Amenhotep drew to a close, I was called into Pharaoh's private presence chamber for the first time. The summons came to me very early one morning. Nava and I were just finishing our breakfast beside the long pool when a gorgeously jeweled official came striding through the women's quarters. He dropped to both knees before me and delivered his message in ringing tones while Kepi, my other maids, and a few curious women from other apartments nearby looked on.

By this time I had gone through enough ceremonial dinners and other events at court to be used to hearing myself acclaimed with such exaggerated praise that I no longer heard a word of it. I only paid attention when the messenger got to the point of his errand—namely, that I was to come at once.

"I am honored to obey Pharaoh's word," I said, rising

from my stool. The man stood up as well and was about to lead me away when Kepi intervened.

"My lady, *naturally* you will be wearing something suitably fine when you greet Pharaoh," she said, blocking my way and trying to steer me back into my rooms. "I will see to it myself that this gentleman is offered refreshments while the girls bring you the appropriate dress and jewelry."

The man's hand fell heavily on Kepi's plump shoulder. "There is no time for that. My lady Nefertiti is to come without delay."

"But, my lord, we haven't even had the chance to paint her eyes or comb her hair or—"

"*Without delay,*" the man boomed, glaring at my maidservant. "These are the words of the living god, the Pharaoh Amenhotep, may he reign forever. You will be punished severely for having the audacity to defy them."

"And *you* will be punished twice as severely if you say one word to bring harm to her," I told him, doing my best to look like Aunt Tiye at her worst. I must have done a good job of it: The man quailed and spouted even more flattery, begging my forgiveness and assuring me that I was renowned for being as merciful as I was beautiful. He was still groveling as he led me away, but not loudly enough to blot out the sound of whispers rising from every corner of the women's quarters as we passed.

I was thankful when he at last fell silent. His constant chatter was too intrusive to let me think, and I had much to think about before I faced the Pharaoh. *Why does he want to see me?* I wondered. *What could be so important that I have to come to him* without delay*? Sweet Isis, I'm afraid! It's been weeks* since *Thutmose raged at me about my spending time with Amenophis. If he were going to denounce me to his father, wouldn't* he have done it sooner? A darker suspicion crossed my mind. *Unless he* wanted *me to think I was safe and then strike when I was off guard. Oh, that snake! Amenophis and I didn't do anything wrong, but will Pharaoh see it that way, or will Thutmose poison his father's judgment against us, or—*

I paused in midstep and closed my eyes. *Enough,* I told myself. *If I start seeing evil schemes behind everything, I'll turn into Aunt Tiye or Thutmose.*

"My lady Nefertiti?" My guide hovered near, alarmed that I'd stopped walking.

I opened my eyes and nodded. "I'm fine."

I was brought to a great audience hall where Pharaoh's throne stood empty under its canopy. The official guided me around the platform to a humble doorway curtained with woven reeds. Through this was Pharaoh's private presence chamber. I'd heard of its existence from Sitamun when she described yet another foreign ambassador who'd come to ask for one of Pharaoh's daughters as a bride for his king. Pharaoh always refused but had the kindness to do it in this chamber, to spare the envoy and his king public humiliation.

I didn't have time to take in my surroundings before Pharaoh spoke to me from the gilded chair in the center of the room. "There you are, my dear Nefertiti. I'm always so happy to see your lovely face. Please"—a rasping cough echoed from the walls—"please come nearer, child. It's been too long since I've enjoyed your company."

I approached Pharaoh with reverence and bowed low,

my hands outstretched to honor the living god. "It's my joy to be here," I said, thankful that our family ties excused me from having to cover him with praise and blessings before actually *talking* to him. "How may I serve you?"

I heard him chuckle, then cough again. "First, by looking at me so that I *can* delight in your beauty."

I did as he asked. A wedge of sunlight bathed the floor between us, but Pharaoh's chair remained in shadow. My eyes had to adjust between the contrasting light and darkness in the room, but when they did, I saw that he and I were the only ones there. *What does it mean?* I thought, trying to stay calm.

"You can come closer than that, can't you?" he said. "I should have ordered the slaves to bring some lamps, but I'm so tired of lamplight. Do you know, as long as you've been with us, I haven't seen your face by daylight more than a handful of times? And I haven't been able to speak more than a few words to you. That saddens me more than you can ever know. I've asked you to come see me because I've finally got the time to correct that." He patted the arm of his chair. "Please."

I crossed the room until I stood with my feet no more than a hand's breadth from his. His smile was a wide, pale gleam in the semidarkness. "You do look like her," he said.

I could guess who he meant. "My mother . . ."

"She was even lovelier than you, Nefertiti. I hope you don't mind my saying that."

I shook my head. "I'm glad to hear it."

"Then you are an exceptional female. My dear Tiye flies into a tantrum if I say one word about another woman's beauty. Sometimes I think that she encouraged your parents to wed so that *I* couldn't marry your mother." He smiled. "The gods must have guided her plans, because if I had made your mother my bride, I wouldn't be seeing *this* exquisite face before me now." He stretched out one hand to cup my chin. His touch was oddly cold and damp. With my eyes now used to the shadows, I could see that his face was no longer full and gleaming with health but dull and haggard.

"My—my lord Pharaoh," I began.

"Sweet girl, you're a princess now, my kin even before you marry my son. You can call me Father. In fact, I insist on it."

"Father . . ." It didn't feel natural, speaking to a living god so familiarly, but I couldn't disobey. "Father, are you—are you well?"

He laughed softly into his fist, though there might have been a fresh cough hidden in the laughter. "Your mother was also very smart; nothing escaped her. Tiye needn't have worried about my marrying that one, no matter how beautiful she was. *One* wife who sees everything is plenty for any man. Tell me, Nefertiti, does your father's second wife have hawk's eyes, too?"

And so my question went unanswered as Pharaoh filled our time together with pleasant, meaningless conversation. My worries about his reasons for wanting to see me drifted away like mist, but a fresh ember of doubt settled in my belly and began to burn: *What is the matter with him?*

At one point, he wanted us to share cakes and wine. He clapped to summon a servant, but his hands shook and made such a weak sound that he looked ashamed. I couldn't bear to see him so dejected, so I raised my voice and called out: "Isis have mercy, Father, how many times do you have to clap before those lazy servants wake up and do their jobs?" Two men charged into the room so fast that they nearly fell all over one another. Pharaoh gave me a grateful look; I'd rescued his pride.

When it was time for me to go, the same well-dressed official who'd brought me into Pharaoh's presence came to escort me back to the women's quarters. Since Pharaoh hadn't called for him, I assumed that the length of my visit had been decided in advance. I was glad that it had gone well and that Amenophis's father and I got along when we could be ourselves. How awkward to be trapped for that long with a man whose company was an ordeal!

On the other hand, it would have been good practice for being married to Thutmose, I told myself grimly as I left the private audience chamber. *I can't go through with it. I have to find a way to get my freedom back, a way that won't let Aunt Tiye retaliate.*

The weeks passed and the season of the Inundation came, bringing great rejoicing. Pharaoh Amenhotep appeared before the people, performing all of his ceremonial duties with a firm step and steady hands. I stood with the rest of the royal family and watched, amazed to see him in such robust health. The vigorous king I saw offering gold and incense to the god Hapy made me wonder if the ailing man I'd visited had been part of a dream.

Maybe he really is *a god on earth,* I thought. I admit that I'd never truly believed that about Pharaoh. I felt guilty for my doubts, and I never dared to mention them to anyone. They came to me when I saw how wan and wasted Pharaoh looked. Gods were supposed to be powerful, greater than we mortals could ever hope to be or even to imagine, and yet . . .

And yet when I'd looked into Pharaoh's face, I'd seen nothing but a badly weakened, ailing man.

That year, the sacred river rose to the perfect level—deep enough to enrich the farthest fields but not so deep that Hapy's waters could wash away the people's homes. It was an unmistakable sign that Pharaoh Amenhotep continued to enjoy the favor of the gods. The Pharaoh and his land were bonded in ways that ordinary people could never hope to understand. (So we were told many, many times.) Pharaoh's health was the same as the health of the Black Land, and the other way around, so nearly all of the Theban priesthoods lifted their voices in hymns of praise for Pharaoh's strength and songs of thanksgiving for his influence with the gods.

Only the priests of Amun kept all of their praises for the god they served, parading images of Amun through the streets daily. Nava, Sitamun, and I liked to watch their processions from one of the palace rooftops. More than once we recognized Thutmose in their midst.

"Why is he with them?" I asked.

Sitamun shrugged. "He told Father that he had a dream where Amun personally demanded that he serve him as faithfully and frequently as he could. Father wasn't happy.

He's been trying his best to curb the priests' sway over his kingdom, and now they've got his oldest son under their influence."

Or the other way around, I thought, remembering what Thutmose had told me about making the powerful Amun priests his allies.

"Anyway, whether Father likes it or not, he can't interfere. It's impossible to argue with the commands of a god."

Even where you're supposed to be a god yourself? I wondered.

The Inundation celebration in Thebes went on for many more days than they had in Akhmin. Pharaoh made an appearance as part of both the solemn rituals and the merry festivities every day, in addition to entertaining his most highly placed nobles and important foreign guests each night. From my place with the other princesses, I saw how intently Aunt Tiye watched his every move. None of the guests would have been able to tell how nervous she was, but I was close enough to see it and to sense the tension leaping through her whole body if a piece of bread slipped form Pharaoh's hand, if his wine goblet trembled, or if his laugh seemed to end with an unusually hoarse sound.

Aunt Tiye wasn't the only one of Pharaoh's wives who attended the Inundation banquets. He often invited a selection of his junior wives who were of royal birth, and sometimes even a few who weren't but whose beauty blazed like the sun. Aunt Tiye's face showed no emotion throughout those dinners, but her eyes reminded me of a dagger's edge, glittering in the dark.

One night, after the last feast to welcome the new

season, I was walking by myself back through the women's quarters when my sandal broke. I kicked it off and tried to slip my foot out of the other one, but my gown got in the way. It was a gift from Aunt Tiye, sent to me just that morning with a "suggestion" to wear it to the banquet. It turned out to be a poor fit, much too big, and the excess fabric tangled around my legs. I stumbled off to lean against a wall so that I could use both hands to remove my second sandal, and I left my little clay lamp on the floor next to my broken one, to make sure I didn't accidentally set that accursed gown—and me!—on fire. Just as I pulled the unbroken sandal from my foot, a wayward breeze whisked past and blew out the lamp. I was left hugging the wall in the dark.

Well, this *will teach me to have a servant escort me back to my rooms,* I thought sourly. *Now what? Do I blunder home in the dark?* I looked to the sky. It was a moonless night and thin clouds blurred the stars. *If I keep one hand on the wall, I can probably feel my way back without falling into one of the garden pools. Oh, it would be so much easier if I could get another lamp! I don't see any lights burning nearby, but maybe someone is still awake in the next courtyard.* I edged slowly along the wall, looking for a speck of light, a sign of life.

I heard the two women's voices before I saw the light of a lamp shining behind a mat-hung doorway. One sounded familiar but only vaguely so. The other was strange to me. I moved toward the glow, about to announce my presence, when the indistinct murmur of their voices suddenly sharpened into words that turned me to stone where I stood.

"—how can you guarantee that my son will be crowned once Pharaoh's dead?" That was the voice I didn't know, shrill and nervous. "I hear that Prince Thutmose is protected by the priests of Amun, and as for that mother of his . . . ! Ugh. She frightens me."

"You jump when you see a mouse." The voice I half-recognized was soft, caressing, and heavy with contempt. "I haven't been wasting my time. I've made . . . a *friend* who'll help us, a powerful nobleman whose wealth and connections can buy us more than enough armed men to defend your son's claim if the queen or any of her pups try to make trouble. The priests of Amun are no fools. They flock to the strongest player in this game."

"Well . . ." The first voice sounded uncertain. "And you're *positive* you can get Pharaoh to name my boy crown prince instead of Thutmose?"

I heard a gusty sigh of exasperation, and then: "You wouldn't question me if you could have seen the way the old man was looking at me tonight. He's been my captive since the day I became his bride, and I won't be asking him for anything alarming."

Now I did recognize that voice. It belonged to one of the junior wives who'd been present at tonight's banquet. The sound of her throaty laugh attracted my attention. I saw her chatting with one of the foreign ambassadors and remembered thinking, *She's so beautiful, she'd make Hathor envious.*

The plans I overheard, standing suspended in silence just outside that doorway, would have made the evil god Set envious, too. I listened for what felt like hours, until I heard a rustle of linen and the voice of the beauty saying, "I'd better work fast. He's getting sick again. If he dares to die before I've arranged things for your son, I might as well jump in the river, but once everything's in place, I'll be happy to push the old man into his tomb myself!" She yawned. "Good night."

I moved as quietly as I could, creeping along the wall, then scrambling to hide myself behind a clump of shrubs. From there I saw her push back a door curtain and emerge, lamp in hand, before heading briskly for her own rooms.

As soon as she was out of sight, I moved as fast as I could in the dark until I stumbled back into a part of the palace where lights still burned for the servants who were carrying away the last traces of the feast.

I grabbed one man's arm as he tramped past with an armful of chair cushions. "Take me to Queen Tiye's apartments at once!"

"The Great Royal Wife has retired for the night," he replied, looking at me in bewilderment. I realized what I must look like—my new gown filthy and my hair in disarray from my time crouched behind that shrub, but my body decked out with a fortune of gold ornaments. No wonder the poor man was confused.

"I am Princess Nefertiti, Queen Tiye's niece," I said. "I have news for her that can't wait until morning."

"My lady, I beg you to excuse me," he pleaded. "You are not aware of the penalty for disturbing the Great Royal Wife at this hour."

"And what's the penalty for wishing that Pharaoh were dead?"

✦ ✦ ✦

The royal palace was in an uproar, feet pounding back and forth through the halls, raised voices bellowing commands, the sound of shrieks and weeping coming from the women's quarters. Through it all, I sat in the center of a tiny spot of calm in my aunt's bedchamber, still in my stained, disheveled dress, my hair in tangles, my body smelling of garden soil, sweat, and the fast-souring remains of the perfumed oil I'd worn for that fateful banquet. I was worn out, desperate for a bath and a soft bed. *Why won't she let me go?* I thought. *I warned her of the danger, I protected our family! Is* this *how she repays me?* My heart thudded wildly at each new tumult from outside.

What have I done? I thought. *What have I done?*

I was not alone. As soon as I'd told Aunt Tiye about the conversation I'd overheard that night, her first act was to summon all of her children to her side. Sitamun and her sisters could have spared themselves the trouble of coming; their mother had nothing to say to them once they arrived except, "There's a plot against us. Stay here." It was only when Thutmose and Amenophis arrived that she bothered to speak of the details, and then only to her elder son.

"Two of your father's junior wives have conspired to rob you of your inheritance. One of them is an ugly sow from Ugarit, sent here twelve years ago as tribute. The gods alone know why your father didn't just send her away to one of the rural places that house his surplus women. There are plenty of those scattered everywhere in this land, for his pleasure when he travels. I suppose it's because she's a *princess.*" Aunt Tiye's tongue dripped scorn. "Anyway, the sow gave birth to a piglet right away—no threat to you until now. *Now* there's a new gift from Ugarit under my roof, an ambitious little hyena who can't give Pharaoh a son herself, so she's joined forces with the sow. The hyena was going to convince your father that having two sons in line for his crown wasn't enough. She'd persuade him to make a third crown prince out of the worthless piglet, and once that was accomplished . . ."

"Kill me?" Thutmose's eyes were aflame, but his face was the color of ashes. Sitamun's sisters gasped and mumbled prayers to avert evil.

"Or find a way to turn your father against you, to have you falsely accused of some crime, to have you exiled, and to do worse than that if nothing else worked. She thought she could. She believed she had the power to make him turn a piglet into a crown prince. And once the piglet had his crown, his mother would have to be regent but *she* would hold the real power. She'd even formed an alliance with one of your father's most trusted and influential men, to guarantee there'd be swords to back up her scheme. Oh, the arrogance!"

"Did . . . did they plan to kill me as well?" Amenophis faltered.

"Why would they bother?" his brother snapped. "The idea of ruling the Black Land must leave you terrified. A child could push you aside. Haven't you always told me that you don't *want* the throne?"

"I only said I don't want *your* throne," Amenophis muttered.

"What?" Thutmose stared at his brother like a hunting hound suddenly seeing an unexpected lion.

"Ignore him, Thutmose. This is no time for your bickering," Aunt Tiye decreed, grabbing both of her sons by the wrist. "We are in *danger*. Do you understand that?"

"I—I—I don't," Amenophis admitted. "Their plans were discovered. Nefertiti warned us—" He gestured to where I sat all bent over on a low stool, hugging my knees and wishing I could block my ears against the sounds of chaos outside.

"Nefertiti is to *blame* for this!" Aunt Tiye cried. Sitamun's sisters broke into shocked murmurings.

My head shot up. *"What did you say?"* I spoke so loudly that I silenced the whispering princesses.

"You can't deny it," Aunt Tiye said, her voice even colder than Thutmose's. "Your selfishness has put us all at risk. If your father hadn't spoiled you so badly, you would be a *proper* girl, listen to those who are wiser than you, and do what you're told. Ah, but I'm not guiltless. I let my affection for my brother blind me. I thought there was no harm in taking the oath that gave you three years' time to get over your silly reluctance to marry my son. I was so wrong, and now my son came far too close to paying the price for *your* stubbornness. If you'd married Thutmose at once, the gods would have blessed us with a son by now and my boy's path to the throne would be secure!"

"You don't know that," I said. "If that woman could turn Pharaoh against Thutmose, why couldn't she turn him against any child Thutmose might have as well?"

"Whose side are you on, you ungrateful girl?" My aunt was no longer willing to hear reason. Her suspicions of plots and conspiracies had just been proved right, and she was even more frightened than before. "Once this affair is settled, you *will* marry my son!"

"Aunt Tiye, you took a public oath," I reminded her, speaking in a soothing voice. We didn't need a shouting match. "You swore before Amun to give me these three years—two, now. I'm not ready to become Thutmose's wife."

"*Get* ready." Once again, my aunt's eyes were dagger blades. "Two years is too long for us to wait. My husband isn't—isn't well." Her expression softened to one of true regret and worry. She did love him, and not merely because he'd given her a crown. Her lapse lasted only a moment. "The women's quarters is a nest of vipers' eggs. More can hatch in two years' time. I won't wait to see it. You'll be my son's bride before the next season of the Inundation. It's settled."

I opened my mouth to protest, but she cut me off: "I know how attached you are to that little slave girl who came with you from Akhmin. I made it my *business* to know. If simple loyalty to your family means nothing to you, maybe you'll act more sensibly for *her* sake."

I surged to my feet. "You can't touch her," I said.

"Because she's *your* slave?" Aunt Tiye looked as if she pitied me. "One word in Pharaoh's ear and she's mine. My husband still loves me, even if he wastes his time and strength with those others." Her mouth twisted in disgust.

"When morning comes, he'll awake to the news of how those two from Ugarit intended to deceive and manipulate him. He'll also learn how well I dealt with the matter, saving him the trouble. He'll be so pleased that he'll give me anything I ask for, and if all I want is one insignificant slave child . . ."

"Nava isn't a slave!" I shouted. I couldn't help it; I couldn't hold back anymore. "I gave her her freedom months ago. Henenu the scribe and your own daughter Sitamun witnessed the document, and Henenu himself carried a copy of it to the shrine of Ma'at, for safekeeping."

"They *would* help you." Aunt Tiye shot a bitter look at her eldest daughter. Sitamun met it calmly. "Whispers run through these halls like mice. You wouldn't believe what people notice. When I first came here as a young bride, I decided to harness those mice to serve me. Every servant under this roof knows he'll be handsomely rewarded for any information I find interesting. It's a shame they can only fetch me scraps of knowledge. Why *does* Henenu meet so often with you and my Sitamun and that Habiru child? Many servants have seen you all climbing to one particular rooftop, day after day, but unfortunately none of them could find any excuse for going after you to learn more."

"If I tell you, you should reward *me*," I said. "For that, and because I was the one who told you about the Ugarit women's plot, not your 'mice.' You owe me a debt, Aunt Tiye: Repay it. Let Nava and me go home."

Aunt Tiye's smile could be more unsettling than her scowl. "But, Nefertiti, you *are* home," she drawled. "Your future is here, on the throne of the Black Land as the next Pharaoh's Great Royal Wife." She grew thoughtful. Seeing the sly look that crept into her eyes made the short hair at the nape of my neck prickle with apprehension. "A common scribe, alone in secret with *two* royal princesses, and no one knows the reason why? That can't be appropriate. He should be questioned. Thutmose, my son, since your promised bride is one of them, can I trust you to do whatever it will take to get the *truth* from Henenu?"

Thutmose's smile was every bit as unnerving as his mother's. "Gladly. You're right as always, Mother: No man but me should spend time alone with my beloved Nefertiti." He gave his brother a hard look. "The scribe will be questioned and punished. I'll have the guards secure him at once." With that, he started for the door.

"You can't be serious!" Sitamun exclaimed, running to block his way. "There was nothing improper about our meetings with Henenu. He was helping us learn how to improve our scribal skills, that's all. I swear it by Ma'at!"

"And so do I!" I cried. I no longer cared if Aunt Tiye found out that I knew how to read and write. Henenu's future was in the balance. Next to that, it didn't matter if she tried to force me to take my mother's place as her new Seshat.

"Sitamun, stand aside!" Aunt Tiye commanded. "Would you throw your own family to the crocodiles? We must take every precaution to defend the security of our royal house. Even a *hint* of scandal could become a weapon for our enemies." She turned toward me. "Even if you swore a thousand oaths, the scribe must be questioned, and the slave—the *freed* slave girl, too." Her eyes never left my face.

The noises from outside the royal apartments had subsided; dawnlight was seeping in through the high, narrow windows. I was weary of Aunt Tiye's game-playing, wholly drained by the events of the night, too worn-out to fight anymore. And how *could* I fight when she'd just shown me she held Nava in the palm of her hand?

All I wanted was peace.

"Will you swear a new oath, Aunt Tiye?" I asked softly. "You know as well as I that Nava and Henenu are blameless. Will you promise to leave them alone if I—if I give you what you want? Promise that, and I swear that before another month passes, Thutmose and I will be—"

"*No!*" The word resounded through the queen's chamber with the might of a lion's roar. "Don't do it, Nefertiti. Marry my brother when *you* want, not an instant sooner!" Amenophis strode across the room on those gawky, comical legs to stand beside Sitamun, barring Thutmose's path, facing his mother's fury. "I won't let you twist her arm like this, Mother. If you complain to Father that Henenu's done something wrong, I'll go to him myself and testify that the scribe is innocent."

"You'd lie for this girl?" There was a dangerous note in Aunt Tiye's voice. "The gods will condemn you for that. Ammut the Devourer will have your heart if you defy me."

"Then let her! You're always talking about how important it is for us to stay *loyal* to our family, to *protect* our family, to work for what's *best* for our family. Are you forgetting that Nefertiti's part of our family, even if she never marries Thutmose? Yet you're willing to bully her into something she doesn't wa—isn't ready for, and you don't care if you destroy innocent people to do it."

271

"You stupid *child*," Aunt Tiye spat. "Apologize to me at once!"

Amenophis folded his arms and said nothing.

"You heard Mother!" Thutmose grabbed his brother, spun him around, and knocked him to the floor with a backhanded blow. "You need more than one lesson in manners. Get up. Get up, if you're a man."

"But I'm not. Didn't you hear what Mother said?" Amenophis's fleshy lips parted in a provoking smile. He clambered back to his feet, blood trickling from his nose, and told his brother: "I'm a child. If you want me to fight you so that you've got an excuse to beat me, you'll be waiting a long time. You'll just have to do it with no excuse at all."

Thutmose let out a hoarse bellow and struck him again. This time Amenophis staggered but didn't fall. Thutmose was about to throw himself on his brother when Aunt Tiye stepped between them.

"Are you my son or are you Set the Destroyer? Let your brother be." She surveyed the room. Sitamun looked ready to fight the next person who said a cross word to her. Her sisters, on the other hand, had withdrawn into a corner and were chattering in undertones among themselves, their eyes darting from Amenophis to Thutmose to their mother. As dearly as I wanted to collapse from carrying the weight of my bones, I forced myself to stand tall when she looked at me.

The queen sighed. "This isn't what I wanted. Go, all of you. No one will be questioned. Nefertiti, it's true that I owe you my thanks for having told me about those creatures and their plot. It was pure luck that you discovered it, but luck is a precious gift. The gods must love you and I . . . I must respect that. My oath before Amun still stands, but hear me: Your part of it does as well. Two more years, girl. Less, if you get the sense to wake up and recognize your opportunity. Now go."

We all did as she commanded, most of us looking thankful to be making our escape. Thutmose stamped off down the hall without a backward look, cursing as he went. Sitamun's sisters scurried away in the opposite direction like a spooked covey of quail. Sitamun, Amenophis, and I didn't say a word to one another, yet somehow we agreed to walk away together until we found ourselves back on the humble rooftop where Henenu had his unofficial classroom. The sun was a thin slice of gold on the horizon.

"I wonder what will happen to them," I said very quietly, sitting in my usual spot. The rooftop was still cool from the night's chill.

"Who?" Sitamun asked.

"The Ugarit women. The nobleman who was going to help the pretty one. The other one's child."

"Father's going to laugh about the whole business and give each of them a handful of gold and a vineyard or two in the country. What do you *think* will happen to them, you straw-head?" Sitamun snapped.

I knew she spoke so sharply only because she was as tired as I was and her nerves were frayed, but her harshness still hurt. Tears spilled down my cheeks. "They'll all be put to death, won't they? Even the boy?"

"Not the boy." Amenophis squatted next to me, looking like a gigantic grasshopper. "He's still Father's son, no matter what his mother's done. There's even a chance that Father will show mercy to those women, exile and imprisonment instead of death. The man, though—his treachery to Pharaoh can't be forgiven; his punishment can't be lessened."

I covered my eyes with one hand. "I wish I'd never overheard that conversation. I mean—I wish I'd never told Aunt Tiye about it. I should have gone directly to Pharaoh, or the vizier, or—or *anyone* else. But I thought that if I told Aunt Tiye first, she'd be so indebted to me that she'd let me go home. Instead—" I raised my head and looked at the fresh marks on Amenophis's good-natured, homely face. "I'm sorry you were hurt again because of me."

He laughed. "I was hurt because my brother's got the temper of a wild jackass."

"That's being kind about it," Sitamun said with a smirk. Her good humor was returning.

"And you, Amenophis," I said, brushing away my tears and smiling again. "You surprised me. You were so brave! You stood up to Aunt Tiye for me, you saved Henenu, you protected Nava, you—"

"If I were brave, I wouldn't have stayed away from you for so long. If I challenged Mother, it's not because I'm brave. I just—I just didn't want you to be unhappy,

Nefertiti," he said, standing up and turning his face to the sun. "Because we're—we're . . . friends."

Had I imagined it, or had his voice stumbled painfully over that final word? I had no chance to know. With his next breath he was halfway down the stairs from the rooftop and gone.

❈ 14 ❈

WALKING ON FEATHERS

In the aftermath of the great plot, the women's quarters became much quieter. Now Pharaoh's other wives eyed me with respect and a little fear whenever we met. A few stared at me with hostility, but only when they thought I couldn't see. One evening I found a dead frog in my bed. I got rid of it before Kepi or the other maids could see it. I didn't need more whispers trailing after me.

My worst fear was that since that night, Aunt Tiye knew about my ability to read and write. I recalled Father's fears that his sister would try to force me into the same role as my mother. Worse, it would be yet another reason for her to keep me in the palace. (Sometimes I really was foolish enough to imagine that she might have a change of heart and let me go home.)

I needn't have worried. About two weeks after the night of the failed plot, Pharaoh became ill again. It was very serious—so serious that not a single hint about his health was allowed to slip out of the royal apartments into the rest of the palace. No one waited on him except slaves, who had more to lose than servants, much more easily, if they talked about anything they'd seen.

Aunt Tiye vanished from the palace halls, except when some keen-eyed servant or official spied her rushing from her husband's apartments to the small audience chamber and back again. Sitamun came to our lessons looking sad and worried.

"I never thought I'd say this, but—poor Mother! When she's not at Father's bedside, scolding his doctors, priests, and magicians, she's working with the vizier and the rest of the royal advisers, receiving ambassadors, hearing pleas, keeping in touch with the local governors. I don't know when she finds the time to eat or sleep."

"Is there anything I can do to help her?" I asked. In spite of what she'd put me through, she was still my aunt, and I knew she loved her husband sincerely. My heart went out to her. "She'll wear herself out and then she'll be sick, too."

Sitamun shook her head. "You might as well ask a lioness if she wants help raising her cubs. All that we can do is wait."

That afternoon, Nava came to me with a piece of broken pottery in her hand. I thought she was bringing me her latest writing lesson, seeking help with a difficult symbol or idea. I did think it was odd that she had it on a shard instead of on the waxed board she normally used. Then she handed it to me, and I gasped to read:

Greetings to you, Nefertiti, from Amenophis, who is forever your friend.

I wish we could meet. No one would notice. My mother's eyes are elsewhere. My brother is always busy, either with her, or with Father, or at the temple of Amun, may the god send his healing to Pharaoh soon. I am so afraid. If we could meet and speak, your kind words would comfort me. May the gods bless you.

I crushed the shard into powder and told Nava to fetch me her practice tablet. "Will you carry my message back to him, Nava? Please?" I asked as I scratched the words into the yielding wax. The child nodded eagerly. "You'll have to be very careful. No one else must see this. Do what you can to make sure no one sees *you*." I handed her the finished letter and watched as she ran to deliver it.

She returned with his reply scrawled across the tablet: *Noon. The stables. I have shown Nava the way. Let her lead you.* When the sun was directly overhead and the palace sank into midday rest, Nava brought me there.

Amenophis was waiting. He was familiar with the stables, going there every day to visit his horses, harnessing them to his chariot for a good gallop and practice with his hunting bow. He knew which parts of the building were the busiest and which were unused. From the look of the healthy spiderwebs in the empty stalls, he'd chosen a section of the stables that hadn't been occupied for a very long time.

We spoke in whispers. Mostly I listened while he poured out his troubled thoughts. He loved his father and he was as terrified as a little child of losing him.

"Don't despair," I told him. "Pharaoh—your father is a strong man. He'll recover."

"I pray you're right," Amenophis said. "I pray to all the gods who have the power of healing, but I don't see any change."

"I pray for him, too," I said. "But I only pray to Isis."

"That might not be enough. You should also call upon Amun, Thoth, Imhotep, Anubis, even Sekhmet!" Even though he was so concerned about his father, he was still able to spare a warm smile for Nava and say: "Maybe our little messenger worships gods of healing that we don't know. Well, Nava? Will you add your prayers and your gods to ours, to help my father?"

Nava shook her head.

"Nava!" I was shocked by her response. "Why won't you help Amenophis's father?"

Again, Nava shook her head, then wrote something on her tablet and showed it to us: *One.*

"One?" Amenophis repeated. "You have just one god of healing? But that's all right, he—or she—might be powerful enough to help."

The child shook her head a third time and jabbed her sharpened reed forcefully at the lone word she'd written. She looked ready to burst with annoyance. What was wrong? Then I remembered the first time she'd used her writing to thank me, to say she loved me, and to tell me her true name. What else was it that she'd written?

May the One bless you always.

"This isn't just your god of healing, is it?" I said, cradling the child's cheek in my palm. "This is your only god." My words worked magic. Nava's frown vanished. Radiant with joy, she dropped her tablet and flung her arms around me. When she looked up at me, her lips moved as if she were trying to speak, but all that emerged were the same rough, uncertain sounds I'd overheard when I'd left her alone with Thutmose's cat.

And then, so very hard to hear that it sounded like the voice of a ghost, Nava whispered: "Yes."

Did I hear that? Did she really speak or do I want her to speak so badly that I'm hearing things that aren't there? I couldn't let it go; I had to know. "Yes, Nava, *yes!*" I cried. "Please, don't be afraid, talk to me!"

Oh, what a fool! I wanted to encourage her; I only scared her back into silence. Her small hand flew to seal her lips and her eyes widened in horror, as if she'd caught herself committing a crime. She whirled about, stooped to grab her tablet, and flew out of the stables. I let out a moan of disappointment.

Amenophis patted my shoulder. "I heard it, too," he said.

"You did?" How could something so small have the power to make me so happy?

"Yes. She will speak again, Nefertiti. You—we have to believe it. But she'll only do it when she's ready, not when you or I want her to do it."

"If only I hadn't talked to her just then . . ." I shook my head over my own rashness. "How stupid."

"Stupid? You? Never. You're impetuous," he said.

"It's been over a year since she lost her voice. Sometimes I lose hope that she'll ever recover it."

"And I—I wonder if Father will ever be well again."

I smiled at him. "You and I will just have to learn to wait for what we want most, Amenophis."

"And pray." He gazed after Nava and grew thoughtful.

We didn't spend much longer together. We didn't dare risk discovery. Before we parted, we agreed that it would be wisest never to meet in the same place twice in a row.

"I know the palace better than you," he said. "I'll send word when I've found a spot that's out of my brother's sight and not too overrun with other people."

"Or it *could* be overrun," I suggested. "No one can blame us for speaking if we happen to meet in the middle of a crowd."

"Ha! That's good. See, I *told* you you're smart!" Those few kind words of his pleased me more profoundly than all of the empty praises and flattery I'd heard since coming to Thebes.

And so the game began, the challenge of finding enough times and places for Amenophis and me to speak with one another without attracting notice. Nava's practice tablet had to be recoated at least twice because we wore away the layer of wax with our messages. Our meetings were brief, and I did miss the times we'd been able to ride freely through Thebes, but I didn't dwell on what was now beyond my reach. It was enough to know that we *could* have them, and that no one could destroy our friendship.

Someday I will be free again, I thought. *May Isis help me, I will find a way. And when that day comes, Amenophis, you and I won't just return to the temples of Karnak, we'll travel everywhere!*

Almost a month passed and Amenophis sent Nava to me with word that he had great news. *Come to the stables again, the place and time you know. It will be safe.* Nava and I got there before he did and were amusing ourselves by trying to play catch with wayward wisps of straw when he came bursting in. He was so happy that he looked ready to sprout wings and fly.

"He's better!" Amenophis cried, his joy making him forget the need to keep our voices down. "Father is *much* better. He made such an improvement overnight that when I left his rooms, the magicians and the doctors were still fighting each other, trying to claim the credit for it. If you ask me, it was all Mother's doing. Father told me that she made it very clear to him that if he died, she'd follow him to the Afterlife and make him miserable for all eternity."

"She *bullied* him back to health?" Knowing Aunt Tiye, I wasn't surprised.

We spent the remainder of our time rejoicing over his father's improving health and talking about what sort of thanksgiving offerings we should make to the gods. Neither one of us thought about what Pharaoh's recovery might mean to our little game.

Within a week, Amenophis's father was holding court and looking after the business of ruling the Black Land. Formal receptions and banquets for important visitors resumed, though the evening's festivities ended much earlier than before. Pharaoh Amenhotep was well but not the man he'd been. His broad face showed more lines, his cheeks sagged, and his skin had lost its healthy glow.

As the season of the Inundation waned, ambassadors

came to Thebes. They brought tribute from one of the many petty kings who ruled the land of Canaan. Sitamun told Nava and me about the audience that was planned to receive them.

"It's going to be splendid, of course—Father always says that the more impressive you make yourself look to your neighbors, the more likely they'll be to think twice before picking a fight with you. But I'm afraid it's not going to be everything he wants it to be. Mother is doing all she can to cut the ceremonies short. She's watching Father so closely these days, afraid that he's going to overexert himself and get sick again! Oh well, I'm sure that however much she shortens the event, it will still be the most remarkable sight those Canaanites ever saw."

When Sitamun said *Canaanites,* Nava pricked up her ears, then began scribbling madly on her tablet. When she was done, she urged us to read it: *My people are Habiru. We come from Canaan. My sister told me so. I want to see my people.*

Sitamun didn't understand why Nava would make such a request. "These Canaanites aren't *your* people, Nava. I think they might be Amorites or something, not Habiru." But Nava insisted, tapping the last sentence on her tablet repeatedly, her eyes pleading.

We decided to give her what she wanted. What harm would it do? As royal princesses, Sitamun and I were free to attend the ambassadors' reception with as many personal attendants as we liked. That was how I happened to be present when Pharaoh made the announcement that this would be the last court event for some time to come.

I'd heard him address the assembled nobles, priests,

and petitioners before. I knew he would speak to them in the affected, artificial style that tradition demanded on such occasions. When he spoke so pompously it always made me want to giggle, because Pharaoh himself was one the most down-to-earth people I knew. Since it would never do for a princess to giggle when Pharaoh spoke, I prepared myself to keep a straight face.

I couldn't prepare myself for what I heard him say: "It is my will to travel to Dendera, to the holy temple of Hathor, the Golden One, the Lady of Life and Beauty, there to worship the goddess for the blessings I have accepted from her. It is likewise my will to depart tomorrow, accompanied by my beloved Great Royal Wife, Queen Tiye. Because of the love I have for him, my son the crown prince Thutmose will be my eyes, my ears, my hands, and my mouth here in Thebes until I return. When he speaks, hear my voice! So will it be."

I smothered a gasp. *Thutmose to reign here, in Pharaoh's place? O Isis, no!* I stole a glance at the crown prince, who was ascending the steps of the throne to stand beside his father. He was grinning like a crocodile.

Pharaoh Amenhotep and my aunt Tiye departed for Dendera the following morning. The royal ship that would take them there was twice as sumptuous as the one that had carried me to Thebes. Even the oars were gilded, and the cabin in the shadow of the towering mast was a finer shelter than many common people's houses. I stood under a blue and gold striped canopy on the dock, watching as the helmsman turned the ship's prow into the current. The painted sail remained furled; the wind wasn't favorable for a downstream journey. Even though the current was on their side, the sailors had to man the oars if they hoped to make any significant progress.

The ship seemed to take an eternity to pass from sight. Thutmose had commanded that all of his sisters, his brother, and I witness Pharaoh's departure. We were ordered to remain standing where we were until the royal ship was truly gone. My legs ached. Sweat trickled down my spine and my mouth became parched. I could hear the priests of Amun chanting prayers for a safe journey, but when I tried to turn my head to see them, a strong hand closed on my shoulder.

"Show respect for your Pharaoh, Nefertiti," Thutmose said, his voice making my skin creep. I tried to edge away from his touch, but his fingers tightened. *"Respect,"* he repeated.

When we were finally permitted to leave, I took off as if a pack of hyenas were after me. I didn't stop running until I was back in my rooms, letting the cool shadows calm me. I was all alone. Nava came and went as she liked. She was growing up and growing bolder. It made me happy to see how much more independent she'd become in only one year's time, but now I was the one who needed somebody to cling to, and I wished she'd been there for me.

"Nefertiti?" I heard Sitamun's voice calling me from the out room. "Nefertiti, are you in here?"

"Back here, Sitamun!" I called. When she joined me, I sat at the edge of Nava's small bed and motioned for her to take a seat on mine. We sat facing each other in silence for some time.

Finally Sitamun took a deep breath and said, "Well, little sister, are you planning to spend the rest of your days hiding away in here?"

"Just until Pharaoh comes back from Dendera," I replied with a smile. "Please remind my servants to shove a plate of food under the bed for me from time to time."

We laughed. Then Sitamun said, "It's time for our writing lesson."

It wasn't. I gave her a quizzical look but didn't question her. There was something about her manner that forbade any argument. I gathered up my scribe's pen case and palette and followed her to our customary rooftop classroom. Nava was already there, bent over her tablet, intently copying words from the papyrus scroll that Henenu held open in front of her. He looked up and smiled when he saw me.

"Greetings, little Seshat. We will begin our lessons soon. While you wait, will you please fix that for us?" He indicated a part of the rooftop where the ropes holding up our shading canopy had come undone. "It's not a good idea to spend too much time under the burning eyes of Ra."

I looked at the half-collapsed canopy. "I don't know if I'm tall enough to reach that."

"Well, I'm certainly not," the little scribe joked.

"Sitamun is taller than—"

"It's no job for Pharaoh's daughter. Try."

More puzzled than before, I went to examine the fallen

canopy. As I lifted one corner of it, a hand darted out of the shadows and clasped mine.

"Ah!" My cry of surprise was answered with an urgent shushing noise from under the folds of cloth. Amenophis huddled against the wall, motioning frantically for me to be quiet. I ducked under the makeshift shelter and crouched beside him. "So *you're* my writing lesson," I said, so very glad to see him.

He wasn't in the mood for humor. "I have something important to say to you, Nefertiti. I—I'm afraid to, but if I don't say it now . . . We can't see or write to each other again until Father and Mother come back. You know that, don't you?"

"I know that Thutmose is going to be worse than ever, now that Pharaoh's left him in charge," I said. "But surely a message or two—it wouldn't have to be in writing. If we asked Sitamun to carry word . . ."

"No. Nothing. We shouldn't even be meeting now, but I don't know how long Father and Mother will be away and I couldn't let there be a long, unexplained silence between us, especially when I—"

"Why must there be *any* silence?" My fierce whisper cut off his words. "Thutmose is frightening, and I'm not looking forward to living under his rule, but I refuse to be afraid of him. He spends so much time with the Amun priests, but he lives as if he's given himself to Set, body and spirit. What is *wrong* with him?"

"What would you do, Nefertiti, if all your life you'd been told that there was only one prize you had to win? And I mean that you *had* to, because if you didn't, you'd be nothing. Less than nothing! How would you feel if every day you were told how wonderful your life was going to be when you finally reached that goal but no one ever asked you if it was what *you* wanted?"

"Oh, I'm pretty sure I know that feeling," I said dryly. "Why do you keep making excuses for him? He's hurt you more than once, and it's obvious that he scorns you. Why do you stand for that? Wait, don't answer." I held up one hand. "You're going to say 'Because he's my brother,' aren't you?"

"No, Nefertiti," Amenophis replied softly. "Because my brother is afraid of me and it breaks my heart. He can't even look at me without believing that my only desire is to take everything away from him. His fear and bitterness and jealousy are a sickness that's eating away at him. When we die, we all must face Ammut, the Devourer of Souls, but Thutmose fights her every day of his life and I—I'm scared he's losing the battle. There's nothing I wouldn't give to see him well again. I want my brother to be my brother, and to love me as I love him."

Amenophis's words touched me deeply. His love and compassion for Thutmose were sincere. *I would feel the same way if it were Bit-Bit who treated me like Thutmose treats him,* I thought. *It* is *a sickness. I couldn't hate her for that.*

I gave Amenophis a quick, strong hug. "All right," I said. "Let's stay apart. We won't do or say anything to feed Thutmose's fears. Because it means so much to you, I promise that I'll do everything I can to reassure him that he has nothing to fear from you. Don't worry, I won't say it *that* way." I smiled. "It *would* be wonderful if the two of us could soothe his mind. And who knows? Maybe there's a different person under all that jealousy, someone I could like enough to marry."

"You would—you would want to marry him?" Amenophis's voice in the shadows was troubled.

"After all I've seen of him, I doubt I could ever *want* to marry him, but since I'll *have* to, someday, I'm going to try to become more like you and hope for the best."

"That's not what I'd call—" The rest was lost. When I asked him to repeat what he'd just said, he was his cheerful self when he replied: "Perhaps you ought to marry Thutmose right away. Once he's certain that no one else can have you, he won't be so touchy about our friendship and we'll be able to see each other freely." He must have seen the look of alarm on my face, despite how dark it was under the tumbled canopy, because he swiftly said, "I'm joking, I'm joking!"

"Sweet Isis, it's a joke I'm sick of," I said. "I've had my fill of people who see me as nothing more than a *marriage* waiting to happen. And what a marriage! Never a single word said about love, only power, and never any power of my own. The high priest of Isis in Akhmin, your mother, your brother, they're all alike, all wanting me to marry so that *they* can get what they desire. I'm tired of being the paddle that the baker uses to pull hot bread out of the oven. When do *I* get to taste the bread? If it were up to me, I'd steal your chariot and drive it so far from here that no one would know me. Then maybe I could *make* something worthwhile of my life, whether I married or not!"

"Nefertiti, your life here is already—" Amenophis began, but his speech was interrupted when the edge of our makeshift refuge was thrown aside. Sitamun stood over us.

"You have to leave, Amenophis," she ordered, face and body taut with anxiety. "You told me that you only wanted to say a few words of farewell to Nefertiti. I wouldn't have arranged this if I knew you'd take *this* long or make so much noise about it." She stared at me meaningfully. "Now go!"

He unfolded his long legs and left without another word. I was still so angry that I wasn't even sorry to see him leave me. With Sitamun's help I reattached the canopy, dropped cross-legged to the floor, and turned my thoughts away from everything except my writing. When Henenu at last called an end to our session, he remarked at how much progress I'd made.

"Let's see if you can be as industrious next time I see you, *without* raising a storm first." He spoke playfully and nodded toward the rehung sunshade. "We thought it was in danger of filling like a sail and blowing away."

I blushed. "I thought I was whispering."

"You whisper loudly, but not loudly enough to carry beyond this rooftop, thank the gods," Sitamun said.

Days passed and I regretted that Amenophis and I had parted so unpleasantly. *If I'm unhappy about my future, I should put my mind to changing it, not complaining about it,* I thought. *I lashed out at the best friend I have.*

I wished there were a way I could let him know how much I regretted my snappishness, but how? We had promised to keep our distance, for Thutmose's sake: no meetings, however secret; no notes, however carefully passed along; not one thing that his ailing mind could pounce on as "proof."

I suppose I could ask Sitamun to tell Amenophis that I'm sorry. Just one whisper and after that, nothing more. She wouldn't even have to bring me back an answer. O Isis, I miss him!

I made my request the next time we shared a lesson with Henenu. Sitamun looked very doubtful, but I coaxed and wheedled until she agreed. "You could wait until my parents return from Dendera," she said primly. "They won't be gone forever, and Amenophis has probably forgotten all about the way you scolded him."

"But I remember it," I said.

"Remember what, Nefertiti?" Thutmose's smiling face popped into sight. He reached the topmost step and joined us on the rooftop. Henenu and Nava fell to their hands and knees. He accepted their display of respect as his due, but when Sitamun and I bowed to him he said, "Please, this isn't the royal court. We're all family here. That's not necessary." He looked so relaxed and spoke so amiably that it was startling.

"Really, brother?" Sitamun arched one brow. "You had a different attitude when we bid farewell to Mother and Father. From the look on your face then, I think you would've ordered your guards to arrest any of us who broke ranks and left before you dismissed us."

"That was days ago, with the priests and nobles watching. They had to see evidence that I was going to be a strong ruler in Father's absence. If I couldn't get them to take me seriously, I'd be betraying the trust Father placed in me by making me regent in his absence." His smile never wavered. "I apologize if I was rough with you, and I intend to atone for it. Tonight we'll have a special dinner, just the family. Will you come?" He was looking at me.

An invitation or a command in disguise? Whichever it was, I wasn't about to test it. I remembered my promise to Amenophis. *Thutmose looks genuinely happy. He has what he's always wanted, even if it's only temporary. If he's found serenity, ruling in his father's place, I'll do all I can to keep him content—*

I recalled the sharp pain of his fingers digging into my arm that day on the dock and the intense, intimidating way he'd demanded "respect."

—but I don't trust him.

15

THE DEVOURER OF SOULS

Thutmose's family dinner lacked nothing. The eight of us shared one of the finest banquets that Pharaoh's cooks could produce. As we entered the room where oil lamps leaped and flickered, Thutmose himself placed flower garlands around our necks and set cones of perfumed wax on top of our heads. As the evening wore on, the wax melted and the room filled with the dizzying scent of blossoms and spices.

Amenophis chose a seat as far from his brother as possible, and equally far from me. That didn't last long. Thutmose was in high spirits, laughing and joking with his sisters. When he noticed where his brother had placed himself, he made a great show of indignation.

"Amenophis, why are you all the way over there? Did I forget to bathe or is it you? Come on, sit here, beside me. We've had our quarrels, but I want tonight to be a gateway to better times." He wouldn't let it go until Amenophis, with much reluctance, took the chair at Thutmose's right side.

Sitamun was seated to her oldest brother's left, and I had the stool next to hers. While Thutmose heaped Amenophis's plate with the best portions from every platter on the table, I was able to whisper to my friend, "Do you believe this?"

Sitamun shrugged and whispered back, "I want to."

As the meal progressed, Thutmose's unusual good humor was contagious. I think that all of his family felt the same way as Sitamun—they *wanted* to believe that their Father's decision to hand over part of his authority to Thutmose—even for a little while—had had a magical effect on their normally cold and distrustful brother. Smiles and laughter were everywhere, all formality and reserve vanished, helped into oblivion by the never-ending streams of wine that poured into our cups.

While we ate and drank, a group of musicians struck up one merry tune after another for our entertainment. Professional dancers leaped, spun, kicked, even did handsprings, their tattooed arms and legs flashing in the lamplight, their belts tinkling. We soon joined the sound of our hands clapping to the crisp beat of the tambourines, the clack of castanets, and the jangle of the sistrums.

At a sign from Thutmose, one of the dancers holding a sistrum adorned with Hathor's face thrust that ankh-shaped rattle into my hands and encouraged me to play along. Others were urging the rest of the royal princesses to accept their instruments, too. The music wrapped itself around us, the rhythm flooded our bodies, the wine made our heads reel. Before I knew it, I was whirling across the floor with Sitamun and her sisters. The dance's captivating spell possessed me and I came within a breath of stripping away my pleated linen gown because it held me back from matching the dancers' most spectacular steps. Because I was the only one who'd chosen not to wear a wig, my hair came undone from the long plait down my back. Joyously I tossed my sistrum to Amenophis, who was closest, reached up, and unbraided my hair completely until it was spinning around me like a cloak. We finished our improvised dance amid cheers and much applause from everyone—Thutmose, Amenophis, the hired dancers, the musicians, even the servants. I returned to my seat flushed and tired but feeling as if I'd just been given a priceless gift from the gods.

A lute player plucked a more languid, dreamy melody as the feast continued. Servants waving huge fans of blue- and red-dyed ostrich plumes stirred sweet breezes through the air. Thutmose leaned toward me in front of Sitamun and offered me a plate of little cakes studded with dates drenched in honey and garnished with a sprinkling of rose petals. As I reached for them, Ta-Miu appeared out of nowhere, leaping onto the table as if she owned it.

"Oh, that cat!" Sitamun exclaimed. Her sisters shrieked with delight to see the elegant animal daintily weaving her way among the golden plates and goblets, sometimes stopping to tap one delicate paw against a precious glass vessel filled with wine until it edged its way toward the rim of the table.

"Stop that," I said with mock severity, seizing the cat

and cradling her to my chest. "You're going to smash something if you're not careful, Ta-Miu." I got a loud, resentful meow for an answer.

"Watch out, Nefertiti!" Sitamun's youngest sister exclaimed, giggling. "Ta-Miu is a sacred animal and she knows it. It's almost the feast of Bast, so you mustn't offend one of the cat-goddess's children or you'll be punished."

"It's true," another of the princesses said eagerly. "Remember when we were all little and they caught that Phoenician merchant trying to smuggle a chest filled with cats out of Thebes? The priests said he'd committed blasphemy and he was *executed.*"

"Cats are *always* sacred, not just during Bast's festival," Thutmose said amiably, taking Ta-Miu from my arms and scratching her sleek brown spotted head in exactly the spot that sent her into ecstasies of purring. "But my Ta-Miu would be special even if the goddess Bast weren't her mother. She's destroyed at least five scorpions that I know of, and countless mice. Her mother killed cobras—just small ones, but still—! It's impossible for a snake to get into the palace, though if one could, no doubt Ta-Miu would prove her own worth as a warrior."

He gave her an additional scratch under the chin and put her down. She promptly jumped back up onto the table and rubbed her head against the glass wine vessel. It wobbled, tottered, and crashed to the floor, splashing my dress. The cat looked around the room with a "who did that?" expression in her huge green eyes. We all laughed.

The only false note amid the joy of Thutmose's party was Amenophis. My friend smiled and laughed, feasted and drank, clapped his hands to the music, and called out compliments to the hired dancers as well as to his sisters and me, but it seemed that there was something hollow in his words and actions.

Perhaps I'm imagining it, I thought. *I've been drinking a lot of wine; I could be seeing things that aren't really there.* But when I took a good, long look at Amenophis, I couldn't deny the touch of sadness I saw in his eyes.

There was nothing I could do about it, no matter how much I wanted to ask him to share his sorrow. Even though Thutmose was behaving like an ordinary young man—one who didn't spend his days seeing conspiracies under every leaf in the gardens and around every corner in the palace— I wasn't going to put him to the test by speaking to his brother right in front of him.

"What are you staring at, my lovely Nefertiti?" Thutmose asked. His question took me off guard, so much so that I realized I hadn't taken my eyes off Amenophis for several long breaths.

"I—nothing," I said.

Thutmose chuckled. "You shouldn't call my brother nothing, Lady Nefertiti. Until I marry and have a son of my own, he's *my* crown prince."

"I didn't mean to stare at him," I protested. Amenophis shifted uneasily in his seat throughout my conversation with his older brother. "My mind was wandering. I must be getting sleepy. I should go back to my rooms."

"Nonsense, the evening has barely begun! Drink a little less, eat a little more, and you'll drop all this silly talk of going to bed. It wouldn't be a party if you left us so soon."

He slipped his arm around my waist. I braced myself for the unpleasant experience of being forcibly propelled back to my seat, but to my surprise, Thutmose gave me only the gentlest touch, a suggestion and not a shove. The expression on his handsome face was gracious and agreeable. I let him help me back to my place, amazed at the change in him.

If he'd been like this when we first met, I might have married him by now, I thought, though it might have been the wine helping me forget that a few hours' kindness was not enough to outweigh his past fits of jealous rage or the bruises he'd left on his brother's face.

"Thank you for consenting to stay with us a while longer, Nefertiti," he said, once more passing me the plate of honeyed date cakes. "I promise that you won't regret it. I have no intention of letting this party last until dawn, though we're all having such a good time that I hate to see it end. But I need my sleep, too. I'm going hunting tomorrow."

"On the river again?" I remembered the last occasion when he'd mentioned a hunting trip to me. It was part of our time of compulsory togetherness, when Aunt Tiye held Thutmose's beloved cat hostage, forcing him to court me. It hadn't been a happy time for either of us.

"Better," he said. "Into the Red Land, where there are lions. I'll be hunting them from my chariot. Shall I bring you a trophy?"

"I'd rather have the chariot ride," I blurted. *Did I just say that out loud? I* was stunned by my own audacity. *Stupid wine. Stupid* me *for drinking so much.* I stuffed a piece of cake into my mouth to cover my embarrassment.

Thutmose put another sweet morsel into my hands and smiled. "Is that true? Then, please, ride with me. I wasn't going to invite you because I thought you might feel compelled to accept. But if it's something you *want* to do . . ." He regarded me hopefully.

I wouldn't lie. "Yes, very much."

"Then we'll go tomorrow morning."

"But you'll miss your lion hunt!" I said. "You shouldn't give it up for me, not if you've been looking forward to it."

His teeth were bright and sharp as the edge of the crescent moon. "There will always be lions to hunt in the Red Land, but how many times have you been so willing to share my company? Rare things must be treasured." I blushed again and ate more cake.

The next morning I woke up feeling ill from having eaten and drunk so greedily the night before. My head throbbed, my stomach was bloated, and I was too queasy to stir from my bed. *I can't ride in a chariot like this!* I thought, and groaned with disappointment.

I called for Kepi and sent her to deliver my regrets to Thutmose. "You must be absolutely certain that he understands I really am sick," I told her. "Swear by the gods, if you must." She acknowledged my request with a low bow and hurried away. When she returned, I didn't even give her the chance to enter my bedroom before showering her with questions: "Did you find him? What did he say? Did he believe you? Was he angry or upset or—?"

"You must judge that for yourself, Lady Nefertiti," she said, crossing the threshold and stepping to one side as Thutmose himself and a stocky old man with a wrinkled monkey's face came in. He was well-dressed, and his neck-lace was adorned with many protective symbols like the Eye of Horus, the ankh, and the scarab. He carried a small clay pot that was giving off a weird odor.

"Nefertiti, this is Ptah-hotep the physician," Thutmose said. "He was one of the healers whose knowledge helped my father. I've brought him in hopes he can cure you so that you won't need to miss our ride."

The old physician strode haughtily to my bedside. "Where is the chief maid?" he demanded. When Kepi bowed before him, he commanded: "You will send one of the other servants to fetch honey. You will bring a large bowl and put it beside the lady's bed." His directions were quickly fulfilled. None of my maids wanted to keep Prince Thutmose waiting. Once he was satisfied with the preparations, he presented me with the little pot. "I was told you have an affliction of the belly, my lady. Drink this, and I swear by the lives of my grandchildren, it will trouble you no more."

I sniffed at the clay pot uncertainly. "What is this?"

"Nothing extraordinary: goose fat, fresh cow's milk, and cumin, boiled together and strained. It is a well-known remedy."

"I think I feel better already," I said, trying to give the vile-looking, hideous-smelling stuff back to him. It was no use. Ptah-Hotep began lecturing me sternly about all of his greatest successes in the healing arts and about the horrible fates of patients who'd been foolish or stubborn enough to refuse his treatments. I gulped down the potion just to silence him. It stayed in my stomach for as long as it took to count to twelve and then I threw up right into the bowl Kepi had brought. Ptah-Hotep nodded, pleased.

"Now a few spoonfuls of honey and you may resume your normal activities," he said. I wanted to argue that I was too drained to do anything, but as soon as Kepi fed me the second dollop of honey, I felt restored. Within the hour I was out of bed, dressed, and accompanying Thutmose to his waiting chariot.

We rode out of the palace and through the streets of Thebes, but we didn't ride alone. Four other chariots galloped with us, each bearing a driver and an armed soldier. The people who saw us coming sprinted to get out of the way of Thutmose's blue and red bronze-trimmed chariot, some of them just barely dodging the flying hooves of his tawny-coated horses. In the wider, more prosperous streets, those who saw us rumble by would raise their hands to the heavens, calling down the gods' blessings on their crown prince, but in places where the streets were only wide enough for one chariot at a time to pass, the folk on foot had to take refuge between vendors' stalls or press themselves flat against the walls of the buildings. Any prayers they uttered were for their own safety. Thutmose took no notice of them as he whipped his horses to go faster and faster until we broke free of the city and were on the same flat plain where Amenophis used to bring me for my lessons with the bow and the chariot.

"Now I'll show you some good horsemanship," he said, and he made the whiplash in his hand crack through the air as it struck the animals' backs. They whinnied shrilly and put on a fresh burst of speed, foam streaming from the corners of their mouths, leaving our accompanying chariots smothered in the dust thrown up by our careening wheels.

"Slow down, please slow down," I gasped, holding on desperately. Speed didn't scare me—I'd braced my feet the way I'd done when Amenophis let me race his chariot—but I knew that these vehicles were clumsy and unreliable at sharp turns. Thutmose paid no attention. He leaned into the wind, entranced, and made the chariot skim and swerve dangerously. His gaze was on the horizon, and he looked as if he were aching for the impossible instant when we would go so fast that all of us—horses and riders together—would sprout hawks' wings and soar into the sun.

I *thought* I'd had that feeling when I'd been the one holding the chariot reins, giving the horses their freedom to race flat out. Now, looking at the spellbound expression on Thutmose's face, I realized that I'd known only the pale ghost of what he was experiencing, body and soul.

He doesn't care how dangerous this is any more than he cared if we trampled innocent people when we were riding through Thebes, I thought, panic rising in me. *He doesn't care how mercilessly he beats the horses, if we crash, if our bones are shattered, even if we die!* "Stop, stop, please *stop,* Thutmose!" I screamed. "For the love of Amun, stop before it's too late!"

Was it wishful thinking or did I sense him tightening his hold on the reins, gradually easing the horses from their heart-straining, headlong rush back down to a more moderate pace? I held my breath as their gallop became a canter, then a trot, and at last—thank the gods!—a walk. While our escorts raced to catch up to us, Thutmose grinned at me like a naughty child who'd done a great mischief and gotten away with it.

"Sweet Isis, what were you thinking?" I cried, trying not to choke on the dust still settling around us.

"I was thinking that you'd enjoy seeing what *real* driving is," he said lightly. "I love it, but it seems that it's too much for you. My apologies, Nefertiti. We won't do that again."

"I wasn't afraid of how fast we were going," I said, on the defensive. "You steered so violently, taking such sharp turns that I thought we were going to flip over."

"But *did* we?" He laughed and handed me the reins. "Why don't you show me the *right* way to drive?"

I looked at him steadily. "You know—?"

"My brother took you riding, showed you the temples, taught you how to use a bow, how to guide a chariot, all of that, yes. You know how riddled with Mother's spies the palace is. I sometimes think that *she* doesn't know how many there are. *You've* even played the spy's part for her, even if it was by accident. Why are you giving me *that* look?" He tucked my loosened hair back behind my ears with an unexpectedly delicate touch. "I'm not insulting you. I'm grateful that you saved us all from the conspiracy of those Ugarit women. But yes, I do know how happily you and Amenophis spent time together. Why do you think I was so very envious of him? You obviously *enjoyed* his company."

"Maybe if you'd given me some sign that you enjoyed

mine, too," I murmured too low for him to hear. I pushed the reins back at him. "I would love to drive these horses, but I can't. Look at them. They're ready to die."

"*Pff!* They're strong enough to survive a little exercise. I'll tell you what: Take them. They're yours, and the chariot too, my gift to you. I'll even see to it that the guards at the palace gate let you come and go as you please, completely on your own"—he paused, looking almost shy—"though I would like it if you'd allow me to go with you at least once, so I can see if my brother's taught you well."

"You rule Thebes," I said softly. "You have the authority to do whatever you want. You don't need to get my permission for anything."

Thutmose didn't react right away. He turned to the four chariots surrounding us and made a slashing gesture. "We don't need you hovering so close. There's no danger here. Move farther off!" He waited until our escorts had put enough distance between themselves and us to give us privacy, then said, "That's not the way it's going to be between us from now on, Nefertiti. When Father proclaimed that he trusted me to rule Thebes in his absence, everything changed. His decision means my place as crown prince is secure. I now stand only one small step away from sharing the rule of all the Black Land with him. He's not well, and a co-regency would ease his burden. Once that's established, who else could possibly be the next Pharaoh but me?"

He held my face tenderly in both of his hands and said: "I don't need to marry you anymore. I give you your freedom." He sealed the promise with a kiss that made my blood sing and my head spin happily, as though I'd drunk unwatered wine.

Of course he apologized afterward. "I'm sorry, I had no right to do that. I couldn't help it. I just wanted to know how it felt to kiss such a beautiful girl, and since I'll never have another chance . . ." He tried to look shamefaced, but his ear-to-ear smile gave away the lie.

My heart was pounding so hard that I could only nod. I couldn't tell if it was the heat of the sun or the blood rushing to my face that made me so uncomfortably hot. *Another chance . . . ,* I thought.

Thutmose leaned forward in the chariot, studying the horses. "They do look done in, don't they? Now that they're yours, I ought to take better care of them or you'll be telling everyone that the crown prince gives second-rate gifts. It might be best if they didn't pull a loaded chariot all the way home." He hailed one of our four escorts. When the driver drew up alongside, Thutmose stepped down from our own chariot and beckoned for me to follow, holding out his arms to catch me. I could have dismounted on my own, but I chose to leap into his waiting embrace, my hands clasping his broad, strong shoulders.

We returned to the palace in the borrowed chariot, leaving its driver and armed guard to walk my new chariot and team back. Thutmose kept the horses to a moderate pace, sometimes even slowing them down when there was no real need for that. As we rode into sight of the city, he asked me if I was feeling well.

"That's a funny question," I said.

"Not really. You were sick this morning, and I gave you

a bone-shaking ride. You should see yourself. You're covered with dust, your gown is torn, your hair is flying in all directions, and your face is one big smudge." He was joking.

"You're no wall painting yourself," I said, tossing the jest right back at him. "I was sick to my stomach this morning but I'm fine now. No matter how bad I look on the outside, it has nothing to do with how my insides are faring."

"And yet if there's a crack in the wine jug, the wine goes sour."

"I am not a wine jug."

"You were last night. It's a good thing old Ptah-Hotep was able to get you emptied out."

"Don't remind me," I said with a shudder.

Abruptly, Thutmose stopped teasing me. "I should send him to you again when we get home. He can give you another dose of medicine."

"Why? I told you, I feel better now."

"Yes, but after the crazy way I was driving, I'm afraid I might've made your stomach churn up again. You feel well now, but suppose you don't feel the effects of all that swaying and bouncing until it's the middle of the night? I couldn't forgive myself if you suffered or went sleepless."

"I'd rather not suffer drinking another one of Ptah-Hotep's vile concoctions."

"Not all of his potions taste like the wrath of Set," Thutmose argued. "I can't force you to do it, but . . . I'd feel better if you would."

"I'll think about it," I said. Thutmose's newly revealed thoughtfulness made it hard to tell him *No* outright.

"Think about this as well, then: If you do fall ill again, how will I be able to send you home?"

"Home? Why would you need to *send* me—?"

"I don't mean *my* home, Nefertiti," he said gruffly, slowing our chariot to a standstill a spear-cast from the city gate. "I mean Akhmin."

Tears stung my eyes. Akhmin! For more than a year I'd yearned to hear from them but hadn't been permitted to receive a single message. And now, to be offered the opportunity to return—!

"Don't taunt me, Thutmose," I said, swallowing my tears. "I know it's impossible. Aunt Tiye would never—"

"She's in Dendera," he cut in. "*I* am here and in command. You will sail to Akhmin in three days' time."

My arms were around his neck before the last word left his lips, and I didn't care how many travelers on the road to and from Thebes saw me kiss him.

He hosted another family dinner that evening, though this one was a simple affair—no fancy dishes, no perfumed cones of wax for our heads, no flowers, and no entertainment. When I came in, he rose to greet me and seated me in the fancy, high-backed chair beside him instead of on the low stool among his sisters where I'd been the previous night.

"Isn't this your brother's place?" I asked. Amenophis was nowhere to be seen.

"Don't fret, Nefertiti, he'll be here soon. He's helping me with preparations for some important business that will take place at my audience tomorrow. You can move elsewhere when he arrives. Can you tolerate being next to me in the meantime?" He smiled.

He filled my plate and my cup with his own hands and urged all of us to eat and drink. When Amenophis finally joined us, I tried to give him his chair but he only shook his head and went to sit with his sisters. He ate and drank very little, and whenever I caught him looking my way it was always with a melancholy smile.

Hathor and Isis be my help, I thought with growing exasperation. *Now* he's *the envious one? And after all he's endured because of Thutmose's jealousy! Oh, I will never understand boys.*

I tried to make things better. I tried to draw Amenophis into conversation. I tried offering to give him back his place at Thutmose's side. I tried making jokes and recounting Kepi's horror when she saw how disheveled I was after my morning chariot ride. I tried everything I could think of, but in the end it was Thutmose who was able to conjure a true smile back to his brother's lips.

"Nefertiti, you're forgetting something. Tell Amenophis about your new gift." He beamed at his brother. "Better yet, let me do it. Amenophis, today I made your friend a present of my chariot and horses. She also has my permission to use her gift freely, coming and going with or without an escort whenever she likes; however"—he raised one finger to draw attention to what he had to say next—"I understand that she's quite the able driver and that you're the one to thank for teaching her that skill. Therefore I would be very happy if you'd promise me to accompany her on her outings as much as possible—with her permission, of course."

"Thutmose . . . ?" Amenophis regarded his brother warily. "Are you really saying . . . ? Uh, I mean . . ." He floundered.

Thutmose looked at him with affection. "Yes, I *do* mean it, brother. Consider it my gift to you, and one that's long overdue. Things haven't been as they should be between us. If I were to die tomorrow, I wouldn't want to stand before Osiris with this regret weighing down my heart. Rather than prepare a feast for Ammut the Devourer, I prefer to make amends with you."

Amenophis stood up and raised his goblet. "May the gods witness the truth between us. Live long, be blessed, and know that I will always be your loyal servant and loving brother." The two of them rushed into each other's arms while the royal princesses and I laughed, cheered, and applauded for joy.

The physician Ptah-Hotep came to my rooms that evening after dinner. He was carrying another small clay pot, but this one steamed with a sweet, tempting fragrance. "Lady Nefertiti, I am here at the command of Prince Thutmose, may he live and reign. He has informed me that you had a rather . . . *unsettling* chariot ride this morning. He requests that I offer you this soothing drink, to assure you of a good night's sleep."

I eyed the steaming clay pot in his hands. It did have a pleasant aroma, but I couldn't get the memory of that morning's goose-fat-and-the-gods-alone-knew-what-else brew out of my mind. Just thinking about it made me gag all over again. While I was debating what to do, a sleepy-eyed

Nava came padding out of the bedroom, woken by our conversation.

"Thank you, Master Ptah-Hotep," I said, lifting the drowsy child onto my lap. "But I believe I'll sleep well enough without help."

He bowed his head. "As you wish. It is my professional opinion that you would be the better for drinking this—it's nothing more than milk, honey, and some soothing herbs— but the decision is yours. I can understand your mistrust. You look at me and see a withered old man almost past his usefulness, passing his days by preparing worthless potions that only serve to make you sicker. You are wise to dismiss me. Perhaps your reluctance is a sign from the gods. I should heed it and retire from the practice of medicine, awaiting the day Anubis comes to lead my soul into the Afterlife."

He looked so aged and doleful that I couldn't stand it. I took the clay pot from his hands and drank. My heart wouldn't let me do otherwise, out of pity for the man. Nava's nose twitched and she stretched out her hands, silently requesting a taste.

Ptah-Hotep smiled. "No harm will come of giving her a sip or two."

I held the clay pot to her lips. The first taste made her greedy and she would have drunk the whole thing if Ptah-Hotep hadn't snatched it away from her. He could react with remarkable speed for a man of his age. "I said a *sip*." He spoke so sternly that Nava jumped off my lap and ran into the bedroom.

"You scared her," I accused him.

"Lady Nefertiti, I don't know what that child is to you, but if you care for her at all, you should thank me. If I scared her, I swear by the wisdom of Thoth, I did it for her own good. The most harmless herbs can still have ill effects if you consume too much of them, just as the most wholesome foods will make you sick if you overeat. I have offered you a dose carefully measured to be beneficial for a young woman. It would be too much for a small child. I swear to you by the wisdom of Thoth that whatever sins I may commit, I will never betray my calling as a physician. I would sooner die than give anyone a potion that I knew would harm them." There were tears in his eyes as he finished.

"I believe you, Master Ptah-Hotep," I said, and to prove it, I drained the last drop from the clay pot in my hands. The physician was visibly pleased.

"Sleep well, Lady Nefertiti," he said, bowing before he left me. His words combined magically with the sweet potion, and I fell into a deep sleep the moment I stretched out in my bed.

That night, for the first time in years, I dreamed of the desert and the monstrous lions of my childhood. I stood in their midst, not knowing how I'd gotten there, and watched in horror as they circled me. Their jaws were stained red with blood, their yellow fangs were spotted black with rot, their ribs protruded from their scrawny, half-starved bodies, but their manes were gorgeously adorned with sparkling beads made out of precious gems and gold. When they opened their mouths to roar, all I heard was a low, indistinct droning, like the chanting of priests from deep within the god's house.

As they drew their circle tighter around me, I felt the sand beneath my feet give way. I sank slowly, unable to fight back, or run away, or move a finger, or even scream. When the sand reached my chin, I saw their looming faces ripple and begin to change like long ago, before I'd found the magic to overcome my nightmares. I waited helplessly for them to become sphinxes and devour me.

Up! Get up! A gigantic voice boomed through my dream. The lions' changing faces became featureless disks of polished bronze, mirrors that flashed my own slowing drowning image back into my eyes. *Get up, Lady Nefertiti, and face your crime!*

I gasped, inhaling dream-sand, and woke to find myself on my feet, held captive between two palace guards. A strange man who smelled strongly of incense stood in front of me, the pottery lamp in his hand casting weird shadows on the walls. He was hairless, well-dressed, and his glittering collar was adorned with a massive golden image of Amun. *A priest?* I thought, still half-mired in sleep. *What's a priest doing in my dream?* But when I tried to ask him what magic he'd used to save me from the hungry sand and the lions, my tongue wouldn't obey me and my words stumbled out of my mouth as nonsense.

"What are you waiting for?" the priest barked at the men holding me. "The crown prince is waiting!"

"Lord . . . ," one of the guards said timidly. "Lord, her chief maidservant is fetching her dress. If she is going to stand trial, she must be clothed."

The priest growled something I couldn't hear, then bellowed, "And how long will that take? Maid! Hear me! If you can't clothe your mistress before I count to five, she'll go before the crown prince and her accusers as naked as the day her mother bore her!"

Kepi came running, one of my dresses draped over her arms. She was followed by my other maids, all of them wailing hysterically. I watched with heavy-lidded eyes as they wept rivers of tears while wrestling the dress onto my languid body, and I smiled because none of this was really happening. The thick darkness beyond the circle of lamplight proved that it was still nighttime, so clearly this was all a lingering dream. If it weren't, all the noise and commotion would have wakened little Nava, but there she was, still sleeping soundly in her bed.

Yes, it was all just a dream.

"Stop fussing, you stupid turtles. That's good enough. Bring her!" The priest sailed out of my rooms and we followed him, leaving Kepi and the other maids sobbing in the dark.

I lurched along between the guards, sometimes tripping over my own feet, sometimes treading on theirs, sometimes almost tripping all of us until it got so bad that one of them swept me up in his arms and carried me until the priest glanced back, caught him at it, and cut him to pieces with his tongue. I had to walk the rest of the way, even though it was much slower going.

They brought me to the small, private audience chamber where I'd once spoken with Pharaoh. I recognized Pharaoh's vizier and two other high-ranking nobles. Judging by their resemblance to the man who'd ordered me here, the five others present were also Amun priests. The vizier and the nobles were bewildered and sleepy. Their clothing was rumpled, as though thrown on in haste. One nobleman's wig sat tilted too far down on one side, making him look like a drunkard. The priests, on the other hand, were neatly dressed and seemed to have no doubt at all about why they were there.

Someone had taken the elaborate throne from the great assembly hall and placed it here, between two wall niches that held flaming alabaster lamps. There were more lights kindled along the other walls and held high in the hands of servants. No effort had been spared to turn night into day.

Thutmose sat on his father's borrowed throne. Head bent, he rested his lips against his interlaced fingers, his eyes lost in thought. He was dressed in the same finely woven white robe he'd worn to public events of the highest importance. His head was covered with the *nemes* crown, a striped ceremonial headcloth adorned with the gold images of the vulture and the cobra, sacred guardians of royalty. Its long sidepieces trailed down his chest, flanking his immense jeweled collar. The scepters that were ancient symbols of Pharaoh's authority, the crook and the flail, lay across his knees. His lowered eyes were elaborately, perfectly painted.

He raised his head and looked at me. "Why did you do it, Nefertiti?" he asked sadly. He reached beneath the throne and pulled out a wad of white cloth. "What did you hope to gain?" With a flick of his wrists, he unfurled it at my feet. It was badly stained and crumpled, but I still recognized it. It was the dress I'd worn on the night of Thutmose's family party. I remembered how Ta-Miu's antics had shattered a glass vessel filled with wine, splashing my gown, but I didn't understand why it was also marked with so many small rips and slashes.

Then I realized that not all of the stains were wine.

"Why, Nefertiti?" Thutmose repeated. "She was Bast's child, she was sacred, but she was also the only creature whose love I could ever trust. Why did you do it? Why did you kill Ta-Miu?"

16

TRIAL

I stared at the bright red spatters of fresh blood among the darker blotches of wine on my dress. At the heart of a spiderweb of scratch marks that had torn the linen, the scarlet imprint of a cat's paw bloomed like a flower.

"N-n-never," I said. My tongue was still like wood. It was a struggle to turn my horrified thoughts into words. "I n-never would hurt—hurt Ta—hurt her."

"Listen to how she stammers!" The priest who'd led the guards into my apartment jabbed his finger at me. "Her voice breaks with guilt because she feels the wrathful breath of Ma'at searing the back of her neck, parching her throat, making her lying tongue shrivel in her head!"

"No!" Thutmose was on his feet, glaring at the priest. "Don't talk to her like that. Let her defend herself."

"She will lie." The priest folded his arms, defying anyone to contradict him. "If she says one word denying her crime, she will double the charges of blasphemy against her."

"Bla-blasphemy?" Why *wasn't* this a dream? It was bizarre enough. "No. N-n-*no*!" I shook my head insistently and raised my hands in a gesture of prayer. If I couldn't speak to clear my name, I'd fight to make them understand and accept my innocence.

One of the other priests laughed at me and ridiculed my attempts to act out my reverence for the gods. Thutmose was nose-to-nose with him in an instant, his face distorted with rage. "Is this the time for laughter, with a life in the balance? Do you find that funny? Or are you mocking my authority here? Go," he snarled. "And offer Amun thanks that you serve him. If you weren't a priest of the supreme god, I would break your bones for such insolence." The priest went white and scuttled out of the room.

Thutmose resumed his place on his father's throne. "Nefertiti, you know that to kill one of Bast's children is sacrilege against that goddess. To lie about it is blasphemy against Ma'at's sacred truth. I want to believe that you are innocent, but how can I, with this evidence in front of me?" He indicated the torn and bloody dress at his feet. "Justice must be done, in my father's name. Please help me see proof that you're guiltless of this dreadful crime."

A dozen protests and a dozen frenzied questions seethed inside me, unable to be expressed. I thought I would choke to death on my frustration. What was wrong with me? Why couldn't I speak, except so clumsily that I might as well have been as mute as Nava? *Is this some act of the gods?* I wondered. But in the next instant, I thrust that thought aside. *Why must it be from the gods? Mortal hands and minds could teach Set himself the art of malice and destruction. If I've been left this vulnerable, may Aten's all-seeing light witness that there's something human behind it. But how was it done to me? And why? And—and—*

—and what good will learning any of those answers do me, if I can't defend myself right now? I remembered the fate of Nava's sister, Mahala, also falsely accused of blasphemy. *You gave up your life to save mine, and now your sacrifice is wasted.*

I clenched my teeth. *No. No, Mahala, you did* not *lose your life in vain. I won't let it be so, I* won't! *Even if my voice fails me, there must be* something *I can do to save the life that you gave back to me.*

I cast a desperate look at the evidence on the chamber floor. The smears of blood on my wine-stained dress mocked my powerlessness. They looked like some of Nava's first failed attempts to try writing with a scribe's brush on papyrus instead of her sharpened reed on wax.

Writing!

I broke away from my guards, throwing myself at the nearest servant who held a lamp. Before he could react I yanked it from his hands and blew out the flame. I spat on my fingers and pinched off a bit of the blackened wick. Then I dropped to my knees and began to scribble across the floor. Every man in that small room gaped at me. They must have thought I'd lost my mind. I ignored their stares and whispers. I wrote on. I had to choose my words with care; the little bit of burnt wick wouldn't last forever. When it crumbled into black ash in my fingers, I spat on them again and wrote more. And when that was gone, I dipped one fingertip into the lamp's spout and scrawled my words in oil.

The men leaned closer, reading as I wrote. When I was done, I sat back on my heels and waited for them to read it all: *I swear by Ma'at, my hands are clean of blood. My dress proves nothing. Anyone could have taken it. Prove that this is Ta-Miu's blood. If she is dead—Bast forbid it!—show her body. Let her wounds accuse me. I say she lives. All cats roam. Wait five days. Her return will prove that I am innocent.*

The muttering began, though only among the vizier and the nobles. The priests kept a stony silence.

"Five days . . . that seems reasonable."

"Cats do go wandering everywhere."

"Were we shown the cat's body? I'm so sleepy, I don't remember."

"I think you would have remembered that. But the girl is right: Anyone could have taken her dress and smeared it with any kind of blood."

"What about that paw print?"

"A live cat can leave paw prints, too. We mustn't act hastily. She's the favored niece of Pharaoh's Great Royal Wife. Do *you* want to tell Queen Tiye—may she live!—that we condemned a member of her family on such chancy evidence?"

With an inarticulate roar of rage, the priest who'd brought me hurled his clay lamp into the center of what I'd written. Flames erupted and raced across the puddled oil. I screamed and jumped back while servants rushed past me to stamp out the fire. When they were done, my words were only a slick, black smear on the floor.

He showed a demon's face to the vizier and the nobles. "Dogs!" he shouted. "Is this how you deal with a case of sacrilege? You fear a mere woman more than you fear the anger of a goddess!"

The vizier's lips tightened and he stood his ground. "Queen Tiye is not a 'mere woman,' nor is Princess Nefertiti. She is the chosen bride of our crown prince. When Pharaoh entrusted me with the office of vizier, I swore to serve the living god by upholding his justice. If sacrilege *has* been committed, the guilty one will be punished, no matter how highborn or powerful he—or she!—may be. But until we have better proof than that rag, I refuse to give my approval to any action against this girl."

"As do I," Thutmose said quietly. I looked at him with grateful eyes. How changed he was from the cold, suspicious person I knew! *Maybe . . . maybe it's done him some good to be free of his mother's shadow,* I thought. It was an unexpected change, but I wanted to believe it. I *needed* to believe it. I was alone and in peril and afraid, confused by my inability to speak clearly when my life depended on it. In my fear, I clung to any hint that Thutmose had found a kinder heart the way an ant clings to a straw when the sacred river sweeps him away.

The other nobles murmured their agreement with Thutmose and the vizier. They, too, wanted more proof. *Isis be praised!*

The priest glowered at them all. "So be it." He turned to one of his attendants. "Bring him now."

The second priest moved swiftly from the room and came back leading a boy almost past the age for wearing the braided youth-lock. The women's quarters teemed with children exactly like him, though he was a little pudgier and fairer-skinned than most. Even so, we might have encountered one another a score of times, and I never would have been able to pick him out of a crowd.

Despite the hour, when most children were deeply sunk in sleep, the boy didn't look at all drowsy. His eyes were bright and keen, like a well-bred hound's when the hunt was on. When he glanced in my direction, I thought I saw a glint of hostility as well, but why would a boy I'd never seen wish me ill?

"My lord vizier," the priest said as pleasantly as if his recent outburst had never happened. "Your proof is in the mouth of this lad. Hear him."

The vizier and the nobles looked as confused as I, but they motioned for the boy to speak. He stepped forward and bowed to Thutmose before he began.

"Hail, my brother. I am Meketre, son of our divine father, Pharaoh Amenhotep—may he rule forever!" His prim, mannered words would have sounded more natural coming from the priest's mouth. "Last night, I had a dream in which the god Amun himself appeared and warned me that my father's life was in great danger, as was your own. He showed me a vision of a garden in the women's quarters where thirteen sycamore trees grow. It's set apart, a place the royal physicians sent my father's wives when they suffered from con-contagious sickness." He stopped, flustered for having tripped over that word, and looked at the priest.

"Yes, we're listening," the man said harshly. "Go *on*."

Meketre recovered his poise and continued with his testimony. "The healing rooms are empty now. Everyone in the women's quarters knows this, and we all thank great Amun daily for his mercy. But when I came there, obeying the god, someone was in the garden." He pointed one shaking finger at me.

My head began to spin as I heard the boy describe how he'd seen me crouch in the moonlight under the branches of the sycamores with Ta-Miu pinned helpless under my hand. "She called on the power of Set the Destroyer. She held a flint knife over the she-cat's body, but when she first tried to kill Bast's sacred child, the cat squirmed free and slashed her dress. She laid hold of it a second time and killed it. She took its blood and mixed it with a handful of soft wax. She made the wax into two figures and gave them the names of my father and my brother, pronouncing ghastly curses against them. Then she crushed them under her feet, she pulled them apart in small pieces, she oblit-*obliterated* them utterly." He inhaled deeply and concluded: "I followed her when she carried the cat's body to the river and threw it in. I watched her return to her rooms. I went back the next day, when she was gone, and with Amun's help I was able to take that dress and bring it to the priests and tell them what I had seen and—and—and I think that's all."

I blinked rapidly, trying to focus my gaze and make sense of what I was hearing. The vizier, the nobles, and Thutmose all heard Meketre's oddly formal recitation with expressions of growing horror. The priests looked grave, but there was no surprise on their faces. I was so overwhelmed by the scope and audacity of the lies filling the chamber that I wouldn't have been able to refute them then and there even if I'd recovered the full use of my tongue.

If I made and destroyed those wax images, where are the pieces? If I killed Ta-Miu with a knife, where is that? And why would I want to curse Pharaoh and Thutmose in the first place? Meketre's story is a tattered fishing net that can't hold the truth. Doesn't anyone else see that?

All that I could do was appeal to the one friend I had: "Th-Thutmose—"

"What would you have me do, Nefertiti?" he asked mournfully. "This boy's—my brother's testimony changes everything."

"He—he isn't tell—telling . . ." My speech was coming back to me, but not fast enough. I shook my head and mimed the act of writing, mutely imploring Thutmose to have someone bring me a pen or a brush, a scrap of papyrus or a shard of broken pottery.

Thutmose closed his eyes and sighed as if his heart were being crushed under a stone. Had he seen my gestures at all? "The penalty for blasphemy—" he began.

A commotion from the back of the chamber interrupted him. A tall figure paused in the doorway chamber. A trick of light and shadow made it look like an impossible monster, a two-headed beast that stalked the shadows just beyond the lamplight's reach.

"What is going on here?" Amenophis used one arm to push his way through the men who stood between him and his brother, the other arm holding Nava to his bony chest.

The instant she saw me, she thrust free of Amenophis's hold and hurled herself into my arms.

"Brother, how did you know—?" Thutmose stared at Amenophis, perplexed.

"She brought me." He pointed at Nava, who was clinging to me as if I were all that stood between her and the jaws of Ammut. "She woke as Nefertiti was being taken away. She followed silently and once she saw where your men brought her, she ran to tell—" He paused. "It doesn't matter *who* she told, only that he was able to tell me. Now in the name of our father's justice, explain this!"

Thutmose did so. He did it gently and graciously, without lashing out at his brother for barging into his presence and making demands. I sat on the floor, rocking Nava in my lap, awed by the man Thutmose had become.

"Where is he?" The mild-mannered Amenophis I'd known was gone. "Where is her accuser?"

"Our *brother* is there," Thutmose responded, pointing to where Meketre cowered among the priests.

Anger transfigured my friend, infused him with strength and authority. He didn't raise his voice when he faced Meketre; he didn't need to. "Hear me, *brother:* I swear by the all-seeing light of Aten's sun-disk, if any harm comes to Nefertiti because of your false words, you will regret it all the days of your life."

Meketre began to cry. The chief priest curled his lip in disgust at the boy's teary, snot-streaked face. "Take him away," he said. Two of his underlings obeyed. "A fine thing, threatening a child!"

"I made no threat," Amenophis said. "I made a promise."

He turned to Thutmose. "We must send word to Dendera at once. Father must hear about this."

"Brother, you forget." Thutmose stood up, his arms crossed on his chest, the crook and the flail in his hands. It was the same commanding stance that I had seen on countless statues and paintings of Pharaohs who had ruled the Black Land in the past and then gone to join the gods. "Our father *is* here," he said solemnly. "I rule in his name."

"Then rule the way *he* would!" Amenophis exclaimed. "With justice."

"What's come over you, Amenophis?" Thutmose asked, his voice and demeanor unnaturally meek. "I've never heard you defend anyone so passionately before, not even yourself. Tell me I can still trust you. Tell me that you haven't betrayed your own brother by stealing the love of my intended bride. Tell me I'm wrong."

"I—I—" Amenophis stammered, caught off guard by the accusation. "I'm only defending her because she's been falsely blamed."

The priest of Amun gave a short, cynical laugh. "You reject Meketre's testimony as blindly as you fight for Nefertiti's innocence. May the gods have pity on you, Prince Amenophis, for I fear you are the victim of this girl's evil enchantments. Her beauty is undeniable. Coupled with her sorcery, it's irresistible. She has enslaved you, poor man. Why else would you question the absolute authority your divine father, Pharaoh Amenhotep, has bestowed upon Prince Thutmose?" A sly look came into his eyes. "Unless this is your way of saying that *you* are more worthy to rule?"

"No!" Amenophis was appalled by the priest's insinuation. "I would never—"

"Then *let* him rule!" The priest shouted him down.

The two brothers looked at one another. "Amenophis, *do* you believe that Father was right to let me speak in his name until he returns from Dendera?" Thutmose asked earnestly. Amenophis held his gaze and I counted five of my rapid heartbeats before Thutmose said, "You hesitate, my brother?"

"Traitor," the priest muttered.

"Amenophis is no traitor!" I cried, and with Isis's healing help the words were able to leave my mouth without bungling into one another. "I swear by Ma'at—"

"Be quiet, you!" The priest closed in on me. Nava gasped, her eyes rolling in terror. *Was this what it was like for her when they came for her sister?* I thought. I pressed her face protectively to my shoulder and met the priest's furious look with one of my own.

"Stand back!" I commanded. "I won't say another word if you leave us alone."

"*You* give *me* orders? Amun curse you for a thousand years, you insolent girl!" He raised his hand as if to strike me.

Acting as one person, Thutmose and Amenophis moved swiftly to shield me. Thutmose touched the ceremonial crook-shaped scepter to the priest's chest. "Do *you* deny my authority, too?" he said. The priest bowed almost double, begging Thutmose's pardon, and took himself to the far side of the little chamber.

Thutmose returned to his throne and resumed his imposing stance. "So, brother, do you think I acted well just now, or do you want to send a message to Father about *that,* too, to see if he would approve?"

Amenophis gazed at his brother with new respect, then went down on one knee before him. "Father was right to give you the power of rule in his absence. I am loyal to you both and I—I love you dearly. All I ask—all I *beg* of you—is that whatever judgment you give tonight will not weigh down your heart when you stand for your own judgment in the court of Osiris."

"Judgment—" Thutmose repeated. He pronounced the word solemnly, sadly. "You speak as if I have a choice, but in this case, there can be none. I rule in our father's name, according to the customs and traditions that you know as well as I. It is in his name that I must pass judgment, even if it breaks my heart. The penalty for sacrilege—"

I clapped my hands over Nava's ears. I couldn't, *wouldn't* let her hear Thutmose utter the same verdict that had taken the life of her sister.

"—is death. The penalty for sorcery is death. The penalty for plotting the destruction of the divine one, my father Pharaoh Amenhotep—may his name be preserved and praised!—is death." He leveled the flail at me. "So it must be."

The guards came at me from either side. They hooked their hands under my arms and lifted me off my feet. Nava tumbled sprawling to the floor. She looked like a gazelle hearing the first distant cry of the hunt. She had no idea at all of what was going on around her, only that I was being taken away. Amenophis was shouting at his brother. The other men were babbling excitedly over my fate. It was only a matter of time before my poor Nava overheard enough to understand what was happening and to hear my fate.

"Nava, go! Get out of here! Run back to the room!" I cried, struggling against my captors. I wanted her far away before it was too late.

"—Great Royal Wife's own niece, his own *bride,* and yet he condemned her—"

"Nava, obey me! *Go!*" I went limp in the guards' grasp, fighting for the chance to let Nava escape before she could hear—

"—to death!"

One of my guards lost patience and slung me over his shoulder like a sack of emmer wheat. As he carried me away, I heard a piteous howl rise up behind us, and then a voice that I had never heard so clearly before calling after me: "Nefertiti! Nefertiti! Don't leave me, *Nefertitiiiiii!*" And the first words that completely broke Nava's long silence ended in a storm of tears.

17

MONSTERS FROM THE SHADOWS

They put me in a room even more isolated than the quarantine apartments in the women's quarters. I could tell that by how quiet it was, though I had no solid idea of where it stood because they'd dragged me there in the dark. It was very small, with a wooden door instead of a curtained archway, and a window that was so high and narrow that if a mouse could scale the outer wall, it would still have to crawl on its belly to get in. At least it was wide enough to let me watch a bit of sky. It was still the color of a crow's wing, but the stars were already losing their light as the night began to seep away.

I had a mat to sleep on, a jug filled with water, and a tiny clay lamp that could hold so little oil that its light would never last me through a whole night. There was also a toilet stool—a wooden frame holding a large clay pot with a heavy lid. I hoped that my jailers would empty it often. I didn't want to think about how foul the air would get in that confined space when the heat of the day rose, even if it were kept covered.

I sat cross-legged on the mat, rested my head in my hands, and tried to make sense of what had happened to me. *O Isis, my head is spinning! I'm so happy that Nava can speak again, but what a dreadful cause for regaining her voice! And what will become of her now? Sweet goddess, help her. Bring Ta-Miu back so that everyone can see living proof that Meketre lied. Why did he do it? I don't know him or that mean-hearted Amun priest; we're strangers, yet both of them stood against me and did everything they could to drag me down. Why?* I stretched out on the mat and closed my eyes, intending only to rest long enough to sort through those mysteries with a clear mind, but instead I plunged into dreamless sleep.

"Nefertiti?" A soothing voice woke me. Daylight filled my small window and I saw Thutmose standing in the doorway of my prison. He still wore the *nemes* crown and looked as impressive as when he'd handed down my death sentence, but instead of the crook and the flail he held a garland of flowers. "These are for you," he said, stooping to place them on my hair as I sat up, rubbing my eyes. He'd brought me roses.

I took off the wreath and laid it aside. "You've done enough. I can't make you leave, but I wish you would go."

"Not without saying what I've come to tell you." He sat down beside me. "You're not going to die."

"Don't do this to me, Thutmose. You were the one who pronounced my death sentence."

"Nefertiti, I had no choice. Meketre's testimony—"

"Meketre's *lies*! Why would a boy I've never seen before want to incriminate me like that? I've done nothing to him."

"Who knows? I was born and raised in this palace and even so, I'm still stunned by how many secrets it holds."

"Now you sound like your mother," I said with a sour smile.

"Instead of scorning her, you should thank my mother for your life when she comes home, Nefertiti. It's because of her that your life is safe until my parents return from Dendera. Last night, after you were arrested and my brother took that crying child away, the talk began about when and how your sentence should be carried out."

I felt as if I'd swallowed stones from the bottom of the river. "What was decided?" *Isis, make me brave!*

"To wait." Thutmose picked up the wreath that I'd set aside and took a deep breath of the roses' fragrance. "I spoke for you, Nefertiti. I told them all: 'Make your choices, carry out this sentence, but remember, you'll have to justify it all on the day Pharaoh returns. You'll have to tell the queen.'"

"The vizier said the same thing before I was sentenced," I said. "All it did was enrage the chief Amun priest. He trampled on my words. I'm no sorceress, but I know that names hold power. He *burned* the name of Ma'at, Thutmose. If he doesn't fear truth, why would he suddenly fear the queen?"

"Because this time, *I* was the one who counseled

caution. I'd pronounced your sentence, so I'd made it clear that I wasn't speaking out of fear or—or love. I'd proved that I put the honor of the gods and the authority of Pharaoh first."

The corner of his mouth lifted slightly; his eyes were sad. "The Amun priests are *very* pleased when we fear the gods. Fear makes us open our hands wider when we give offerings to the temples. The priests' wealth and influence make them almost Pharaoh's equals. They're cunning enough to know that their best interests lie in working *with* the ruler of the Black Land, as long as he is also willing to work with them. They make bad enemies."

"I know," I said sullenly.

"They were the ones who woke me from a sound sleep with Meketre's story. I immediately ordered my servants to search everywhere for Ta-Miu, but even when they couldn't find her, I didn't believe that boy's wild tale. Like you, I thought she'd simply gone following the moon. All the same, I couldn't simply send them away, not with that bloodstained dress in front of my eyes and Meketre's testimony. It would look like I was turning my back on sacrilege and sorcery just because of how I felt for—" His fingers clenched, tearing away a handful of rose petals. "I *had* to bring you to judgment. The evidence *demanded* the sentence I pronounced against you. But because I did all that, the Amun priests trust my integrity. When *I* said we should fear the consequences of carrying out your sentence before Pharaoh's return, they listened."

I took the half-crushed garland from his hands and

placed it on my hair. "I hope she comes back," I said. "I hope Ta-Miu shows that *who, me?* face of hers before another day goes by."

"Of course you do," Thutmose said, taking my hand in his. I didn't pull it away. "You'd be saved."

"That's not the only reason I want her back." I squeezed his hand. "It's for your sake. I know how much you love her. I remember how it hurt you when your mother took her away from you. I don't want you to go through that again."

"You say such kind things. I think you have that gift because you were raised with kindness." He sighed deeply. "I wish I could say the same." His fingertips brushed the flowers, sending a few petals tumbling into my lap. "I've ruined this. I'm sorry. I'll bring you a new garland tomorrow, something beautiful to sweeten your captivity."

"I'd rather have something else," I said. "If it's permitted."

"Name it and it's yours. Remember, I speak for Pharaoh." His face was even more handsome when he smiled.

"I want to send a message home, one that I *know* will get there. I want to let my family know that I'm all right."

He cocked one eyebrow. "You have a strange idea of being 'all right,' Nefertiti."

"But I *will* be once your parents come back; we both know it. And when that happens, I—I'd like it very much if you and I could make a new beginning."

"I'd like nothing better." He went to the door of my prison and gave orders. I heard a scurry of retreating feet and, before too long, the sound of them returning. A guards-man came in carrying my heavy stone scribal palette, my pen case and burnisher, and several rolls of papyrus. I wel-comed them like long-lost friends and laid out one papyrus sheet right away. Thutmose watched me work diligently, scraping the nubbly surface smooth with the burnisher, and didn't even try to hide his amusement.

"Such obsession! You *are* a sorceress: I've been turned invisible," he teased. "Once you've got your writing tools in hand, you don't need anyone's company, do you?"

I looked up. "I'll always need my friends."

"Like my brother," he said softly, kneeling beside me.

"And Henenu, and Sitamun, and—" I gazed into his eyes and remembered how he'd freed me from the obliga-tion to marry him. I recalled how he'd stood up for me against the priests at my trial. *Where he pronounced your death sentence!* a fierce voice whispered in my mind. *Where he de-layed it, too,* I replied. *Even a stone can soften. I want to give him a chance to show me that he's changed.*

I set aside the scraper and clasped his hand. "And you."

His fingers closed warmly around mine for an instant before he let go again. "What an honor, to be included in such company. I don't know how to thank you for this."

"Thutmose—" I hesitated for an instant. *I want to trust you. I want to believe you* can *be my friend, that you'll make sure this message reaches my family, that perhaps you've even got the power to let me receive word* from *them at last, after all this time!* "Thutmose, could I have visitors? Please?"

"Visitors . . ." I thought I saw a flicker of the old, mis-trustful look in his eyes, but it vanished in the flash of a grin before I could be sure. "Of course. Why not? I'll arrange it; however"—he grew thoughtful—"I think that it should be only my sister, at first. You heard the chief priest: He believes you cast a spell over Amenophis. He'd probably suspect the same if you were allowed to have any male visitors."

"Except you," I joked. "My 'evil' magic can't touch you, O prince!"

"Don't be so sure of that," he said, and kissed me.

My lips were still burning when he left. I sat there, staring at the door, trying to make sense of everything that I was feeling. It all turned into tangles in my head. At last I made myself put it aside and concentrated on preparing the papyrus for my message home.

I was still working on the letter when a servant came in with food and fresh water. He also brought me a short-handled ostrich plume fan. "From Prince Thutmose, for the heat of the day," he said, bowing. I asked him to wait until I finished writing to my family, then told him to take the finished message to his master. "He'll know what to do." I spent the rest of that day wandering from daydreams of freedom to the maze of events from the previous night. Bits and pieces of memory nagged at me, insisting, *Something in all this makes no sense, something is wrong! You must discover it or—*

But then I would stir the heavy air with Thutmose's beautiful gift, and inhale the fragrance of the dying roses, and remember his kiss, and fall back into daydreams.

Much later that day, when the shadow grew long and the light in my lone, narrow window turned from gold to amber, my door swung open and an armed guard announced, "Her royal highness, beloved of Amun, great in beauty, Princess Sitamun." He scarcely finished speaking before my friend pushed past him and hugged me to her so fiercely that it squeezed me breathless.

Then she let me go and began to curse. It was amazing to hear her. Where did a royal princess learn such language? The guard was just as dumbstruck as I, and a second guard leaned against the doorpost to gawk as well. Sitamun's stream of fiery words was overwhelming, vicious, and thorough. She named no names—only "he"—but the unknown object of her fury was doomed to all sorts of sickness, accident, disfigurement, misery, and affliction while he lived, and condemned to be the prey of every demon and agony that the Afterlife could provide after he was dead.

Her blind rage was terrifying and fascinating, so much so that it was only after she fell silent that I noticed the guards had shut the door to my prison and that Sitamun wasn't my only visitor that evening. Wide-eyed and quivering like a cornered rabbit, Nava peeked up at me from behind the princess. Her little hands clutched a leather bag.

"Nefertiti?" Her voice had lost its rough, unused edge. It was just an ordinary child's voice now but sweeter than any music to me.

"Oh, Nava!" I knelt and opened my arms. She dropped the bag and was on me in an instant, babbling my name over and over, begging me to tell her that everything was going to be all right.

"Shhh, don't worry," I said, patting her back. "Nothing is going to happen to me, unless"—I grinned at Sitamun—"unless *you* ever get angry at me. By Bes, Sitamun, you could peel the skin off a crocodile with that language! Who's the unlucky soul that made you *that* mad?"

Her face was flint. "The gods will punish me for my words, but I don't care: It's my brother Thutmose." She spoke his name so low it was almost a whisper.

"Oh, Sitamun, no!" I exclaimed. "You don't understand." And I repeated everything that he had told me, all the reasons that excused him for having ordered my death, all the things he was doing to save me. "You know that your father will never permit my execution, and he's sure to get to the bottom of this when he comes back. If I'm locked up, it's just to pacify the priests, but I'm in no real danger. Do you see?"

She looked unconvinced, so I added: "Thutmose is—I think he likes me now." *More than* likes *me,* I thought, and my heart beat a little faster. "He's doing whatever he can to make my imprisonment comfortable. You wouldn't be allowed to visit if not for him. And look, he brought me this and sent me that"—I indicated my garland and the feathered fan. "Best of all, he let me have those"—I pointed at my scribe's tools—"so that at last I could write a letter home that *will* reach my family!"

Sitamun bent to pick up the sack Nava had dropped. She pulled out a wrinkled tattered scrap and handed it to me. It was so mangled that I asked myself why my friend was giving me such a rag. Then I saw my own handwriting and recognized a shred of the letter I'd written with such care and love.

"He was reading this when he sent for me, to tell me I could visit you," Sitamun said. "By Amun, how he laughed!

When he was through, he tore it to pieces and threw them on the floor. My brother is strong, to be able to tear papyrus like that. Most men wouldn't make the effort." She sneered. "I thought I glimpsed your name on one of the scraps, so I asked him what it was. He told me to mind my own business." Her sneer became a satisfied smile. "So I did. The servant who gathered up the pieces is a little richer for it."

I closed my eyes. Tears slid down my cheeks. "Nefertiti?" Nava put her arms around my neck. "Don't cry."

Sitamun knelt and put her arms around me, too. "Listen to her, my friend. He's not worth your tears."

"But why am I worth his hate?" I tore the wreath from my head and threw it at the door. I was about to do the same with the fan, but she grabbed my wrist and stopped me.

"Nefertiti, control yourself," she murmured. "Throw that and it will attract attention. There are two pairs of ears on the other side of that door, two tattling tongues that are in my brother's pay. Why do you think I've been keeping my voice down? Your life's in peril because of all the secrets he's kept from you. Let's try to keep some from him."

"Keeping secrets from me is no challenge," I said bitterly. "I'm easily blinded. The smallest kindness dazzles me, the least bit of attention from a good-looking young man is like a donkey's kick: It scrambles my brains. I should have suspected him from the moment I saw how perfectly dressed and groomed he was at my trial. Who paints his eyes at that hour of the night? The Amun priests didn't set my doom in motion; he did. It was right in front of me and I didn't see it." I shook my head. "Stupid, stupid, *stupid*."

"You're *not* stupid," Nava said staunchly. "Remember

the funny milk we drank? It made me sleepy, and my head was all fuzzy, and I only had a little. You had *lots* more."

"Funny milk?" Sitamun looked at me quizzically. I told her about another of her brother's "kindnesses," sending the old physician Ptah-hotep to my room. "A sleeping potion . . . no wonder you had trouble speaking in your own defense against that boy's testimony."

"Poor Meketre," I said. "Thutmose must have terrorized him into telling such awful lies."

"You can save your pity," Sitamun said. "Meketre acted willingly."

"Why would he? I don't know him; I never did anything to him."

"Not to *him,*" she said. "To his mother. He's the son of one of the Ugarit women whose conspiracy you discovered."

"Oh!" Comprehension struck me like a blow. "Was she—was she executed?"

"Exiled. Her friend didn't fare as well, nor the nobleman who worked with them, but Father was merciful to her, for Meketre's sake. He divorced her and sent her to the farthest reaches of Nubia as a gift for one of his officials. She might as well be dead, as far as Meketre's concerned. When Thutmose wanted his help, that boy must have leaped at the chance for revenge."

"Thutmose must be happy to have a brother who's like him, for a change," I said. "No wonder he didn't challenge any of the holes in Meketre's testimony."

My limbs felt suddenly heavy. It wasn't enough for Thutmose to condemn and imprison me; he'd played games with me, filling me with hopes he knew were nothing but smoke and dust. And why take such pains to hurt me now, when he'd achieved his dream and had one foot firmly on the steps to the throne? The answers hammered inside my head:

Because you preferred his brother, and how could you do that when he knows he's so much stronger, more handsome, more important than Amenophis? Because your choice wounded his pride. Because Amenophis can never have anything without Thutmose believing it was wrenched away from him, whether he ever wanted it or not. You helped the thief, and now you have to pay.

"Nefertiti?" Nava's voice shook. "Nefertiti, last night when the nice prince carried me back to our rooms, Kepi asked him what was happening and—and he told her that— that the reason you're shut up in here is that Ta-Miu is dead. Is it true?"

"Not at all, little bird, I swear it," I said. If Ma'at couldn't forgive me for that lie, I didn't care.

Nava was unconvinced. "I know you'd never hurt her, but someone else who wants you blamed for it could have—have killed . . ." Her lower lip trembled.

I stilled it with the touch of my finger. "Prince Thutmose loves Ta-Miu very much. He doesn't like me, but no matter how much he wants to punish me, he would never sacrifice her to do it."

"Oh. Good." Nava believed me now. I wished I could believe myself.

Before Sitamun and Nava left me, they emptied the leather bag that had held my ruined letter and gave me a comb, a fresh gown, and a little flask of perfume.

"We'll bring you more nice things tomorrow," Nava promised, and kissed me goodbye. She would have thought I was silly if I'd told her that the sound of her restored voice was the nicest gift of all.

I was left alone with my anger and my thoughts. At first, all I could do was imagine all the things I'd like to do to Thutmose for the way he'd deceived me, but once I'd exhausted my nastiest dreams of revenge, I realized that they were never going to happen. *And not just because I haven't got the strength or the means to accomplish them,* I thought. *If I'd do such things to punish him, then I* become *him, and that is something I must never do.*

A servant brought me more food and drink—bread, a pair of roasted quail, a few dates, a jug of weak beer. There was also a note from Thutmose: *Be happy, Nefertiti. The letter to your parents has already left the palace.* I could just picture him saying such lies and felt a fleeting urge to slap them off his lips.

Nefertiti, control yourself. Sitamun's words came back to me. I conquered the impulse to throw his note out of my window or into the clay pot on my toilet stool. Instead I tucked it under my sleeping mat, just as if I were still starry-eyed over him.

Let him see it like this the next time he comes here, I thought, placing it deliberately so that one corner stuck out from under the mat. *He mustn't discover that I know exactly what he's done to me. He thinks he's won, but this little game of Hounds and Jackals isn't over yet. I swear by Isis, I'll do everything in my power to outplay him.*

I ate my dinner at peace with myself. The light in my window turned scarlet and began to fade. One of my guards came in to kindle my tiny lamp. I knew that its comforting flame wouldn't last long, so I used its light to write down a question that I needed to ask Sitamun but that I didn't dare voice where Nava could hear: *How long do I have until he sends me to my death?* It was a reasonable question. Thutmose claimed I was safe until his parents returned, but he'd lied about everything else. I had to know.

Once that was done, I stretched out on my mat, said a prayer to Isis to keep scorpions out of my room, and went to sleep. I woke up to a day like the one that had gone before. Thutmose came to see me, bearing a fresh garland of flowers. How the gods must have laughed to see the two of us together, trading false smiles, dueling with deceit. He mentioned his brother, the way a hunter uses a lure to attract his quarry, but I brushed aside Amenophis's name and turned our talk to other things. *If you want an excuse to fuel your hate, I won't give it to you,* I thought. He left disappointed, and I gloated over it.

Sitamun and Nava came to see me at noon. Once again they'd brought the leather bag, and I couldn't help being curious about what it might hold this time. Nava also brought her harp, and while she played and sang strange songs in the Habiru tongue, I found the opportunity to slip Sitamun my question. She read it, crushed the scrap into a ball in one fist, and said, "Even a blind hawk sometimes catches his rabbit. You will be kept here until my parents return."

"So he told me the truth about that?" I raised my eyebrows. "Now I've witnessed a miracle."

"Not a very big one. It was Father's vizier who persuaded the others to delay your . . . fate."

"How did you find that out?"

"Rumors fly through this palace like bats. But that isn't all." Her mouth became a flat line. "He did his best to hide his feelings, but my brother was *not* pleased when the vizier was able to sway things your way. Oh, Thutmose's tame priests put up a token argument, but then the vizier asked, 'Shall I tell Pharaoh that *you* take full responsibility for this—'" She glanced at Nava and her voice dropped to a whisper. "'—this death?' That was when the chief priest solemnly pronounced that the gods were eternal and could wait to see justice done."

I studied my friend's face. "So I'm safe here for now. Shouldn't you look happier?"

"My brother was *not* pleased," Sitamun repeated. "And you have nowhere to run."

That was true. "You think that Thutmose would—?" I said.

"I don't know. He's my brother, and I love him, but I don't recognize him anymore. With every year that passes, the sickness in his mind grows worse, and he becomes more and more of a stranger to me. What will become of him, Nefertiti? Who will he be when he finally stands before Osiris and Anubis weighs the sins in his heart?" She was on the point of tears.

"Sitamun, I promise you this: When Thutmose faces

the gods, his heart won't be weighed down by my blood. I can't wager my life on guessing what his sickness will make him do, or spend my days just *wishing* he won't touch me before your parents return. I'm getting out of here."

"How?"

I had to answer honestly: "I don't know. I don't even know where I'll go once I get out, but maybe Isis will come to me in my dreams and lend me a little of her cleverness." I gave her a weak smile. "It's my only hope."

Sitamun embraced me. "Not while you have friends."

We spent the rest of our time together that day proposing ideas for how to get me out of my prison, out of the palace, out of Thebes, where I should go once I had my freedom, and how to transport me there. While we whispered together, we had Nava sing and play her harp as loudly as she could to keep the guards in ignorance. She gleefully obeyed. What child wouldn't welcome the chance to make as much noise as possible, especially one who'd been silent for so long?

"You could go home," Sitamun said. "Your family will protect you."

"That's the trouble," I replied. "Father would die to defend me, but until my name is cleared, he'd be shielding a criminal. His enemies and mine would be justified in punishing our whole family. I won't do that to them." I thought about my choices some more, then said: "Dendera. I won't wait for Pharaoh to come back here, I'll take my case to him."

"Good idea." Sitamun touched the gold necklace she

wore. "This will buy a boatman to take you downriver. I'll take care of that. Now all we have to do is figure out how to get you *to* the boat."

"Details, details," I said, smiling.

"I'm going to speak with Master Henenu and Amenophis about this," Sitamun said. "They may have some good ideas."

"Not Amenophis." I raised my hands. "He mustn't be involved. If Thutmose found out, he'd have him convicted of treachery."

"But he wouldn't dare execute him for it."

"He can't do that to me, either, and yet we both know I'm still in danger. Keep Amenophis out of this. Please."

Before Sitamun and Nava left, my little friend told me, "I brought you a present, Nefertiti." She opened the leather bag and handed me a large clay bottle.

"This is a *lot* of perfume," I joked.

"It's not perfume," Nava said. "It's oil for your lamp. Lady Sitamun got it, but it was my idea. I don't want you to be alone in the dark. You might be afraid."

I gave her a hug. "Isis bless you, Nava."

"And may the One bless you, too," she said, her small face the image of adult solemnity.

"The one what, dear?" I asked, so distracted by my plight that, for a moment, I forgot that Nava worshipped only one god.

She looked at me as if I'd asked if water was wet. "The *One,*" she said again. "When I pray, I ask Him to—"

"I hear the guards changing shifts. The new ones will be poking their noses in here any moment. If we linger too long, they'll report it to Thutmose. We'd better go," Sitamun said, interrupting Nava, and leaving me behind.

I was deeply grateful to Nava for her gift. It took me a long time to fall asleep that night, what with my mind whirling over possible escape plans, so it was comforting to have a lasting light to keep the demons of doubt at bay. When the third day of my captivity came, she and Sitamun arrived even earlier than before, with fresh lamp oil and a different kind of gift.

"Here," Sitamun said. She took my hands and closed them around a bronze pin adorned with a scarab.

"Thank you, it's very pretty," I said, turning it in the light.

"It's better than pretty, it's—Nava, dear, sing a little *louder* for us, won't you?—it's part of your escape. May Bes give his blessing to Master Henenu, our teacher is as wise as Thoth. 'Don't underrate Nefertiti,' he said when I told him where Thutmose is keeping you. 'You talk as if we need an army to rescue her when all *she* really needs is this.' " Sitamun pointed at the bronze pin.

"Oh, it's a *magic* pin," I said dryly.

She giggled. "It's a pin you'll use to secure your dress so that once you get out of this room all you'll have to do is climb a wall and make your way to the river, where a boat will be waiting. 'She can do that in her sleep,' he said. 'She's a dancer, strong and nimble, but more importantly, she's brave.' "

"I'll have to be invisible, too," I said. "If—*when*— I escape this prison, how do I reach that wall without being seen?"

"Don't worry about your guards. Master Henenu has plans for them."

"What about anyone else I might meet while I'm trying to reach that wall?"

Sitamun tilted her head. "You really don't know where you are, do you?"

"Only that it's quiet."

"Your prison is an outbuilding that stands alone in what used to be a part of the old servant's quarters. I think it was once surrounded by a vegetable garden, but in any case, once you're out, you won't have to worry about passing through any part of the palace. The wall between you and the river is just a little way outside that door."

We parted a little after noon, with Sitamun's pledge to do everything she could to arrange things with Henenu that would hasten the day of my escape. "The longer we wait, the greater the risk that some 'accident' will befall you."

I cast a leery glance at the remains of my latest meal. "Maybe you should bring me my food from now on," I suggested.

She shook her head. "If your food was tainted, the crime would be examined much too closely for my brother's comfort. If he does intend to be rid of you, poison never looks like an accident."

Thutmose didn't come to visit me that day. I was just as glad to have him leave me alone. It was tiring, pretending that everything was the same between us, and how would I react if he kissed me again?

I didn't waste my hours: I danced. I didn't want to grow soft by just lying on my mat all day, especially not when my escape was going to depend on how fast and how easily I'd be able to get over a wall. When I wasn't dancing to keep myself fit, I worked at finding the best way to pin up my dress so that it wouldn't come loose and entangle my legs midclimb. I was so focused that I was almost caught at it when the servant brought my dinner.

I tried to eat, but I kept remembering Thutmose. When I looked at the food, all I could think was *What if—? What if—? What if—?* Since I couldn't eat, I decided that at least I ought to drink something, but when I served myself some beer, it smelled strange. I poured it into my toilet stool, covered the pot to hide the faintly flowery scent, and tore up the rest of my dinner to make it look like I'd eaten something when the servant came back to take away the dishes. I stripped off my dress, placed it with my scribe's kit beside my mat, and lay down to sleep.

The night wore on and I learned the hard lesson that an empty belly makes a bad mattress. No matter how still I lay, hoping for sleep, the rumbling of my cheated stomach kept me awake. I tried counting as high as I could go, then tried losing myself in the pattern of shadows on the ceiling cast by my flickering oil lamp. Once more I was thankful for Nava's gift of extra oil. The only thing worse than lying awake and hungry in my prison would have been doing so in the dark.

As a last resort I tried closing my eyes and imitating the slow, regular breath of sleep. I don't know if it worked. I *think* I dreamed, or maybe I was only in that peculiar place between sleep and waking where wandering thoughts sometimes counterfeit dreams. My mind drifted over the wastes of the Red Land, the sandy stretches where my nightmare lions dwelled. I walked alone across barren ground, expecting to encounter them at any moment. My eyes swept the desert, waiting for the first telltale stirring of the sands before the monsters leaped out at me. Instead, all that I saw was an odd series of wavy tracks, and my ears echoed with a faint, unfamiliar sizzling sound.

Why are you wandering here, Nefertiti? A great voice rolled across the desert. The air rippled with heat, and through the shimmering haze I saw a titanic figure striding toward me. The Great Sphinx's lion-pawed stride devoured the distance between us and his human face was grim as death. *Why do you sleep while your enemies wake? Get up! Get up! Open your eyes while you can and—!* The rest of his words were drowned out as the buzzing noise surged louder and louder around us until the Red Land shook with it and the wavy tracks in the sand split open into a chasm at my feet. I plunged into the depths, crying out to my sphinx to save me, save me!

Save yourself, Nefertiti! came the answer, and I woke with a start on my mat.

The buzzing was still there. I lay very still, listening. It was coming from the far side of my prison, where the high, narrow window framed a small piece of the midnight sky. By the light of my lamp I saw a leather sack in the shadows. The sizzling sound was coming from it. As I sat very slowly on my mat, I saw the folds of leather stir, and a small, pear-shaped head with prominent black eyes lifted itself clear of the bag. The snake paused for a moment, tongue flickering, then poured itself onto the floor, draping its pale brown, rust- and white-patterned body into curves.

I knew what it was: a viper, and one of the most deadly in the Black Land. I remembered traveling from Akhmin into the countryside with Mery, to visit relatives of hers who farmed the land. When we reached their village, we found them in mourning, and I saw the corpse of exactly such a snake laid out beside the body of Mery's cousin. He was young and strong, but the snake's bite had killed him.

Time stopped. My thoughts became remarkably sharp and clear, like a shard of shattered crystal: *I should call for help. Wait. No, not that. Someone threw that bag into my room. This place stands alone; no one can approach it without the guards hearing them. So the guards must know. They won't help me. They might even burst in here and do something to make sure the serpent bites me. Very well, then. I'm all the help I'll have.*

I continued to eye the snake. I was astonished at how calm I felt. I was looking at death; if I couldn't escape it, what good would it do me to panic? The creature swung its head back and forth, then stopped, black eyes glittering at me. Did it see me or did it sense my presence some other way? It began to move its coils together quickly, rubbing its scales against one another, and the strident buzzing sound was back.

Save yourself, Nefertiti!

The sphinx's words echoed in my ears. I searched the room. There was no way out, nowhere to hide, no place high enough to climb that would take me out of reach of those venomous fangs. I couldn't run.

I wouldn't run. I would fight.

The snake sprang toward me. I grabbed my dress with both hands and threw it like a net. The viper's body tangled in the folds of sheer linen and the creature thrashed wildly, trying to get free. The buzzing of scales scraping together grew louder and angrier. The snub-nosed head poked out from beneath the edge of the cloth, but too late: I had my scribe's palette in a tight grip and I brought it down hard again and again on the viper's skull.

18

DAWN

The day was only a pale hint of brightness in my window when Thutmose came barging into my room the next morning. He greeted the guards cheerfully a moment before he threw the door wide open, and I seized that moment as time enough to sprawl on my mat with my one remaining dress covering my body and my eyes staring glassily at the ceiling. I was very proud of the way I held that pose when he bent over me and smiled.

I wish I could have shifted my gaze a little, just to be able to see his expression when he spotted the smashed snake wrapped in my ruined gown, but dead people don't do that. I had to content myself with hearing him gasp and splutter with confusion.

I sat up, grinned right into his shocked, bone-white face, and chirped: "Good morning, my prince. I slept *so* well last night, thanks to whatever that was in my beer, but I had the *funniest* dream and now—isn't it awful?—I'm going to need a new dress."

He stormed out of the room, slamming the door behind him. I rolled back and forth on my mat, laughing so hard that I almost couldn't hear the sound of Thutmose bawling out my guards.

After a while, I heard him stomp away, cursing. The door opened and one of the guards came in looking like a whipped dog. Without a word, he bundled up my dress and the dead snake. "Maybe you should have warned Prince Thutmose about what he was going to find in here this morning!" I called after him. "He could've prepared himself for disappointment."

"Shut up," the guard muttered, closing the door.

I just laughed some more. I had no qualms about mocking him or his partner. Even if they hadn't been the ones who dropped that leather bag into my room last night, they'd certainly been in on it. "I *know* you heard the racket I made killing the viper," I shouted at the door. "You could've peeked in after things got quiet, just to see who'd won, me or the snake, but you stayed put. Cowards!"

"I said shut up!" the guard bellowed back. "Shut up or I'll come in there and—"

"And I'll give you what I gave that snake!"

The silence that followed was as sweet to me as a mouthful of honey.

Later on, I ate every bite of my breakfast. I wasn't being foolhardy. When the servant who brought it set the dishes on the floor, he managed to murmur for my ears alone,

"With the compliments of Princess Sitamun." He was wearing a pair of gold earrings that looked much too fine for a person of his rank.

I looked forward to seeing Sitamun, to thank her for looking out for me, but the day went on and she didn't come. The guards changed shifts and the afternoon was nearly gone before my prison door opened again and Nava came in with her harp, alone.

"Where is Sitamun?" I asked as the child seated herself on the floor and prepared to play. Nava didn't answer, but her fingers glided along the harp's wooden frame until they touched a piece of papyrus stuck to the wood. She strummed a few notes with one hand and began to sing loudly while the other hand peeled the note from the harp frame and gave it to me to read.

What happened last night? Thutmose summoned me this morning. He was ranting about something you'd done, calling you an unnatural woman, but I couldn't piece together anything sensible from his ravings. He forbids me to see you. He says the guards are ordered to turn me away if I come. I pray that they will let Nava pass. A child is harmless. Tell her everything and send her back to me. Whatever you did has set a monster free. May the gods shield you, my sister.

I didn't want to do it. How could I tell Nava what had almost happened to me? It would petrify her.

Yes, but if I spare her, I may lose my chance for freedom, I thought. *My chance for life.*

"Nava?" I whispered. "Nava, can you be brave?"

Nava left me shortly after I gave her my message. My

little Habiru didn't go straight back to Sitamun. I listened at the crack of the door as she talked with the guards. They were charmed.

"You remind me of my little sister, when she was a tyke," one of them said. "Except she couldn't even get decent sounds out of a sistrum!" They all laughed.

"What would you like me to play for you?" Nava asked sweetly. They called for a few popular tunes and clapped mightily as she finished each one. "I have to go now," she said after the fifth song. "But I can play some more when I come back later."

"You come back any time you like while we're on duty, girlie!"

"Bah, just come any time," the second man said. "We'll tell the lads who've got the other shifts that you're all right."

"Poor donkeys," said the first guard. "They got their ears yanked off them by Prince Thutmose. Any idea what they did?"

"Don't ask me." I could picture the other guard shrugging. "It doesn't pay to rub shoulders with anyone that gets on *his* bad side."

"I heard he's having fits because something happened to that cat of his and that *this* one"—he rapped on my prison door—"is to blame."

"What, that cat he used to take everywhere, the one with the white star on its forehead? Huh. I could've sworn I saw a cat like that just yesterday, when I was passing through the royal quarters."

"And all the lads know why you were in *that* part of the palace," his friend teased. "So, you're romancing the queen's hairdresser and you noticed a *cat*? That's not what catches *my* eye when I'm with my sweetheart. Hey, little girlie, take some advice." He was talking to Nava again. "Never marry a man who puts you second to a cat."

"No, Master," Nava said docilely.

"Good girl. You remember that and grow up to be a *smart* woman, eh? Keep your nose clean and your mouth shut and you won't end up like the one we've got behind *this* door."

"Yes, Master."

"All right, all right, let's see that pretty smile of yours again. That's it. And you remember what I told you: Come back and see us any time."

"Oh, I will, Master! Thank you very much." I heard the sound of her little feet running off.

Clever Nava! Thutmose might not forbid her to return, but the chastened guards might have gotten more officious and done it. She'd prevented that by opening a good path between them. I wanted to cheer, but all I could do was smile. I couldn't wait to see her again and praise her for her shrewdness in making my guards her friends.

I didn't wait long. I heard one of the guards call out, "Well, look who it is!" and then: "What's this, sweetheart? Brought us something, did you?"

"It's cake," Nava said. "Honey cake, my favorite! My mistress, Princess Sitamun, wants you to have it so you'll treat Lady Nefertiti nicely, because she likes her."

"Hmmm, something for *us* from Princess Sitamun?" The second guard sounded dubious. "She's not allowed to visit anymore. You think we should trust this stuff?"

There was a lot of muttering on the other side of the door and then Nava's voice saying, "Can *I* have it if you don't want it?" Then I heard her gobbling.

"Hey, save some for us!" Soon the guards were digging into the cake as well. I could still hear them stuffing their faces when they let Nava into my room.

This time Sitamun's message was folded up small and tucked into the wide belt of Nava's dress: *The child told me everything. I am so afraid. If you stay, I know Thutmose will try again to kill you, and this time he won't underestimate you. He'll see to it that you have nothing you can use as a weapon, then he'll destroy you and make it seem to be mischance. May Imhotep heal my brother, he has a demon in him. You must flee tonight. I am doing all that I can to make this happen. We have help—I won't say who, in case this message reaches the wrong eyes. May the gods grant that we meet again in this life, my sweet sister, and not in the Field of Reeds.*

I gave the papyrus back to Nava, who was strumming her harp but not singing yet. "Did you read this?" I asked under my breath. She looked embarrassed, but she nodded. "Good. Because—don't stop playing, Nava—because this means that when I leave, you're coming with me."

"Oh, I knew *that*," Nava replied. She smiled at me and began to sing. Soon the two of us were singing together.

She left me when the servant came with my dinner and to light my lamp. I didn't have any of the extra oil left, but that didn't matter. I wouldn't need it tonight. *Who's going to go out first, me or the lamp?* I thought, trying to hearten myself with a lame joke.

The servant was the same man who'd brought my breakfast, so I ate my dinner just as confidently. Even so, I sniffed everything I was given, food and drink alike, just to be sure nothing smelled like last night's beer or that "funny milk." As I was disposing of the last mouthful, I heard the guards take notice of something.

"Well, look who's back! It's our little girlie. Brought us more honey cake?"

"Whoa, what's in that monstrous huge jar you've got there? It's bigger than you!"

"Looks like a beer jug to me. Is that it, girlie? You bringing the lady some beer?"

Nava's voice came through the door: "It's not beer; it's wine. Princess Sitamun sent it. She said not to drop it or spill even *one* splash or I'm in trouble."

"Hmph. Must be pretty good wine, then."

I heard a slap and then an exasperated: "Of *course* it's good wine, you dung-brain! *From* a princess *for* a princess, it's not going to be like that sour swill you and I get to drink when we're lucky. By Bes, I hate that stuff!"

"You drink enough of it when you can."

"Well, it makes a change from beer."

Nava spoke up again: "It *is* good. Really good. I tried it."

"What, a little tadpole like you got to drink royal wine? You've got a generous mistress if she's giving you this stuff." There was a silence, then the guard's voice again: "Ohhhh. So *that's* how it is. Look at that guilty little face! She didn't give you any; you helped yourself."

"Let me see that jar," the other guard said. "Aha! The seal's broken." Both of them clucked their tongues so loudly that there was no doubt they were clowning.

"Please, Master, don't tell Princess Sitamun!" Nava cried.

"Welllll . . . maybe we won't tell if you share a little of that wine with us," one guard said. The other chuckled.

"Oh, I can't do that!" Nava said. "This is for Lady Nefertiti."

"That didn't stop you from dipping *your* beak into it, my fine little goose." The men were enjoying this. Guard duty was tedious, and they were glad to have any kind of diversion.

"Come on, just a taste," the other wheedled.

"*No.*" Nava was unbending. "You can't have a taste. You can't have *any*. I won't let you!"

"We'll see about that," came the good-humored response. There was a scuffle and the sound of Nava's protests, though they weren't very loud. Judging by what I heard next, the guards were passing the jar back and forth between them.

"Say, this *is* good."

"Save some for me, you guzzler."

"Stop whining, you had some."

"And you're having plenty! Give it back."

"Stop it! Stop it!" Nava cried. "You're going to drink it all! Don't you *dare*, or I'll—I'll—"

"Oh ho, making threats now?" one guard said. "I'm so scared. I guess we'd better obey her before—" He took such a big slurp that the noise carried through my prison door, followed by the sound of something heavy dropping to the ground. "Awww, too late. Sorry, girlie."

"You're mean! I *hate* you!" Nava exclaimed. I pressed one eye to the crack between the door hinges and saw her pelting away while the guards doubled over laughing.

I sighed. Some men were nothing but overgrown boys who never got over the "fun" of teasing girls, just to get noticed. *They'll be sorry about this in a little while,* I thought. *They'll apologize to Nava when she returns.* I knew she would—how else was I going to receive Sitamun's next message, the one that would tell me the plan to free me from prison?

I looked up at my window. Night had fallen. I caught a glimpse of the moon, showing half his face. *I hope she comes back soon.* I gathered up the loose material of my dress and secured it with the pin Sitamun had left me. I wanted to be ready. Then I sat down on my sleeping mat and pricked up my ears, waiting to hear the guards hailing Nava's return and begging their "little girlie's" pardon.

Time passed and I heard nothing, not even the sound of the guards' voices. Where was Nava? What was wrong? Had Sitamun's scheme to free me been discovered? If Thutmose had found out what his sister was planning, everyone would suffer for it. *Not Nava,* I prayed. *Please, sweet Isis, not the child!*

I was praying fervently, my eyes closed, my arms extended in supplication, when I heard the creak of the door edging open.

"Nefertiti?" Nava clung to the doorpost, her face painted with the oil lamp's dancing shadows.

We crept away together, past the sprawled and snoring bodies of my guards. Nava took impish joy in telling me how she'd tricked the men into drinking the "funny wine."

"Master Henenu went to that old doctor and told him he couldn't sleep. Then *he* gave the medicine to Princess Sitamun, and *she* put it in the wine, but it was *me* who got them to drink it, every drop! That's because I told them *no.*"

I patted her head and murmured praises. I did feel a pang of pity for those men—Thutmose would have their hides for this—but my life was at stake, and now others' as well.

I found everything as Sitamun had described it. The small building where I'd been kept was all by itself in a deserted enclosure; the wall that Nava led me to was high, but not so high that I couldn't boost her to the top and climb up after. The beautiful sound of the sacred river's flowing waters came to us from a distance. I jumped down from the wall and caught Nava in my arms as she dropped. With the child's hand in mine, we moved swiftly to the riverbank, seeking the boat that Sitamun had promised.

By the moon's weak light, I saw a dark shape rocking in the shallows. The small vessel was the same type that poor Mahala had used when she saved me from drowning, made of bundled papyrus lashed together and curving up at both ends. The ferryman crouched by the oar, his bent body cloaked head to heels, though the night wasn't that cold. I couldn't see his face, only one hand silently beckoning us to board. As Nava and I picked our way forward, I saw that the bottom of the boat held bags of supplies and bulging water-skins. I thanked Sitamun in my heart and hoped she'd also sent me another dress to wear.

There was a short delay in launching our boat. The ferryman seemed to be having an unusual amount of trouble getting his craft under way. I decided that he was probably either very old and feeble or very young and inexperienced, though I'd have to wait for a better look at him before I could tell which.

And then we were on the river. We had no sail, only the big steering oar and the current to take us where we were bound, downstream to Dendera. I noticed that the ferryman wasn't merely allowing the boat to ride the river north but was working hard to steer the boat to the western bank as well.

"What a good idea, crossing the river," I murmured to Nava. "That side's where the royal tombs lie. We'll have far less chance of being seen if we sail along that bank instead of the eastern one."

"Do you think the bad prince will chase us?" Nava asked with a yawn. She'd had a busy day and was growing sleepy.

"Are you afraid he will?" I asked.

"No," she said, though she didn't sound confident. "I'm brave, remember?" She looked over the side of our boat at the dark water. "But I don't like the river. It's got crocodiles and things, and it's nighttime so we can't see them if they sneak up on us. This boat is safe, yes? The crocodiles can't knock it over?"

"If they try, I'll take that big oar and knock some manners into their ugly heads," I told her. "I'll do the same to anybody Prince Thutmose sends after us, too." *And he* will *do that*, I thought. *Once he learns I've escaped, he'll want revenge. He doesn't know where we're going, but he's got countless soldiers, officials, and servants to put to the task. He might even send word to the farming villages up and down the river. It's very good we're being ferried over to the western bank, where there are tombs instead of towns.*

"Now don't worry about the crocodiles anymore tonight," I told her. Once we have this big river between us and Prince Thutmose, we'll only sail during daylight, when we can see the crocodiles before they see us. Isn't that right, Ferryman?" Our lone rower only grunted, but it was enough to satisfy Nava.

"Good," she said. She curled up in the bottom of the boat like a little mouse in its nest and went to sleep. She didn't wake when our boat reached the western shore and bumped and rolled in the reedy shallows. The ferryman had some trouble with a tangled line and made a huge splash when he finally heaved the stone anchor over the side. Drenched, Nava slept through that as well.

"Poor thing," I said, kneeling to pick her up. Once I had her in my arms, I realized how difficult it would be to get out of the boat and wade to the bank while carrying the sleeping child in my arms. I stood in the prow, holding her to my chest, unsure of what to do.

The ferryman leaped into the water and came to my aid. The folds of his cloak that had been draped over his head fell back as he held out his arms. He said, "Give her to me, Nefertiti." By the half-moon's light, I saw Amenophis looking up at me.

"Sweet Isis, what are you doing here?" I cried.

"Helping you," he said mildly. "Please give me Nava so I can get to the shore. I think the fish are starting to nibble on my ankles."

I handed him the sleeping child and waded ashore after them. "Answer my question," I said.

He did, but not until he'd given Nava back to me. I sat on the sandy ground, the child cradled in my lap, hearing him out while he went back and forth from the boat, unloading supplies. "I already told you: I'm helping you reach Dendera so that you can get Father's protection. If you want to go by land, you'll have to transport food and water and sometimes Nava. If you go by boat, you'll need an extra pair of arms for the oar, and in case you run into a difficult stretch of river, or a bad-tempered bull hippo, or one of Nava's crocodiles."

"Or a school of those ankle-eating fish?" I said, with a little smile.

"Oh yes, they can be deadly," he joked back. "You need someone to watch your back when my brother sends his underlings after you, someone to hunt and fish for you when your food runs out along the way, someone who's *been* to Dendera, knows the way there, and knows where to find Pharaoh once we reach the city." He placed the last bundle from the boat between us. "You need me."

"But I didn't want you mixed up in this! I told Sitamun that specifically"—I knit my brow—"and apparently she ignored my wishes. So did you."

Amenophis sat down beside me. "Sitamun didn't say one word to me about the arrangements for your escape. Thutmose banned me from visiting you, so I was going to my sister's rooms to see if she could give me any news. I overheard her speaking with Henenu about the plan, I waylaid him when he left, and I made him see the wisdom of letting me be your ferryman. So you see"—he showed me his wonderful smile—"it was fated. Don't blame Sitamun for my being here, Nefertiti. Blame the gods."

"Thutmose will kill you when he finds out about this."

Amenophis's smile vanished. "Thutmose tried to kill *you*."

"So you know about that. Rumor again?"

"The palace was humming with talk of how a viper got into your room when nobody's ever seen so much as a harmless little sand snake inside the walls."

"You also must have heard that I managed to deal with the serpent on my own?" I challenged him.

He leaned closer and looked intently into my eyes. "Nefertiti, I knew long ago that you can take care of yourself. All I'm saying is, you don't *have* to do it alone. If you really count me as your friend, then let me share this with you. Please."

I could see that there would be no arguing with him. "Stubborn donkey," I muttered.

In my lap, Nava stirred and woke up. "Donkey?" she said drowsily. "Where?"

"Nowhere, dear one, go back to sleep," I said.

"I can't. I don't want to. I had a bad dream." She put her arms around me. "There was a lion."

"Shhh, it's only a dream, it can't hurt you. Look, sweetheart, our friend Amenophis is here now. You're with us." I touched his arm and smiled. "We're not afraid of lions."

AFTERWORD

In my previous books, *Nobody's Princess* and *Nobody's Prize,* I wrote about Helen of Troy, a woman of legendary beauty whose life was mythical but very well might have been historical, too. Many people believed that the Troy that Homer described in his epic poem *The Iliad* was purely the stuff of myth, until nineteenth-century amateur archaeologist Heinrich Schliemann used that same epic poem to help him uncover the remains of a *real* Troy that had been attacked, conquered, and put to the torch at the time Helen would have been living.

Now I'm writing about Nefertiti, another beautiful woman, except this time she's a historical person who very well might have been mythical!

There's much that we know about Nefertiti and much that remains a mystery. One of the most wonderful parts of this puzzle is the world-famous statue of this fascinating Egyptian queen, a carved and painted bust that has preserved her beauty through the centuries. Much of ancient Egyptian art depicting members of the royal family was formalized, which is to say that if Pharaoh or any of his relatives had physical imperfections, the artist did not show them. Think of it as the great-great-great-to-the-nth-degree-grandfather of Photoshopping.

Nefertiti lived during one of the most interesting and dangerous periods in ancient Egyptian history, the Amarna Period. It was a time of new ideas and concepts, which is especially exciting when you remember that we're talking about a millennia-old civilization that did *not* handle change well (to put it mildly). One of the changes of the Amarna Period was Pharaoh Akhenaten's decree that artists should portray him and his family realistically. This says a lot about Akhenaten, since his surviving statues show him with a pot-belly, an oddly shaped head, and numerous other physical characteristics that might lead some people to describe him by saying, "But he has a *great* personality!"

It speaks highly of Akhenaten's character that he was willing to be immortalized warts and all (even if he didn't have warts). It also tells us something about Nefertiti: If the famous bust of this Egyptian queen shows us a beautiful woman, then she really *was* a beautiful woman. Amarna Period art was honest.

I suppose it was lucky for Nefertiti that she was beautiful, since her name means "The beautiful woman has come." Imagine having to live up to a name like that! And everyone would know, because her name was in the language used throughout Egypt. Modern names have meanings, too, but they often come from foreign or dead languages. If you're named Hope or Brooke or Heather, everyone knows what your name means. But what about Alexandra ("man's defender") or Madison ("son [yes, *son*!] of the mighty warrior") or Emma ("embracing everything")?

Nefertiti was as beautiful as her name, but aside from that, we don't know a lot about her before she became Egypt's queen. The name of her father is known, as well as her stepmother's and her half sister's, but what was her *mother's* name? There's further debate about her ancestry, too. Did Nefertiti come from a purely Egyptian family, or was she of foreign blood? Was she born into the nobility, or was she a commoner?

We do know that there was more to her than just her looks, because she is portrayed many times on walls and monuments acting not merely as Pharaoh's wife but as an independent ruler, a monarch in her own right. Some evidence suggests that she might have ruled Egypt for a time when her husband could no longer do so. What's more, it's theorized that she didn't rule as regent but as Pharaoh, using a male name. There is even one carving that shows her destroying the enemies of Egypt with her own hands! (All right, maybe Amarna Period artists sometimes *did* stretch the truth just a bit.) But whether she acted alone or with her royal husband, she challenged many powerful men who didn't want to give up even the smallest bit of their wealth and influence. Even for a queen, that took courage.

Then . . . she was gone.

There are no official records of her death. Her tomb has never been found. Recent discoveries in Egypt have raised hopes that her mummy has finally been located, but this has not yet been confirmed to the point where we can say, "Yes, that's Nefertiti, no doubt about it."

That's the historical Nefertiti, a flash of beauty, bravery, and wisdom who stepped out of the shadows of mystery and back again. We still don't know where she came from or why she vanished, but we can look at the exquisitely painted image of The-beautiful-woman-has-come and let our imaginations supply those parts of her story that history still conceals.

Above all, we can remember that she was much more than just another pretty face.

ABOUT THE AUTHOR

Nebula Award winner **Esther Friesner** is the author of thirty-one novels and over 150 short stories, including "Thunderbolt" in Random House's *Young Warriors* anthology, which led to her novels about Helen of Troy, *Nobody's Princess* and *Nobody's Prize*. She is also the editor of seven popular anthologies. Her work has been published in the United States, the United Kingdom, Japan, Germany, Russia, France, Poland, and Italy. She is also a published poet and a playwright and once wrote an advice column, "Ask Auntie Esther." Her articles on fiction writing have appeared in *Writer's Market* and other Writer's Digest Books.

Besides winning two Nebula Awards in succession for Best Short Story (1995 and 1996), she was a Nebula finalist three times, as well as a Hugo finalist. She received the Skylark Award from the New England Science Fiction Association and the award for Most Promising New Fantasy Writer of 1986 from *Romantic Times*.

Ms. Friesner's latest publications include the novel *Temping Fate;* a short-story collection, *Death and the Librarian and Other Stories;* and *Turn the Other Chick,* fifth in the popular Chicks in Chainmail series, which she created and edits. She is currently working on the sequel to *Sphinx's Princess.*

Educated at Vassar College, receiving a BA in both Spanish and drama, she went on to receive her MA and PhD in Spanish from Yale University, where she taught for a number of years. She is married and the mother of two, harbors cats, and lives in Connecticut.

The story continues in

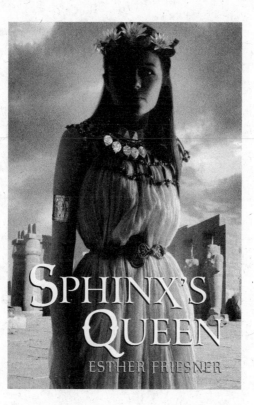

SPHINX'S QUEEN
ESTHER FRIESNER

Read on for a sneak preview of Nefertiti's
extraordinary adventures in ancient Egypt!

Excerpt copyright © 2010 by Esther Friesner.
Published by Random House Children's Books,
a division of Random House, Inc., New York.

THE LAND OF THE DEAD

The hippo's square jaws gaped, his terrifying tusks dripping with water and foam. His breath enveloped us in a wave of heat and the smell of rotting greens as his bellow of blind rage dinned in our ears. Nava shrieked and dug her fingers deep into my skin. While Amenophis and I had been whispering shaky reassurances to the little girl, we'd kept our gazes on the herd of hippopotamuses lolling on the eastern bank. We'd neglected to turn our eyes west, even for a glance. If we'd done that, perhaps we might have spied two wickedly flicking ears just above the waterline, a pair of tiny, spiteful eyes watching us, even a telltale trail of bubbles on the river's surface.

We hadn't, and now it was too late. The solitary beast attacked.

I grabbed Nava even tighter than she'd seized me and scrambled backward in the boat, dragging her as far from the raging creature as possible. The boat pitched and tossed crazily under my feet. I heard Amenophis calling my name. From the corner of my eye, I caught sight of him raising the big steering oar and swinging it at the hippo. The wooden blade bounced off the monster's shoulder as if it were a fly. I watched, my blood as cold as the deepest night, as the hippo turned and snapped his jaws shut on the oar so forcefully that he nearly yanked Amenophis into the river before he crushed the wood to splinters.

Then, as suddenly as he'd attacked us, the hippo sank back beneath the river. I dropped to my knees, hugging Nava, looking up into Amenophis's ashen face. My heart was thumping so loudly, I thought that it would overwhelm my labored, panting breath.

Just as I drew a long breath of fresh air into my lungs, the beast burst from the water a second time, only a hand's breadth from the stern, and plowed headfirst into the side of our boat. Our vessel heeled steeply as we all struggled to keep from sliding overboard. Panic began to choke me as I clawed for something, anything, to save me from the water. Slivers of reed slid under my fingernails as I fought to hang on to the boat with one hand and to Nava with the other. Sky and water teetered before my eyes for one heart-stopping instant, and then—

Then a fresh bellow from the beast, a second blow to the boat, and our watercraft turned over, spilling us into the river along with everything aboard. As the water closed over my head, Nava's small hand slipped from my fingers. I kicked my feet frantically and broke the surface, hair plastered across my eyes. My ears were filled with the sound of brutal crunching as the hippo demolished our capsized boat.

He tore the bundled reeds into flying, floating debris mouthful by mouthful in a mad, mindless riot of destruction.

"Nava! Nava, Amenophis, where are you?" I called, desperately scanning the water. The river's current was carrying me along, away from the rampaging animal. I used my hands the way I'd used the oar, steering myself toward the shore. My head throbbed with prayers: *O great Hapy, lord of the sacred river, save them! Lady Isis, loving and gentle, powerful and wise, bring them safely out of the monster's jaws!*

My legs began to ache and tire. I thought that I was near the bank, but no matter how energetically I kicked and paddled with my hands, the land didn't seem to get any closer. My neck grew stiff from the effort of keeping my head above the surface, and I choked when a wavelet slapped me across the face, filling my nose and mouth with water.

Blinking my eyes rapidly to clear them, I cast heartsick looks everywhere, seeking one glimpse of Nava, of Amenophis, of any sign that the sacred river had spared them. All I saw were three great boats with sails set to catch the wind that would carry them upstream. Some nobleman was traveling south to Thebes or beyond with his family or followers. Laughter and loud music drifted to my ears from the brightly painted ships. I shouted for help, but no one aboard those magnificent vessels heard my voice over the beat of the drums and the jangling of the sistrums. If my cries reached them at all, they must have sounded as faint as birdcalls on the wind.

Every kick I made to stay afloat became more and more difficult. Weariness was a rope lashed around my ankles, relentlessly dragging me down, and despair at seeing no sign of Nava or Amenophis turned my heart heavy as a stone. Something bumped into my shoulder. I turned my head and saw a big bundle of reeds, part of the wreckage of our boat. I threw my arms over it and let it carry me along, but I was too numb with gloom to rejoice over this unexpected, life-saving gift of the river.

Hugging the reed bundle, I was able to rest until my legs recovered enough for me to resume kicking. Every hope I'd clung to since the hippo's attack was gone, swallowed up by the river, whose banks and surface showed no sign that Nava and Amenophis were still in the land of the living. My face was wet with river water, wetter with tears, but sheer stubbornness made me go on, fighting to guide my tiny float to shore.

At last I felt the blessed sensation of muddy ground underfoot. I staggered out of the river, through shallow places where papyrus plants towered over my head. Waterfowl heard me coming and took flight, squawking angrily. I let the bundle of reeds bob away back into the current, and I sprawled on the bank, my cheek pressed to the warm, welcoming earth. I took one deep breath before my chest tore open with loud, inconsolable sobs for everything that had been wrenched away from me.

"Nava, little Nava . . . Amenophis, my friend, my dear, brave . . . Oh, gods, why?" I howled, and beat my hands against the ground. "Why, why, *why*?"

I don't know how long I lay there, crying out my sorrow. In the end, grief stole the last scrap of my strength and I fell into a deep sleep. There were no dreams. When I awoke, Ra's great sun-ship was well on its way to entering the gates of the underworld, past the western horizon. Beyond that gate lay darkness and the giant serpent, Apep, whose one purpose was to devour Ra and his ship, leaving us to perish in an endless night. It was no wonder that so many of Pharaoh's royal ancestors had ordered their tombs carved into the rocks of the sacred river's western shore. This was the land of the dead.

I pushed myself up and sat back on my knees, gazing at the sun. My throat felt raw, and my palms were red, badly scraped and stinging. I tucked them under my arms and hugged myself, taking deep, steadying breaths.

Dendera . . . The name slipped into my mind unbidden. *I can't stay here. If I don't move, I'll die. If hunger and thirst don't kill me, I'll shrivel to dust in the sun, or be found by some hungry beast who prowls the night. I must get up. I must go on. I have to reach Dendera.*

"Dendera," I whispered. "Yes. Nava and Amenophis risked—lost their lives to save me from Thutmose's plotting." Fresh tears trickled from my eyes. I wiped them away and stood up. I knew with all my soul that if I didn't go on, stand before Pharaoh, let him know the injustice that his crown prince had committed in his name, there would be more than my life at stake. Could someone like Thutmose be trusted to rule if he worshipped his own desires and scorned the goddess Ma'at's holy truth? The gods would avenge it; all of the Black Land would suffer.

Pharaoh Amenhotep has many sons. A wicked, insinuating doubt disturbed my thoughts. *Many, but only two are Tiye's children. He adored her enough to raise her to the position of Great Royal Wife, even though she wasn't nobly born. She still holds power over him. How will he react when he hears one of his favorite sons has been accused of so much wrongdoing and learns that the other died trying the save the accuser? More important than that, how will she react? Who will suffer then?*

I clenched my hands, even though it made the pain worse. *"No!"* I shouted, stamping my foot. Wings whirred up out of the papyrus thicket, but I didn't see the birds I'd startled with my outburst. "No, no, *no*!" I shook my head violently, my eyes squeezed shut, as if that would banish the evil whisper that I knew came from my own weakness. "I won't turn back. I won't run away."

Why not? it came again, cajoling. *Pharaoh has many sons, but you have only one life. Why gamble it when you could live it? You have a scribe's skills, and cleverness, and you can dance as well as many of the girls who earn their bread by entertaining at banquets. Forget Dendera. Seek your fortune somewhere else, far from Dendera, from Thebes, from the royal court, from—*

"Not from the gods," I said quietly. "Not from Father, Mother, Bit-Bit, all that I love. Even if I'm punished for Amenophis's death, I'll see them again. No matter how enraged and vengeful Aunt Tiye will be, even she's not cruel enough to deny me that." I opened my eyes. "And even if she is so pitiless, I'm still going to Dendera." I knew that I was alone on the riverbank, talking to the air, but it gave me courage.

The sacred river showed itself in lingering flashes of brilliance through the green thickets of fringe-topped papyrus plants. There were more boats sailing along its deep blue surface now, though none of them steered a course close to my side of the wide water. Would one of them come to help me if I could hail them loudly enough, or would they just sail on, indifferent?

Even if a boat answered my call, could I blindly trust my fate to whomever took me aboard? If all men's hearts were good, upright, and honest, Lord Osiris wouldn't need to keep ever-hungry Ammut at his side when he judged the dead. *Better to walk than take that chance,* I decided, and took the first steps of my renewed journey.

I headed inland first, seeking a clearer way, one where I wouldn't have to push aside the plants that grew so thickly at the water's edge. I was overjoyed when I happened upon an irrigation canal. Its banks would be well maintained, providing me with an easier path. It might also lead me to the farmers who used it to raise their crops. In any case, I'd never go thirsty as long as I could dip my hands into its sweet water.

Water alone wouldn't sustain me. The western bank of the sacred river was where the sun sank into the dark land of many dangers. It was the place where generations of our pharaohs, their families, their highest-ranking and most honored nobles were entombed, an empire of the dead. The living dwelled here, too, but this side of the river wasn't as thickly settled as the other. How far along the canal would I have to travel before I met another human being? If I was going to reach Dendera on my own, I had to find other people or I'd starve.

And what will you do once you find them? Oh, that horrible voice of doubt, haunting me! *How will you persuade them to give you anything to eat? You're no one to them, a stranger, a grubby beggar from who knows where!*

Mery—my second mother—always gave bread to any beggar at our door, I thought, fighting back against my own misgivings.

She could afford *to be charitable! She wasn't a farmer's wife with a brood of children to feed. It's easy to give away a loaf of bread when you've got five on the table, ten more coming out of the oven, and thirty jars of grain in the storeroom!*

I shook my head again, as if that would force out my troubling thoughts, and walked faster, following the line of the canal. As I strode along, I muttered prayers: "O Isis, have mercy. Let me meet another human being soon. I don't dare stray too far from the river. If I lose my way and there's no one to help me find it again . . . Goddess, please, don't let that happen. Guide me. Help me. Hear me!"

But if the goddess heard my words, she gave no sign. Daylight was fading, and the track of the canal wasn't bringing me any closer to finding a peasant's home or even a boy sent out to herd goats for his family. Hunger dug deep into my belly. How grateful I would have been for a mouthful of bread, even if it was as hard as baked clay! I paused, torn between following the canal a little longer or giving up on my search. The land was silent except for the chirr of insects and the distant cries of birds. *Not even a dog's bark,* I thought. I took a deep breath through my nostrils. *Not even the smell of a cookfire.* That decided me. Reluctant but resigned, I turned my back on Ra's sinking sun-ship and headed toward the river.

I don't know if I walked faster because of the coming night or if I'd simply taken a shorter route than following the irrigation ditch, but it felt as if I'd taken less time to return to the sacred river than to leave it. As I neared the water's edge, I heard the sound of raised voices. Moving cautiously, I crept closer until I saw two men loudly arguing as they waded through the shallows, hauling a boat between them. It was a larger version of the one the rogue hippo had destroyed, except this one was laden with baskets brimming with the feathered bodies of dead ducks and other game birds. One of the men looked much older than the other, perhaps his father. I hoped he wasn't. No son should fling so many curses and complaints at his father's head.

"Why I have to listen to you, you worthless frog skin! It's more my hard work than yours that's filled this boat! Stupid old bag of bones, you're already blind in one eye and the other's halfway gone. I'm the one who killed all these birds, and you think you can claim *half*?"

"You couldn't kill 'em if you couldn't find 'em," the older man replied just as hotly. "You're a poor excuse for a hunter. You'd waste your days sticking this boat into every patch of reeds on the river and praying to Lady Neith for luck. And that's the only way you *would* find your quarry. The gods might've stolen the light from my left eye, but my right's still sharp enough to read the game signs and know where the birds are."

"Pfff! Sharp as *mud,* you mean. You nearly steered us onto a bank full of crocodiles!"

"No such thing! Tell a few more whoppers like that, boy, and you won't have to worry about Ammut gobbling up your heart. Your mother'll do the job first. Trust me, I know my sister's temper when it comes to liars."

"Ah, Ma's not that bad," the younger man replied with a snort.

"Oh no? How d'you think I *really* lost sight in this eye?"

The two of them laughed over that and the harsh mood was broken.

I watched them secure their boat and build a small fire using whatever they could scrounge that would burn. I stayed where I was, hidden in a stand of dead reeds. Hapy had withdrawn his waters from them and left me thankful for a hiding place where I could wait out the night. I was close enough to the hunters' fire to discourage any wild beasts from bothering me. As for encountering any crawling things—insects, lizards, or serpents—I'd have to pray to Isis for protection and take my chances. I was too afraid to risk letting them see me, though when they began to eat their modest evening meal of bread and cheese, my empty stomach complained stridently that some risks were worth taking. I fought back the aching emptiness, folded my arms around me, and squatted down in my nest of reeds.

I didn't think I'd fall asleep where I sat. I honestly expected that my fears and sorrows wouldn't let me nod off, especially after that who-knows-how-long slumber I'd had earlier that day after crying myself into collapse. But in spite of all that, fatigue stole over me, body and mind, and sleep followed.

I awoke to the sound of a loud crash and found myself flat on my back in the dead reeds, staring up at the moon and stars. When I'd fallen asleep, I'd *really* fallen, toppling backward, rattling and crushing the plants around me. Before I could take a breath, I heard the old man shout out, "What's that? Who's there?" and saw shadowy hands shove aside the few reeds left standing.

"Well, look at this, Uncle!" The young man's expression was hard to read in the dark, but it seemed he could see me well enough. His hands shot out and grabbed my wrists, yanking me to my feet and hauling me out of the reeds to the side of the fading fire. "You might know where the ducks nest, but I've caught something better." He laughed. I hoped it was a friendly laugh; it *had* to be!